THE HUNTED SERIES

Devotion

IVY SMOAK

Thank you.

Without your devotion to these characters,
I'd have nothing to write about.

PART 1

CHAPTER 1

Friday

It almost felt like I was dreaming as I walked out into the pouring rain. Steam rising off the hot pavement gave Main Street an eerie look. Everything looked dull and lifeless. Or maybe it was just me. Without James, I felt dull and lifeless. I willingly lost myself in him. And what was left of me now? An empty shell? I wiped under my eyes. I wasn't sure if it was rain or tears on my cheeks.

This wasn't real. This couldn't be real. I ran my thumb across the spot where my engagement ring once sat. *How is this happening?* I tried to feel the rain on my shoulders. I tried to focus on anything but the ache in my chest. This definitely wasn't a dream. If anything, my reality was a nightmare.

I knew better than to put my self-worth into someone else's hands. Hadn't I learned anything from my relationship with Austin? I was so naive back then. I stopped outside the restaurant of our last date. That awful double date that Melissa had forced me to go on. It was the same night that James and I had shared our first kiss. I had called James, wanting to tempt him, knowing he'd come to make sure I was okay. He was trying to stay away from me, but I wouldn't let him. I wasn't just naive, I was immature and awful. He could still be here teaching if not for me. He could be happy.

Maybe James was right when he called me greedy. I wasn't in the sense of financial gain. I didn't care about his money. But I was greedy when it came to him. I liked monopolizing his time. I liked when his eyes were on me and me alone. Maybe he had me pegged exactly right. I was greedy. Had that bothered him? Me wanting him and needing him? I thought we were happy. But maybe I had been suffocating him the whole time.

I looked down the street at the coffee shop. I thought seeing it would be comforting, but it had the opposite effect. It made me think of how our whole relationship had started on lies. Lies about my age and lies about his past. He didn't trust me then, and he didn't trust me now. His words cut through my thoughts like a knife. *You're not my problem anymore.* That's what I was, a problem. Something to take care of. An annoyance.

His words made it seem like he put up with me for the benefit of getting my body in return. To do whatever he wanted with. That's all it ever had been. There was no other reason why he pursued me in school. I wasn't a good speaker. He couldn't have been attracted to me because of what I said in class. So was that it? Just physical attraction? I touched the center of my chest. It was more than that to me. How could I have been so blind? I pressed harder on the center of my chest. There was an ache there that didn't seem to want to fade.

I sat down on the curb outside of the restaurant. There was a huge puddle, but it didn't matter, I was already soaked. This really was just like that night we had shared our first kiss. I was depressed and it was pouring. But there was one main difference. That night, James was there when I needed him. Why wasn't he here now? I still needed him.

Stop torturing yourself. I pulled out my phone. There were still no calls or texts from him. He wanted me to leave. He told me he never wanted to see me again. But all I wanted to do was run back to him. I wanted to stay and fight for him. I couldn't go back to New York if he didn't want to be with me, though. I couldn't bear to run into him if he was going to look at me with hate instead of love. So why did I come here? To walk around feeling his presence? His ghosts were everywhere. Being here was like torturing myself. I knew the answer, and it was a pathetic one. Because I knew my life was nothing without him. I needed something to hold on to. A little piece of him. This was the best I could do.

This time I knew that I was wiping away tears. I thought I had grown. I thought the two of us had grown together. But I was so wrong. I was still naive. I was still pathetic. I was still immature. I so badly tried to act like I had my shit together. I wanted James to take me seriously. But the truth was, he never had. He never cared enough to. He never really saw me. I was an object. And now he had cast me aside. It felt like the past few years had meant nothing to him and everything to me.

Fuck this. I searched my phone for flights that were leaving soon. I didn't have my passport. And I barely had any money. I couldn't afford to blow it all on a flight. But I needed to get out of here. I needed to leave before I lost myself to grief. I was stronger than this. Wandering around chasing memories wasn't going to help me. And the only person that could help me was myself.

I clicked on the cheapest flight that was leaving this afternoon. A one way ticket to Chicago cost $103. I didn't know a thing about Chicago and I didn't know anyone who lived there. It made me think about our decision to leave Newark. Would things have been different if we had moved to a place that we were both unfamiliar with? Away from Isabella and Rachel and every toxic thing in the city? I thought agreeing to go to New York would make him happy.

I looked down the street at the coffee shop. There was no choice here. If I stayed, I'd drown. I clicked on the flight and pulled my debit card out of my purse. Before I could change my mind, I typed in all the necessary info and purchased the ticket. I had a couple thousand dollars in my account. That was enough. I had a good GPA from a great school. My stomach twisted in knots. Possible employers would ask why I transferred schools. They'd ask why I didn't finish my internship at Hunter Tech. I didn't have a single letter of recommendation.

I abruptly stood up. I'd figure it out. Despite what James had said, I was a competent adult. I took a deep breath. In my heart I knew I had grown. I had come a long way since I used to live here. Just because I had thought what I wanted was James, it didn't mean my life was over. I'd find new goals and new dreams in Chicago.

James had been my other half. He was gone, but that didn't mean I was half a person. I was more than that relationship. Before I could stop myself, I clicked on his name in my phone. I waited for the voicemail to click on. Hearing his voice brought tears to my eyes. *Stop it.*

"Hi, James, it's me." I tried to say it sternly, but my voice cracked, giving me away. I took a deep breath. *I can do this.* "I just wanted to let you know that I gave Ian my keys and credit card. And I'm out of New York, like you wanted. Could you maybe mail some of my things to my parents' house? I'll have them send them to me when I settle down." What things were even mine, really? I bit my lip. *Nothing.* My clothes, my computer, my phone, he had bought all of it. "Actually, never mind. You can just donate all that stuff or whatever you want to do. I don't want it. And you can cancel my cell phone too. I'll have that figured out before you get your next bill, I promise." Why was I promising him things when all his promises meant nothing? I thought about my wedding dress hanging in my closet. *His closet.* I wiped the tears off my cheeks. I wished I had called the apartment line. Then maybe he'd hear me and pick up. Instead, he'd probably delete this message before he even listened to it. So it didn't even matter what I said. I wrapped my free arm tightly around myself to help make the feeling of loneliness fade. It didn't work. "You promised you wouldn't push me away again, James. You promised."

I moved the phone away from my mouth as I tried to hold back a sob. I quickly ended the call and sunk back down onto the ground. I wanted to scream and throw my phone. Instead I put my face in my hands and started to cry uncontrollably. I wasn't sure how long I sat there crying. My phone buzzing finally made me lift my head.

My heart let me hope for one second that it was James. I quickly grabbed my phone. *Please be James.* Tyler's name flashed across my screen. Of course it was Tyler. He'd want to know if I needed help decorating for the rehearsal dinner. Or writing my vows. Or something else sweet because that's the kind of guy he was. I laughed. It sounded strange in my throat. No, he wasn't calling to be sweet. He probably wanted to know why he suddenly had 20 million dollars in his bank account. No one else I knew had reached out to me because no one else knew what had happened. My parents were sitting in some hotel in New York, still thinking I was getting married tomorrow. I wanted to ignore Tyler's call. I wanted to be alone to wallow. But I owed him an explanation.

I slid my finger across the screen. "Hey, Tyler."

"Hey, Penny."

The awkward silence made my chest hurt even more. He knew. *God, he knows.* I pulled my knees to my chest.

Tyler cleared his throat. "I think we need to talk. Can you come over?"

"I'm not in New York."

"Where are you?"

"Sitting in the rain on Main Street."

"Main Street? Are you in Newark?"

"Yeah."

"Okay, well first of all, get out of the rain, weirdo."

I laughed. This time it didn't sound as strange. "I like the rain." *It reminds me of him.*

"You don't want to be sick for your wedding."

I closed my eyes. It was so obvious that Tyler knew. Why was he torturing me like this? "I'm not getting married." My words were greeted by silence. I stood up and stepped under the overhang of the roof to block some of the rain. I didn't care about being sick, but if my phone broke I'd be even worse off. I wiped off some of the rain and put it back to my ear. "Tyler, are you still there?"

"I need to see you."

"I'm not going to be here by the time you get here."

"Penny, please."

"I already booked a flight. "

"Where?"

"Chicago. Could you maybe not tell anyone? I just...I need to do this on my own."

"You don't need to do it on your own. Let me come with you."

"What?"

"I want to come with you. I fucking hate New York."

"You don't hate New York. You love it there. You have an amazing job and a great apartment. Melissa just moved in. You're happy."

"Happy?" He sighed. "Penny, I don't want to be here if you're not here with me."

"Tyler, stop."

"You know how I feel about you, you know that I'd..."

"You're dating my best friend!"

"I love you, Penny. I've never stopped loving you."

"What are you talking about? That's all in the past. We're friends. We've been friends for years."

"Because you put me there. I still want you. And James is a fucking asshole for hurting you. I don't want to be having this conversation on the phone. Please, let me meet you in Chicago. We need to talk about this in person. Please, Penny."

I sighed and leaned against the brick wall. No wonder James had jumped to the conclusion that he had. He knew. How did I not know? I thought Tyler and I were good. I thought we were on the same page. "Okay. Yeah, we need to talk about this."

"Yeah? What airport are you flying into? I'll book the flight right now."

"Just come here."

"You'll wait for me?" His words made the ache in my chest even worse. He had been waiting for me this whole time.

"I'll get a later flight."

"Get out of the rain, but don't leave Newark. I'll be there by...9 o'clock, okay?"

"Okay."

"See you soon, Penny." The line went dead.

I stuffed my phone back into my purse and walked back into the rain. I just wanted to be alone.

CHAPTER 2
Friday

It was weird being back here. I looked down at the worn steps of Tyler's frat house. It was also hard to think about how different my life would be if I had never slept with my professor. Maybe I'd be with Tyler. Maybe I'd be happy. But I couldn't go back in time. I couldn't change what had happened, and honestly, I wouldn't want to. I meant nothing to James, but he meant something to me. Hell, he meant everything to me. I had a sickening feeling that the past few years would be the best years of my life. Anything going forward would be tainted by that. It wasn't all a lie to me, it was real. I loved him. And this hurt so much because I still loved him.

I looked down at the text I had gotten from Rob an hour ago. "You forgot your ring."

I had written back telling him to give it back to James. It wasn't really mine. If I kept it, it would just remind me of everything I had lost. I didn't need that reminder. My solitude would be reminder enough. The ache in my chest would be reminder enough. Falling asleep and waking up alone...it was all enough.

I stared at the text from Rob that I hadn't responded to yet. "Don't leave like this. It'll kill him. You know it'll kill him. I'm begging you, Penny. Please come back. I'll drive you back home. You two will work it out, I know you will. He needs you."

There wasn't anything to say back. Rob was wrong. This was James' decision. I was just doing what he wanted.

If James reached out to me, I'd talk to him. But that wasn't the case. I hadn't heard from him since he kicked me out. He was done with me and there wasn't anything I could do about it. James would be fine. His friends and family would support him. He had a strong foundation. He was going to be okay. James had never really needed me. I was the one that needed him.

The word "home" made me feel even worse. My parents' house was no longer my home. Newark was no longer my home. And now New York was no longer my home. Home to me was wherever James was. It had been ever since we met. Now I had nowhere to go. I had to start over. Sure, I could go to my parents' house and find the key under the potted plant and let myself in. I could wallow away in my childhood bedroom, remembering. But I refused to hurt my parents. I refused to hurt my friends, what I had left of them. And I refused to just give up on life just because one person told me I was worthless. I wasn't worthless. I just lost myself. Which meant I could find myself again.

I wiped away my tears with the back of my hand. The problem was that I didn't want to find myself. Not without him. I wanted to believe in what we had, even if it was all a charade to him. Because it wasn't to me. It was real. All of it. I grabbed my purse, pulled out the notebook that I had been carrying around for weeks, and stared at the vows I had been working on. The words blurred in front of me as I started to cry harder. I didn't ever want to forget him. I wanted to remember every little thing. The way my skin tingled when he brushed his fingertips against me. The way I immediately smiled when his eyes met mine across a room. If I could somehow put those feelings into words, maybe I'd have something to hold on to. Something that would make it feel like I wasn't drowning.

I shoved the notebook back into my purse. I couldn't capture him on paper. I couldn't verbalize the way he made me feel. I put my hand on the center of my chest. No one had ever told me that when your heart breaks it actually hurts. It felt like my chest was caving in. I took a deep, shaky breath.

"God, Penny, I'm so sorry."

I looked up at Tyler rushing toward me. My eyes immediately landed on the bruise along the left side of his jawbone. The scruff on his chin didn't hide it nearly as well as he probably hoped. I quickly wiped away the rest of my tears. "What the hell happened to your face?"

"It's nothing." He immediately put his arms around me. "Are you okay?"

"No, I'm not okay. Let me see your face."

But he kept his arms wrapped firmly around me. He ran his hand up and down my back. "I'm fine. God, you're soaked. Let me..."

"You're not fine." I pushed on the middle of his chest until he let me back up a fraction of an inch. He didn't need to say anything. I knew. It was written all over his face. I lightly touched the side of his jaw with my fingertips. "James did that, didn't he?"

"There may have been an altercation late last night."

I closed my eyes. "Tyler, I'm so, so sorry." Mason was with James. Apparently none of his friends were good at keeping him out of trouble. It also meant Ian had probably driven him there when I specifically told him not to take James anywhere. But Ian didn't have to listen to me. I was never his boss.

IVY SMOAK

"There's nothing to apologize about." Tyler put his hand on the back of my head and pressed my face to his chest.

There was something so comforting about being in Tyler's arms. Despite his move to New York and all his success, he still smelled the same. Like freshly cut grass and mint. I wasn't even sure how that was possible. There was barely any grass in New York and he wasn't a land-scaper. I wrapped my arms around his back. It was selfish, but I needed this right now. I needed my friend. I could tell Tyler wanted to talk, but I wrapped my arms tighter around him. I just needed a few more seconds.

Tyler kissed the top of my head and ran his fingers through my hair. "It's going to be okay, Penny."

No. It's not. I shook my head against his chest and let my arms drop from his back.

He grabbed my shoulders and pushed me back so he could look at my face. There was so much hope in his blue eyes. And it killed me.

"How much do you know about what happened?" I asked.

"Everything I need to know."

"Which is?"

"That you and James broke up. And that he thinks I convinced you to run away with me." He searched my face.

So Rob really hadn't talked to James. Neither had his parents. He didn't know. Or maybe he didn't believe them either.

"So now I'm here to actually convince you to run away with me." He lightly touched the bottom of my chin so that I'd look into his eyes.

A part of me wanted to say yes. I wanted to feel the comfort of his arms around me. And see that smile that always made me smile too. The only problem was that I didn't love Tyler. It wouldn't be fair to him or...*fuck, Melissa*.

"I'm still in love with him," I said.

Tyler shook his head. "You broke up. You left him and New York. You're standing in the rain crying because of him. And I'm here for you. We can go wherever you want. We can start a new life together."

"I'm still in love with him," I said again, a little quieter.

He let go of my shoulders. "Okay, but that feeling will fade. You have to move forward."

I shook my head.

"What, so you're going to go through your whole life missing him?"

"What else am I supposed to do, Tyler? He was it for me. There is nothing after him. I was ready to give my whole life to him. That feeling doesn't just disappear after a fight."

"Be with me. I'm right here. I've always been here for you. I'd never do anything to hurt you. Let me fill that void."

"I can't."

"Why? I know you love me. We're great together. I know you felt it back in school. I know you can feel it again."

"I could never hurt Melissa like that."

"We already broke up."

"What?"

"I broke up with her before I came here."

"Why did you do that? You only just started dating."
God, she's going to hate me.

"I thought you were getting married. I was at peace with that. Or in denial or something. These past few years haven't been a lie, I was your friend. I enjoyed being your friend." He scratched the back of his neck with his hand. "But when I found out you two broke up, all I wanted to do was see you. I think I had buried my feelings. I don't know. But I just knew I needed to see you. I never stopped loving you, Penny. And I'll never stop loving you."

I shook my head back and forth.

"I didn't want this to happen. All I've ever wanted was for you to be happy. I thought that James was that for you, so I just accepted where I was. But when I found out it was over...it feels like my second chance. Our second chance."

"I'm sorry. But it's like you just said. Except, I never stopped loving *him*. And I'll never stop loving *him*."

"I can wait. I'm used to waiting. I'll wait my whole life for you, Penny. Don't you see that?" He put his hand on the side of my face.

"Tyler, I don't want you to wait."

"Don't say that. I know you need time to heal from this. I'll wait until you're ready."

"I'll never be ready."

He shook his head. "I love you. Tell me to stay. Choose me. Penny, please give us a chance. I need you. Meet me halfway."

"You don't need me. You need some sweet girl who will put you first. Who thinks the sun rises and sets with you. You deserve that. I can't give you that."

"I'll take whatever you can give me."

"All I can offer you is friendship. Honestly, Tyler, you're my best friend. You've always been there for me..."

"I can't be your friend anymore." He let his hand fall from my cheek. "I thought I could be. But now? No. I need more than that. I can't live my whole life in denial."

"I'm sorry."

He shoved his hands into his pockets. "So...Chicago?"

I nodded. "My new flight leaves tonight. I think maybe I need to do a little soul searching."

"And you know for sure that what you're looking for isn't me?" He gave me a sheepish smile that ripped my heart in half. "How are you so sure?"

I pressed my lips together. There was something else that I hadn't told him. But I didn't want to. It wasn't fair. It was just in my head.

"Tell me."

I shook my head.

He grabbed my hand. "Tell me. If it's something I can fix..."

"No." I swallowed hard. "Seeing you reminds me that it's my fault that James broke up with me. Because I insisted on being your friend. I made this happen."

"It hurts you to see me?"

I closed my eyes and nodded.

He dropped my hand. "I'd do anything for you. You know that right?"

I wiped away the tears that had started to fall down my cheeks again.

"Penny, look at me."

I slowly opened my eyes. The hurt on his face was palpable.

"Everything in my gut is telling me to stay and fight for you. But if you want me to leave, I'll leave. Is that what you want?"

"I'm sorry."

His Adam's apple rose and fell. "I can't be your friend anymore."

"I know."

He nodded his head. "I guess this is goodbye then?"

"Where are you going to go?" I thought about his apartment in New York. Melissa was probably waiting there, seething. Hating both of us.

"I think maybe I need a fresh start too," he said. "Somewhere...sunnier."

I nodded. "I hope you find what you're looking for."

"I already found what I was looking for," Tyler said with a sigh. "Now...now I'm running away because it hurts too fucking much."

"Tyler..."

"Go back to New York, Penny. Don't spend your whole life missing him. It's exhausting to deny yourself what you want, to spend your whole life dreaming about what you're missing."

The fact that he was talking about me made my chest hurt even more.

"I really hope that you two work it out," he said.

"Thanks, Tyler." I took a step toward him to hug him goodbye, but he immediately took a step back.

"Bye, Penny." He turned around and walked away from me. I watched him climb back into his car. I lifted my hand to wave goodbye, but he didn't look back as he pulled away from the curb and out of my life.

CHAPTER 3
Friday

My Uber was going to arrive any minute to take me to the airport. The car was going to come to the coffee shop. Up until this point I had avoided it. I had walked all around campus, remembering, savoring the happy and sad memories, the joy and the pain. I was filled up with fleeting images of James. It was time to go. I couldn't stay here living like this.

It felt like déjà vu walking toward the coffee shop. I had walked this path so many times. Good and bad memories flooded back to me in a rush. I wanted to focus on the good, but my mind wouldn't let me. It was like I was transported back in time to when James had broken up with me back at school. Only this was worse. He didn't need time now. What he did need was someone that wasn't me. Someone better.

I was numb before, walking through the rain and mist, but now the ache in my chest was all I could feel. I wanted to think about meeting him for the first time. I stopped outside the coffee shop. It was open now and locals were inside, enjoying their Friday mornings. But all I could see was James bursting through the door on that day that changed my life. His hands had steadied me. He had always grounded me. He was always there to catch me when it felt like I was falling. I was falling now. Where was he?

I closed my eyes and I pictured the rose petals on the floor. I could imagine the candles on the tables perfectly. I could see James down on one knee. His words were all around me. Promises of a future. Confessions of his feelings. He talked about how hard he had fallen for me. Had he lied? I turned around and looked out at the falling rain. I didn't feel defeated anymore. I was angry. How could he throw away what we had? How could he do this to me? I had given him everything I could. I had given him every single piece of me.

I pulled my phone out of my purse. He said he didn't want to see me, but I'd make him hear my voice. Didn't we owe it to ourselves to talk this out? I dialed the number for our apartment. *His apartment.* This time, he'd listen to me. I'd make him listen to me. After several rings, the voicemail came on. It was a cheery message with both of us talking. It ended with me saying, "and the future Mrs. Hunter." Stupid, naive, pathetic girl. The voicemail beeped, signaling that it was time to leave a message.

"Answer the phone, James. Talk to me! Don't cut me out like I meant nothing. Please!" My voice cracked. "James, please. You're supposed to believe me. You're supposed to trust me! Answer the fucking phone! Listen to what I have to say. Stop pretending like I mean nothing to you. Stop pushing me away! Pick up!" I was choking on my words. "Damn it, James, pick up the phone. Please."

"He's not here, Penny."

My heart starting beating fast. I hadn't realized that someone had answered the phone. "Mason? Is that you?"

"Hey." He sounded pissed. "You can stop yelling now."

"Put him on, Mason. Please, I have to talk to him."

"No, I mean, he's seriously not here. I'd force him to talk to you if he was."

"Where is he?"

"I don't know. I woke up this morning and he was gone."

Shit. "Have you looked for him?"

"What the fuck do you think I've been doing?" He sounded on edge.

"I'm sorry, I..."

"You shouldn't have walked out on him, Penny. He's a fucking mess because of you. Why would you leave him like that?"

"I didn't leave him. He kicked me out."

Mason sighed. "God, where the hell did he go? Where would he have gone?"

"I don't know." I looked behind me at the coffee shop. "Maybe somewhere that we used to go together? Maybe the Tavern on the Green? Or our old apartment? He didn't sell it yet. He could have gone there." But those were all suggestions if he was missing me. I wasn't sure if that was the case. The thought was chilling. I wrapped my free arm around myself.

"I already looked in both those places. Think, Penny."

My heart sunk. Then he definitely wasn't going somewhere to think about me. "Have you tried to call Isabella?" It pained me to say the words, but it was a possibility. A terrible, awful possibility.

"He wouldn't go there."

"How do you know?"

"Because he loves you."

"I'd try Isabella," I said. I thought back to our fight here on campus. He had broken up with me and he ran right back to her. It was always her. It had never been me.

He had loved her and he had lied to me about it. Maybe he still did love her.

"Can you just come help me look?" Mason asked.

"I have a flight to catch."

"Where the hell are you going? Aren't you going to try to fix this? I spent all night trying to defend you, and now you're fucking leaving? What the hell is wrong with you?"

"Mason, I..."

"He's missing, Penny. I woke up at 6 a.m. and he was gone. He's not answering my calls. I can't find him anywhere. Something's wrong. I don't know what else to do here. Don't you care at all?"

"Of course I care."

"Then what the hell are you waiting for? Get your ass back here and help me find him, he needs you."

I swallowed hard. "He doesn't need me, Mason. He needs you, his friends, his family. Not me. He made that pretty clear last night. You weren't there. You didn't hear what he said. He never needed me. He just needed to realize what he already had. You and Matt, Rob and Jen, his parents if he'd give them another chance. He doesn't even love himself, I don't know why I ever thought he was capable of loving me." My Uber car pulled up in front of me.

"Just because someone doesn't think they're capable of love, it doesn't mean they haven't loved. He's just...broken."

"And I can't fix him."

"That's bullshit and you know it."

"I have to go."

"Penny, don't give up on him. And what about me? And Bee? Rob and Jen and Matt? Do we mean nothing to you either? You said we were your family. You don't just walk out on family."

That's not fair. "When you find him, tell him I'll always love him. And that I'm sorry...about everything."

"Penny, don't..."

I hung up the phone. I had lost James. I had lost my new family. Tyler was gone. Melissa would probably never speak to me again. I had no one. Didn't Mason see that? Didn't he realize how much it killed me to walk away? But that's what James wanted. He asked me to leave. He never wanted to see me again. I had to go. I had to disappear. I grabbed the door handle and climbed into the car.

"Where are you heading?" the driver asked.

Despite what Mason thought, I did care. That's why I was leaving. I looked down at the phone in my hand. What if James was hurt, though? What if something really was wrong? Mason sounded concerned. I would never forgive myself if something happened to him because of me. Because of what I had done.

I thought about what Tyler had said about going through your whole life wanting someone. Why was I running away? That wasn't what I wanted. I wanted to fight for James. He didn't know why I had done what I had. He didn't understand that I was trying to protect him. He didn't understand that I did it out of love. And he was hurting. He was missing. This was my fault. I needed to fix it. I needed to make him understand. I needed to find him before it was too late.

Fuck. "I'm sorry," I said to the driver. "Just charge me whatever it would have cost."

"That's not how it works..."

But I was already climbing out of the car. I needed to talk to Rob. He'd know what to do. He'd know where to find James. He'd help me. He had to help me. I slammed the car door and turned back toward Rob's apartment.

And I ran straight into someone. No, not someone. All I could smell was him. All I could feel was his grip on my arms. *James.* It didn't feel real. I didn't want to look up and realize it was just a memory. I'd always be haunted by him. I'd never stop wanting him.

"You came here too." His voice was gruff, like he hadn't used it since he had woken up. Or maybe he had never slept. But it was definitely him. He had come back to me. He had been drawn to the coffee shop just like I had.

I looked up at his face. He was as soaked as me. Droplets of water clung to the scruff on his face. His eyes were red and there were dark circles underneath. But even when he looked a mess, he was still the most handsome man I had ever seen.

"James, I thought something had happened to you." I put my hands on both sides of his face. "Thank God you're okay."

He wiped his thumb under my eye, where I wasn't even aware a tear had fallen. "Why did you come here?"

I had the vague sense that maybe he had been walking around remembering too. Like he thought this was some kind of dream or nightmare too. "Where else would I have gone, James?"

"I thought you'd be with Tyler." The pain on his face made me want to cry. But before I had a chance to say anything, he said, "Penny, I don't care why you did it. I just need to know if you want me instead of him. I need to know that you'll always choose me. Please choose me. Please tell me I'm not too late."

He really didn't know the truth. No one had told him. But he was still here. He still wanted me despite what he thought had happened, and that meant everything. "I'll always choose you."

His lips crashed against mine before I even knew what was happening. Part of me wanted to push him off and slap him. He had hurt me too. He hadn't apologized to me. His hand moved to my hair and he gripped it hard. But I wanted this too. The kiss was salty, and I wasn't sure if it was from my tears or his. I had never meant to hurt him. His fingers slipped underneath the back of my wet tank top. *No, this isn't right.* He needed to know what had really happened. He had diminished our relationship to nothing. He had hurt me. We needed to talk about everything. I turned my head away from him and tried to catch my breath.

His fingers intertwined in my hair again and he pressed his forehead against mine. "I thought I'd never see you again. I thought I lost you. I thought..." his throat made a desperate gasp, holding back a sob that made me start to cry again.

I closed my eyes. "Then why did you push me away? Why didn't you believe me?"

"Because a part of me has always thought that you'd be better off with Tyler. That he could make you happier than I ever could. I feel like I've always just been standing in your way, holding you back from what you deserve." His forehead was still pressed against mine. Droplets of water were falling down my face, a mixture of tears and rain.

"I love you and only you."

He didn't say anything. And I knew it was because he didn't believe me. He thought I didn't love him. He thought I didn't care. He thought I stole money from him so that I could run away with another man.

"James, I've only ever loved you. I only ever will love you."

He lifted his head away from mine. "But maybe you're too young to realize what you really want."

I was trying to stay calm for his sake. I was sad and upset, but I was also angry. I was angry at him for telling me to leave. I was angry at him for not listening to me, for not trusting me. I pulled back and pushed his hands off me. "Don't throw my age in my face. Why do you always do that? Yes, I'm younger than you. But I'm an adult. I can make my own choices. And every choice I have ever made since meeting you has revolved around you. Not because I'm immature, but because you're what I want. You make me happy. Why can't you see that? I didn't take the money so that Tyler could have it. Isabella..."

"Stop." His voice was icy. He ran his hand through his hair. "Jesus, I don't care about what happened. All I care about is the fact that you're here right now with me and not with him. I forgive you. I just want to move forward. Please don't talk about him."

He forgives me? He was here right now, so why did my chest still hurt? Why did it still feel like I was drowning? "We need to talk about what happened, James. We can't move forward unless we talk about it."

"You said we were being blackmailed. I'll take your word for it. It's over now. We're going to be okay. We have to be okay."

It wasn't over now. Isabella was still out there, probably planning her next diabolical move. And despite what James said, it didn't sound like he believed me at all. "Then why didn't you call me back? Why did you just disappear?"

"Because I want what's best for you."

Before I even realized what was happening, I had slapped him hard across the face.

He looked shocked. And pissed. God, he looked so pissed. But he didn't get to be upset with me. He was the one that pushed me away. He was the one that wouldn't hear me out.

"What's best for me? How would you know what's best for me if you don't listen to me, James?" I poked him hard in the middle of the chest. "When you prefer to listen to your ex-wife instead?" I poked him again. "What's best for me certainly isn't hearing that I'm ugly on the inside. That you only ever wanted me for sex." I poked him again. "That you never loved me!" I was choking on my words.

"Penny..."

"How could you say that to me? How could you not listen to what I had to say? You never hear me, James. You never listen."

"I'm sorry. You know I didn't mean any of that. I was upset. I thought...I thought you were leaving me."

"That doesn't take it back. That doesn't undo all the hurtful things you said. All the lies..."

"I never lied to you!"

"You loved Isabella, James! I saw the notes. Every intimate detail. You talked about how excited you were to marry her. And how much you wanted children with her."

He ran his hand through his wet hair. "You don't understand."

"Then help me understand. Talk to me. Stop cutting me out of your life. Stop hiding from me!"

He lowered both his eyebrows and looked toward the coffee shop. "You're soaked. We should get out of the rain."

I wanted to slap him again. "We need to talk, James. Now. Somewhere more private than that."

He nodded. There was so much pain in his eyes, and it made me wonder if there was something else he had hidden from me. "Okay."

We both stood there awkwardly for a moment, watching each other in the rain. I wanted him to put his arms around me. I wanted him to kiss me like nothing was wrong. But I needed to know the truth and so did he. We needed to figure this out. We had to. I folded my arms across my chest.

"Where's your ring?" His eyes were locked on my naked hand.

"I left it with Rob."

"Baby..." his voice trailed off. "Please don't leave me. Please, I can't live without you." This time when he stepped toward me, I didn't push him away. I'd never leave him. The only reason I had walked out was to make sure he didn't. Because he was drunk. I didn't want him to get hurt. He needed to know that I wasn't going anywhere. So I let him put his hands on me. I let him kiss me, softly at first and then more savagely. I let myself get lost in the kiss because I needed it too. I needed to know that what we had wasn't a lie. And that maybe we could go back. Maybe we didn't have to be over. This time I didn't push him away when his palm slipped up the back of my shirt or his fingers tugged on my hair. He pulled me tightly against him. I knew he was trying to forget. I wanted to forget too. But we couldn't do that. We had to talk about what had happened. I lightly touched his chest.

"Tell me I'm not too late," he sighed. "Tell me I can fix this." His hand cupped the side of my face.

"We can fix it. But I need you to tell me everything, James. You have to let me in."

CHAPTER 4

Friday

James slid an access card into the scanner outside the elevator. I didn't ask him why he still had a key to this apartment. Whether or not he paid for Rob's place wasn't what I cared about. I kept my arms folded in front of my chest and stepped onto the elevator as soon as the doors parted. James leaned against the opposite side of the elevator with that wanting look on his face. He had given me the same look when I refused to hold his hand on the way back here. I loved him, but we weren't okay. He needed to understand that. If I gave into him, we'd never talk. We'd never get past this. And I needed to get past this.

The elevator stopped and James pressed in the code. The doors slid open.

Rob came running over to the elevator. He slid across the marble due to the socks he was wearing and skidded to a stop. "Hey. I'm glad you guys decided to talk. I may or may not have been spying on you from the window." He gave me a wink.

I wanted to laugh. I knew he was trying to cheer me up, but I didn't feel like laughing. I gave him a weak smile instead.

"So, are you two okay now?" he asked.

I glanced over at James. He stayed silent and so did I. He was staring at my hand where my ring had once sat.

"Rob, do you have my ring?"

"Um...yeah." He gave James a weird look and walked over to the kitchen. My ring was still sitting on the kitchen counter. "Right here." He picked it up.

I walked over to him and took it from his hand. James seemed to be focused on this one thing. If he was going to open up to me, I needed him to be focused on me and not my hand. I slid the ring back on my finger.

"So, you're good?" Rob asked.

"We have a lot to talk about."

"Okay, well, you guys are soaked. I folded your dress and put it on the bed in the first guest room. I was hoping you'd be back." He gave my shoulder a reassuring squeeze. "James," he said as he stepped away from me, "want to borrow something?"

"Yeah, that would be great." James didn't take his eyes off me as he followed Rob to his bedroom. It was as if he thought I was going to run away again. Did he not remember last night? I didn't run, he forced me to leave.

I walked through the dining area and living room and opened the door to the hallway. This part of the apartment looked the same as when James had lived here. I opened up the door to the first guest room. My dress was folded neatly on the foot of the bed. My bra and thong were sitting next to it. I tried not to think about how awkward that was as I changed back into the clothes I had come in. My shoes were sitting next to the bed, but I had no desire to wear high heels right now.

I walked back into the kitchen just as James and Rob were coming out of the master bedroom. Rob was shorter than James and apparently wore different sized clothes. The tight t-shirt clung to every single one of James' muscles. I quickly moved my eyes back to his face. I wasn't going to be the one that led us astray during our conversation. James and I had always seemed to communicate best with our bodies. And it chilled me to think that that was all he wanted from me. We needed to have a serious conversation. No touching would be involved in that.

"So..." Rob let his voice fade away. "Is now a good time to tell you that I slept with Penny last night?"

I knew he was just trying to lighten the mood, but I seriously wanted to kill him.

James lowered both his eyebrows. "I swear to God, Rob, if you so much as..."

"I'm just kidding, man." Rob put his hands up in the air to show his innocence. "We fell asleep together on the couch. Nothing actually happened except for some light snuggling. Lighten up." He punched James' shoulder.

James looked down at his shoulder and then back at Rob. "Can we maybe have some privacy?"

"Um, yeah. I just talked to Mason before you got here to let him know you were okay. And it sounded like he needed some help with the decorations for the rehearsal dinner tonight. He clearly has no idea what he's doing."

James had called off our wedding. That meant there was no rehearsal or rehearsal dinner tonight. There was nothing to decorate for. I glanced up at James. Had he not told Rob?

I turned back to Rob. "Rob, I don't know if..."

"You'll be back to New York in time?" Rob said. He glanced at the time on the oven. "The rehearsal doesn't start until 6. You have plenty of time. Bee's going to come help too, I'm sure we'll need a woman's touch. But we'll have it all done in time, I promise."

I pressed my lips together. Why was I being forced to break the news to Rob? This wasn't what I wanted. But James wasn't stepping in. "There's no reason to decorate," I said.

Rob laughed. "Why? You're still getting married, right?"

"We haven't..."

"Yes," James said, cutting me off.

I let myself glance at him. He was staring at me so intently. I wanted to marry the man he was before last night. The man who loved me unconditionally, who trusted me. I wasn't sure if that man even existed. It felt like I didn't know him at all.

James turned to his brother. "That would be great if you helped Mason out. We'll be there before it starts."

"Okay, well, that's probably my cue. I'll leave you two alone to talk. And I'll see you both tonight." The way he said it made it seem like he had no doubt that what he said was true.

"Thanks," James said.

I kind of wished Rob was staying. It was like he sucked any last remaining joy out with him as he stepped onto the elevator. He gave me a small smile and a wave as the doors closed.

As soon as we were alone, James put his hand on my shoulder.

"You know that I didn't mean anything I said last night. Penny, you have to know that."

"Then why did you say it?"

"Because you hurt me. You betrayed my trust. I thought..."

"I didn't. You just weren't listening."

- 31 -

"You must understand how it looked."

"Of course I do. But I also expect you to believe me instead of your ex, James. Do you have any idea how that made me feel?"

"Probably the same way it made me feel when I thought you were running away with Tyler." He let go of my shoulder and ran his hand through his hair. "Can we please just move past this? Let's just forget last night ever happened."

"No, James. I want to talk about this. From the beginning."

"The beginning? There's nothing to talk about. We both just jumped to conclusions..."

"My conclusions were very meticulously planned by your psychopath of an ex-wife."

He sighed. "Psychopath? Penny, that's..."

"Stop, okay? Would you just listen to me for two seconds? You have no idea what that bitch put me through. Put *us* through. Just hear me out, okay?"

He shrugged his shoulders. "Okay. I'm listening." He sat down at one of the stools at the kitchen counter and stared up at me.

I finally had his undivided attention. I sat down too, leaving one stool in between us. He was going to listen to everything I had to say. He had to. "When you left for your bachelor party, Isabella started sending me stuff. Envelopes full of pictures of you and Rachel hugging and of you and Isabella kissing. There were notes about how you'd never love me as much as you loved Rachel and how your addiction problem is a sickness and you can't control yourself. She knew how to get in my head. She must have known you were away and that I couldn't talk to you. And I was fighting with Melissa. I just...I'd never felt so alone."

"Why didn't you tell me when I got back?" He moved to the stool that had separated us before. "Baby, I would have listened to you."

"Why? Because I could show you the evidence?"

He frowned. "Penny, I said I was sorry. I don't know what else you want me to say." He put his hand on my knee.

"Don't touch me." I knew I was being dramatic, but I needed us to talk. "Please don't touch me. Let me just finish what I have to say."

He removed his hand. His silence made it seem like he wanted me to keep going.

"She sent me a box full of notes that you wrote her. Love letters. All about how Isabella was the love of your life. And that you dreamed about marrying her your whole life. You talked about how no one understood you better than her. How much you missed her when you were apart, and how beautiful she was. You talked about being ready to have children with her. And that you thought she'd be a great mother. I read them all James."

I thought he might jump in here, but he just looked down at his hands, which were clasped together on his lap.

"Isabella left a note on the box about how your love is as fleeting as your addictions. And that you were just trying to escape your reality by being with me. Because you're addicted to me."

I waited again, wondering if he'd say anything about that. He continued to look down at his hands.

"The last envelope I got was pictures of you fucking some girl. Isabella made it seem like it was from your bachelor party. I mean, she didn't say it was, but with everything else she had sent...I was doubting whether you even liked me, let alone love me. It seemed like you didn't care about me at all. She was so in my head, I don't even think I was thinking clearly anymore. I just felt so alone.

"When you came back from your bachelor party, you didn't seem guilty though. I could tell you genuinely missed me. And I thought I should let it go. Isabella was clearly just messing with me. I knew she was trying to get under my skin. I talked to Rob and he said you were just by the pool all weekend. I wanted to believe him. I wanted to believe you. And honestly, you kept talking about how you thought she had changed and how nice she had been recently. I didn't even think you'd believe me."

He continued to look down at his hands.

"I think she thought that would ruin us. But it didn't. I thought it was over. I thought we had won. But then yesterday, she sent me a message about wiring her 20 million dollars or she'd leak the photos of Tyler and me at my bachelorette party. I ignored it. I was done playing her games. And those photos didn't mean anything. Tyler was comforting me when I couldn't get a hold of you. He asked Melissa to be his girlfriend right after that lunch. And my friends just made me do stupid stuff at my bachelorette party. For the record, I wanted to stay in and watch a movie."

He nodded his head, but he still didn't look up at me.

"When I didn't reply to Isabella, she forwarded me pictures of you and me having sex in your office. She must have put a camera in there when she kissed you or something. I don't know. Either way, she said she'd leak them to tabloids if I didn't wire her the money. And she gave me her bank account number.

"I had already ruined your teaching career. I didn't want to be the reason you were part of a scandal again. My first thought was to tell you. I went to your office and was about to open the door when she texted me. She said if I went to you, she'd leak the photos. She was watching me, listening to me. I didn't have a choice. I was trying to protect you. So I did what she said. I had no idea the money was going into Tyler's account. James, I didn't know.

"And before I went home, she said I couldn't tell you she was involved or she'd leak the photos. That's why I just said we were being blackmailed. I couldn't tell you by who. I see now how stupid I was. That those photos weren't as important as you. I never meant to hurt you. I was just trying to protect you."

James didn't say anything. But he slowly lifted his head. He stared at me like he was seeing me for the first time.

"When you kicked me out, I didn't have anywhere to go. All I could think about was how much I loved you. I couldn't stand the thought of you going back to Isabella, because she's not good for you. You need someone who supports you and loves you and sees how great you are, even when you can't see it." Now I looked away from him. "So I went to your parents' house. Isabella never said I couldn't tell them. I told them everything. I showed them the text messages. Your father found this camera sticker thing on my phone. I think Austin put it there in the bar. Isabella really had been watching and listening to me. Your parents said they'd take care of it. I thought they would have called you. But I guess I did tell them that we had broken up. I think your mom seemed kind of relieved about that.

"Rob found me after that, walking back to the city. He agreed to take me back here. You asked me to disappear. I just...I needed to be near you. This was the best I could do. And I feel so dumb, because you were right about Tyler. You weren't wrong to jump to the conclusions you did."

James' back seemed to stiffen.

"Not about me wanting to run away with him. I don't love him, you have to know that. But he did still like me. We talked this morning and I told him I'd always love you. Even if you didn't want to be with me anymore. He's moving out of New York. He said he couldn't be just my friend anymore. I think that's probably for the best. You don't have to worry about him stealing me away now. I officially lost the last friend that was just mine.

"You were wrong about everything else though, James. And the things you said...they hurt me. Especially how I came from nothing. I didn't come from nothing. I didn't need saving. I never asked you to give me anything." I put my hand on his knee. "But I feel like I'm nothing without you."

He stood up, letting my hand fall from his knee. "I..." he let his voice trail off as he put his fingers through his hair. "You're not nothing without me. You're everything to me. Baby..." his voice trailed off and he took a step toward me. "I'm sorry. I'm so, so sorry. I never meant to hurt you. Please let me touch you. I need to touch you. I need to know we're okay. It's the only way I know we're okay."

"James, what are you talking about? What we're doing right now is going to show us that we're okay. We need to communicate. Having sex isn't going to fix anything. Why can't we just talk this out?"

"Because I'm addicted to you!" He put the back of his hand over his mouth and shook his head. "I lied. I didn't mean to. I thought I was better. But I'm sick. Isabella was right. I'm sick. Penny...I'll always be sick."

"You're not sick." I thought about what Rob had said to me last night. "James, you're not addicted to me. You're devoted to me."

He shook his head. "No. No, I've been lying to myself. I told myself it was okay because you're good for me. But I have an addictive personality. I can be addicted to something even if it's good. And you're so good. Baby, you're the best thing that has ever happened to me." He took a step back from me. "God, I'm addicted to you. How did I not realize I was addicted to you? How did I not see it before?"

I wanted him to calm down. I wanted him to talk to me. "James, you love me. That's what this is. Just like I love you." I stood up and put my hands on both sides of his face. "You're not addicted to me. You're not."

"Yes I am!"

"No, you're not!" I let go of his face. I wasn't sure if I was screaming because I was upset, or because I thought it was true.

"You have no idea what runs through my head when we're apart. When I thought you were leaving me," his voice cracked. "You have no idea how much I need you."

"Then tell me. James..."

He took a step forward, sandwiching me between him and the kitchen counter. "I'm addicted to your lips on mine. I'm addicted to how you taste." He grabbed the back of my neck and kissed me hard.

I was done fighting him. He had heard what I needed to say. And now? Now he was hurting. Now I needed to make him feel better. If he needed this, then I'd give it to him. We could talk later. I grabbed the front of his t-shirt, pulling him closer to me. Our kisses weren't usually like this. I was used to slow, passionate kisses. This was urgent and raw and...emotional. He was kissing me like he didn't need air. Just me.

He grabbed my thighs and wrapped my legs around his waist, pushing my back against the counter.

I tilted my head away from his. "That's not addiction, James. That's love. I feel it too."

"No." His voice sounded pained. "I'm addicted to the smell of that perfume you put behind your ears." He kissed the side my neck. "And the smell of your shampoo." He kissed my neck again. "The softness of your skin." He put his hand on the side of my neck, rubbing his thumb against my jaw line. "The sight of your face, your beauty. I'm addicted to the curves of your body." His hand slid down to my left breast. "I'm addicted to the goosebumps you get when I turn you on." He tightened his other hand on my thigh.

A small moan escaped my lips.

"And that. That sexy little noise you make when you want me inside of you. I'm addicted to that noise. I could live in moments like this. Where I have you in my arms. I need this. Whenever I'm not with you, I crave these moments. It's all I think about. You're all that I think about."

"That's love."

"Not when you're sick. Not for me."

"Don't say that."

"I'm an addict."

"No. You *were* an addict. You're good. We're good."

"It doesn't go away. I just found something healthier. For me. Not for you. You deserve better than this."

"Stop. Nothing is better than this. This is love. What we have is love." I put my hand on the left side of his chest. "You're labeling this wrong."

"No I'm not. I'm addicted to the way you make me feel. I'm addicted to you, Penny." He pushed the hem of my dress up, trailing his fingers against my skin.

"No, James. That's love. That's just love. I feel the same as you. I do. James, it's okay. We're okay."

He grabbed my hips and pulled my thong hard, ripping the lacy fabric in his hands. "I need you all the time."

Holy shit. I could feel his erection pressed against me. It was so hard to focus on his words when I was so incredibly turned on. "I need you the same way you need me. Don't you see that?"

"But it's just like you said. You didn't need saving, Penny. I did." He thrust into me hard.

Fuck. My fingertips dug into his back. "I thought I lost you," I moaned.

"I thought I lost you," he said back as he thrust even deeper inside of me.

"You'll never lose me." This was love. This was our love. And to me, it was the best kind of love possible.

He pushed my dress up and I lifted my arms up so he could pull it the rest of the way off. He made short work of my bra. And as soon as his hands touched my breasts he moaned into my mouth.

"I'm addicted to every inch of your body, baby. Every fucking inch." He slammed into me hard. My back was digging into the edge of the granite counter top.

I knew he was exhausted and upset. But he was also wrong. He was just plain wrong. This was not unrequited love, it never had been. He wasn't addicted to me. He was in love with me.

I grabbed a fistful of his hair to pull his mouth off mine. "I love your smile. And your laugh. Whenever I smell your body wash or cologne I get turned on." I felt the same as him. And it wasn't a sickness. It was love.

"Penny."

"I love having your arms wrapped around me. And the way you absentmindedly run your fingers through your hair. I love the color of your eyes and the way that they're always on me. And I love this," I said as I tightened my legs around him. "I crave this too. I miss you when we're apart. I love every inch of you too. Love, James. Not addiction. It's love. I love you."

"Penny."

"So how about you stop fucking me and make love to me because that's what we have."

"Baby, I'm so sorry." He pulled my face against his chest. "I'm so sorry." He held me like that for a moment. My hair was wet, so maybe I imagined it, but it felt like his tears were falling on the top of my head. I hadn't been wrong. I hadn't imagined it. We had grown together. What we had was real.

"Make love to me, James," I whispered against his chest.

"I always make love to you. Always, Penny." He grabbed my hips firmly and walked over to the master bedroom. He kicked the door open with his foot.

"Not here, James. Not in Rob's bed."

"It's our bed. Remember?" He threw me down onto it.

"Of course I remember." I looked up into his eyes. There was something there that I had never seen before. They almost looked stormy. Like something was brewing in his mind and it couldn't be stopped. I watched him pull off his t-shirt.

"We've always been wrong. You were my student for Christ's sake. We were never supposed to happen."

"But we did happen. Because despite what you think, we've always been right."

Something crossed over his face and he climbed on top of me on the bed. His strong hands pushed my thighs apart as the tip of his cock pressed against me. "We were always wrong, Penny. But it's always felt so fucking right." He pressed into me slowly this time, gently, lovingly. "And that's what's so terrifying," he whispered.

I barely heard him say it. But I definitely heard it. He was finally opening up to me. It felt like he was finally ready to share his heart completely. I let myself get lost in the moment. I let myself get lost in him.

CHAPTER 5

Friday

I listened to the sound of his heart beating. It felt like he wanted to talk. I was just going to wait until he did.

Several minutes later, he kissed the top of my head. "I think we need to talk."

I ran my index finger through the outlines of his six pack. "I think maybe I just need to listen."

He interlaced his fingers with mine and gently kissed my wrist. "Okay." He ran his other hand down my back, stopping right above my ass. "I don't even know where to start."

I didn't say anything. I just wanted him to tell me whatever he needed to tell me.

He sighed. "I'm always happy when we're together. But sometimes when we're apart I feel...guilty. I don't know if that's exactly the right word. It just feels like I cheated fate. I was your professor. There's responsibilities that come with that. I was supposed to protect you. I was supposed to guide you. I wasn't supposed to sleep with you. I feel bad about that. I didn't act like your professor, I was thinking with my heart and my dick instead of my head. I crossed a line. And it feels like I shouldn't be allowed to be happy when I broke the rules. That guilt eats at me. You deserved better than that. I should have never put you in that position."

I kissed his chest. "I didn't know you still felt bad about that. James, that was just as much my fault as yours. I pushed you. I wanted you to..."

"No. I was in the position of authority. That was on me."

"Still." I splayed my hand against his chest and lifted my head so I could look at him. "Okay, maybe you didn't protect me the way you should have as my professor. But you've done nothing but protect me since then. I think you've more than made up for it. Maybe you could start to try and let that guilt go?"

"But what if by doing all that, I ruined your life."

"You didn't."

"What if you were supposed to end up with Tyler?" The agony in his voice was almost palpable. "I worry that you'll be taken away from me like every other good thing I've ever had in my life. I don't deserve you, Penny. What if we were never supposed to happen?"

"I was never supposed to end up with Tyler. It's always been you. I wouldn't be happy with anyone else. I promise."

He grabbed my hand and kissed my wrist again. "I don't know how to let that go."

"Maybe it'll be easier once we're married. Once you hear my vows. Maybe then?"

"Are you sure that's what you really want? Penny, if I'm addicted to you..." he let his voice trail off. "I don't want to ruin your life. I can't let you."

"The only way you could ruin my life is by not being a part of it."

He moved his fingers up my back and ran them through my hair. "It's scary. I know you don't see my being

- 43 -

an addict as a problem because I seem to have it under control. But that's the thing, it's all about control. It hit a nerve hearing you talk about the notes Isabella left you. She always made me feel worthless. She made my problems worse than they were. I learned to doubt myself. It reminded me about how easily my control can shatter. But even if I am addicted to you, I still love you. I'm sorry about what I said. Of course I love you. I'm just worried that it's more complicated than that."

"I don't believe that you're sick, James. I think you're perfect. A little self-deprecating, but perfect."

He gave me a small smile.

"And I'm pretty sure we've proved that we're good at complicated. Our relationship was built on complicated." I kissed his chest.

"What happens if I lose control again?"

"Then I'll be there to help you get it back."

"But what kind of life is that?"

"The one that I want," I said.

"You're terrible at making decisions that are good for you. You realize that, right?"

"Luckily I have someone to take care of me."

He kissed the top of my head. "I'm sorry about what I said during our fight. You're not a problem. I know you could take care of yourself. I was just upset. I didn't mean anything I said. None of it. I'm so sorry."

"It's okay." I closed my eyes and listened to his heartbeat. "I forgive you." I waited a second. "Do you forgive me?"

"There's nothing to forgive. All of it was my fault."

"It wasn't your fault. You shouldn't put so much weight on your shoulders. You can't take responsibility for your ex-wife's decisions."

"I didn't know she was sending you stuff. I wish you had told me. I don't want you to ever feel like you're alone. I'm sorry you had to go through all that on your own."

"I'm sorry I didn't tell you. I know I should have. I think I thought that it would just go away if I ignored it."

He ran his fingers through my hair.

"Rob told me about what really happened between you and Rachel. I don't understand why you didn't tell me the truth about how you two ended."

"I didn't mean to lie, it's just easier for me if I remember it the way I told you. Her cutting me off...it nearly killed me. And when I found out it was because my parents paid her to stop seeing me? It made all those old feelings come up, which is probably why I jumped to conclusions about what you had done. It's something I'm sensitive about. I was raised to be suspicious of people's motivations to be close to me."

"I wish you had talked to me about it."

"I'm sorry. I should have. I just didn't want you to think that there was anything to worry about. I didn't want you to be jealous of something that didn't matter."

I looked up at him and pursed my lips. "Jealous? I'm never jealous."

"Mhm." He raised his left eyebrow.

I laughed. "So...there's nothing to be jealous of? You don't have feelings for her anymore?"

"No. No, I don't have feelings for Rachel. That was a long time ago. I think I liked her more for what she represented than who she really was. I built her up as a symbol for what my life could be without following my parents' wishes and dreams. I was young and naive and...stupidly opportunistic."

"But you loved her once."

"Maybe. It wasn't anything like this though." He kissed the top of my head.

"I'm sorry that your parents did what they did. I'm sorry that happened to you."

"I'm not." He let go of my hand and touched the side of my face. "If that didn't happen, I might not be here with you right now. I wouldn't change a thing."

I turned my head and kissed his palm. "There is one more thing I want to talk about."

"Isabella?"

I nodded.

"All I want to do right now is kill her," he said.

"You don't mean that."

"I wouldn't have said it if I didn't mean it."

"Can we maybe not commit murder the night before our wedding? I was hoping to just focus on us."

He smiled. "Does that mean you still want to marry me?"

"James, I never didn't want to marry you. You kicked me out. Because you believed the word of your ex-wife over me. I'd like to know why."

"It's not that I believed her over you. My whole life I grew up hearing my parents say I wasn't good enough. I married Isabella and heard it even more. It was ingrained in my head that no one would ever really love me, they'd just love my money. And combined with the guilt I feel about how our relationship started...it wore me down. All those nagging thoughts were swirling around in my head.

You couldn't give me a name and it just seemed..." his voice trailed off. "It seemed like everything I was ever told was true. And I was drunk. And I was hurting. That's not an excuse. It's just what happened. I didn't believe her over you. I just believed what I thought was true, what I've always thought was true."

I nodded. "Okay."

"I'm sorry."

"I know."

"So...you forgive me?" he asked.

I bit my lip. "There's one more thing. All those notes you wrote her. James, it really seemed like you were in love with her. I don't know why you didn't just tell me that. There's a reason why you wanted to have kids with her and not me. There's a reason why you trust her more than you trust me. There's a reason."

"No. Baby."

I looked down at his chest.

"Penny, look at me." He put his fingers under my chin and tilted my face toward his. "I hated my life. I forced myself to write those notes, trying to convince myself that I was happy. But I was drowning. Everything I wrote was a part of the facade. It's what I thought I was expected to say. I was going through the motions. And when I didn't feel like I was suffocating, I was completely numb. My life was meaningless. I was so depressed. You want to know why I really don't want to have kids? It's not just because I worry about my own problems. Yes, I worry that I'll slip and not be there for them. But mainly I just don't want to fuck them up like my parents did to me. I worry about not being good enough. The same worries I have about you.

But if you want kids, let's have kids. We can make babies right now. I want to give you whatever you want."

I smiled up at him as I rested my chin on his chest. "I do understand. We don't have to have kids, I just want to be with you. It just hurt so much to see that you wanted children with her."

"I would have killed myself if I had a bunch of demon spawn running around."

I think he thought it would be funny, but I didn't find it humorous at all. There was something in the back of my head that had worried me for awhile. I had read books and articles about addiction. It was insinuated that addiction was linked with mental illness. And he had just said that he had been depressed. "Have you ever thought about that?" I swallowed hard. "Killing yourself?"

"Penny, I would never leave you."

"I know. I just mean...before we knew each other. Did you ever think about it?" I realized I was holding my breath as I waited for his answer.

"Once, maybe. I remember sitting in my office at Blive Tech. I had a press conference that I was running late for and my office phone was ringing and my cell phone was ringing and I had a million unanswered emails that I was staring at on my computer. I looked out the window at Central Park and realized that I wanted to be anywhere in the world but where I was. And maybe for a second, I thought about just how high up my window was."

I exhaled slowly.

"I had already been thinking about selling the company. I had been fighting with Isabella about it for months. And in that moment, I just knew I couldn't keep going the way I was going. So, I went to the press conference and talked about how I was stepping down instead of whatever I was supposed to be talking about. I don't think I ever would have killed myself. I just...I needed that moment of clarity to push myself into finally making a decision for myself for once in my life."

"And you decided to be a professor instead?"

He ran his fingers through my hair. "Yeah."

"Had you always wanted to teach?"

"I had been thinking about it for awhile. It felt so much more meaningful than what I was doing."

"And you loved it?"

"Yes. More so here than in New York, though. Moving to Newark really was my fresh start. Teaching in New York still felt stifling. Maybe because I was still living with Isabella. But yes, I loved teaching. It really felt like I was making a difference."

I smiled. "Do you ever miss it?"

"My first priority is always you."

I knew that he meant what he said. But there was also another truth in it. He missed teaching. Why had he never told me he missed being a professor? I let go of his hand and shifted so that I was straddling him. "Okay, here's the deal, Professor Hunter."

He smiled at me calling him that.

"I will marry you tomorrow under one condition. You have to start teaching again."

He put his hands behind his head and smiled up at me. "That's quite the ultimatum, Miss Taylor."

I shook my head. "Not really, because I'm pretty sure you want both those things."

"I don't really want to sell Hunter Tech. I think we're doing a lot of good. We're so close on a breakthrough for a new energy source."

"Mhm. Yet you had tons of money invested in oil stocks?"

"It's good to diversify. Wait, did you sell my oil stocks?"

"Maybe a few."

He laughed.

"You're so environmentally conscious. I think I did you a favor."

"I guess I owe you a thank you." His hand moved to my waist.

I laughed. "What about my ultimatum? Don't you want to teach again? You don't even have to sell your company. You just need to find someone else to run it. Maybe unload some of the stress?"

He smiled up at me. "You think I'm stressed out too? Rob was just telling me that the other day. Maybe I should just retire and we can move to the country."

"Maybe." Despite what he thought, I didn't save him. Becoming a professor did. And as his soon-to-be wife, I'd do anything I could to ensure that he was happy. "You can retire if you want, but I want you to consider teaching again. Besides, you'd be bored out of your mind if you didn't do anything at all."

"I didn't say I wouldn't be doing anything." His hand slid up my thigh.

"James!" I laughed. "I just want you to think about it."

"Okay. I'll consider teaching again. Will you accept those conditions?"

"Conditions accepted." I stuck out my hand for him.

DEVOTION

"Oh, I have a better way to acknowledge our deal." He pulled me against him as he rolled over, pressing my back against the mattress.

This is so much better.

CHAPTER 6

Friday

James drove straight instead of turning right toward our apartment. The whole drive back to New York had been fun and relaxing. We had so desperately needed some alone time. And now I felt closer to him than ever. He had finally opened up to me about his worries and fears. I was so in love with him. Maybe he didn't want this car ride to end either. He made another turn, in the opposite direction of our apartment.

"Where are we going?"

"The police station."

"Why?"

He glanced at me for a second and then looked back at the road. "Blackmail is a felony, Penny. I'm not letting this go."

"You're going to report it to the police?"

"Of course I am. I'm sick of dealing with her shit. I told her to leave us alone. I gave her fair warning."

"James, I don't even know if there is any evidence of her blackmailing us. The money was sent to Tyler, not her. I feel like she was careful about covering her tracks."

"So they'll call Tyler about it."

"No, I mean, there's no evidence that she was even the one that sent it there. Yes, I was getting text messages from her, but it was from a restricted number. They might not be able to trace it."

"Her handwriting was on the pictures and notes she sent you too."

"Maybe. Or maybe someone was helping her."

"Well, that's what the police are supposed to find out. She should go to prison for this. It's not like 20 million dollars is a petty crime. I don't care about the money, but I'm not just letting this go. And we can at least file a restraining order while we're there. I'm not going to risk her showing up to our wedding. Not after all this."

"You think she'd try to stop it?"

"I think that's all she's been trying to do. She can't accept that I'm happy with someone that's not her." James pulled to a stop outside of the precinct. "I think maybe you were right when you called her a psychopath."

I laughed, but stopped when he didn't even so much as smile. "I don't think she'd ever try to hurt us or anything though. Right?"

"Well, I never would have thought she'd blackmail me either."

"James, technically you blackmailed her in order to get her to sign the divorce papers. Maybe she was just returning the favor. What if she gets arrested and brings that up?"

"A one minute conversation where I never even exchanged anything with her won't hold up in court. Besides, what she got from that conversation was half my money. And there isn't a shred of evidence anyway."

"There were photos..."

"Penny. I took care of that. Let me take care of this too."

"When I talked to your parents, they said they'd handle this. Maybe you should check with them first. Maybe they already filed a complaint."

"A complaint?" He laughed. "They invited her to our engagement party. As far as I'm concerned they're just as much to blame." He climbed out of the car and slammed the door.

I quickly climbed out of the passenger's side. "James, your parents seemed sorry about that. Especially your father. You should call them."

"Penny, Isabella tortured you for a week. She tried to break us up. She threatened you. She stole our money. Those are crimes. She doesn't deserve to be out there walking the streets. You said yourself that she had a back-up plan when her original pictures and notes didn't work. What if she's planning something else? I won't have peace of mind until she's behind bars."

"Okay. If you think we should, then let's do it."

He grabbed my hand. "You seem like you're scared to go in there."

"A little nervous, maybe. I've never even been pulled over before. "I'm awkward around authority figures."

James laughed. "Oh, is that why we ended up together? Maybe I shouldn't let you in there then."

"No. That was different." I shoved his arm playfully. "I mean law enforcement. Those detectives that questioned us at the University of New Castle really knew how to crawl under my skin."

"You have nothing to worry about. Like you said, you've never even been pulled over for speeding. Which is great, because I have a terrible record. They'll trust your word more than mine."

"I didn't even think about that."

He pulled me toward the front doors. As soon as we stepped inside, the air turned stale. It didn't look anything like it did in shows and movies. No one was jumping up to talk to us, eager to close a case. There was a large desk where officers sat behind glass and their eyes were glued to their computer screens. I couldn't help but think that the glass they were behind was bullet proof. It made me glance over at the people sitting in waiting chairs. They looked harmless enough. One of them was clearly homeless. Well, at least the police officers were nice, letting him stay here like this. It was so hot in New York in the summer and it was definitely cooler in here.

I heard a fly and glanced toward my right. I grabbed James' arm. "Oh my God, there's blood on the floor," I hissed.

James laughed. "I'm pretty sure that's soda. Probably. Come on."

My eyes stayed glued on the spot as we approached the desk.

"Good afternoon officers, we'd like to report a crime," James said calmly.

The woman on the computer didn't look at us. "Is anyone dead or in immediate danger?" she asked as she typed something on her keyboard.

"Not yet," James said.

I elbowed him in the ribs at his joke. "Not funny," I mouthed silently.

The woman paused and looked up at us. "If you could please fill out this form," she said and shoved a clipboard under a small slot in the glass partition. "We'll be with you shortly."

"Thank you," I said.

James lifted up the pen and quickly filled out the information as I tried not to stare at the blood stain. He pushed the clipboard back through the slot and we walked over toward the seating area. Before we even had a chance to sit down, we heard a beeping noise. I looked over my shoulder at an officer who had just opened up a door.

"James Hunter, please come with me," the officer said.

That was fast. James kept his hand in mine as we followed the police officer through the door. We walked down a narrow corridor into a larger room with tons of desks. This was actually a lot more like T.V. shows and movies. Detective and police officers were on phones, a few guys were handcuffed to chairs, and there was a buzz of electricity in the air. There were even maps on the walls and pictures of wanted subjects. We followed the officer to a desk and sat down.

"I'm Officer Daugherty and I'll be handling your case." He glanced at his notepad. "I understand you're filing a complaint about blackmail against Isabella Hunter. Correct?"

"Yes," James said.

"Wife?" he asked as he jotted something down in his notebook.

"Ex-wife. I'm getting remarried tomorrow."

Officer Daugherty looked up and eyed me coolly. "Name?" he said.

"Penny Taylor."

"Okay." He turned to his computer and typed something on his keyboard. He scrolled with his mouse and glanced at me once more. "You have a much better record than your future husband."

It took every ounce of restraint not to ask about James' record. That was one thing I still didn't know about.

I knew he had been arrested in the past. I just didn't know all the details. "Um...thanks," I said instead.

The officer smiled. "I'll need to know the specifics of the blackmail. What were the demands and what were the compromising materials that Isabella Hunter had against you?" He started typing on his computer again.

"Right," James said. "She had photos of us having sex in my office that she was going to leak to tabloids if we didn't send her 20 million dollars." He shifted uncomfortably in his seat.

Officer Daugherty paused in his typing and looked up at him. "Did you say 20 million dollars?"

"That is correct," James said. "And we gave it to her."

"Okay, well, that escalates this to a felony. Do you know if your ex-wife is currently in New York City? We're going to need to bring her in for questioning."

"I have no idea," James said.

Officer Daugherty typed something into his computer. "Do you have any documentation of her demands and threats?"

"She had been sending pictures and notes to Penny all week trying to get in her head. And then she sent her some text messages about the money yesterday. Show him, Penny."

I pulled my phone out of my purse, clicked on the text message thread, and slid it toward Officer Daugherty.

He picked up the phone and thumbed through the messages. "Okay, give me one second." He lifted up his desk phone and typed in the number from my cell phone into his phone. He immediately hung up. "The phone used for these texts has been disconnected. Are you sure it was her?"

"It was definitely her," I said.

"Were the photos and notes she had sent you signed?"

"No. But one of the things she sent was notes that James had written her when they were married."

"Was there anything else?"

I tried to think. "Yes, there were emails too that she sent me at work. But they were just from a random email account and she didn't say her name."

"Okay, we're going to need access to those as well. I can send an officer with you to pick up the pictures and notes she sent you. We will need access to your work email."

"I can give you temporary access to our server," James said and gestured for Officer Daugherty to hand him his pen and notebook. James quickly jotted down something in the notebook and pushed it back toward Officer Daugherty.

"Alright," he said. "Do you know what bank this account is in? We'll need to verify the amount you're claiming as well."

"Actually, she said it was her account as you can see from the text. But it went to one of my friends," I said.

"And you assume that this friend wasn't the one behind the threats?"

"No. Absolutely not," I said.

I could feel James' eyes on me. I knew what he was thinking. We knew Austin was working with Isabella. So why not Tyler? But I knew Tyler. He never would have done something like that. Even if he was still in love with me. Really, the fact that he loved me made it even less likely.

"Why would your ex-wife send your soon-to-be new wife's friend 20 million dollars?"

"She was trying to get us to break up," I said.

Officer Daugherty nodded, but it didn't really look like he believed me. "Right, right. Do you have this friend's contact information?"

"Yes. Tyler Stevens. His number is in my phone."

"Okay, great. I'm going to give your friend a call real quick."

"I don't really think that's necessary," I said. I pictured Tyler walking away from me back on campus. He had been so upset. This wasn't the way to tell him that James and I had worked things out. This wasn't right.

"It'll just take a second," the officer said as he lifted up his desk phone again.

"It wasn't him," I said. "He had nothing to do with this."

"I'm just verifying the bank account information."

"It did go to him," James said, clearly understanding my distress. "I talked to my bank and they said the name belonging to that account was Tyler Stevens. You can just verify it with my bank."

"Do you know what bank the money went to?"

"No, he didn't say. But I can find out if you want."

"That would be great. How about you give your bank a call while I give Mr. Stevens a call." He lifted up his phone before I could say anything else to stop him.

"Hello, Tyler Stevens?" He paused. "This is Officer Daugherty with the NYPD." Pause. "No, everything is fine. For now." He gave me an accusatory glance.

Why is this happening right now?

"I'm going to call my bank," James said and squeezed my arm. "Don't worry, we're going to figure this out." He stood up and walked toward an empty desk to make his call. I focused back on what Officer Daugherty was saying. He was reading the account information to Tyler.

"No?" Officer Daugherty said. "Yes, if you wouldn't mind checking your account." Pause. "Are you sure, Mr. Stevens?" Pause. "Yes," he said as he glanced up at me. "I'm sitting with her right now." Pause. "I will let her know. If you'll please just keep an eye on your account. We may need to contact you again." Pause. "I'm sure she'll be happy to fill you in. In the meantime, please don't discuss this incident with any outside parties." Pause. "You too, Mr. Stevens." Officer Daugherty hung up the phone and typed something in his computer.

"What did he say?" I asked.

"He said he wanted you to call him."

I thought back to our conversation on campus. We had never talked about the money. He had never even asked about it.

"Did he have the money?" James asked as he sat down next to me.

"No," Officer Daugherty said. "He claims that account doesn't belong to him and that he doesn't have the money." He glanced down at his computer. "His account currently holds only $24,000. According to him." He leaned back in his chair and crossed his arms. "If there is any more information that you haven't provided, now would be the time."

"My bank verified again that the money was transferred to Tyler Stevens," James said. "The account number was from a Bank of America in New York City."

"Mr. Stevens said he banks at WSFS. Whatever that is," Officer Daugherty said.

"It's a bank in Wilmington," I said. "He grew up in Delaware like me. I use the same bank. When I talked to him earlier today, he didn't mention anything about the money. He would have brought it up if it just suddenly appeared in his account. Maybe Isabella just opened an account under his name?"

"You can't just open an account under a random name that isn't your own," Officer Daugherty said. They'd want verification. That would be breaking all sorts of laws."

"Which Isabella doesn't seem to care about," I said.

"Either way, we're going to need to bring Mr. Stevens in for questioning."

"I'm not sure he's even in New York anymore," I said. "He said he was moving this morning."

Officer Daugherty leaned forward, resting his elbows on his desk. "You must see how that looks."

"It looks like I hurt him and he can't stand to run into me in the city."

"No, it looks like he's fleeing with 20 million dollars. Look," Officer Daugherty said. "If you want my honest opinion, all the facts point to him being your guy. If you want me to open this case, he will be one of the key suspects."

"I don't want him to be a suspect."

"That's not how it works..."

"Officer Daugherty," James cut in. "We don't want Tyler to be a part of the investigation. We're just worried about Isabella. That's it."

"Okay. We'll look into it as best we can. If we can't find the money, though, you don't mind if Mr. Stevens just...keeps it? Is that what you're saying?"

James looked at me. "Yes. Because I know Isabella has it."

Officer Daugherty sighed. "Okay. We'll try to track the cell phone and emails. And we'll work on fingerprints from the notes and pictures you'll be giving us. If that leads to a dead end, we'll have to drop the case, though."

"That's fine," James said.

"Is there anything else I can help you with?" Officer Daugherty said as he typed something on his computer.

"We'd also like to file a restraining order against Isabella Hunter. For both of us."

Officer Daugherty looked up at him. "Even before you know she's guilty?"

"She's guilty," James said.

"Okay. Well, restraining orders take one to two days to process. We should be able to get you a court hearing within a few weeks. Let me get the paperwork for you."

"Two weeks? Officer, this is kind of an emergency," James said. The calmness was gone from his voice.

"We can look into having the hearing later this week, but that's the earliest we can do it."

"I'm worried about the safety of my fiancée. Isn't there anything you can do?"

"Has Isabella made any threats against your person?"

"No, but..."

"Then as far as the state of New York is concerned, she is not an imminent threat."

"She just stole 20 million dollars from us!" James slammed his fist against the desk.

"James." I grabbed his arm.

"If you would please calm down," Officer Daugherty said.

"This is ridiculous," James said as he stood up.

Officer Daugherty stayed completely calm. "Officer Kemp will be by your residence within an hour or so to pick up the evidence."

"Thanks a lot," James said. He started to walk away. "New York's finest, my ass," he said under his breath.

Officer Daugherty looked angry now. "What did you just say?"

"He didn't mean that, Officer," I quickly said. "We really appreciate all your help. And we'll have the evidence ready when Officer Kemp arrives." I glanced back at James who was pushing through the door. "Thank you so much," I said and stood up.

"We need a signature if you want to file that restraining order, and a little more information," Officer Daugherty said.

"That's okay, I think we're going to pass on that. But thank you," I said again.

"No problem. I'm sure you'll have plenty of experience filling out those forms soon enough," Officer Daugherty said coolly.

"What?" I turned back toward him.

"I just mean, with his list of priors I don't doubt you'll be filing one against him in your near future."

Fuck you. I didn't lose my temper as easily as James, but I wanted to punch this guy in the face. "You know, I'm pretty sure James donates a lot of money to the New York City police department. He might reconsider that now."

Officer Daugherty laughed. "Great. We'll make sure to put your blackmail case with missing suspects at the top of the priority list," he said sarcastically and turned back to his computer.

I should have kept my mouth shut. "I hope you have a great weekend," I said as nicely as I could muster as I walked after James. He wasn't in the waiting area. I walked outside and blinked from the bright sun. James was pacing on the sidewalk, yelling something into his phone. I ran over to him.

"James."

He put his finger up. "No, not in half an hour. Now." He hung up his phone as he ran his hand through his hair.

"Are you okay? James, I don't think there was anything he could do. That's just how restraining orders work."

"That guy was an asshole."

"Yeah, maybe. But you can't call him an ass to his face. He's a police officer."

"Freedom of speech, Penny."

"No. That's insulting a police officer. He probably could have arrested you for that."

He lowered both his eyebrows.

"Take a deep breath, okay?"

He laughed.

"James, this isn't funny. They don't believe Isabella did it. They think it was Tyler. I don't even know if they believed us."

"Because they're fucking idiots!" He gestured rudely to the building.

"Get in the car before you get us arrested." I shoved his shoulder.

When I climbed into my side, James had his forehead resting on the steering wheel. I gave him a second to calm down before I touched his arm. "So, what now?"

He lifted his head and ran his hands down his face. "I called my security detail."

"You really think she'd try to hurt us?"

"I have no idea. All she cares about is status. And as soon as we get married, her status goes down."

"Didn't it go down when you two got divorced?"

"She played the whole divorce card really well. The whole, 'woe is me' thing really worked in her favor especially after everyone found out I was dating a student. The press ate it up."

"I didn't think people actually believed her."

"People believe whatever they want to believe."

I looked out the window. I knew that. That's why I had to transfer to NYCU in the middle of college. I could feel James' eyes on me. I knew what he was thinking. He didn't have to say anything. "He didn't have anything to do with it, James."

He put his hand on my knee. "If you're sure, I'm sure."

I turned my head toward him. "I'm sure."

He nodded.

"I may have said something to Officer Daugherty about how you'd be reconsidering your generous donations to the police force. And he may have insinuated that our case was now a low priority. I'm sorry." There was no need to talk about why I had snapped. This wasn't the time for that. I'd ask James about his record later.

James laughed. "I kind of figured that about our case anyway. My private investigator is coming by the apartment in about half an hour. I wanted to make sure he saw the pictures and notes before the police took them."

"You have a private investigator?"

James nodded.

"And a security detail?"

He nodded again.

"Have you ever used them before?"

"I've used the private investigator to help get Isabella to sign the divorce papers. And I may have gotten him to give me some information about you before we started dating."

I laughed. But it didn't look like he was kidding. "Seriously?"

"It's not like I found anything out. Like I said earlier, you don't have a record or anything. All he got me was that you were a good student and your home address or something like that."

I shook my head. "You're so ridiculous. And what about the security detail? Have you used them before?"

"I use them all the time."

"Since we've been together?"

"Especially since we've been together."

"Why have I never seen them before then?"

"I pay them to not be seen. But they'll be swinging by the apartment too. I'll want you to know who they are if you see something or if you feel like you're in danger."

"What do they do exactly?"

"They do hourly perimeter checks outside our apartment and office. And they attend any functions we go to. They were even at the party my parents threw us."

"Wait, really? Where were they when Isabella slapped me?"

"Isabella hadn't been on the list of potential threats. We probably should have told Officer Daugherty that she hit you. He might have taken us more seriously then."

"List of potential threats?" I asked, ignoring his comment about being slapped. Officer Daugherty definitely wasn't going to help us now either way. "Who is on the list?"

"Just a handful of people."

"Like...who?"

"They're just possible threats, Penny. It's nothing serious."

"Who's on the list?"

He shifted in his seat. "Only a few people. Joseph Moreno, the CEO of an online security company I had to fire for security breaches. He wasn't happy with the loss of the Blive Tech account, and made some disturbing promises that I hope he doesn't deliver on. Richard Sutton, who filed a lawsuit against me after he claimed I stole his idea. I didn't, by the way. Brian Vega, who founded a startup that I buried when I launched Hunter Tech. His technology advancements were outdated as soon as we launched. I've gotten death threats from him. Albert Dalton, who owns an oil company. One I definitely wasn't invested in. He sends me threatening letters sometimes about how I'm ruining the economy by looking for new energy sources. Marc Hatfield, a Harvard acquaintance who's always asking me for money. I actually have no idea who he is. I'm pretty sure he's crazy. And Kristen Dwyer. It's really not a big deal. It's just in case. I like to be proactive."

"Kristen Dwyer? Who is that?"

"Just a student I had that I thought was stalking me. I should probably remove her from the list. It was a long time ago."

"From New York or Newark?"

"Newark. I had her the same time I was teaching you actually."

"And you thought she was stalking you?"

"Yeah, I'm pretty sure she was. But she has a boyfriend now and I really don't think she's a threat anymore."

"Did your private investigator find that out for you?"

"No, actually, I ran into her during my bachelor party."

"Did she follow you there?"

He laughed. "No, she was there for her friend's bachelorette party. By the way, did Rob tell you about Daphne yet?"

"Daphne? No. I was too self-absorbed last night. You know, crying everywhere and missing you."

He grabbed my hand. "Well, you're going to like her. I think she's coming to the rehearsal dinner tonight."

"Wait, Rob is dating someone?"

"You sound surprised."

"Of course I'm surprised. He never stays in one place for more than five minutes. He must really like her."

"I think he does. And she's good for him. She seems really grounded. He needs that."

I smiled. "I think you're right about that. Maybe he's finally ready for some roots. Is she from New York?"

"Yeah, she lives like fifteen minutes away from us.

"That's even better. It would be awesome if Rob moved to New York. Besides, the girls he was chasing on campus were much too young for him."

James laughed. "Maybe it's a Hunter thing."

I pressed my lips together and shook my head. "Maybe." I scooted over in my seat and leaned my head against James' shoulder.

He immediately put his arm around me.

"I love you so much, James."

He kissed my temple. "Thank you for forgiving me. Thank you for giving me another chance. I love you too."

His arm had tightened around me when he spoke. Isabella had gotten into his head too. I could tell that he was still struggling with the fact that he thought his love was twisted with addiction because of her. But that was okay. We'd work through that together. I had my whole life to convince him that what we had was purely love. I had my whole life to convince him just how amazing he was.

CHAPTER 7

Friday

"Penny!" Bee yelled as she jumped off a chair and tossed Mason the streamers. She ran over and threw her arms around me. "Why didn't you call me? I was so worried about you. I left you like a hundred texts."

It was so good to see her. I had convinced myself I had lost her friendship. I immediately hugged her back. "I just...I thought if James broke up with me..."

"What? That I wouldn't be your friend anymore? Are you crazy?" She held me at arm's length. "Penny, you're one of my best friends. No matter what."

"Thanks, Bee."

"I can't believe you didn't think you could talk to me." She hugged me again. "I'm always here for you. Always."

I couldn't help it. I had felt so alone last night and this morning. To know that the friends I thought I lost were still my friends made the tears flow again. My chosen family was still choosing me back. I was so full I couldn't help but burst.

"Welcome back, Penny." I felt Mason's hand on my back.

Bee released me from her hug so I could look up at Mason. "Thanks, Mason. I'm sorry I hung up on you this morning. I didn't want to walk away. I didn't..."

He laughed. "I know that. I was trying to guilt trip you."

I wiped underneath my eyes. "Well it worked. You know me so well."

"Don't cry, Penny." He leaned down and hugged me hard. "Just for the record though, I'll always have your back."

"I know. And thanks for being with James last night when I couldn't be."

"I would never let anything happen to him either. Family, Penny." He patted my back and released me from his hug. He gave me a warm smile that just made me cry even more.

How did I get this lucky?

"Don't make her cry again," James said. "I'm pretty sure she's already dehydrated."

"Yeah, because of you, asshole," Mason said and tossed the roll of streamers at him. He winked at me.

"Why was no one on my side last night?" James said.

"Because you're an idiot," Rob said. He patted James' shoulder as he walked over to me. "Told ya you'd be back in time," he said to me with a smile.

"Thanks for everything, Rob." I stood on my tiptoes as I threw my arms around his neck.

"That's what family is for."

"You know what I mean," I whispered in his ear. "For being there when you didn't have to be."

"That's what family is for," he said again and kissed my cheek. "And you're super hot when you've been walking around in the rain."

"Rob!" I laughed as I released his neck and lightly punched his shoulder. "I heard you're dating someone."

He smiled. "I'm assuming James told you that?"

"Mhm. Why didn't you?"

"Because you were upset last night. I didn't think it was the right time to brag about my new relationship. Especially when you were convinced that you weren't part of the family anymore. Which was ridiculous."

"You look happy."

He smiled. "I am. She's...really something."

"Is she coming tonight?"

"Yeah. I mean, if that's okay. James said..."

"Of course it's okay. I can't wait to meet her."

"I think you're going to like her."

"Does this mean you aren't going to say super inappropriate things about me anymore?" I made a pouty face.

Rob laughed. "No one can stop me from doing that. It's our thing."

"Our thing?"

"Yeah, our thing. I say hilarious stuff and you pretend to be upset about it."

I laughed. "Right." I laughed again as James wrapped his arms around me from behind.

"We have an hour before we have to be at the rehearsal, so we need to finish this in forty minutes," Bee said and clapped her hands.

"Where's Matt?" I asked.

"He went to go buy more streamers," Bee said. "Can you try to get a hold of Melissa? We could really use her help. She's not returning any of my texts. And Jen should be here any minute. Ian left like an hour and a half ago to go pick her up. I'm not sure what's taking them so long."

"Okay, I'll give Melissa a call. What else do you want us to do?"

Bee smiled. "Go get ready. Relax. We got this." She picked up a roll of streamers off the ground.

"Come with me," James whispered in my ear. He grabbed my hand and led me toward the stairs. As I walked up the stairs, I glanced over my shoulder at my friends decorating our apartment. *Yes, I was lucky.* And I was so happy to be home.

James lead me into our bedroom and then the bathroom. He dropped my hand and pulled his shirt off.

"I should call Melissa. She'll want to know what's going on."

"Not right now." He turned on the shower.

"James, we should really be helping them decorate. And making sure everything's set for tonight."

"We can do all that. But first, we both need a shower. We need to relax. We need to unwind from earlier." He grabbed the bottom of my dress and pushed it up my thighs.

I lifted my arms in the air as he pulled it the rest of the way off.

"Besides," he said and kissed the side of my neck. "Our friends have got it covered." He unhooked my bra and pushed my thong down my hips.

"What about Officer Kemp? And your investigator? And..."

He put his finger to my lips. "We're getting married tomorrow. Let's just take this one moment to focus on that." He pushed his shorts and boxers to the floor and stepped into the shower.

I bit my lip. I did need to shower. And get ready. And about a million other things in forty minutes. I laughed as he grabbed my arm and pulled me in after him. I looked up at his handsome features, covered in the cascading water. A smile was planted on his face.

"I can't wait to marry you."

"I can't wait either." I placed my hands on the scruff on his cheeks. "Thank you for coming after me. Thank you for fighting for us."

"Wherever you are, I am. I'll always fight for us. Close your eyes, baby."

I smiled and closed my eyes. I heard him open the bottle of shampoo. His fingers immediately started massaging my scalp. It felt amazing. He was washing off last night and this morning and everything in between, cleansing me of every worry and fear.

I kept my eyes closed as he started to massage my shoulders. "You're perfect, Penny," he said as he kissed my neck and moved his hands down my arms. I sighed and leaned back against his chest as he washed my breasts and stomach. His fingers ran over my most intimate areas and down my thighs. He shifted behind me as he got low enough to wash my legs and feet. *Oh my God, my feet. This feels amazing.* I pressed my hand against the shower wall as he placed a kiss against my ass cheek.

He pulled me back under the water and grabbed my hair, tilting my head back, making sure I didn't get any soap in my eyes. "There," he said as he let go of my hair.

I slowly opened my eyes and sighed. "That was just what I needed."

He kissed my forehead. "I hoped so. Go get ready, baby. I'll be out in a second."

"Let me do you."

"You take longer to get ready than me," he said as he grabbed his shampoo bottle.

I grabbed the bottle from him. "You need this too." I poured some soap in my hand. "Let me."

He smiled and stepped out of the water. He closed his eyes and put his hands on my hips as I started to massage the soap into his hair.

A quiet groan escaped from his lips, which put a smile onto mine. I placed a kiss on the tip of his nose as I began to lather up his shoulders. I massaged his lower back. I knew it bothered him from sitting at a desk all day. He groaned again. "That feels so good, baby."

I massaged him another minute before running my soapy hands down his chiseled abs and over his growing erection. He groaned again. This would definitely relax him. I tightened my hand around his hard cock.

"Fuck." He laughed and opened his eyes. "As much as I want to do that, we don't have enough time." He stepped under the water and rinsed the soap out of his hair. "Go get ready. Now." He slapped my ass.

"So demanding."

"We can revisit this later," he said and winked at me.

"When? We're not sharing a hotel room tonight."

"Shit, I forgot about that. Maybe we should make time."

"I want you to want me tomorrow night," I said as I stepped out of the shower.

"Penny, I always want you." Something crossed over his face and he turned away from me. "I'll be done in a sec," he said into the water.

I tried not to let it bother me as I wrapped a towel around myself. I knew he had talked to his therapist about me. James had even told me that his therapist agreed that he wasn't addicted to me. Why was James doubting his word? *Should I find a way to contact him?* Maybe James needed to talk to him, to help calm down.

That desperate feeling that he had gotten when he told me to leave wasn't addiction. Because I felt it too. It was...pain. Loss. Heartbreak. I quickly combed my hair and grabbed the blow-dryer. By the time I was done drying my hair, James had turned off the water.

He stepped out of the shower and wrapped a towel around his waist. I would never tire of seeing him like this. Beads of water dripped down his perfectly sculpted torso. God, he was so sexy.

He walked over next to me and ran his hand through his hair. "Do you want me to shave?" he asked.

I smiled at his reflection in the mirror. "No. I like your stubble."

He kissed my cheek. "What color tie should I wear?"

"Um." I turned toward him. I hadn't thought much about what I wanted to wear. "I'll let you know when I figure out what I'm wearing."

"How about gray suit, black tie? Can't go wrong with that."

"That's sounds perfect."

"Come downstairs as soon as you're ready. I want you to meet the security detail before we head over."

"Okay."

He put his hand under my chin. "Remember the first night we moved here? I had wanted to take you out to a fancy dinner. We both got super dressed up and were walking through Central Park to go to the restaurant when you convinced me you just wanted to try a New York hot dog? We ended up just spending the entire night talking and laughing on a bench. And I got mustard all over my suit jacket." He smiled.

"Of course I remember." My eyes had gotten teary remembering.

"I loved that night. And you looked beautiful in that dress." He placed a soft kiss against my lips. "Wear that one."

"Okay."

He kissed me once more and I watched him walk out of the bathroom. I couldn't believe he remembered what I was wearing that night. I smiled to myself. He had been wearing a gray suit and a black tie. I quickly wiped under my eyes. If I started crying again right now, I'd never be able to get ready. It seemed like all I did was cry recently. I plugged in my curling iron and did my makeup as fast as I could. When I was done, the curling iron still wasn't hot enough.

I grabbed my phone and clicked on Melissa's name. The phone rang a few times and then went to voicemail. My stomach sunk. "Hey, Melissa, it's me. I just wanted to make sure you were going to be at the Tavern on the Green by 6. I know we have a lot to talk about. And we can talk about it after the dinner tonight. Please just be there. I love you. And I'm sorry about everything. I'll see you soon. Bye, Melissa." I hung up before I started to ramble about Tyler.

Shit, Tyler. I put my hand over the curling iron and felt the heat rising off of it. I was going to need to talk to Tyler and curl my hair at the same time in order to finish getting ready. I pressed on Tyler's name in my phone and balanced my cell phone between my ear and shoulder as I started to curl the ends of my hair.

"Hey," he said. "I was hoping you'd call." He sighed. "So you took my advice? You two made up?"

"Yeah. Thank you, Tyler. For everything."

"The wedding is back on then?"

"It is. Tyler, if you're still in New York, you should come tonight."

"No. I mean...I never went back to New York. I'm at some diner in Pennsylvania right now, actually. I just needed to drive."

"I'm sorry."

"Don't apologize. I get it. And I am happy for you. Really, Penny, I am."

"Thank you." I quickly wiped under my eyes again. *God, don't start crying again.*

"So," Tyler said. "The police think I stole money from James? Is that about right?"

"Yeah. But it was Isabella. Don't worry about it, okay? We're going to clear it up. We went to the police station to try and get her arrested and it just...they twisted everything around." I moved the phone to my other ear so I could finish my hair.

"I don't really understand why my name came up. Should I be worried about this?"

"No. I promise I'll take care of it. I'm sorry you got dragged into this. I just wanted to call to make sure you knew it was going to be okay."

"Yeah. Hey, it's 5:30. Don't you have to get going to your rehearsal?"

"I have a few minutes."

We were both silent for a moment. I unplugged the curling iron.

"Penny, I said I couldn't be your friend anymore. We can't...*I* can't do this." His breathing sounded heavy.

"I know." I walked out of the bathroom. I couldn't stand to look at my reflection in the mirror. It was hard being so happy when Tyler was so sad. Because of me. "Okay. Thank you for taking my call."

"Penny." His voice sounded pained. "I'm sorry that I'm not going to be there. I just...I need time."

"It's okay. I understand." I was blinking fast so that I wouldn't start crying.

"Maybe one day down the road we can try this whole friend thing again."

It was at least a small shred of hope. Time could heal this. Tyler would find someone and she would heal him. He'd know what true love really was.

"Call me when that happens. I'm going to miss you."

"I'm going to miss you too."

There was another awkward pause.

"Good luck tomorrow," he said.

"Thanks, Tyler."

"Bye, Penny."

"Bye." I listened to the phone disconnect on his end before hanging up. He was going to be okay. He just needed time. I took a deep breath as I walked into my closet.

I moved my dresses around until I found the one James wanted. I lifted up the hanger and held it out in front of me. James was right. That night had been wonderful. And this dress would be perfect tonight too. I quickly changed into it. Luckily it still fit just right. It was a strapless white dress that stopped mid thigh and had a teacup-like skirt. I had thought the poof of it looked sophisticated and fun at the same time. I grabbed a pair of white high heels. As I put them on, I spotted a pair of red ones. That would be more fun. Tonight was all about celebrating me and James. It was supposed to be fun. I slipped on the red stilettos instead. *James will like these.*

I ran back into the bathroom and applied some red lipstick and a pair of dangling diamond earrings. I stared at my reflection in the mirror. Tomorrow morning I would be marrying James Hunter. There was no dwelling on the past. There was no worrying about the future. I was focused on this moment. Because I wanted to remember tonight for the rest of my life.

CHAPTER 8

Friday

James was talking to two men in the foyer as I made my way down the stairs. He turned his head when he heard me and a smile broke over his face. It was easy to live in the moment when he looked at me like that. My heels clicked on the marble as I made my way over to him.

"May I formally introduce you to Penny," James said to the two gentleman. "Penny, this is Porter and Briggs. Our security team."

"Are those your first names or last names?" I asked.

"Last names. I'm Porter, ma'am," the one on the left said and stuck out his hand for me to shake. His grip was like iron. He was the taller of the two and had a shaved head and steely gray eyes.

"Briggs," said the other. If possible, his grip was even stronger. He had a buzz cut and blue eyes. They were both impossibly intimidating.

"It's nice to meet both of you. So, what are your first names?"

"That's classified, ma'am," Briggs said.

"Oh. Well, you can just call me Penny, if that's alright."

"We prefer last names, Miss Taylor," Porter said.

These guys were so serious. And, now that I was looking at them, they seemed familiar. "Actually, I do recognize both of you."

Briggs gave Porter a nervous glance. James had said he paid them to not be noticed. I wasn't trying to get them in trouble.

"I mean, only because I walk past you every day. Porter, you're always sitting on a bench outside Central Park drinking...tea not coffee. Because there's a little tea tab sticking out of your cup. And Briggs, I always see you sitting outside James' office building after work. Eating a hot dog and reading the newspaper."

"I thought you were laying off the hot dogs," Porter said. "You know that's incredibly unhealthy."

"I'm not *always* eating a hot dog," Briggs said defensively.

Porter cleared his throat. "Sorry, ma'am. We'll try to be more discreet in the future."

I pressed my lips together. I certainly hadn't meant to get them in trouble. "I never would have guessed you were security. And, hot dogs are delicious, I totally get it."

Briggs gave me a small smile.

"Mr. Hunter, we'll work on it," Porter said with a very serious nod.

I was surprised to see James smiling. "No, that's fine. I'm glad to know that she's being perceptive. I debriefed them on the Isabella situation. They'll be looking for her. If you don't notice her first."

I sighed with relief. "Great."

James put his arm around my shoulders. "We should probably get going."

"Did everybody else already head over?"

"Mhm."

"What about your detective friend?"

"Already taken care of."

"And Officer Kemp?"

"It's all taken care of. Let's go enjoy our night." He let go of my shoulder and slipped his hand into mine as he led me to the door.

"So everything went smoothly?" I asked as we stepped onto the elevator. I was surprised that Porter and Briggs didn't follow us on.

"Yes. You can stop worrying about it. It's going to be fine."

I nodded. If he thought it was fine, then I believed him. "Aren't Porter and Briggs supposed to be watching us?"

"They'll get the next elevator. It's not very discreet if they stay a foot away from us all the time. Besides, Isabella can't get into our apartment building, the front desk knows about the situation."

"So...what are their first names?"

James laughed.

"No, really, I'm dying to know."

"I think I should let you wheedle that out of them."

"You're seriously not going to tell me?"

"I don't want them to be mad at me," James said. He held my hand as we walked out onto the busy street and stopped on the crosswalk.

"Is this one of those things you'll tell me as soon as we're married? Like when Mason's going to propose to Bee?"

"Did I say I would tell you that? I don't remember saying that."

"James," I said and squeezed his hand. "You promised you'd tell me."

"Hmm. I promised?"

I laughed. "You know I'll get the information out of you."

"Oh, I have no doubt that you're capable of that." He smiled down at me. "You look beautiful, Penny."

"And you look very handsome." I ran my fingers down his tie. "Are you nervous at all?"

"About what? Tonight or tomorrow?"

"Both. Isn't it like a bad omen or something if the rehearsal goes poorly?"

"I don't think I've ever heard that before. But no, I'm not nervous. Are you?"

"Of course I am."

He turned his head away from me and stared at the Tavern on the Green in the distance.

"Not anything about you, James. I'm so sure about what we have. I just want everything to go perfectly, though. And our parents...James," I said and stopped in the middle of the path, almost making him trip. "We didn't tell your parents the wedding was back on! Did you call them?"

"Um...no. I didn't."

"We have to call them."

He lowered both his eyebrows. "No."

"You didn't hear your father last night. They care about you so much. They just..."

"They care about me?" James laughed. "If they cared about me at all, they would have called me last night to see if I was okay. They clearly didn't care that we broke up. So, fuck them. Both of them."

"My parents are expecting to meet them at the dinner tonight."

"I think they'll understand after the way they behaved at the engagement party they threw us."

"Well, I didn't tell them about that."

"Why not?"

"Because I didn't want my parents to dislike your parents before they even met them."

An exasperated laugh came out of James' mouth. "They should dislike them. I dislike them. Everyone dislikes them!"

"I just wanted to give them the benefit of the doubt."

James shook his head.

"If you think they knew about what Isabella was planning, they didn't. Your mom looked so shocked that her perfect daughter in law would do something like that. And your father stuck up for me in front of her. He wanted to hear what I had to say. It was the best conversation we had ever had, and I don't think it was just because they knew they had gotten rid of me. Your mom even asked if I loved you. They care."

"I'm sure Jen told them that the wedding was still on. If they want to be there tonight, they'll be there."

"It's different if they hear it from you, James. That you want them to come."

"But I don't want them to come. Penny. Hey." He put his hand on my cheek. "Tonight is about us. Not about anyone else. There could be no one at the dinner tonight or the wedding tomorrow, and I wouldn't care. I'm only going to focus on you either way. This is about us agreeing to spend the rest of our lives together."

"I know. But James, it's also about our families coming together."

"And our family is going to be there. Rob, Mason, Bee, Matt, Jen, Melissa...that's our family. You're my family."

"You know what I mean."

His fingers slid down my neck. "And your parents. And Mason and Matt's parents."

"Mr. and Mrs. Caldwell aren't your parents, though."

"I know. They're better than my parents. They were always nice to me growing up. Their house was like a safe haven."

"I just don't want you to regret your parents not being there."

"Like I said, it's their choice."

I took a deep breath. "Okay."

He leaned down and placed a soft kiss against my lips. "We're going to be late," he said and kissed me again.

"You know, I never understood the point of a rehearsal. Isn't it just walking down an aisle and standing there?"

He laughed. "Come on, Penny." He grabbed my hand and we quickened our pace toward the restaurant. As we approached, I could see the big tree with the lights strung through it. To me, that tree exuded all things romance. And tomorrow night, James and I would be getting married underneath it. Chairs were already set up on either side of an aisle. My mom and dad were sitting in the front row to the left. Mr. & Mrs. Caldwell were sitting in the front row on the right. James' parents hadn't come. It hurt my heart, but James didn't seem to have any reaction.

"James!" Jen was the first one rushing toward us. She threw her arms around James' neck and he lifted her off her feet. "How's California treating you?" he said as he set her back down.

"Really, that's the intro you're going with? I heard you almost blew it with the best thing that's ever happened to you and you want to talk about California? Priorities, James," she said as she straightened his tie.

She threw her arms around me. "You look stunning. I never would have let this wedding not happen." She kissed my cheek and released me from her embrace.

I laughed and looked up at James. He was straightening his tie back to the way it had been before Jen had touched it. He met my gaze and smiled.

"Okay, so all they've said so far is that the bride's parents will sit on the left and the groom's on the right. Penny, is your dad walking you down the aisle?"

"Yes."

"Okay, I'll go grab him." She rushed off as quickly as she had come.

"So, what are we supposed to be doing?" James whispered in my ear.

I laughed. "I have no idea." I caught sight of Melissa standing off to the side, completely engrossed by her phone.

"Melissa?"

She immediately looked up from her phone and gave me a huge smile. "Penny, you look amazing in that dress," she said.

That had not been the reaction I was expecting at all. More like, tears and shoe throwing.

"Thanks, Melissa. Did you get my message? I know you probably..."

"It's okay. You know, sometimes I hate being right, but, it's really okay. I kind of knew it wasn't going to be a long term thing. Even though I was hoping it could be more. But I'm seriously okay."

She was saying 'okay' way too many times for someone who was actually okay. "Do you want to talk about what happened?"

"No. Not tonight. Penny, I still feel horrible about acting like such a terrible friend the past few weeks. I'm going to put this on hold until after I'm done with my maid of honor duties. I can do that," she said more to herself than to me. She seemed to take a deep breath. "You do owe me one week of sitting in pajamas and eating ice cream after your honeymoon, though."

"Deal."

Melissa laughed.

"Thank you, Melissa," I said and gave her a hug.

She didn't say anything, she just hugged me back.

Someone whistling made us pull apart.

"Alright, everyone in the bridal party, bride's father, groom's mother, and the pastor, please get in the back of the aisle for a super quick meeting," our wedding planner announced. "I was promised dinner tonight and I'm hungry."

I laughed. The reason we had picked Justin to be our wedding planner was because we thought he was hilarious. He also always seemed so calm, which I certainly appreciated. Melissa and I walked over toward the rest of the bridal party.

"I heard you got cold feet," Matt said to me.

"No joking around about that before the wedding," Justin said and gave him a dirty look.

Mason elbowed Matt in the ribs. "That's not...I didn't tell him that's what happened," Mason said defensively.

"It's fine. Hey, Matt," I said and gave him a hug.

"I'm glad you decided to show," he said and gave me a kiss on the cheek.

"Okay, everyone, pay attention," Justin said. "Leave the hugging for later. By the way, Penny and James, you both look amazing as always."

"Thanks, Justin." That was the other thing. He always gave me compliments. Just being around him inflated my self confidence.

"God, now I'm chit chatting. We'll never eat at this rate. Focus, people," he said and clapped his hands together. "What order did you want everyone standing beside you in? That dreaded question...who's the favorite?"

"Melissa is the maid of honor and Rob is my best man," James said, gesturing toward Melissa and Rob.

"They'll come in right before you two then. No flower girls or ring bearers, right?"

"Nope," James said.

"Good, just double checking. Kids ruin weddings. Absolutely ruin."

I laughed.

"No, seriously. They steal all the attention when they shit their pants on the aisle or throw petals in someone's face. Yes, I've seen both those happen. Who will be walking down the aisle before Melissa and Rob?"

"Well, I don't know, we never really discussed it. I think it would be nice if Bee and Mason walked down the aisle together," I said.

Bee smiled. "Really, whatever way you pair us is fine," she said.

"No, that sounds good," James said and winked at Mason.

Mason pressed his lips together and shook his head.

I laughed and Mason's frown turned into a smile. He shook his head again, as if he knew James had told me he was going to pop the question soon.

"Okay, Bee and Mason and then you two," he said and pointed dismissively at Jen and Matt.

"Thanks. I feel so special," Matt said.

"You know you wanted to walk with me," Jen said.

"No bickering. Hey!" Justin said and clapped again. "James, did you want to start everything off by walking down with your mom?" He pointed at Mrs. Caldwell.

"No," James said quickly. "I'll walk alone."

Mason patted his back. No one pointed out the fact that James' parents actually weren't there.

"Whatever suits you," Justin said. "The less family drama the better if you ask me. You first then, handsome," he said to our pastor. "I almost forgot about you. And go slowly, it's not a race." He pointed to the aisle.

Pastor John laughed.

"And now the man of the hour," Justin said and grabbed James' arm. "Just wait until he's halfway down the aisle and it's your turn to shine. Wait for it. Wait for it."

"See you up there," James said. He ran his fingers gently from my elbow to my wrist. The gesture gave me shivers. Or maybe it was the fact that this was all actually going to be happening in a day.

"Now!" Justin said, like it was the most magical moment of his own life. "What's your name again?" Justin said as he spun around and pointed at Matt.

"Matt."

"Okay, Matt, hold your arm in front of yourself like you're holding a baby," Justin said and showed him what he meant.

Matt made a funny face.

"And Jen, just grab his muscle and hold on tight."

"What muscle?" she said with a laugh.

"Don't pretend you haven't noticed that I'm ripped now," Matt said.

"Mhm. Whatever you say," Jen said and grabbed his arm.

"What did I just say about bickering! Now hold this rose. No, lower. Just pretend it's a whole beautiful bouquet like you'll have tomorrow. Yes, there, perfect! Now put on a smile and follow that handsome man down the aisle."

"Ew, Matt?"

"No, James of course! The man of the hour. Have you never seen him or something?"

"He's my brother."

"Your loss, honey. Go, now," Justin said and snapped his fingers.

"Hey, Pen."

I turned around to see my dad standing behind me. "Hi, Dad." I gave him a hug, tuning out my friends squabbling and Justin giving orders to everyone.

"Nervous about tomorrow?" he asked.

"More excited than nervous."

"That's my girl."

I laughed and unwrapped my arms from around him. "What about you?" I asked. "Are you worried that you're going to trip?"

"Absolutely," he said. "And if I do, I'm pulling you down with me."

"Fair enough."

"Pen, I can't believe..."

"Your turn, future Mrs. Hunter," Justin said, cutting my dad off. "Okay, slip your hand around his arm and hold this flower. You want it low so that everyone can see your gorgeous dress." He grabbed my hand and lowered it.

"Now, Dad, it's your job to make sure this goes smoothly. You've been taking care of her ever since she was a little girl. Don't ruin the last time you're the only man in her life. Got it, Dad?"

My Dad looked a little flustered that Justin kept calling him Dad.

"Okay, now walk slowly, and gracefully. Try to float. Head up, shoulders back. Work it!"

I laughed, which made my dad laugh too.

"Laugh all you want now, tomorrow I know you'll be crying. God, I'd be crying if I was marrying a hunk of meat like that."

And those comments were the reason why James hadn't wanted to hire him. But, I liked Justin too much to care if he was a little inappropriate sometimes. He was just excitable.

"And go. Now." He motioned for us to start walking.

"He's quite the character," my dad whispered to me as soon as we were out of earshot.

"No talking down the aisle!" Justin yelled after us.

"That he is."

"Great, great," Justin said from right behind us, making me jump. "You guys look perfect. Now stop here. Give your daughter a kiss on the cheek."

"Good luck, Pen." He reached up and squeezed my cheek like he used to do when I was little.

"I said a kiss, not a weird squeeze," Justin said. "Do it for the pictures."

My dad smiled down at me. "You look beautiful, Pen. And I'm so glad you found someone to make you happy." He kissed my cheek.

My eyes were getting watery already.

"Now, Dad, sit down next to Mom. And Penny, gracefully float up to your soon-to-be husband."

James' eyes were glued on me as I walked toward him.

When he opened his mouth, I thought he was going to say something romantic, but he said, "I kind of wish this had been the real thing. The video footage would have been hilarious."

Pastor John laughed.

It reminded me that the vows I had been working on for months weren't going to be heard by just James. They were going to be heard by the pastor and all our friends and family. I was suddenly extremely nervous.

"Pretend you like each other!" Justin shouted and pushed his hands closer together to show us we were standing too far apart.

James laughed and grabbed my waist, pulling me against his chest. "How about this?" he said more toward me than to Justin.

"Okay, pretend you like each other a little less than that."

James kissed the tip of my nose and let go of my waist. I took a step back. James held out his hands for me and I grabbed them. All I could focus on were his eyes. The same eyes that had captivated me when I was his student. I never thought we'd wind up here. But I was so thankful that we had.

"Bridesmaids, each take half a step to your left," Justin said. "No not that much! God, I'll just make some kind of markings so you know where to stand tomorrow. Forget about it. Pastor, get your thing on."

Pastor John laughed. "Right, well, I'm going to make a few jokes, which I'll keep to myself for now. I want to get you laughing on your wedding day. I'll do the normal spiel about love and what this commitment means. Normally right now, I would just have you practice reciting the vows after me, but you've decided to read your own vows, correct?"

James squeezed my hands. "Correct."

"Well, then after you exchange vows, I will simply say, do you James take Penny to be your lawfully wedded wife?"

James ran his thumbs against the backs of my hands. "I do."

"And Penny, I'd say, do you Penny take James to be your lawfully wedded husband? And you'd answer 'I do.' But don't say it now, it's only the rehearsal."

I laughed. "I do," I mouthed silently to James.

He raised his left eyebrow.

"And then I'd say, by the power vested in me, by the state of New York, I now pronounce you husband and wife. You may now kiss the bride. And you'd..."

James pulled me against him and pressed his lips against mine. His tongue darted across my lips and I opened my mouth, inviting him in. His fingers tangled in my hair as mine pressed against his neck, deepening a kiss that was already too sexual for public.

"Ow ow!" Melissa yelled.

"Get a room," Rob said.

I laughed and pressed on James' chest.

"God, I can't wait for tomorrow," he said.

I kept my hand on his neck and smiled up at him.

"Less tongue tomorrow, yes?" Justin said from the seat he had taken in the second row. "Now after that, you'd walk hand in hand back down the aisle with huge wedding bliss smiles. I love newlyweds."

James gave me a playful smile.

I wanted to tell him to follow Justin's instructions. But that smile of his was my favorite. It meant he was so caught up in this moment, that nothing else in the world mattered. Just him and me. "Whatever you're thinking of doing, do it. I dare you."

"Dare accepted." He leaned down and lifted me over his shoulder.

I squealed as he put his hand on my ass. I wasn't sure if he just wanted to touch me or if he didn't want me to moon all of Central Park. I laughed the whole way down the aisle.

"Piggyback time, Melissa!" Rob said from behind us.

I heard Melissa laugh and I didn't doubt at all that Rob was giving her a piggyback ride down the aisle.

"No!" Justin shouted. "No, no, no! The exit is supposed to be elegant and...ugh! I give up. Rehearsal done."

James set me back down on my feet. "I'm pretty sure we just got hitched."

"I didn't say 'I do'."

"I saw you say it, baby." He tucked a loose strand of hair behind my ear.

"No paper, no proof."

"You got me there. Tomorrow I'll get the signed evidence."

"I can't wait."

CHAPTER 9

Friday

My friends had been doing a fantastic job decorating. But when I stepped back into our apartment, my jaw dropped. Justin's assistants had rearranged all the furniture so that there was room for long tables with elegant tablecloths and huge flowery centerpieces. The caterers were all set up and the food smelled amazing. Everyone was bustling around, doing last minute preparations.

"Told you I'd make it beautiful," Justin said. "What do you kids think?"

James smiled at me, only caring about what I had to say.

"It's perfect, Justin. Thank you."

"Does that mean I get an A?" he said with a wink to James.

James laughed. "Absolutely."

Justin clapped his hands. "Okay, people! Everyone not in the bridal party will be arriving in fifteen minutes! Places everyone! Places!"

We had originally wanted to keep our rehearsal dinner small. Just the people that were a part of the wedding. But with so many people coming in from out of town, we decided to make it a bigger thing. Mostly James' friends that I had never met. I was a little nervous to meet them. I wanted to hear their stories. I wanted to know what James was like in college.

Bee looped her arm in mine. "I feel like I just got completely schooled in party decorating."

I laughed. "I like the streamers. It's exactly what I would have done."

She smiled. "We'll learn how to step up our party throwing game together. Sometimes I still feel so out of place in all," she gestured with her hand, "this."

"Yeah, I know what you mean." I looked over at James. He was standing with my mom, introducing himself to the caterer. No matter the situation, he always looked so in his element. I looked back at Bee. "I'm glad I have you to figure it out with."

"Here's to that. God, I need a drink. These shoes are killing me. I have no idea what I was thinking, they just looked so cute with this dress."

Her shoes matched her dress perfectly. But they were also at least 7 inches tall. "They are really cute."

She laughed. "Thank you. Can I get you something?"

"No, I'm good." Ever since James had kicked me out, my stomach had felt uneasy. I knew it was probably just nerves now, but I didn't want to add alcohol to the mix.

"Penny! Come over here for a second," my mom said and waved her arm toward the caterer. She had been very insistent on hiring the catering staff by herself. Whoever she had chosen, it smelled amazing. I walked over toward her and James.

"Remember La Patisserie? Your favorite restaurant in Philly?"

"Of course."

"This is Rory, he used to work there."

"Oh yeah? You're an amazing chef." I tried not to look directly at him. I used to love going to La Patisserie because he was as mouth watering as his food. I had never even had a boyfriend in high school. I may have day-dreamed quite a lot about Rory. It had been a few years since I had seen him, but he looked exactly the same.

"Thank you. It's nice to meet you, Penny," he said and stuck out his hand for me.

I quickly shook it.

"James, this is a funny story," my mom said and lightly touched his arm. "In high school, Penny always wanted to go to that restaurant. The food was really good. But I have to say, I was completely convinced that she had a crush on Rory."

"Oh my God. Mom." I was completely mortified. "That's not...the food was just..."

Rory and James both laughed.

"I never really thought about it before, but I guess she's always had a thing for older men." My mom shrugged. "But, either way, you did love his food, so...here he is. The chef himself! And James, you've had his food before too. The first time you came to our house. You know, when you told us who you really were. Oh, Peter was so angry that day." She laughed. "Anyway, I'm going to go try some of the appetizers." She walked toward one of the servers.

"I am so sorry," I said to Rory and James.

James laughed and put his arm around my shoulders. "Such great memories."

"Geez, parents can be so embarrassing sometimes," Rory said with a smile.

"You have no idea," I said.

Rory laughed.

"So, you started your own catering company?"

"Yeah. We only just opened a couple weeks ago, but your mom sought us out. I actually just have my friends helping me out tonight because I haven't had time to find staff." He pointed them out to us. "Connor, Jackson, and my wife, Keira."

Keira glanced over and smiled at Rory when she heard her name. She was arranging some delicious looking appetizers on a serving tray.

"Well, everything looks amazing," James said. "Hopefully tonight will go better than the first time I ate at her parents' house. Because that was pretty much a disaster."

Rory laughed. "If not, hopefully it won't be due to a mistake on my part. Actually, if you'll excuse me for one second. I promise they'll all be professional by the time the rest of the guests get here." Rory rushed past us to go talk to his friends.

I glanced over my shoulder. It looked like Jackson and Justin were arguing heatedly over decorations. And Conner was sitting down across from Melissa at one of the tables talking to her. I laughed.

"So, you had a crush on him, huh?" James asked.

"That was a long time ago."

"Any traces of that remaining?"

"No," I said and placed my fingers behind his neck. "Not one lingering trace."

"Why did we invite all these people over to our house again?" he whispered in my ear.

"Wishing we were alone right now?"

"So badly. About not sharing a room tonight...I think we should discuss that."

"You're not excited to have a slumber party with all your friends tonight?"

He laughed. "Not in the least."

"Talk about an upgrade," someone said from behind us. I hadn't even realized that guests had started arriving. "She's stunning."

James let go of my waist. "Luke. Geez, how many years has it been?"

Luke embraced him in a huge bear hug. "Too many, man."

"So, you must be Penny," he said and put his hand out for me.

I recognized him from the one picture James had of him and his frat brothers. "It's so nice to meet you."

"The pleasure is all mine," he said.

"You knew James in college, huh? I would love to hear some stories."

"Just you wait till Benny and Mike get here and the beers start flowing. There will be plenty of stories."

I couldn't help but notice that James looked a little uncomfortable. "I can't wait," I said.

"Definitely a keeper," he said to James as he pointed at me. "Are any of the guys here yet?"

"Mason is here somewhere." James looked around the room.

Out of the corner of my eye, I saw one of my oldest friends walk in. "If you'll excuse me, it was great meeting you," I said to Luke and gravitated toward the door. "Mila!"

"Penny! It's so great to see you!" She gave me a huge hug. "Oh my God, this place is amazing. Do you seriously live here?"

"We just moved in, yeah."

"Geez, I'm so sorry, I'm being incredibly rude. This is my boyfriend, J.J.," she said and gestured to the guy smiling beside her. He was so tan it looked like he spent all his time on the beach. "J.J., this is Penny."

"It's so nice to meet you," I said and shook his hand. "It's so funny, Mila, the last time I saw you, we were both boyfriend-less. It was actually your going away party. Before you left me and moved to Cali."

"I know. I'm sorry I've been missing in action the last few years. Geez, time flies, doesn't it?"

"It does. I'm just really, really glad you could make it."

"I wouldn't have missed your wedding for anything in the world. I'm so happy for you, Penny. I've really missed you."

I was getting teary eyed again. God, what was wrong with me tonight? "Are you moving back to the east coast anytime soon?"

"We're actually thinking about it," J.J. said. "We both grew up on the east coast. We're just waiting to hear back on some job offers."

"Who are your friends?" James asked as he slid his arm around my waist.

"Mila was my best friend growing up. She went to UCLA and dropped off the face of the earth for awhile."

Mila laughed.

"And this is her boyfriend, J.J."

"It's great to meet both of you," James said and shook their hands. "That means you were the neighbor growing up, right?"

"Yes, that's me. What terrible things has Penny been telling people about me?"

"Only good things. Mrs. Bennett on the other hand..."

"You've met Mrs. Bennett? She was the nosiest neighbor in the history of nosey neighbors. Please tell me she's not behind me right now?"

I laughed. "No. Mrs. Bennett is surely patrolling the neighborhood as we speak."

"I feel so out of the loop right now," J.J. said with a laugh.

"Trust me, you don't want to be in the loop on this," I said. "Mila, my parents were looking forward to seeing you."

"I can't wait to see them either. I need to stop disappearing for years. I'll go say hi to them. Congrats, Penny," she said as she passed me and squeezed my shoulder.

"Did you two get in all sorts of trouble growing up?" James asked.

"If by trouble you mean staying in and watching movies and eating popcorn in pajamas? Or catching fireflies? Or playing with Barbie dolls? Then yes, we were in trouble constantly."

He kissed my temple. "I'm envious of your childhood."

When he said things like that, my chest actually ached. "You know, whenever I picture your childhood, I see little you locked in your room being denied anything good."

"It wasn't quite that bad."

"What was a normal day like in the summer? Didn't you do anything fun? I bet you were probably holed up in your tree house terrorizing Jen."

"Hey, Daphne's here."

I knew he was purposely trying to distract me. But I was dying to meet Rob's girlfriend. Or friend that was a girl. I wasn't going to throw out terms and freak them out.

I just couldn't believe that Rob was actually dating some-one. "Which one is she?"

"The one with brown hair standing right by the door. She doesn't know anyone else here and Rob hasn't spotted her yet. Come on, let's go save her." He grabbed my hand.

"So, you already know her pretty well then?"

"Yeah, we actually got to talk quite a bit during my bachelor party weekend."

"Anything I should know? I don't want to say some-thing stupid."

"You'll be fine." He squeezed my hand.

I was nervous. This girl could potentially be a huge part of my life if she was able to get Rob to settle down. Plus she must be magical if she was dating Rob. Rob never dated anyone.

"Oh, hey, James," Daphne said. "I hope it's okay that I just walked in. Rob didn't really say if..."

"It's fine. It's great to see you again." He gave her a quick hug. "This is my fiancée, Penny."

"Hi. Wow, I've heard a ton about you, Penny. I'm su-per excited to finally meet you in person." She stuck out her hand for me and I shook it.

"What terrible things has Rob told you about me?"

"Mostly good things, I promise. He's super excited to have you officially be his little sister, I know that."

"Did he really say that?"

"A couple times, yeah."

That's so sweet. "Well, I think that's a total lie. He just loves tormenting me. A big brother thing I guess?" I said with a laugh.

"I'm pretty sure that's what little sisters are for," she said. She glanced past us, probably looking for Rob.

James' grip tightened slightly on my waist.

Had I said something wrong? "I wouldn't know. I'm an only child."

"I've heard you and Rob had quite the exciting week," James said.

She gave him a small smile. "Yes. God, he's...it was probably the best week of my life. After Costa Rica we flew to Paris. And then we went to Venice before coming back here. I think he might already have tickets to go to Sydney next week. He's so full of surprises. I never know what to expect next."

"Welcome to my life," James said.

I laughed. "Rob is certainly full of surprises. Always good though."

"Stop freaking Daphne out," Rob said. He had suddenly appeared next to Daphne. He grabbed her waist and pulled her in for a kiss. And she melted into his kiss. She so clearly adored him. "Hey," he whispered to her, but it was loud enough for us to hear. "You look amazing." Her face blushed. "I see that you've met my super annoying soon-to-be little sister."

Was that the new way he was going to torture me? "Annoying? Thanks, Rob."

"I'm just kidding. You know you're my favorite sister. And definitely sexier than Jen. You know...since Jen is actually my sister and that would be disgusting if I thought she was sexy. But it's still okay if I think you are." He winked at me. "Speaking of which, Daphne, you have to come meet my real sister, not the fake one."

There were some weird things mixed in with that rant about sisters and I was happy to see that Daphne laughed.

She must have already realized that Rob was an endless flirt.

"It was really great meeting you, Penny," she said.

"You too."

"And you have a lovely home." Before she could say anything else, Rob whisked her away.

"She seemed really nice. Did I say something wrong, though? I feel like I might have."

"Yeah. She actually lost her brother only a year and a half ago. She's having a hard time with it."

"James. I just asked if there was anything I should know before talking to her."

"I didn't think it would come up." He shrugged.

I pursed my lips together. "I feel awful. Do you know what happened to her brother? Was it an accident?"

James shifted uncomfortably. "He died of an overdose."

"That's horrible." I looked over at Daphne. She was meeting Mason and Matt's parents. "She probably hates me now."

James laughed. "I don't think so, Penny. Are you okay? It seems like you were nervous about getting her approval."

"Of course I am. If she marries Rob, then we're going to be sisters. And I don't want her to hate me. I blew it."

"You're incredibly cute. You didn't do anything wrong."

"Is there anything else I should know about some of your friends I'm meeting tonight? Like horrible things in their past I shouldn't talk about lightly?"

"Try not to talk about Davy Jones' missing eye. He's very sensitive about it."

"Which one is Davy Jones? And how did he lose his eye? I don't want to mention whatever did it either."

"You're kidding, right? Davy Jones? Like the pirate? I was just joking, Penny."

"So, you don't have a friend named Davy Jones?"

He laughed and pulled me in for a kiss. "No. I'm not a pirate, so I don't have any super awesome pirate friends."

I laughed against his chest.

"What are you so nervous about tonight? All these people are here because they love us. There's nothing to be nervous about."

I looked up into his eyes. "Honestly, I just want tonight to be more memorable than your rehearsal dinner with Isabella."

"Penny..."

"I'm sorry. It's just hard for me not to think about what might be running through your head. And I just want..."

"There is no comparison, baby," he said and grabbed the side of my face. "None."

I nodded.

"So, stop being nervous. Let's just enjoy tonight. Let me get you a drink."

"No, that's okay. My stomach has been kind of upset."

He lowered his eyebrows. "Are you alright?"

"Yeah, I'm fine. I just don't want to make it worse."

"I'm going to go grab you something for that. I'll be right back." He kissed the tip of my nose and walked toward the bathroom. I watched Mrs. Caldwell stop him and give him a hug. Tonight was perfect. It was exactly as it should be.

I noticed Ellen helping the caterers with something. She was used to preparing our meals and I knew she was probably having a hard time being our guest tonight. She never seemed to stop moving. I walked over to her and lightly touched her shoulder. "Ellen, you don't have to do anything tonight. We invited you to be part of the celebration."

"I like to help, dear," she said with a smile.

"Please just sit down and enjoy yourself. You do so much for me and James. The caterers can handle all this."

She smiled and patted my cheek. "I just want it to be perfect."

"Thank you." James' parents might not be here, but between Mrs. Caldwell and Ellen, he definitely had a motherly influence. "But really, just relax."

She nodded. "I packed up all your things and James' too for tomorrow. Your suitcases are by the bedroom door. I left his tux and your dress in the closet though. I didn't want them to get wrinkled."

"Thanks, Ellen. You're the best." I gave her a hug.

"Just keep making him happy. I already know I'm going to cry my eyes out during the ceremony tomorrow. James asked me to look over his vows and..." she put her hand over her heart. "He loves you so dearly."

It felt like I had written my vows a thousand times and they still weren't perfect. "Were his funny at all? Or were they completely serious?"

Ellen laughed. "You know I'd never say a word. I need to go make sure they know where the extra glasses are. Then I promise to join the fun."

"Okay."

"Speak from your heart, though, Penny. That's the most important thing." She quickly walked back into the kitchen. There was no way she was actually going to relax tonight.

Speak from your heart. That was better advice than she probably realized. I was pretty sure that meant James' vows were sweet. I'd be the one crying my eyes out, not Ellen. Maybe I needed to take out a few jokes from mine. What had I been thinking?

"I still can't believe this is actually happening," Melissa said from beside me.

"What do you mean?"

"I don't know. It's just crazy to think my best friend, who never took any risks, slept with her billionaire professor and now they're getting married. It's insane."

"Yeah." *I guess?*

"Don't you ever feel like you're going to wake up and all this will be a dream?"

Yes. I glanced at James again. Someone else had stopped him and was hugging him. Maybe one of his friends. "Yeah, sometimes."

"You have to enjoy moments like this. Because they can be taken away like that." She snapped her fingers when she said the word 'that.'

I frowned. Was this seriously her idea of a good conversation for a rehearsal dinner? "What do you mean by that?" I folded my arms in front of my chest. I had almost lost James. We had only just made up this morning. I had already thought about what we had disappearing enough for one day. Especially today of all days.

"I just mean I'm happy that you finally learned how to live in the moment. Now, I'm not quite as sure that you have. What's going on?"

I sighed. "I don't know. I just feel kind of on edge tonight. James is worried Isabella's just going to show up and...I don't know exactly." *Hurt us?*

"I'm sure that's not going to happen."

"I hope not."

"All I meant was that your life is kind of like a fairytale." She squeezed my arm. "Handsome prince. A castle of an apartment." She smiled. "A happily ever after."

Melissa still didn't know about James' problems. At least, I had never told her. It wasn't something I had shared with anyone. It wasn't my secret to share. Yes, James was the light of my life. But there was darkness there too. Worry. Fear. Especially now that he thought he was addicted to me. I had a pit in my stomach that seemed to be growing by the second. What if James decided at the last minute that he couldn't be with me? That I wasn't good for him because of something he had built up in his head that wasn't true at all?

"Are you okay?" Melissa asked. "You look a little pale."

"Yeah, I'm just not feeling very well."

"Maid of honor, at your service. What do you need?"

"A hug."

She laughed. "I think I can arrange that." She put her arms around me and ran her hand up and down my back. "I didn't mean to upset you. If anything, I was just saying how envious I am of you."

"Melissa, I'm so sorry about..."

"No. We're not talking about that until after your honeymoon. Not another word."

I laughed.

"Take a deep breath. And try to do what I thought you were already doing. Enjoy tonight. Remember every second. You only get one rehearsal dinner your whole life. Unless you're James."

I laughed again. "Ugh. God, I've been thinking about that too. I just want all of this to be better than whatever he had with Isabella."

"It's better by default. Because this time he's marrying you." She put her hands on my shoulders and held me at arm's length. "And you, Penny, are my best friend in the world. James is the lucky one."

"Thanks, Melissa."

"You don't think Penny is a little lucky to have wound up with me?" James said with a smile. "Here, take this." He handed me a few pills and a glass of water.

"Of course she's lucky." Melissa squeezed his arm. "You're both lucky. And you're seriously the happiest, cutest, most amazing couple I know. Was any of that good? I'm so nervous about my speech tomorrow. I feel like you're going to be grading me."

James laughed. "Something along those lines would be perfect."

"Oh, good. I'm definitely going to pay attention to Mr. and Mrs. Caldwell's speech tonight to get some ideas on what to say."

"They're giving a speech?" James asked.

"Um, of course. I thought you knew that?"

"No, they didn't say anything to me about it," he said.

"That's really sweet of them," I said and looped my arm in James'.

"They don't have to do that."

"Yeah," I said. "They want to do it. That's the sweet part."

He laughed. "I guess so." He glanced over at Mr. and Mrs. Caldwell. He said he was envious of my childhood. Was he envious of Mason and Matt's too? As far as I could see, Mr. and Mrs. Caldwell had been better parents to him than his own.

Despite how much I thought it might hurt him, James had made the right call. His parents shouldn't be here. Tonight was supposed to be fun with the people we were closest to. That wasn't James' parents. And to me, it seemed pretty clear that that was on them, not James. I was done pushing it. I just wanted us to be happy. We had enough negativity that we couldn't shake. I didn't need to add to it.

"I can't wait to hear their speech," I said.

"Me too." James smiled. "Although, I have no idea what they're planning to say."

"Probably something about how lucky Penny is to have you," Melissa said with a smile. "Okay, I have no segue. But what's the deal with that caterer over there? God, he's gorgeous isn't he?"

"So gorgeous," someone said from behind us.

I turned around. "Hi, Kendra."

"Girl, you were not lying about the plethora of single men. It's like walking into a very elegant candy shop. Now I just need to find the right flavor lollipop."

I laughed.

"Don't be gross," Marie said from beside her. "Hey guys," she said and gave me and James each a hug.

"Congratulations, you two," her husband, Carter, said. He gave me a hug and James a handshake. "Kendra has been talking non-stop about weird, sexual candy references the whole taxi ride over here. I need a drink."

James laughed. "Come with me."

"I still can't believe you snagged the sexiest bachelor in New York," Kendra sighed.

"We were just talking about that," Melissa said.

"Wait, you're referring to Carter, right?" Marie said.

We all laughed. I don't know what I had been so worried about. Tonight was going so well.

CHAPTER 10
Friday

Yes, I may have had a crush on Rory in high school. But that in no way reflected on the fact that his food seriously was amazing. It was even better than the restaurant he used to work at. La Patisserie was probably going out of business without him. Plus, after the stress of the day, I hadn't realized how hungry I was until there was food right in front of me.

It took me awhile to realize that James was staring at me. I wiped my napkin across my mouth. "Sorry," I whispered.

"About what?"

I laughed. "Eating like a ravenous animal."

He smiled. "That's not why I was staring at you."

"Then why were you staring?"

He grabbed my hand on top of the table and ran his thumb along my palm. Whenever he did that, I automatically felt comforted. "Because I'm so happy that we're here. And that you forgave me. This morning, I woke up and realized what I had done and I...I couldn't breathe. I thought I lost you. Baby, I don't ever not want to be staring at you when I wake up."

He had said something similar to me once before. About how his house growing up felt stifling, like he couldn't breathe. He used to escape to his tree house. And when he grew up he found other devices; booze, drugs, sex, anything that made him feel like he was still breathing.

Why did he keep saying stuff like this to me? Why was he tainting what we had with his insecurities? What we had was so much more than booze or drugs or sex. We had talked about this, and I thought he was going to accept that our love was just that...love. But it seemed like he was going backwards. I didn't know how to make him stop falling.

"James..."

The clinking of a glass made us turn our heads.

Mr. and Mrs. Caldwell slowly stood up. "For those of you who don't know us, we're Mason and Matthew's parents." Mrs. Caldwell gestured to her sons. "Our boys and James basically grew up together, mostly getting in all sorts of trouble. And I'm not excluding you, Rob," she said and pointed to him. "He was the most troublesome of the four."

Rob laughed and winked at James.

"James, you have always been a part of our family. And I just want you to know how much we care about you. And how happy we are that you found someone who sees you the way we see you. Max," she said and squeezed her husband's arm. She had grabbed a napkin and was blotting her eyes.

Mr. Caldwell cleared his throat. "James. I see the lives that you and my boys have carved out, and I can't help but feel proud. I know you're not my son, but I knew you as a baby. I saw you grow up. I taught you how to play catch and ride a bike, and..." he cleared his throat again. "I'll always be there for you. We'll always be there for you." He put his arm around Mrs. Caldwell. "And Penny. You make him happier than we've ever seen him." He smiled at me and raised his glass. "Here's to hoping that your life will be blessed with children as wonderful as ours and an extended family that shares equal space in your hearts." He lifted up his glass. "We love you both. And we're so happy for you. Here's to the happy couple."

James and I clinked our glasses together.

A slow clapping from the doorway made me turn my head. James' parents were standing there. "Maxwell, that was a wonderful speech," Mrs. Hunter said. She laughed, but it came out icy. "I always wondered why James begged us to play little league. Such a waste of time if you ask me. I guess we can blame that on you. I should have known. Honestly, Maxwell, you really should have asked us if it was okay."

Okay to play catch with their son who wanted to be outdoors? Laughing and having fun and just being a kid? Was she being serious right now?

Jen was the first one to acknowledge the awkwardness of the situation. She quickly stood up and walked over to them. "Mom, Dad! I didn't think you were coming." She kissed them both on the cheek.

"We didn't even realize the wedding was back on. We had to hear it through the grapevine. The girl told me it was over."

The girl? God, did she even know my name?

I saw some people turn toward me and James out of the corner of my eye. Only a few people knew about last night. My parents weren't among them. *Shit.*

James cleared his throat. "Mr. and Mrs. Caldwell, thank you so much for that wonderful toast. Being at your house was the highlight of my childhood. As you might have guessed. I'm sorry, if you'll all excuse me." He tossed his napkin on the table. His chair squeaked against the floor and he made his way over to his parents. He walked out the front door without saying a word to either of them. Mrs. Hunter smiled at me and then followed her son out of the apartment with her husband in tow.

"You knew and you didn't tell me," James said coolly as the door closed behind them. But even after the door closed, you could still hear their voices. "Why didn't you call me? She came to you because she couldn't come to me and you just let her leave? Do you have any idea what I was going through? Did you even care?"

"Of course we care about you," his mother said back. "That's why we were happy it was over."

"Then why the fuck are you even here?"

"Do not raise your voice at me, James."

God, everyone can hear this. Music! "Rob!"

He was staring at the door in horror.

"Rob, do you know how the sound system works? Could you put some music on?"

"Yeah, Penny." He shook his head and stood up. In a few seconds music was blaring through the apartment. I was surprised to see Rob slip out the front door.

Everyone was either staring at me or the door and I had no idea what to do. I felt frozen. What could I possibly say that would make this better? I gave Jen a pleading look. She was so good with people. *Please make this better.*

Jen laughed awkwardly. "For those of you who don't know my parents, this is just classic Hunter family drama."

It sounded like possibly one person laughed.

"I'm going to go see if they can calm down just a bit for normal social interactions." She smiled and excused herself from the table.

Don't leave me!

Times like this reminded me of how young I really was. All I wanted to do was run to my room and hide and let my parents take care of it. But my parents had no idea what was going on. Everyone was staring at me, wondering what to do. At least the conversation in the hall could no longer be heard. I awkwardly cleared my throat.

"For those of you who don't know, those are my soon-to-be mother and father in-law. They're still adjusting to the idea."

Mason laughed. "They don't like anybody, Penny. Don't worry about it."

A few of James' friends from college laughed too.

"Seriously," Matt said. "I'm still not even sure they know my name and I've known them my whole life. So...are you going to go out there and argue with your new family too?"

"What exactly are they arguing about?" my father said.

I hadn't told my parents about James' parents so that they wouldn't have preconceived notions going into meeting them. I just wanted everyone to get along. It didn't seem like that was a realistic option though. It was time to tell them. "Could I talk to you and mom for a second?" I excused myself and walked into the kitchen. Rory and his friends were all awkwardly standing in there, most likely hiding from what was going on.

"Could you guys maybe go ahead and serve dessert? Hopefully your delicious food will distract everyone."

"Sure thing." Keira gave me a sympathetic smile and dropped the dish she had been scrubbing.

"In-laws," Rory said with a shrug. "They're the worst."

Keira swatted his arm playfully. "You love my parents."

He laughed and grabbed a tray of decadent looking desserts. "Mhm."

She shook her head and grabbed one of the trays. The rest of his friends followed suit as my parents walked into the kitchen.

"What's going on, sweetie?" my mom said. She looked shocked by what had just occurred with James' parents.

"James has a...complicated relationship with his parents." What was the best way to say this? "They never really supported his decisions growing up. And they don't exactly support his decision to marry me."

"When were you planning on telling us this?" my mom asked.

"I'm sorry. I just wanted you to make your own opinions of them. I had this idea in my head that we were all going to be this happy family. But I should have told you. James didn't even want them to come to the wedding. I pushed him to invite them. This," I said and gestured to the door, "is all my fault. They hate me. The worst part is that James thinks they hate him. And I know that's not true, they just have a horrible way of showing that they care. I was just trying to fix it. I just wanted us to be able to get along."

"Pen," my dad said with a laugh. "Not everyone you meet is going to like you."

"I know that. But they're going to be my family. I thought they could at least pretend. Their son is getting married."

"From what I can tell, you have a pretty great group of friends out there. That's your new family. You can't force something if it's not meant to be, sweetie," my mom said.

"Now, what's this about them thinking the wedding was off?"

"James and I had a fight last night."

"About what?"

I never went to my parents with my problems. Not since before college. I used to share everything with my mom. But now it felt like something separated us. I knew it was in my head, but it was there, a line I could no longer seem to cross.

"Just...issues we've been having. It was bad."

"But everything is okay now?"

I looked toward the front door. It wasn't really okay. James thought he was addicted to me. And he was out in the hallway fighting with his parents the night before our wedding. Isabella was out there somewhere, and the cops didn't seem to care. I had lost one of my best friends. And that cop's words kept nagging me in the back of my head. James had a record and I had no idea what he had done. But it was going to be okay. Our love was enough for everything to be okay. *Right?* "Yeah, everything is okay now. I just don't know what to do about his parents."

"Did he ask you to fix it?"

"No, but..."

"That's your answer, sweetie. Marriage is a partnership. You have to be a team. If he's distant with his parents, you shouldn't force it. You have to have his back."

"You're right." God, I had been such an idiot. Maybe if I hadn't pushed him inviting his parents we never would have fought last night. I had caused this whole mess. It was about time I fixed it. "I'll be right back."

"Don't you think you should give them a minute?" my dad asked, but I was already walking toward the door.

"Robert Hunter if you say one more..." Mrs. Hunter's voice died away as I stepped out into the hallway.

I expected to see James yelling when I came out. Instead, Rob was standing in front of him and his face was bright red like he had just exploded.

"Why are you protecting her?" yelled Rob. "Isabella's trying to ruin his life. What the hell is wrong with you? All of this is on you. Both of you. Jesus Christ, when will you let this go? Why can't you just let him be happy for once in his life?"

I was wrong. He was still exploding. I put my hand on his shoulder. Rob jumped at my touch. He hadn't heard me come into the hall. He shook his head when he saw me and ran his hand through his hair. It was the same gesture that James did so often. Even if he hadn't been yelling, I would have known he was upset just by that one action. Everyone was completely silent now.

"Rob and Jen, do you mind if we have a minute?" I asked.

"Yeah," Rob said. "But don't listen to them, Penny. They know where she is. They're full of shit."

"Robert!" his mother said in a stern voice.

Rob shook his head and pushed through the door. And that's what I loved so much about Rob. He always had James' back no matter what. And mine. I had learned that last night. His loyalty was almost tangible.

"Sorry," Jen whispered silently to me and followed Rob.

"We do not know where Isabella is," Mrs. Hunter said. "She hasn't been returning our calls. You're not honestly scared of her, are you? She's just upset because you ruined her reputation. She has a right to be."

"I ruined it?" James said.

"This is not the time or place for this discussion, James."

"It's never the time or place! You know what happened between us was not my fault. And in case you don't remember, let me just clear the record. She slept around behind my back! She ruined her own damn reputation. But am I happy that it's over? Yes. Marrying her was the worst fucking decision I ever made in my life. Letting you two pressure me into something that was never in my best interest, just in yours. Screw both of you. What the fuck are you even doing here?"

"Both my sons seem to lose their vocabulary when they're angry," Mrs. Hunter said and shook her head. "Honestly, James, do you really think it's appropriate to curse at your mother? Especially when we went out of our way to come to this...celebration."

"We really don't know where Isabella is, James," his father said, cutting off his mother. "And either way, I don't think she's a physical threat. You have nothing to worry about."

"And 24 hours ago you never would have guessed that she would steal from me either."

"That is not proven yet. It's her word against Isabella's," his mother said and pointed at me.

"Then it's proven." James slipped his hand into mine. "Penny would never lie to me."

"James, don't be simple. How can you..."

"Stop." James' voice was more stern than I had ever heard it before. And his grip on my hand had tightened so that it almost hurt. "What the hell did we just talk about? If you say one more bad thing about Penny, you cannot come into our home. Ever. I won't remind you again."

"Susan," his dad said. "Stop trying to fight this. It's done. You can't always get what you want." He sounded spiteful. For the first time, I wondered how good their relationship was.

Mrs. Hunter frowned and folded her arms across her chest. "I still think it's a mistake."

"No one asked you for your opinion," James said. "I tried it the way you wanted. It didn't work. Neither one of us was happy. It wasn't just on me. You know that."

Mrs. Hunter made a weird noise with her throat and shook her head.

"Mr. and Mrs. Hunter," I said. It was time for me to say what I had come out here to say. I didn't want to hear them fighting about Isabella. I didn't want to think about James' past. Not tonight. Tonight was about our future. "I pressured James to reach out to you because I wanted us to be a family. I realize now that that wasn't really my place. Because it's not James that has the issues here. It's you. You're the ones that need to grow."

"Excuse me?" his mother said.

"I don't want to get into that right now. All I mean is that your son has done nothing wrong. And as his parents, that should always be your first assumption. Not taking the side of his ex-wife. That aside, everyone in our apartment is here because they love and support us. I wish I didn't have to question your motivations for coming. But..." I glanced at James, "you're invited to our wedding festivities only if that applies to you. We want this weekend to be memorable in a good way. No fighting. No wishing I was someone else. No making James feel bad. And absolutely no talking about Isabella. Put whatever problems you have on the backburner for this weekend. Your son is getting married. I don't think I should have to say anything else. If you agree to that, I'd love for you to come in."

James pressed his lips together. Maybe he just wanted them to leave. I was about to ask him when his father broke the awkward silence.

"I wouldn't have come for any other reason," Mr. Hunter said. "I don't want to fight. James, I'm sorry."

I wasn't even sure what specifically his dad was apologizing for, but this was a huge step.

James put his hand out for his dad who eagerly shook it.

"Thanks for coming," James said way too formally for a son to his father. But it was a start.

"Thanks for having us." He glanced at his wife. "I hope to see you inside, Susan." He turned and walked into our apartment.

"I didn't come to make a scene," Mrs. Hunter said. "Obviously. But how was I supposed to feel when we were uninvited. And we walked in on a toast from the Caldwells." She made the now familiar sound of disgust with her throat.

"We're both really close to the Caldwells," I said. "I've grown quite fond of them over the years." I emphasized the word years. Unlike Mrs. Hunter, the Caldwells had welcomed us into their home with open arms. They had never been anything but nice and supportive. I loved them both dearly.

"Still. It's the groom's parents' job to toast the couple at the rehearsal dinner. It's tradition."

"And no one's stopping you. We'd love to have you make a toast."

She eyed me for a second. "Very well. I'd like that very much."

"Okay." I looked up at James. He was busy staring at his mom. He looked like he was in shock.

"Well, are you going to invite me in or not? Honestly..."

"Welcome," I said to his mom. "My parents can't wait to meet you."

"I'm sure they can't," she said and walked through the front door.

"What just happened?" James said when the door closed.

"James, I'm so sorry. I never should have pushed you to invite them. I should have respected how your relationship was with them. I want us to be a team. We should be making decisions together. And I'm so, so sorry."

"Penny." He grabbed my waist. "I get it. I see the way you were raised. You expected to be marrying into one big happy family. I understand why you wanted a relationship with them."

"But I never should have forced it."

"You didn't force it. I wanted it because you wanted it."

I put my hand on the side of his face. "Well, I was wrong. All I want is you."

He smiled. "Well, they're here now."

I laughed. "I'm sorry."

"Don't be. I think maybe you're right. I would have been disappointed if they hadn't shown. The timing could have been better though."

DEVOTION

"I loved Mr. Caldwell's speech. You never told me all those things about your relationship with him. James, he considers you to be one of his sons."

"I didn't know that before tonight."

"Open your eyes, James. Everyone loves you."

"Hmm." He touched the side of my face. "Maybe."

"They do."

"I kind of wish we didn't have a whole house full of people right now. I can't take my eyes off you. This brings me back to when we first moved here." He ran his fingers across the fabric of my dress. "Do you remember what we did after walking around Central Park that night?"

I'd never forget. "We christened the new apartment." Several rooms of it.

"Exactly." He pushed my back against the wall and buried his face in my neck.

Fuck.

"I know everyone's waiting for us, but I want you so badly right now." He grabbed my thigh and pushed my skirt up. "Tell me to stop now, or I'll be too far gone."

I laughed and grabbed his face. "I'd like to be there to introduce our parents to each other."

"That's not going to go well."

"So optimistic." I looked up into his dark brown eyes.

He smiled. His dimples pooled in his cheeks. "Just honest."

"Do you think your mom is really going to make a speech?"

James lowered both his eyebrows. "You're right, we should probably get in there." He let go of my leg. "But, just for the record, I will have you one last time as my fiancée."

I smiled. "I can't wait." Although I had no idea when he was planning to fit that in.

He grabbed my hand and held it tightly as we walked back into our home. I was surprised to see James' father and Mr. Caldwell sitting together laughing. James' mother was at the bar. Out of the corner of my eye, I saw Daphne kiss Rob's cheek and whisper something in his ear. He had a bad temper like his brother and I was surprised to see that he had calmed down so quickly. Daphne must have secret powers. Maybe she could tell me how she did it. I couldn't wait to get to know her better.

"So where are your parents, darling?" Mrs. Hunter said as she walked up to us. She drew out the word darling. She was clearly mocking me, but I didn't really care.

My mom peered out of the kitchen. She pulled my father out beside her and came over to us.

"You must be James' mother," my mom said. "I'm Julia, Penny's mom. You have such a lovely son."

"Do you know my son well?"

"Well, yes. We all try to get together a few times a month for dinner and board games. James is the undefeated champion of Sequence."

"That doesn't surprise me at all."

"It's a team game, though," my mom said. "Penny's always his partner. They make such a good team."

"Mhm."

"And I'm Peter," my dad said. "Penny's father."

"Are either of you employed?" Mrs. Hunter asked.

"Excuse me?" my father said.

"My husband is missing all the niceties. Jonathan, get over here," she said. "Now."

Mr. Hunter clapped Mr. Caldwell on the back as he stood up. He walked over with a smile on his face. "You must be Penny's parents," he said. "You can call me Jon." He stuck his hand out for my dad.

I was shocked at the exchange. James' dad had always seemed as snooty as his wife. But here he was making an effort at least. He was so much warmer than Mrs. Hunter.

"We are so happy to finally meet you," he said with a smile.

Finally? He had only just met me a few weeks ago. I didn't care if it was just a show, it was nice of him to try. He looked genuinely pleased to meet them.

"We love your son dearly," my mom said as she shook his hand. "He's such a wonderful addition to our family."

Mrs. Hunter frowned. "I'd like to make a toast," she said loudly so that everyone could hear. "Can someone turn off that retched music?"

I saw Rory press some buttons on the sound system. First it got louder and then he successfully turned it off. He gave me a thumbs up.

"Honestly, you should get some better help," Mrs. Hunter mumbled.

Rory's friend that had been flirting with Melissa laughed. After getting a death stare from Mrs. Hunter, he grabbed Rory's arm and they both retreated into the kitchen.

Mrs. Hunter cleared her throat and lifted her drink in the air. "I'd just like to make a toast to the happy couple. Clearly there is some kind of substance there since they're actually going through with this whole thing. It's definitely not the arrangement we would have hoped for." She glanced at me. "Clearly. I admire a girl for marrying up, but how this young girl got her claws in..."

"What my wife is trying to say," Mr. Hunter interrupted and grabbed the glass out of her hand, "is that we are very happy that the two of you found each other. Happiness is the most important thing in this world. Life is much too short. It goes by in a flash. So hold on to each other. Hold on to that feeling that you have right now. And, Penny, you seem like such a lovely girl. My wife and I are both excited to get to know you better. I'm just sorry it took so long. Welcome to the family. Cheers to the happy couple." He raised the glass in the air.

Everyone clinked glasses.

"We're happy for you, son," he said and put his hand on James' shoulder.

James looked down at his dad's hand like it was a foreign object. "Thanks." He said it more like a question than a statement.

"If you'll excuse us for a second." He grabbed his wife's arm and pulled her toward the kitchen. A second later, the catering staff came running out.

"I think your father might be having a midlife crisis," I said.

"Yeah. Or maybe he's finally trying to be a good dad."

"They both seem lovely," my mom said cheerily. But I could tell by her face that she was shocked. Sometimes she was as bad as me at hiding her emotions.

"A little stuck up if you ask me," my dad said under his breath.

"Dad!"

But James laughed. "You have no idea."

My dad smiled. "And they're the ones that convinced you to root for the Giants? I'll make an Eagles fan out of you yet."

"Good luck with that. I think it's much more likely I'll make a Giants fan out of Penny."

"Not a chance," my dad said.

They both laughed.

My dad had made a habit of coming up whenever the Eagles played the Giants. He'd watch the games with us. Rob, Mason, and Matt would all come over too and cheer on the Giants. It was just me and my dad rooting for the Eagles. Sometimes Bee would come over and cheer on the Eagles with us. I'm pretty sure it drove James crazy that he couldn't convert me into a Giants fan. But I had grown up watching the Eagles with my dad. That was one thing James couldn't get his way with. Besides, I'm pretty sure he enjoyed the ongoing bets we had on the games.

"Have any of you gotten dessert yet?" Rory's friend Jackson asked. "It's delightful on your palate. You simply have to try it." He held up the tray of decadent chocolate pastries.

"Absolutely." I grabbed one off the tray and took a bite. "Oh my God, this is amazing." I took another huge bite.

"You really have been hungry," James whispered in my ear. "Your declaration of love for that dessert was almost orgasmic."

I laughed and elbowed him in the ribs. "It was not."

He gave me a playful smile.

Someone pinching the side of my waist made me jump. I laughed when I looked up at Brendan.

"I'm glad I didn't miss all the family drama," Brendan said. "It's always the best thing about weddings."

James shook his head. "Laughing at my torture?"

"Always." They clapped each other on the back. "Beautiful as always, Penny," he said and gave me a swift kiss on the cheek.

"Thanks, Brendan."

"Still can't believe you're marrying this clown. At least he's not your professor anymore. It actually seems like his parents disapprove of you more than your parents disapprove of him. That's pretty twisted."

James laughed. Brendan and him had grown really close ever since James had calmed down about him kissing me. I was surprised that James was able to forget about that. Maybe he had repressed it like me. Either way, they were friends now. James loved talking to Brendan about his latest development projects.

"That's actually incredibly accurate," I said.

Brendan laughed. "My parents would have loved you, Penny."

"And that's why I didn't ask you to be a groomsman," James said.

"What? If I had known my flirting with Penny was keeping me out of that race I would have stopped ages ago."

"We both know that's not true," James said.

Brendan shrugged his shoulders. "I can't help what I say around beautiful women." He winked at me. "How do you like the new place? James and I had a blast designing it together."

I looked at James. "You left that part out."

James shrugged his shoulders. "It was mostly me."

"Yeah, right," Brendan said. "Without me, your plumbing and electricity would have been a fucking mess and you know it."

"Fair enough. But aesthetically, I planned most of it."

"Well, you both did a fantastic job," I said.

"I'm pretty sure James designed it with the sole idea of how many places he could bang you," Brendan said with a laugh.

"Inappropriate," James said to Brendan. "And you would have made such a great groomsman too."

Brendan gave him an exaggerated frown.

"I'm going to leave you two alone to find more dessert," I said. As I made my way toward the desserts, I saw Luke and Mason with two guys I hadn't met yet. I was promised a few stories, and I was not going to miss out on this opportunity. I walked over to their group. "Hey, guys."

"We were just talking about you," Luke said. He sounded a little drunk.

"Yeah? Hi, I'm Penny," I said to the two guys I hadn't met yet. I recognized both of them from the picture of James' frat brothers, though.

"Oh, this is Benny and Mike," Luke said and gestured to the two guys next to him.

"Ben," the taller of the two said and stuck out his hand for me to shake. "College was a long time ago but these assholes still insist on calling me Benny."

"You'll always be Benny to us," the shorter one said. "Hi, Penny, I'm Mike. It's a pleasure to meet you."

"It's great to meet you guys too. So...you were talking about me?"

"Nothing bad, I promise," Mason said.

"We were just talking about how much better you are than Isabella," Luke said.

I tried not to flinch at the mention of her name.

"I don't even know you and I can tell you're better," Benny said.

I laughed awkwardly. "Thanks, I guess." I didn't want to be talking about Isabella. "Luke promised me some stories once the two of you arrived."

"That I did," Luke said and took a sip from his glass of scotch. "Have you ever heard the professor story?"

"The professor story? I don't think so." I felt James hand slip protectively onto my lower back.

"Mason has already told Penny plenty of stories," James said.

"Surely not the ones we're going to tell," said Luke.

Mason laughed. "I have told her lots of stories."

"But Penny wants to hear embarrassing stories about James," Mike said. "Right, Penny?"

Mason smiled at me. "I've already told her loads of those too."

"See," James said. "Penny, didn't you want to go find some dessert?"

"Oh, no," I said. "I want to hear their embarrassing stories. Starting with the professor story."

James groaned. I was pretty sure I was the only one that heard it though.

"It was hilarious," Luke said. "We were all taking poli-sci together sophomore year."

"They forced me to go to it," James said. "I wanted us all to take psych."

"But no one else wanted to take that," Luke continued. "So we had all agreed to take poli-sci." He emphasized the word agreed. "When we showed up on the first day of class, the professor was late. So James here," he put his hand on James' shoulder, "decided that he was going to teach it. He walked up to the front of the class and started talking about how politics is all about the distribution of power and resources. Actually, the lecture wasn't half bad. He made some valid points about how elections are basically popularity contests..."

"You're missing the punch line," Mike said.

"Right, right." Luke took another sip of his drink. "So he asks for volunteers and makes Mason, Benny, Mike, and I go to the front of the room too. And he makes the class vote on who they'd want to listen to speak next."

"I won," Mason said matter-of-factly.

"Beside the point," Luke said and waived his hand dismissively. "But as the professor walks in, James grabs Mason's face and says, 'You voted for your new president based on his pretty face. Suck it America, politics are a sham.' And then he made an incredibly rude gesture to the whole class."

I started laughing. Before today I wouldn't have been able to imagine James doing that. But I was pretty sure he had made the same rude gesture outside of the police station earlier.

"We ended up all getting kicked out of the class," Mike said. "And the only class left with four openings was psych. The evil bastard."

James shrugged his shoulders.

"I never got to take poli-sci," Benny said. "I'm still pissed about that."

James laughed. "You guys ended up loving psych. Don't lie."

Benny shook his head. "What? I hated psych. We had to memorize all those stupid studies instead of just having awesome debates in poli-sci. You screwed us."

"Wait, Mason, please tell me you've told Penny about the streaking incident," Luke said.

Mason started laughing. "No, I never tell anyone that story. It makes all of us look bad."

"That's true," Mike said. "I thought we promised never to discuss the night of November 9th ever again."

"Well now you have to tell me," I said.

They all looked at each other.

"No, you have to tell me now. You can't just put that out there and not deliver."

Luke laughed. "Fine. I'm not ashamed. They're the ones that got the street wrong, so it doesn't make me look bad at all."

"We were all completely wasted," Benny said. "That included you."

"But I wasn't the one that pulled out a map and was rambling about all the hottest chicks. Here's what happened, Penny. It was homecoming our senior year. All the fraternities and sororities were having huge parties. It was almost a competition every year to see who could throw the wildest one. So Mike here got this brilliant idea..."

"It wasn't me," Mike said. "It was James."

I glanced up at James. I wasn't sure I had ever seen him trying so hard not to laugh.

"What? Don't blame this on me," James said. "I'm pretty sure Mason..."

"Fine blame me. I'm completely comfortable with my body," Mason said.

Luke laughed. "Either way. One of these idiots decided that in order to prove that we had the craziest party, we had to end the night with streaking."

"Makes sense," I said as I tried to stifle a laugh.

"Right? So when everyone was starting to pass out on our front lawn, we decided it was time. We were going to shove it to the sororities by streaking through sorority lane. But we went to the wrong street because our party really was fucking crazy. Were we stoned too? I feel like we were."

"We definitely were," Mike said.

"Anyway, we made our way to the street we thought the sorority houses were. And we started running butt naked down the street. When we were about halfway done, we started hearing all these catcalls. So we turned around and all these guys were cheering us on."

"No, we thought they were cheering us on," Benny cut in. "Turns out we had accidently streaked through a neighborhood where there was only one house belonging to a frat. The only gay frat house on campus."

I started laughing.

"They were cheering us on, but also hitting on us," Luke said. "But at the time we didn't realize they were checking us out, so we stopped and were like doing cartwheels and stuff. Really working the crowd. Some of this." He put his hands on his hips and stuck his butt out.

"Oh my God," I said through my laughter.

"For months after that our frat house got invites to all their social events. Our phone wouldn't stop ringing."

I put my hand over my mouth. I couldn't picture James doing that at all. He used to be so carefree.

His eyes looked twinkly as he stared down at me. A huge smile was plastered on his face.

"I can't even picture you doing a cartwheel," I said. "Let alone doing one naked in public."

"Like they said...I was wasted. And stoned."

"Still."

"Let's do a redo tonight!" Benny said. "We're barely ever together anymore. Let's make tonight a night to re-member!"

"It already is," James said and smiled down at me.

"Aw, so cute," Luke said. "Wait, can we hear your sto-ry real quick? We've all heard tons of rumors. And obviously, we know that she was your student. But what really happened?"

James smiled down at me the whole time he told them about how we met. He talked about how he couldn't keep his eyes off of me in class. And how he wasn't at all ashamed of our story. And neither was I. Two and a half years ago I fell in love with my professor. In a strange twist of fate, it was the first time in my life I hadn't worried about following the rules. We were meant to be. There was no other explanation.

CHAPTER 11
Friday

As the rehearsal dinner drew to a close, I wandered into the kitchen. For some reason I had been craving a juice box all night. I opened up the fridge and pulled one out. When I turned around, I was surprised to see James' father behind me.

"Hi," I said. It came out awkward, despite my best attempt. "Did you want one? Or we have plenty of other things to drink. Maybe a soda?"

"No." He smiled. "I'm good. I actually came in here to talk to you."

"About what?" I wasn't sure I could handle another fight tonight. I was exhausted.

He sighed and leaned against the fridge. "For what it's worth. I believed you last night. And I could see how hard it was for you to walk away from my son. You care about him. And that's all the convincing I need that you're in this for the right reasons."

"Thank you." I felt incredibly awkward holding a juice box while talking to James' father. I set it down on the counter.

"I just wanted you to know that. But I'd be here either way. I'm done directing my son's life." He looked out the door of the kitchen. "All of my children's lives."

He was tossing me a bone. I should have been grateful, but all I could think about was why now? Why after torturing his son for almost 30 years had he decided to let

James make his own decisions for once? "I thought you agreed with your wife? I thought you wanted him to get back together with Isabella?"

He laughed. "No. Susan expects things to be a certain way. Give her more time. I can't apologize enough for what she's said."

"I don't understand, Mr. Hunter. It seemed like you agreed."

"Please, call me Jon," he said with a smile.

"Okay. Jon, it always seemed like you agreed with her. When we were in your office and she was giving me the check...it seemed like you wanted me to take it too."

"My wife is manipulative. She knows just what to say to convince anyone of anything. Except you, apparently."

"And what has she been trying to convince me of? That I'm not good enough for her son? I know that." An exasperated laugh escaped my lips. "I know how lucky I am that he chose me. Ever since I've met him, I've been trying to figure that out. But at the same time, I don't think she has any idea who her son really is." I picked up the juice box. I refused to care about what James' father thought about me. I just wanted to be myself. Tonight, that included drinking from a juice box like a little kid. He could deal with it. He had certainly put James through enough hell.

"Neither one of us has ever understood James' motivations. For anything really. My whole life, and my parents' lives before mine...we have always been motivated by money. How to get ahead. How to grow our wealth. No matter who we had to step on. James wasn't like that. He wanted to make a difference. He didn't care about the same things that I did or that his mother did. Actually, none of our kids do really. We were hard on him because we want our name to mean something. As the oldest son, it was his responsibility. Look at Mason and his dad, Max. They had a falling out because Mason refused to take over Max's company. They patched things up, but that was partially because Matt stepped up. Max had another son that wanted the responsibility. One that cared about their legacy. And Rob...Rob doesn't care about anything but himself."

I wasn't sure what made my blood boil more. The talk about legacy and a name that James had only made better, or the fact that he didn't understand Rob at all. *Fuck him.* "The Hunter name does mean something, more so because of James. James started two great companies. Not only do they both make money, but they make a difference like you said he wanted. He was a great professor too. And it made him so happy. If he'd listen to me, he'd still be doing that. As for Rob, you clearly don't know him at all. He has the biggest heart of anyone I know. He cares more about his siblings than himself. He was there for James during some of the worst moments of his life, because he didn't have anyone else. And that includes you. You abandoned him when he needed you the most. I'm lucky that tomorrow I can call Rob a brother. And I'm lucky to be marrying the most caring, strong, and loving person in the world tomorrow. It's a shame that you don't know him. You're the one that is missing out."

He gave me a curious look. "I wasn't trying to upset you."

I took a deep breath. "Then you shouldn't be throwing blind accusations."

"You're good for him. I can tell you're strong. He needs that."

"James is stronger than you give him credit for. He's overcome so much. A lot of which he wouldn't have had to if it weren't for you and your wife."

Jon smiled. "Even if he is strong, it's nice to know you have his back. That you'll fight for him. In our own way, that's what we were trying to do for him when he was younger. We made some mistakes, of course. I realize that. I want to make it better. I want to fix it."

I didn't say anything to that. He wanted to fix it. Just like I had wanted to fix it. But it wasn't up to us, it was up to James.

"And I don't doubt that he was a great professor."

"Why are you saying these things to me instead of him?"

"He wouldn't listen to me. James doesn't give second chances."

"That's not true. He's given me more chances than I can count."

"Maybe only to the people in his life that he loves then."

"If he doesn't love you, it's only because he thinks you don't love him. He's incredibly defensive."

"He gets that from his mother."

"Ugh." *Shit.* I had not meant to say that out loud. "I mean..."

Jon laughed. "It's fine. She is his mother, though. She always said she knew what was best. Maybe you'll understand when you're a parent. You want what you think is best for your children."

"I think happiness is the most important thing."

He nodded his head. "You're right. Happiness is the most important thing." He paused and stared out into the other room. "You see what it's like to defy her. It's easier to let her have her way. I've been taking the easy way out my whole life. I let her direct my family's lives and mine long enough, though."

"Maybe try taking James' side sometimes. He needs that."

He was quiet for a moment as he stared out into the other room. "Fifteen years ago, I decided to get divorced. I realized my life was built on the wrong foundation. There was no happiness, as you put it. Our house was filled with tension. It didn't feel like a home. Our children did everything they could to be away. We were all miserable. But I didn't want to abandon my family. I didn't want to cop out. It seemed unfair to leave them to suffer and for me to get to escape. Especially when I had helped make our home toxic. When I had sat back and done nothing to make it a real home. I failed as a father. I realize that. I went to my lawyer to file the necessary paperwork, but I couldn't do it. I stayed, but it didn't make anything better. I just suffered alongside of my children. I was hard on James because in reality, I wasn't strong. I wanted him to be better than me. I've always wanted what was best for him. But me staying made me an even worse father. I was hard on all my kids. I took it out on them." He shook his head. "I finally filed the papers with my lawyer this morning. Susan doesn't know. None of my children know. I want to make all of this better. I spent 15 years being a coward. I have a lot to make up for, I realize that. But I'm going to start trying."

James was so much like his father. They both carried the weight of the world on their shoulders. They suffered to make others happy. "Why are you telling me this?"

"To show you how much I do care about my family. I love all of my children. And I want to be a part of your lives. Right now you're the closest to giving me grandchildren." He gave me a playful smile that reminded me so much of James.

I laughed. "Not that close. We're going to wait awhile."

"It's good to take the time to enjoy each other." He opened up the fridge and grabbed a juice box. "You know, my wife never allowed these in the house."

"I know." I smiled as I watched him drink from the tiny straw. "You need to tell James everything you just told me. He needs to hear it from you."

"Hear what from him?" James walked through the doorway and wrapped his arm protectively around my waist. "You okay?"

I glanced at Jon. "I'm great. But I think you two need to talk." I stepped away from James' arm and smiled up at him.

"You found yourself a great girl," Jon said.

James' eyes left mine and he lowered both his eyebrows.

That was probably my cue to leave. "Thanks, Jon."

James folded his arms across his chest as I left them alone. He was already closing himself off. I hoped he'd listen to his dad. Maybe they could fix this. I hoped that they could.

CHAPTER 12

Friday

Most everyone had left by the time I walked back into the living room. The bridal party had moved to the couches and they were all laughing about something. I collapsed between Melissa and Bee.

"I'm officially exhausted," I said.

Bee laughed. "But our slumber party hasn't even started yet!"

I sighed and put my head on Melissa's shoulder. I glanced around at my friends. Mason's arm was wrapped firmly around Bee's shoulders. Daphne was sitting on Rob's lap. They looked so comfortable together. And everyone else was smiling like they just had a blast, despite all the awkwardness. Tonight had officially been a success. Especially if James could patch things up with his dad.

"What time do you think the lingerie pillow fight will start?" Rob asked. "I need to know when to casually stop by to check on you ladies tonight."

"Ew, Rob," Jen said and tossed a pillow at him. She stuck her tongue out at him and turned to face me. "So, what were you talking to my dad about?"

"I was just getting to know him." It wasn't my place to tell Jen or Rob about their dad filing for divorce. I wondered if they'd be happy or sad. Based on how they all acted around their parents, they'd probably be relieved. "He was wondering when he could expect grandchildren."

Jen laughed. "Having kids is the last thing on my mind right now. I'm not even dating anyone." She glanced at Rob.

Rob smiled. "Geez, it's a little soon. We've barely been dating a week." He tossed the pillow back at his sister. "But I am excited to be an uncle." He winked at me.

I shook my head. "I'm betting that Rob will have kids first."

Daphne laughed.

"What are you laughing about?" Rob asked. He tickled her side and she laughed again.

"Nothing," Daphne said. "It's just that you probably will have kids first. You're incredibly irresponsible."

"Burn," Matt said.

Rob laughed. "We could go be irresponsible right now." He kissed the side of Daphne's neck.

"Actually, I should probably get going." She slid off his lap. "I guess I'll see all of you tomorrow?"

"You should stay," I said.

"What?"

"We rented a hotel room for just us girls tonight. Kind of a slumber party like Bee said. The guys are staying in a room down the hall from us."

"Oh, I don't want to impose..."

"No, please stay. It'll be fun."

Rob smiled at me.

"Um, okay, if you're sure?" Daphne said.

"I'm positive."

I expected anything Rob to do to be fast and crazy. Maybe they'd be walking down the aisle before Bee and Mason. I wanted to get to know Daphne. After our wedding we'd be leaving for our honeymoon. It would be fun to get to know her tonight.

"I should probably go home real quick to grab some stuff though."

"We can just stop on the way. Don't worry about it."

"Get lost, boys," Bee said and kissed Mason on the cheek. "It's time to get this party started!"

He laughed. "I'm going to need more than that." I looked away as they started making out.

Melissa rolled her eyes. I was so happy that she wasn't upset right now. She was handling the break up well. And probably her anger toward me for my part in it.

"I need to get my beauty sleep," Matt said. He stood up and stretched. "I need to be on my game tomorrow to scope out the hot single ladies. Unless Melissa or Jen just wants to agree to join me in my hotel room tomorrow night."

Jen laughed. "In your dreams, Matt."

Melissa just laughed and didn't say anything.

"I'm taking that as a yes, Melissa."

"I did not say yes."

"But you didn't say no either." He grabbed her hand and pulled her to her feet. He whispered something in her ear that made her face flush. "And besides, I'm great at rebound sex."

"You're such a tool." She pushed on his chest so he'd let go of her.

He laughed. "I'll let you know my room number to-morrow."

"Not necessary." She sat back down next to me.

"Everyone ready to go?" James asked.

I glanced over his shoulder, but I didn't see his father. He must have already slipped out. "Yeah. Ellen packed our bags. I'll come grab them with you." I walked silently beside him up the staircase. I thought he might say what he talked about with his dad. But he wasn't saying anything at all.

"She left my dress and your tux in the closet," I said. I opened up my suitcase really quick to make sure I had everything. Of course, Ellen had packed it to perfection. I'd need to thank her again tomorrow.

"Wow, this is heavy," he said as he lifted up my dress. A cover was draped over it so that he couldn't see it.

"You should have seen how heavy some of the other ones were." I waited for another moment. "What did your father say?"

"He apologized."

"Is that it?"

"I think you may have broken my dad."

I laughed. "He seemed different tonight."

"You mean like he didn't have a stick up his ass? Yeah, I guess."

"I talked to him for awhile. He seemed sorry."

"He should be sorry," said James.

"It's a start."

"I guess so." He wrapped his arms around me and rested his chin on the top of my head. "Baby, I really just want to focus on us right now. Everything else can wait till later. But I'm glad he's trying. Thank you for that."

"You're welcome."

"Maybe we can keep the divorce to ourselves? I don't want...my mom doesn't even know."

"I wasn't going to tell anyone anyway."

"Thank you." He continued to hold me. "Do you want to just stay here tonight? I already had to sleep without you last night."

I tilted my head back. "One last night apart. And then after that, you never have to fall asleep without me again."

He leaned down and placed a soft kiss against my lips. "If that's what you want."

"It's tradition."

"Okay, baby. How's your stomach feeling?"

"So much better, thank you. I was just nervous and hungry and," I sighed, "nervous."

"You said nervous twice."

"That's because I'm super nervous."

He smiled. "Nothing to be nervous about. Let's get you and your heavy dress to your hotel room. Porter is going to stay outside your room tonight to make sure you're all safe."

"Is that really necessary?"

"I'd feel better if you'd let him."

"Okay. If that's what you want."

"What I want is to stay here." He gave me one of his smiles that was hard to say no to.

I laughed. "I'll see you at the altar tomorrow, James."

"What, you're not even sharing a car to the hotel with me?"

"No, because I know you'll end up convincing me to turn it around and come back here."

He laughed. "Well in that case." He grabbed the back of my neck and kissed me hard. His other hand slid to my ass as he pulled me against him. I ran my fingers through his hair as his kiss deepened.

"Stop having sex you guys!" Rob yelled from downstairs. "We're all waiting for you."

James groaned into my mouth. "I feel like we just wasted time. They all thought we were having sex anyway."

"Tomorrow." I patted his chest.

He kissed me once more. "Tomorrow."

***

"Truth or dare, Daphne?" Jen asked.

"Um. Truth," said Daphne.

Jen smiled. "Are you in love with my brother?"

"Which one?" Bee asked. "You should really be more specific." She grabbed the bowl of popcorn out of Jen's hand.

Jen laughed. "Rob of course."

"It's so soon," Daphne said. "I mean, that's crazy."

"I didn't ask if it was crazy or too soon. I just asked if you loved him. Yes or no?"

Daphne pressed her lips together. It looked like she was trying not to smile. "Yes."

Jen squealed. "I know I said it was just a yes or no. But now I need to know everything. How serious are you guys?"

"I don't know. He's talking about moving to New York. I mean, he wanted me to meet all of you. I know it's fast, but," she smiled, "I can't stop thinking about him. He just has this positive energy about him. I really need that in my life. He just makes me so happy."

"I'm so happy for you guys," I said. "You just seem so nice and sweet and understanding."

"Can I ask you something personal, Penny?" asked Daphne.

"Of course."

"Before you dated James, did you date Rob?"

I laughed. "Wait, what? Why would you ask that?"

"He just talks about you in a weird way. Like super flirtatiously, I guess. I'm sorry, I didn't mean anything by it. I was just wondering."

"No, I never dated Rob. We're just like...the best of friends. That's just the way he is."

"It's true," Bee said. "You should hear some of the inappropriate things he's said to me. But he doesn't mean it. He's just being funny. We barely notice it anymore."

Daphne laughed. "Oh, good. I was just worried you had all slept with him. I mean, not you Jen, obviously."

Jen pretended to vomit.

Melissa shoved a huge handful of popcorn in her mouth and nodded along. I was hoping she wouldn't mention the fact that she had slept with Rob a few years ago. Especially since it meant nothing to Melissa or Rob. Surely Rob would tell her eventually, but it wasn't necessary right now. I wanted us all to be able to be friends.

"Okay, truth or dare, Penny?" Daphne asked.

"Truth." None of us were choosing dare. We all just wanted to talk. This was just a fun way to do it with a new person in our group.

"Are you nervous at all about tomorrow?"

I had some unanswered questions about James. But the answers wouldn't affect my decision to marry him. I had wanted to be with him ever since I had run into him in that coffee shop. It had always been us. There wasn't a doubt in my mind about that. "Not about marrying him.

More so just about everything going smoothly. It's silly, but I don't want him to be thinking about his first wedding at all. I want it to be perfect so that there is no comparison."

"He won't be," Jen said and squeezed my knee. "I'm pretty sure he was stoned when he married Isabella."

"Really?"

"Yeah. I doubt he even remembers it. He was a mess."

I thought about that for a second. "And even that makes me a little nervous. I'm worried he's going to change his mind at the last minute and not show up. I know it's ridiculous. But you know, like if he realizes he's making a mistake again."

"I don't think you have to worry about that," Melissa said. "James has been obsessed with you ever since you first met. He wanted to marry you as soon as you moved to New York. The only reason it took this long was because you wanted to graduate first."

"I know." I shrugged my shoulders. "It's still scary."

"Mason would never let him skip town," Bee said. "I actually made him promise not to lose track of him tonight after what happened this morning. I got your back, girl."

I laughed. "Thanks. I have no idea why I'm nervous, I just am. I feel like my stomach is filled with butterflies."

"That's why you should be drinking with us," Jen said and raised her glass.

"No way. I don't want to have a hangover for my wedding."

"I sure do."

I laughed. "Okay, Jen. Truth or dare," I said.

"Since everyone is being super lame, dare!"

"I knew you'd say that. I dare you to ask Ian on a date tomorrow."

"Ian? As in, your driver Ian?"

"What other Ian would I be talking about?"

She laughed and took a sip of her drink. "Ian's not interested in me. Besides, even if he was, I live on the other side of the country. And it would just never work."

"See. You didn't say anything about not liking *him*."

"Of course I like him. He's sweet and funny. And he always goes out of his way to help me. But that's his job. He doesn't like me like that."

"Trust me, he likes you."

"Did he say that?"

"You should hear how excited he gets whenever you're coming to visit."

"Stop messing with me, Penny."

"I'm serious! Besides, you have to ask him out tomorrow. You can't break a dare."

"Fine, I'll ask him. But he's going to say no. And then I'll be mortified and never be able to come back to New York."

"He's going to say yes and then you'll be the first ones running about with grandchildren for your parents."

Daphne laughed. "Good. That was too much pressure for me."

We all laughed.

"Geez, kids," Bee said. "I can't even picture that right now. That seems like a million years away. We should seriously all plan to have kids at the same time. They can all grow up and be best friends too."

"I'm not even dating anyone," Melissa said.

"It sounded like Matt wanted to change that," Jen said.

"Matt isn't interested in a relationship. He just wants sex. It seems like that's all anyone ever wants with me. Tyler and I lasted for like 5 seconds. I don't even know how to be in a relationship anymore. I really liked him. I thought...God I don't know what I thought. He was such a nice guy. And even he just used me. I'm such an idiot."

I knew that Tyler didn't use Melissa for sex. He did like her. He just didn't love her. It still hurt to think that Tyler wouldn't be at my wedding tomorrow. And it hurt to know that he was hurting and Melissa was hurting and it was all because of me.

"I'm so sorry," I said. "Melissa, I know you said you didn't want to talk about it, but..."

"I'm not mad at you. It's not your fault. It's me. Everyone always leaves me. I have some internal flaw that disgusts people or something."

Daphne laughed.

Melissa glared at her.

"I mean, Melissa, I know I don't know you very well. But couldn't your flaw be that you expect everyone to leave you? So maybe you push them away a little bit?"

"I don't think I do that. Do I do that?" she looked at me.

I shrugged my shoulders. "I don't know. Do you?"

She bit her lip.

"I'm sorry," Daphne said. "It's just that I've always been terrified of losing people. So I stopped getting close to people. And if you're doing that too, you should stop. You're going to miss out on someone great if you don't."

"Maybe I push people away. I don't know if it's that exactly. I don't mind being alone. I'm kick ass at being single."

"Here's to that," Jen said.

"I'm just worried about getting hurt. I'm defensive. I hate feeling like I'm not in control of a situation."

"Sounds pretty similar to me," Bee said. "I think you should give Matt a chance. I know him better than you guys because he is literally at our apartment all the freaking time. He has a sweet side just like Rob. You just have to dig a little deeper."

"I think that's true," Daphne said. "Obviously I don't know him as well as any of you. But Rob told me that Matt gets sad at weddings. Because it reminds him that he's alone."

"Matt seriously said that?" Melissa asked.

"That's what Rob said."

"Hm."

"Whose turn is it? Jen?" I asked.

"Guilty," she said.

"Dare Melissa to hang out with Matt tomorrow."

"Too obvious," Jen said. "I'm pretty sure she's going to do that anyway now that she knows he's not a mindless sex robot."

Melissa laughed. "Yeah, maybe."

"Do you want a dare?" Jen asked.

"Sure, why not?" Melissa said.

"Okay. Then I dare you to go find out Porter's first name. And do whatever it takes." She winked.

"I'm not going to give the security guard a blowjob to figure out his first name."

"Oh, please, Melissa, I'm dying to know!" I said.

"Ew. Then you go blow him." She tossed a pillow at me.

I laughed. "I'm going to go tell him to come in here."

"Don't you dare!" Melissa shrieked when I stood up. "I'll go out there and ask by myself. No sexual favors. I'm just going to ask."

"At least pull your shirt down," Jen said.

"And your shorts up," Bee added.

Daphne laughed. "I'm so glad I keep picking truth."

Melissa opened up the hotel door and stepped out, closing it behind her. We all watched the door, especially after a few minutes had passed. Finally she came back in.

"Did he tell you?" I asked.

"Maybe."

"Shut up, he did not," Jen said. "I swear the only person that knows is James. And I guess Porter's mother."

"You're right, he didn't. And just for the record, I was very flirtatious."

"Fine. I guess you met your dare." Jen laughed.

"Truth or dare?" Melissa said and pointed at me.

"Now I kind of want to pick dare just to see what you'll come up with. But I'm going with truth because I don't want to do whatever crazy thing you would come up with."

"So lame."

"Fine, fine. Dare."

"I dare you to go up to the roof."

"Of the building?"

"Yeah."

I laughed. "Why?"

"I don't have to have a reason. It's a dare."

"Can you even get on the roof of this hotel? I told James I'd stay in the room."

Melissa started making chicken noises and flapped her arms.

I laughed. "You look ridiculous. Come on, just make me do something else."

"The dare has already been announced," Bee said. "Technically you have to do it now."

"Will you guys at least come with me?"

"Nah," Jen said. "You got this."

"I'll come if you want," Daphne said.

"Thanks, that would be..."

"Nope," Melissa said. "You have to go alone."

"Why?"

She laughed. "Sometimes you're so clueless. It's exactly midnight. All of us are trying to get you to the roof. And we're all refusing to go with you. Think about it." She winked at me.

I smiled. "James is up there?"

"Don't tell him I ruined it. Blame it on Daphne."

"What? I didn't even know." She laughed.

"What's he doing up there?"

"I don't know. He just sent us all a text a half hour ago about how we needed to get you on the roof at midnight. And I didn't want to risk going up there with you in case he's naked or something. Not that the sight wouldn't be great. It would just be hard to hang out with him after I saw how he was hanging."

I laughed. "He's very well-endowed."

Jen put her hands over her ears. "Gross! Stop talking now."

I laughed.

"It's very tempting to text Ian while you're gone." She reached over and grabbed her phone off the nightstand. "But someone should probably stop me because I am officially drunk."

I grabbed her phone and tossed it at Melissa. "I'll let you guys handle that while I'm gone. I'll be right back." I tied the sash around my new robe and walked over to the door. Bee had given it to me right when we got to the hotel. It was silky and said bride on the back. It was the most comfortable thing ever.

"Sure," Melissa said. She stretched the word out tauntingly. "You're never right back when it comes to James. And if you two uncontrollable love birds are banging, it'll be like an hour."

Jen put her hands back over her ears as I stepped out in the hall. Porter immediately stood up from the chair he was sitting on.

"You don't have to get up," I said. "I'm meeting James on the roof."

"Yes, ma'am. He asked me to escort you."

"Oh. Okay, then. Thanks, Porter."

He nodded.

As we made our way to the elevator he kept trying to walk behind me. So I kept slowing down, trying to get him to walk beside me. Maybe I imagined it, but I thought I saw him smile briefly.

He hit the elevator button for me and folded his arms.

"So what's your first name?"

He looked down at me. "I'd prefer to keep this professional."

The doors dinged and we both stepped onto the elevator.

"I know. It would just make me more comfortable if I could use your real name. Like if there's an emergency and I need to call your name. Your full name would get your attention better."

"Porter will do just fine." There was a small smile at the corner of his mouth again. There was no denying it this time.

"Sorry about Melissa earlier."

"It's fine. She was just asking me random security questions. I thought you were checking up on me to see if I was qualified. I assure you that I am."

"She didn't ask you what your first name was?"

"No, ma'am."

Melissa! I should have known she didn't ask him for his first name. The doors dinged open to another floor. "How do we get to the roof?"

"Right this way," he said and stepped out of the elevator.

I followed him toward a set of stairs. "How did you and James meet?" I asked.

He glanced at me out of the corner of his eye. "It's not my place to say."

If I thought James used to be full of secrets, Porter was on a whole other level.

"That's okay. I'll find out eventually, you know." I stopped at the top of the steps and smiled at him.

"James said you'd try to get information out of me."

"Did he?"

The corners of Porter's mouth curved up ever so slightly again. "He did."

"I just think it would be nice if we got to know each other."

"I already know everything about you." He opened up the door.

I should have been shocked by what he had said, but I wasn't. He probably did know all about me. If James hadn't told him, he had been following me for God knows how long. It was his job to know me. Besides, I was too distracted by the view in front of me. The New York skyline stretched out in front of me, the buildings all lit up in the dark, casting a magical glow. James was standing with his back turned to me, staring out at the view. He was still wearing his suit from earlier. His hands were in his pockets and his hair was blowing slightly in the wind. The view of the city was spectacular, but it had nothing on the view of my future husband.

"I'll be waiting to take you back down," Porter said and closed the door.

James turned around when he heard the door close. His smile was breathtaking. It had only been an hour since I had said goodnight to him, but I had missed him. There was always something missing when he wasn't with me. And I knew why he had asked me up here. He had told me he wanted me one last time before I became his wife. It was incredibly romantic. I wanted him one last time as my fiancé too. We had been together for a long time now. A marriage certificate wasn't going to change how I felt about him. But it did make things different. We were going to be married for the rest of our lives. He'd only be my fiancé for one more night. There was something sexy about that.

I walked over to him, very aware of his eyes wandering down my body.

"This is new," he said once I reached him. He grabbed the strings of my robe and pulled.

"Bee got it for me." I pushed my hair aside for him to see the word bride scrawled across the back.

"I like it. But you're not a bride quite yet." He pushed the silky fabric off my shoulders. "You're a single woman for one more night."

I wasn't wearing anything sexy underneath. I was wearing an old baggy t-shirt and a pair of drawstring pajama shorts. It was a classic slumber party outfit, but not an outfit meant to excite anyone. But James was looking at me like he had never seen me more appealing. It almost felt like we were back at the University of New Castle and he was running into me for the first time. He was looking at me in the hungry way that always made me instantly wet. I swallowed hard.

"Tell me what you want to do on your last night of freedom."

"I want you."

He smiled and grabbed my waist. He lifted me up and set me on the ledge of the building. I should have been scared of falling. But James would never let me fall. He'd never let anything bad happen to me.

"Tomorrow I'm going to make love to you." He slid his fingers up the insides of my thighs. "Tell me what you want me to do to you tonight."

"Porter is right inside the door, James. What if he comes up here?"

"The idea of getting caught has always made you want me even more. Besides, he's blocking the door so we won't have any unexpected visitors." He kissed the side of my neck. "I want you to remember tonight. I want you to remember what it was like to choose me because you wanted me, not because we had a slip of paper that said you had to. But because you can't resist me. Because I'm the only one that can make you scream. Because the thought of my cock makes your pussy ache. Because you can't fucking live without me."

I moaned as his fingers brushed against my thong. I could smell the scotch on his breath. I knew he wasn't drunk, though. He was just horny. And God, I was too.

"Tell me, baby. Tell me what you want."

I wanted to go back to where we started. I never wanted that passion to fade. "Fuck me, James. Just like you did in your office that first time."

"I was punishing you that day." His fingers pushed my thong to the side and he gently touched my wetness. "Have you been a bad girl?"

I moaned again as I spread my legs for him.

"Tell me how bad you've been." The tip of his finger slowly encircled me.

His dirty words just made me want him even more. "So bad. Punish me, James."

He grabbed my waist and pulled me off the . He pushed my shirt up. In a matter of seconds I was completely naked. I had only managed to undo all the buttons on his shirt. His hands were still so much more experienced than mine.

"Turn around, Penny."

I stared at his chiseled abs that were barely visible behind his tie. I wanted to reach up and undo it. I wanted to run my fingers along the contours of his muscles.

"Penny. Turn around and put your hands on the ledge. Now."

I loved when he talked to me like that. I loved everything about him. I turned around and placed my hands on the cold concrete ledge. Normally the view would have my full attention. But I could feel him staring at me. It was like every inch of my body was aware of his presence. I arched my back slightly and he groaned from behind me.

He pushed my thighs apart

"You're so beautiful, baby." His voice sounded tight. He slapped my ass hard.

I lifted my ass higher in the air. I loved the sting of his palm. I loved when he took control of my body. And he loved it too.

"And so fucking naughty." He spanked me again.

I gripped the ledge.

His fingers gently traced where he had just spanked. "You made me wait two and a half fucking years to marry you." He spanked me again. "I hate waiting." He spanked me even harder. His palm stayed pressed against my ass as his other hand slipped between my thighs.

Fuck.

"You're dripping wet, baby." Two of his fingers sunk deep inside of me.

God yes.

"I can feel how much you want me. Beg me for my cock, baby. Tell me how much you need me." He spanked me again.

"James." I was panting now. "Please."

He continued to slowly move his fingers in and out of me. His palm landed on my ass harder than it ever had before.

"James!"

"Tell me that you need me!"

Something was wrong. I could hear it in his voice. I could feel it in the way he was holding me. Our conversation from this morning hadn't calmed him down like it had me. He still didn't believe me. If my surrendering to him helped him understand, then fine. I'd always be willing to surrender myself to him. "I need you."

"Then why did you walk out on me when I needed you the most?!" He thrust inside of me hard.

Fuck! This morning he had been distraught and lost. And now he was angry.

His fingers dug into my hips as he slammed into me again. "Why did you not trust me enough to tell me what was happening? Why do you leave me in the dark when I try so hard every day to be your light?" He grabbed a fistful of my hair to make me arch my back more.

"I'm sorry."

"Why do you refuse to let me protect you?"

I don't know. Tears started to come to my eyes.

"Why? Tell me why!"

"I don't know!" I clenched my jaw. He was being rough, but it didn't hurt. What hurt was that he was right. I hadn't realized I was doing it. But I purposely kept things to myself because I didn't want to add to the constant burden he carried. The one he wouldn't let me help him hold. I didn't want to add anything else because I was worried he might slip. And I couldn't lose him. I couldn't be the reason that he slipped.

His fingers eased on my hips and one of his hands slid down my stomach. He gently massaged his thumb against my clit.

"I don't like when you lie to me."

"I'm not lying to you. Keep fucking me, James." I needed him to get whatever was in his system out. This was the only way I knew how. I thought making love to him this morning would fix this, but I was wrong. "Make me scream your name. Show me how good this feels. Show me how much you need me too."

He groaned as he thrust into me faster.

"Harder!" I closed my eyes. The intensity was too much. The weight of what this all meant was too much.

"Fuck." He slammed into me as his fingers dug into my skin. "Come for me, Penny."

It was easy to follow his command. All I could feel was him relentlessly fucking me. The mixture of pleasure and pain had almost made me come when we had only just started. "James!" I moaned and pushed back against him. I opened my eyes as I started to come. And I had the strangest sensation that I was flying. The city stretched out below me. And I knew as soon as I came down from this high, the reality of what had just happened would make it feel like I was falling. I wanted to fly for as long as I could. I pushed back against the ledge. James hadn't cum yet. I didn't have to fall yet.

But James immediately pulled out of me.

No.

He grabbed my arm and turned me around. His other hand was slowly pumping up and down his erection. He pushed down on my shoulders until I was kneeling in front of him. I usually liked when he did this. And I knew he liked it. He had told me he liked seeing his cum drip down my breasts. It made me feel sexy too. But it didn't seem like that tonight. He was doing it because he felt insecure. As if this somehow claimed me. Why couldn't he see that I was already his?

His first shot landed on the center of my chest. There was no bliss on his face. Only agony. Two more hit each of my breasts. After his last stream hit my stomach he turned around and quickly started to get dressed. The silence was unnerving.

I wiped off his semen with my t-shirt and then pulled my robe on. "James." I stood up and put my hand on his arm, but he pulled away.

"I'm sorry," he said. "I don't know what came over me. You asked me to punish you and I was thinking of reasons why I should. I got carried away."

Why wasn't he facing me?

He exhaled loudly. "Did I hurt you?"

"No." This time when I touched his arm, he didn't flinch. I walked around him and looked up into his eyes. "Talk to me."

"Why do you keep me in the dark?" He was looking at me like he knew the answer. Like it had been part of the burden he was carrying this whole time.

The thought made me feel so guilty. I had been adding to it when I was trying to do the exact opposite. "Because I'm scared you'll slip. I'm scared if anything ever goes wrong you'll slip. And I won't be able to get you back."

"Well I did." He reached into his pocket. He pulled something out and tossed it to me.

I caught it in my hand. It looked like a small bag of baby powder. "What is this?"

He ran his hand through his hair.

"Tell me you didn't take this, James. Tell me you didn't do this."

"You left me."

"You kicked me out! Tell me you didn't take this!" I threw the bag back at him.

"I didn't take it."

An exasperated laugh escaped my lips. "Don't just say that because it's what I want to hear. Tell me the truth."

"I didn't take it. But the moment that you left...that's when I knew I was addicted to you. That's the moment I knew that I was still sick. I wanted to dull the pain. I wanted something, anything to dull that pain."

"That means you wanted something because you were hurting. That doesn't mean you're addicted to me."

"Don't you get it, Penny? My life sucks without you. I don't need anything to dull the pain when I'm with you because you dull it. You're my drug."

The way he said "you" made my chest hurt.

"It doesn't matter if it's this," he grabbed the bag off the ground, "or alcohol or you. I'm an addict. I've always been an addict. And I'll always be an addict. You hide things from me because you're scared of what will happen if I slip. I've already slipped. Every time I fuck you I'm slipping. Can't you see that? Can't you see that I have no fucking control? I almost hurt you..."

"Stop."

"Penny, I can't..."

"Stop!" My words seemed to echo in the silent night. "You didn't hurt me. I love when you're rough with me. You fucked me like that because I asked you to. Nothing has changed from this morning. What you see as addiction, I see as love. And the fact that you didn't take whatever is in that bag means you're not an addict."

"Because it wouldn't compare to you! I'm broken, Penny. I'm weak. I'm not worthy of you."

"James." I tried to keep my voice as even as I could. "I'm not scared about you slipping because you're weak. I'm scared because I don't know what that side of you is like. All I've ever known is the you that I see in front of me. As far as I'm concerned that's the only you that exists. I'm so sorry I kept you in the dark. I'm sorry that I hurt you. I didn't mean to."

"I know." He walked past me and put his elbows on the ledge.

When I had come out here, I thought this moment was so perfect. I wish I could go back in time and ask him to make love to me. Now I was just tired and upset and James was refusing to look at me. This wasn't how it was supposed to be the night before we got married.

"I thought when you found the right person, things were supposed to be easy," he said more to the skyline than to me. "Why does it feel like this relationship is always so much work?"

"I know what you're doing. You're trying to push me away. Again. Like you always do." I leaned against the ledge beside him. "It's like you're stuck in reverse. Why do you not believe in what we have? Why do you keep pushing me away? You and I both know that I didn't walk away from you. This isn't about me. This is about you being scared. And that doesn't make you weak. I'm scared too."

He shook his head.

"Talk to me."

He turned his head to me. "Tomorrow, after I say I do, that's it for me. It's my fresh start. You're my fresh start. If something happens to that, I'm done. I can't live without you. I can't even function without you. You say you don't care if I'm addicted to you. That's your decision. I'm not going to stop you from marrying me because I don't want to. All I've ever wanted was for you to be mine. But yeah, it's fucking terrifying. Because there are no guarantees in life. Who knows what'll happen the next day or the day after that. I've given myself so completely to you that there's nothing left of me without you. There is no me without you."

"James, I feel exactly the same way. And I didn't realize how true that was until our fight last night. And that's why you're feeling that way. Because now you know what it's like to lose me. But I'm not going anywhere."

"You don't know that."

"I'm healthy. And I'm careful. And we have security guards following us around protecting us."

James shook his head. "I'm worried about Isabella. I can't explain it. I just...I know she's planning something. I can feel it. Maybe I'm just unsettled. I realize that no one else thinks Isabella would hurt anyone. But she's out there somewhere, and I'm scared that she'll try."

"We're going to be okay." I put my hand on top of his. "Anything else you need to get off your chest?"

"I want to know that you'll let me protect you."

"I'm letting Porter follow me around. They can hang out with us all the time if that's what you need."

"No, I like being alone with you." He smiled for the first time since we had sex. "I'm sorry." He sighed. "I don't know what's wrong with me. Maybe I'm just finally getting nervous about tomorrow too."

I ducked underneath his arm and let him wrap himself around me. "I promise I'm going to show up."

He laughed. "What about you? Is there anything you need to get off your chest before tomorrow?"

I thought about how I kept things from him before. I wasn't going to do that anymore. "I was wondering if maybe you should call your therapist? I know it's late, so in the morning maybe? To talk to him about the fact that you think you're addicted to me."

"We've already talked about it. He'll say that I'm not."

"So why don't you believe him or me?"

"Because I can't properly express how it felt when you left last night. I can't make someone understand when they don't know how it feels."

"But that's what I've been trying to tell you. I know how it feels. Because I love you."

"Your first reaction wasn't to go out and buy cocaine though."

"Only because I've never done cocaine before. Maybe it would have been. Who knows?"

James laughed. He ran his fingers through my hair. "I'll call him in the morning if it'll make you feel better."

"I just want you to go into tomorrow knowing that what we have is love," I said.

"Okay. I'll call him. Anything else?"

I hated bringing up more stuff. But I had to. This had become a night of confessions. There was no point holding back now. "At the precinct today, that cop said something about how I'd probably have to fill out a lot of restraining orders if I was marrying you. Or something like that. What have you been arrested for, James?"

"Nothing that serious."

"Just tell me the list."

"Isabella filed a restraining order against me after I beat up the guy she was screwing behind my back. She said she was scared I'd come after her next. It was ridiculous. I never laid a hand on her. She was just trying to pretend to be the victim."

"Okay." That had to be what the officer was referring too. But I wanted to hear it all. "What else?"

"Just minor things."

"Then tell me."

He released me from his embrace so he could look down at me. "It was a long time ago."

"I promise I'm not going to judge you."

"Okay." He ran his hand through his hair. "There were a few fights once or twice that got pretty ugly during summer breaks of college. I hated coming home. I was angry all the time." He shook his head. "I think I got something for peeing in a bush in Central Park once. I don't even really remember. Public drunkenness. I wrote some threatening letters to one of Jen's ex-boyfriends. He deserved it. I don't regret that at all. That was another restraining order. And I've been arrested for being in possession of drugs. Nothing since the restraining order from Isabella, though. Nothing since I've met you."

"How are you not in jail right now?"

"I have a really good lawyer. And a lot of money."

I shook my head. "So no fights recently?"

"I don't have anything to be angry about anymore."

"You punched Tyler in the face."

"Tyler fucking deserved that."

"He didn't take your money."

"But he wanted you the whole fucking time we were together. And I trusted him. I let you hang out with him every Friday night for the past year because I trusted him."

"He was trustworthy. And he still is. He only ever said anything to me when he realized you broke up with me. Which he found out about because you showed up at his place and punched him in the face. I didn't tell him."

James raised his eyebrow at me.

"Please don't punch anyone else. And don't yell at cops. And don't buy cocaine."

He sighed.

"I feel like those are things most people don't need to be reminded of," I said.

"I'm not most people."

"I know." I touched the side of his face. "You're so much better. Thank you for telling me. Geez, that cop made it seem like you had a rap sheet of beating up women."

"I would never hurt you."

"It hurts me when you try to push me away."

He pulled me back against his chest. "Then I'm done pushing you away." He kissed the top of my head. "I'm sorry that I ruined tonight."

"Tonight was perfect. It finally feels like there's nothing left unspoken between us. Do you have any idea how relieved I feel?"

"I feel it too."

"There is one more thing, though," I said.

I felt his body tense.

"Does a small part of you just want to hop on the next flight out of here and get married somewhere obscure?"

He laughed. "Maybe a small part. If it means I could have you all to myself."

"You already have me all to yourself."

CHAPTER 13
Saturday

"I have a gift for the bride," Rob said as he peered around the door. "Everyone decent?"

I laughed. My hair and makeup were done, but I was still in my robe. All I had left to do was put my dress on. "It's just me and Jen. And we're both good." The rest of my bridesmaids had gone for a coffee run. And my mom was on the phone outside giving last minute directions to relatives.

He closed the door and walked in.

"How is James? Is he nervous?"

Rob smiled. "I think excited is a better word for it. You look beautiful, Penny."

"Thanks, Rob. You look very handsome in your tux."

"I better. Because this tie makes it feel like someone is fucking strangling me."

I laughed. "I know James appreciates you wearing one. And I do too."

"You know I'd do anything for you. What's your dress like? Can I see it?"

"Did James ask you to report back to him about that?"

"What? No. Psh. Your veil looks nice." He gently touched the veil that the hair stylist had already gotten perfectly in place.

"I'll take that as a yes."

Rob shrugged. "Worth a try. I figured you'd already have it on, actually. I think he just wants to know whether or not he's going to have to hide a boner or not."

"Ew, Rob," Jen said from behind us. "But yeah, it's that kind of dress."

"Score." Rob winked at me.

"You really should be cutting down on this whole inappropriate comments thing now that you're dating Daphne."

"Boners are uncontrollable, Penny. Fuck, now I'm worried I'm gonna get one."

I laughed and took the box that he handed me. There was a note folded beneath the ribbon. I couldn't wait to read it.

"Is there anything else you need?" Rob asked. "I have very specific instructions to give you anything that you might want." He raised his left eyebrow just like James always did.

"Oh, I think I'm good. Thanks, though."

"You sure? It's your last chance to take me up on my offer. I'll fuck you right now, Penny. Just say the magic word."

I scrunched up my face.

"The magic word is please. Just in case you were wondering."

"Rob! Seriously, you have a girlfriend," Jen said. "Stop being gross."

"She'd understand. Penny and I have both been wanting this for so long." He winked at me again.

"You're ridiculous," I said.

Jen laughed. "Rob, get out of here. None of us need anything. Go bother James."

"And that's why Penny is my favorite sister. Seriously, Penny. You look gorgeous."

"Thank you. You're sure James is good? He's still planning on showing up?"

Rob laughed. "He's good. You have nothing to worry about."

"Okay." I took a deep breath.

"And I can tell him you're still planning on walking down the aisle, right?"

I smiled. "Of course."

"I'd kiss your cheek, but I'd probably mess something up. And I don't want to do anything inappropriate." He frowned at Jen. "Fist bump?" He put his fist out to me.

I laughed and bumped his fist with mine.

He made an exploding noise. "See you girls in a bit. Text me if you need anything. And open that in private, Penny. James said it was personal."

"I won't look," Jen said and started rummaging through her purse as Rob left the room. "Even though I'm dying to know."

"I'm sure I can tell you. Just give me a second." I walked a few steps away from her and pulled the note out from under the ribbon.

Penny,

I can't believe this day is finally here. I've been waiting my whole life to feel the way I do when I'm with you. You're everything to me. And today I finally get to make you mine.

I promise not to slip, Penny. I promise to apply to another teaching job like you want. And I promise to love you for the rest of my life. As long as I have you, I'll never need this. And I like to think it's because you make me whole. Not because I'm addicted to you. Give me time. Please don't give up on me. Our love is forever. And I'll never do anything that would cut our forever short."

I love you with all my heart, Penny.

-James

Need this? I pulled the string and opened up the box. The bag of cocaine was sitting there. I hadn't even seen him grab it back last night. *What the hell am I supposed to do with this?* Luckily Jen was preoccupied on her phone instead of staring at me opening the present. I quickly excused myself to the bathroom and poured the powder into the toilet. It mostly dissolved, but I flushed the toilet anyway. I watched it spin away until it was gone. I tossed the bag in the trash. The gesture was sweet, but he really knew how to give me a heart attack when I was already nervous enough.

For the first time I saw that there was something else in the box. I lifted up a picture. It was a picture of a tattoo that looked like the lines on an EKG. The ones you see on heart monitors. The beginning of it was flat and there was a date on it, and then the lines started up and down. It was the date of when we first met, two and half years ago in that coffee shop.

I turned the picture over. It said, "My life began the day I met you," on the back.

I grabbed a tissue and quickly blotted my eyes. He got a tattoo. For me. If that wasn't permanent, I didn't know what was. When had he gotten it? He had kept his shirt on last night. Had he done that on purpose so that I wouldn't see it?

I walked back out into the room and grabbed my phone to send him a text, but there was already one from him waiting for me: "Thank you for the watch. I love it. And I love you. One more hour until you're mine."

I smiled. The watch I had given him seemed so lame in comparison to what he had done. An engraving on a watch wasn't exactly on par with an engraving on your body. I quickly typed out a text back to him.

"James, that was the sweetest gift you could have given me. I feel the same. That was the best day of my life. Besides for today maybe. Where exactly did you desecrate your perfect body?"

His response came almost immediately. "You'll have to find it tonight. I'll see you soon, baby."

"What did he give you?" Jen asked.

I knew that James wanted me to open it in private because of the drugs. But something felt private about the tattoo too. He got it for me. And depending on where it was, I might be the only one to ever see it. "Something personal."

"Sounds juicy." She smiled but didn't press me for more information.

"Coffee!" Melissa said, carrying in a tray of to-go cups. "What are you all teary-eyed about?" she asked and handed me a cup. She looked funny carrying takeout in her fancy dress.

"James gave Penny some top secret wedding present," Jen said.

"What was it?" Bee asked as she set down a bag of pastries.

I quickly closed the lid of the box. "Just, something personal. Please tell me you got raspberry Danish."

"I know you well." She slid the bag toward me.

I picked one up out the bag. We had been so busy getting ready that we had all completely forgotten about lunch. My mom had insisted that if I didn't eat I was going to faint, which I really didn't want to happen. I took a big bite.

My mom came into the room. "Okay, Aunt Margery is officially no longer lost. Oh my goodness, Penny, you need to get dressed! We have to leave in fifteen minutes!"

"Mrs. Taylor, she's eating like you just said she needed to," Melissa reminded her.

"Sorry," my mom said with a laugh. "I'm just nervous."

"You're nervous?" I said. "I'm the one that's going to trip down the aisle and faint in front of hundreds of people."

"Finish your lunch," my mom said. "I'll go get your dress." I heard her unzipping the bag it was in as I took the last bite.

Bee handed me a napkin from the bag of pastries.

"Thanks."

"Okay, shoes first." Melissa placed my sparkly heels in front of me. "Or else you'll never be able to get them on. Your dress is super tight. It's good that you and James did some late night tangoing, or you'd be torturing him all day."

My mom cleared her throat.

I would never be comfortable talking to my mom about that kind of stuff. I lightly slapped Melissa's arm.

She just laughed. "What? The cat's kind of out of the bag after tonight anyway," she whispered.

"Still." I strapped on my heels. Luckily my mom didn't say anything about it when I walked over to her. I stepped into my dress and she pulled it into place as I removed my robe.

My mom immediately started crying after she finished zippering the back.

"Mom, don't cry, you're going to make me cry."

"I can't help it. You look so beautiful, sweetie." She gestured for me to look in the mirror.

I turned around and stared at my reflection in the mirror. James was going to love this. He liked me when I just wore one of his shirts. I smiled to myself. Maybe he would get a boner when I walked down the aisle. Those would be some hilarious wedding pictures.

My red hair cascaded down my back in loose curls. The makeup that the stylist did was better than anything I had ever done myself. I barely recognized the woman staring back at me. I was an adult. James was right about this being a fresh start. I wasn't a student anymore. And he wasn't my professor. Today we left our pasts behind us. I couldn't believe this was actually happening.

Someone knocked on the door and then it opened. Justin poked his head in. "All the hot studs have officially left the hotel. If you're ready, we can head over." He came in as soon as he saw I was dressed. "Honey, you look gorgeous." He walked over to me and kissed each of my cheeks. "The most beautiful bride I've ever had the pleasure of working with."

I laughed. Justin worked with famous people. I was just a lucky girl from Delaware. I knew he was just being nice, but it still made me smile. "Thanks." I took a deep breath. "I think we're all ready."

"Okay, ladies." Justin snapped his fingers. "Grab your bouquets. And someone pick up Penny's train. You," he said and pointed at Melissa. "That's your job."

"Aye aye," Melissa said and picked up the back of my dress as she handed me my bouquet.

"Now hold my arm, Penny," Justin said. "If you fall and break your ankle in those heels I will literally kill myself."

I laughed at his poor use of the word literally and grabbed his arm. I was happy to have the support.

***

I pulled back the lacy curtain and peered out of the window. All the guests were seated in front of the big tree outside the restaurant. I don't know how many times James and I had eaten at a table right under that tree. And in just a few minutes I'd be marrying him underneath it.

James had just emerged from the restaurant. I watched him walk toward the aisle. He greeted a few people as he made his way up to stand beside the pastor. Normally the mother would walk the groom down the aisle. But it was better this way. James was independent. And his mother didn't approve of me. I glanced toward the guests that were on his side. His mother and father were sitting beside Mr. and Mrs. Caldwell in the front row. I was happy to see that they had come.

There was an arch that hadn't been there the night before. It had flowers and ivy hanging from it. The lights dangling from the tree above made the whole scene even more romantic. I held my breath as James stepped beneath it. He shook the pastor's hand and they both laughed about something.

James smiled and turned toward the window where I was spying on him from. Almost like he could sense where I was. I felt that with him too. My eyes seemed to always gravitate toward him. I closed the curtains before we made eye contact. I didn't want him to see me until I was walking down the aisle.

"It's time, ladies," Justin said and walked into the room. "Bridesmaids, follow me."

Jen gave me two thumbs up before she followed Justin out.

"Don't lock your knees, it makes you faint," Bee said and gave me a quick hug. "I heard that somewhere."

I laughed. "Thanks for the advice."

"Take a deep breath. There's nothing to be nervous about. You look gorgeous and everyone out there loves you so much."

I took a deep breath and smiled.

"See you up there." Bee hurried out after Jen.

"Penny," Melissa said. Her eyes were slightly teary.

"Don't you dare cry, Melissa."

She laughed. "I'm sorry, I'm just so happy for you."

"Miss maid of honor. You're holding us up," Justin said from the door.

Melissa quickly hugged me. "I love you, Penny. And I may have found your vows in your purse and read them last night. But don't be mad because they're great."

I laughed. "I'm still not really sure what I'm going to say. Any last minute changes?"

"No. He's going to love them exactly as they are."

"Now," Justin said and stomped his foot.

Melissa laughed and released me from her hug. "Good luck." She lifted up the bottom of her dress and ran after Justin.

I pulled back the curtain again and peered outside. Jen and Matt were already standing on opposite sides of the arch and Mason and Bee had just reached the front. I smiled when he gave her a chaste kiss before they went separate ways. Any day now he'd be popping the question. I could just feel it.

A knock on the door made me turn my head. My dad was standing in the doorway. He smiled. "I was told to come get you. Pen, you look so...grown up."

For the first time I was worried that maybe my dress was a little too sexy. I had wanted to look sophisticated and classy.

He shook his head as if seeing the worry in my eyes. "It's just...I still picture you running around with grass stains on your knees."

I laughed.

"You look absolutely beautiful."

"Thanks, Dad." I walked over to him.

"I just want you to know how proud I am of you. For fighting for what you want. And not listening to all the noise. You are strong and independent. Don't let anyone tell you otherwise."

No one ever called me strong. My dad knew me and he had chosen an adjective that I strived for. He saw my struggles and fears and he believed in me. I didn't know weddings were going to be so emotional. I hadn't even realized how much love I had in my life. Especially after yesterday when I had felt so alone. The contrast was too much. I felt completely overwhelmed.

My dad handed me his handkerchief. He was one of the only people I knew that still used them.

I quickly wiped under my eyes.

"It's time," Justin said. He was smiling from ear to ear.

I heard the violins start playing the processional.

"You ready, Pen?" my dad said.

I took a deep breath. "I'm ready." I grabbed his arm. It felt like a dream as I walked out the doors. It could have been a thousand degrees and I wouldn't have noticed. All I could see was him.

And when we made eye contact, I had to blink away my tears. I felt it in every fiber of my being. This was love. This was the kind of love you read about in fairytales. And I suddenly knew exactly what I would say in my vows. James smiled at me as I walked down the aisle. That smile made me instantly less nervous. There were so many things in my life that seemed uncertain. But not him. James was everything to me.

We stopped and my dad turned me toward him. "Penny, I love James like a son. You couldn't have made a better choice." He kissed my cheek just like Justin had instructed him to do. But then he pinched it too, because that was us. It made me smile.

"Thanks, Dad."

It felt like I was floating up to James. His hands grabbing mine pulled me back down to earth. I didn't even hear what the pastor said, but I heard people laugh. James rubbed his thumbs against my palms like he did so often. It felt like it was just us. His intoxicating brown eyes were staring at me so intently, like he thought I might disappear at any second, as if this whole thing was a dream. I squeezed his hands. We weren't dreaming.

"You look beautiful," he whispered.

I smiled. He wasn't paying attention to anything but us either. "You look so handsome," I whispered back. And he did. Whoever made his tux should have been the only person in the world allowed to design men's clothes. It fit him perfectly. He was wearing an emerald colored bowtie that matched the bridesmaid dresses. He looked even more like he had stepped out of the pages of a magazine than he normally did. The thought made me smile. It was one of the first things I had ever thought about him.

He lowered his eyebrows slightly. "You're shaking," he whispered and inched a little closer to me.

"I'm just excited." I swallowed hard when the corner of his mouth turned up in a smile.

He glanced at the pastor and cleared his throat. Apparently he had been paying better attention than I had. Rob handed him something and he grabbed my hand.

"Penny," he said as he slid my wedding band onto my finger. He paused for a second and I watched his Adam's apple rise and fall. "You once asked me if I was a believer in fate. I wasn't. But I am now because of you. When you fell into my arms, I had no idea that my life was about to change forever. But you knew. You fought for me when I didn't deserve anyone on my side. Your persistence and stubbornness and beauty brought me to my knee after only knowing you for two months. And now we're here. I know that we can get through anything together, I know that we're strong enough together.

"I'm crazy about you and I can't wait for our future. I can't wait for our lives together with you as my wife. You showed me that our pasts don't matter. You see a goodness in me that I was never able to see in myself. You make me want to be a better man for you. You saved me,

Penny. You are the air I breathe. You are the dreams I dream. You are the light of my life. I'm consumed by your beauty, inside and out. I'm the lucky one. And I don't know why you picked me. But I'm grateful every day. When I wake up every morning and see your face, I'm reminded that I am the luckiest man alive.

"I will never push you away again. Penny, I swear to you I won't. And I'm so sorry. I want you to be able to rely on me. I need you to know that you can always fall into my arms. I'll always be there to catch you."

He wiped away my tears with his thumbs. "Don't cry, baby," he whispered. "It hurts me to see you cry."

I pressed my lips together and shook my head. "I'm crying because I'm so happy."

He grabbed my chin in his hand. "It's your turn."

I nodded. I turned around and took James' wedding ring from Melissa. My throat suddenly felt dry. Public speaking had never been my forte. And everyone was waiting on me. I grabbed James' hand and slid the ring onto his finger. I knew he could feel my hands trembling.

He stepped forward and put his hands on my waist. "Don't be nervous. Just talk to me. Pretend it's just us."

That was easier than he probably realized. When we were together all I noticed was him. But it didn't make me less nervous. Because I needed him to listen to me. I needed him to understand. I took a deep breath and stared up into his eyes.

"James, I love you with everything that I am. I could go on for hours about all the things I love about you. Days probably. When I look at you, I still get stars in my eyes. I don't even know how it's possible, but I love you more and more each day."

He smiled.

"But what I need to tell you right now is that I forgive you. I forgive you for not always believing in what we have."

He lowered his eyebrows.

"Because I've always known why you push me away. Deep down that fear was always there. I understand. But you're wrong, James. You're always right about everything else, but you're so wrong about this. Because *this* is love." I put my hand on his chest. "This is all consuming, terrifying, heart stopping love. It's the greatest kind of love. And I'm going to spend my whole life proving to you that that's what this is. And how good and honest and full of light you are."

A single tear slid down his left cheek.

"Forever and always, James." I reached up and ran my fingers across his cheek, wiping away his tears. "There is no me without you. I want you to protect me and cherish me and whatever else normal vows say."

He smiled.

"I want it all with you. And only you. I love the way we met. I would never change a thing. And I love the way we've grown together. As long as you're by my side, I'm not scared of the future. Because I've always known what I wanted." I touched the side of his face. "You. You're all that I've ever wanted, James."

"You're all that I've ever wanted." He pulled me against him and kissed me. I knew it wasn't time. We hadn't said our 'I do's.' But we had said everything that we needed to. We were now one. Nothing would ever come between us again.

The pastor cleared his throat.

James removed his lips from mine, but he kept me in his arms. "Penny, this is the best day of my life."

I smiled up at him. "Mine too."

"James, do you take Penny to be your lawfully wedded wife? To have and to hold until death do you part?" the pastor said quickly.

James smiled down at me. The playful smile. The one I wished he always had. One not tortured by his past or his fears for the future. "I do."

"Penny, do you take James to be your lawfully wedded husband? To have and to hold until death do you part?"

"I do."

"Then by the power vested in me by the state of New York, I now pronounce you husband and wife. You may *now* kiss the bride," he said with a smile.

James laughed and leaned down to kiss me again. Etiquette be damned. This was my first kiss with my husband. I was going to make it count. I grabbed the lapel of his jacket to deepen our kiss as his hands slid dangerously close to my ass.

Someone whistled. But nothing else mattered. Just us. I was drunk on him. I had been since the day we met. I pulled back and looked up into his eyes.

"James, we're married."

He shook his head like he couldn't believe it. "We're married." He bent down and scooped me up in his arms.

I laughed as he carried me down the aisle in his arms. Everyone around us stood up and cheered. I heard laughter and knew that the groomsmen were most likely giving the bridesmaids piggyback rides, much to Justin's horror. And I wouldn't have it any other way.

James carried me through the doors of the restaurant and into the room he must have been in with his groomsmen. "This dress? Really?" He set me down on my feet and pushed my back against the wall. "Are you trying to kill me?"

"Does that mean you like it?"

"Especially this part," he said and trailed his fingers down the V in the front. "You are the most beautiful bride. And officially all mine." His index finger stopped its descent when he hit the lacy fabric again.

"I've always been yours."

"Not like this." He leaned down and kissed me softly. "Not as my wife." He kissed the side of my neck. "Not with my last name." He kissed between my breasts. "You look so beautiful, but all I want to do is rip this off of you." He kissed between my breasts again.

I heard Rob's unmistakable laugh.

James' head was between my breasts. I immediately pushed on his shoulders. He stood up and put his hands on either side of me, effectively sandwiching me between him and the wall. "We need a minute," he said to Rob while still staring at me.

"I'd say," Rob said and laughed again. "I was told to fetch you for pictures. I'll say I haven't found you yet. It'll look suspicious if you're more than a few minutes, though." He winked and walked out of the room, closing the door behind him.

James leaned forward and pressed his forehead against mine. "I meant what I said, Penny. This is the best day of my life."

I put my hands on either side of his face. "I meant it too." We stood there for a second, breathing in each other's breaths. It felt like something was passing between us. Some unspoken connection. I didn't think the words 'I do' could make me feel any closer to him, but they did. After everything we'd been through, this moment was pure perfection.

"Pictures," James said slowly and lifted his forehead off mine. "If I'm not mistaken, that was one of the many reasons you wanted a big wedding. The photographic evidence."

"I never said that."

He laughed. "Well, I wanted it. Let's go get a million pictures of you in this dress so I can take it off you even sooner."

I laughed. "Tonight at the hotel you mean?"

"That's not what I mean at all." His playful smile was contagious.

CHAPTER 14

Saturday

"Perfect!" the photographer said and took what seemed like the millionth shot. "Are there any other pictures you want before I move on to all the candid shots of the reception?"

"Please no," Rob groaned as he loosened his tie.

James laughed. "I think we're good. Right?" he asked me.

I nodded and clasped my hands behind his neck. "So good."

"Stop looking at me like that," he whispered.

"Like what?"

"Like you want to make love to me." He smiled and tucked a loose strand of hair behind my ear.

"I'm just looking at you like I am in love with you." I took a second to savor this moment. We had been walking all over Central Park taking pictures and now we were outside the restaurant again. I could hear the buzz of excitement of our cocktail hour behind us. James had his arms wrapped tightly around my waist. I couldn't believe that we had finally gotten married. I was officially Penny Hunter. Nothing could compare to how I felt in this moment. Secure. Happy. Complete.

"Come on, you two," Melissa said. "They're about to announce the happy couple."

I looked over my shoulder to see Jen and Matt already walking into the reception area and people cheering.

James touched the side of my face so that I'd look back up at him. "Thank you, Penny. For all of this."

"You helped plan it too."

He shook his head. "I mean for taking a chance on me." His hand slipped to my shoulder. "For trusting me with your future."

"It just so happens that there is no future without you."

"I'm not going to mess this up. I promise you, baby. I know I almost fucked everything up last..."

"It's okay. It was my fault too."

"No." He closed his eyes as if he was in pain. "You were right about what you said in your speech." He opened his eyes again, but his brow remained furrowed. "The doubt had always been there. But I'm not going to slip, Penny. We're going to grow old and gray together."

"Hmm." I ran my hand along his jaw line that was already getting a 5 o'clock shadow. "I think you'll look very handsome when you go gray."

He laughed. "And you'll look beautiful when your hair turns white." He lightly tugged one of my loose curls. "It's just you and me, baby."

"It's always been just you and me."

He nodded and placed a soft kiss on my forehead. "Thank you for believing in me."

"James, there isn't any part of you that I don't believe in. And even when you have pushed me away, I knew it was because you cared about me. I'll never stop believing in you. Never." I placed the side of my face against his chest.

"Time is going by too fast. I want tonight to last forever."

"For the first time ever, may I present, Mr. and Mrs. James Hunter!" the D.J. said from behind me.

James pulled back and smiled down at me. "Are you ready for this?"

"I've been ready for this ever since we met."

He smiled. "Come with me, Penny Hunter," he said with a wink.

We walked into the space that had been designed for our ceremony. It had been completely transformed for the reception. Tables with elegant centerpieces had been arranged around the area that would be used for dancing later. I knew the restaurant had been hesitant to let us do this. They usually held receptions inside, but I had really wanted it to be outside. Justin said he could make it happen. He had definitely delivered.

James lifted my hand in the air as everyone started cheering and clapping. All our friends and family were around us. Hugs, smiles, and applause. We were so completely surrounded by love.

"Penny!" someone called from behind me.

I turned around to see my fellow interns walking toward us. Sierra and Zach were holding hands and she was pulling him toward me. Tavon was a few paces behind them with his arms crossed in front of his chest.

"I thought you might want them here," James whispered. "One of the many surprises of tonight."

"Many?"

"Oh yeah. You're going to love Rob's speech."

I laughed. "Thank you." I had felt so guilty that I had finally gotten to know the other interns on the day that I left. I knew they had wanted to come. James was so considerate.

"Congrats, Fight Club," Zach said and gave me a swift hug. He shook James' hand.

"That was the most beautiful ceremony I've ever seen," Sierra said and gave me a hug. "I haven't been to many weddings, but I know I'll never experience one like this again."

I laughed. "I'm glad you're having fun."

"So much fun." She nodded her head discreetly at Zach.

I smiled. I had already seen them holding hands. I was glad that she was happy.

"Ugh," Tavon said from behind her.

Sierra stepped out of his way to give James a hug.

"Congrats, Penny," Tavon said. "Although, I still think you're way too young to get married. Too late now, I guess."

James laughed.

"No offense to you, of course," Tavon said. "Congrats," he said and shook James' hand.

"I think they're about to serve dinner," Sierra said. "We should probably go find our seats. Thank you so much for inviting us." The three of them walked off together.

"You're amazing," I said to James.

He kissed my cheek and escorted me through the crowd of people. There was a long table where the altar had been earlier. The bridal party was already seated and salads were being passed out by the waiters. James pulled my seat out for me and I sat down next to Melissa.

"You really know how to throw a party," Melissa said and picked up her fork. "I know speeches are about to start, but I'm starving."

"I can't wait to see what you have to say."

Melissa took a big bite. "When I'm not stumbling over my words, it's good."

I laughed. "I'm sure you'll be great."

"Can the father of the bride, maid of honor, and best man please meet me up here," the D.J. said.

"Do I have any lettuce in my teeth," Melissa said and smiled.

"You're good."

"Remember, I'm totally getting you back for this when I get married. I know how much you love public speaking." She followed Rob over toward the D.J.

"Any idea what your Dad or Melissa are going to say?" James asked as he put his arm around my shoulders.

"None. At least you know what Rob is going to say."

"I was just kidding earlier. I wanted him to surprise us."

"So he's uncensored?"

James laughed. "What, are you afraid he's going to embarrass you?"

"Of course he's going to embarrass me. It's like his life goal to mortify me as much as possible."

"That's why this is going to be so much fun."

I scrunched up my face and James laughed again.

My dad cleared his throat. "Pen, you know how much your mother and I care about you. And all we've ever wanted was what was best for your future. The road that you took with James swayed a little from the path we wanted for you. But I'm so glad that you veered right. I'm so proud of you for following your heart. Thank you, James. Thank you for making our daughter happier than she's ever been. We couldn't have asked for a better son-in-law. Even if you are a Giants fan."

Everyone laughed and Mason yelled, "the Eagles suck!"

My dad laughed. "We'll see about that this year, Mason." He smiled. "I wish you both a lifetime of happiness. And I'm confident that you'll have it. The two of you can get through anything together. That's the sign of lasting love, having each other's backs through thick and thin. You two have it. Savor it and never let it go. Welcome, officially, to the family, James." He lifted up his glass of champagne. "To the newlyweds!"

James and I clinked our glasses together.

"I'm glad you veered right too," James said and squeezed my shoulder.

I leaned toward him and kissed his cheek. "Thanks for being there to catch me when I fell."

He smiled at my reference to his vows. "Always, baby." He placed a soft kiss against my lips.

"And there they go again," I heard Melissa say into the microphone.

A few people laughed.

I'm sure my cheeks were red when I turned toward Melissa.

"For those of you who don't know me, I'm Penny's best friend. We met freshman year of college. And I have to tell you, when we met, I was almost certain she was doomed to a lifetime of being a cat lady."

Oh please, God, no.

James laughed.

"Don't encourage her." I playfully hit his arm.

"I had to drag her out to parties and had to actively push her to be social," Melissa said. "And actually, without poor influence, I'm not sure Penny and you ever would have hit it off."

"Thanks, Melissa," James said.

She smiled. "When Penny told me she was dating her professor, I didn't even believe her. I thought for sure she was joking. I didn't understand how such a goody two-shoes could take such a crazy leap. But then I met James. And it instantly made sense. These two were made for each other.

"Penny, you're my best friend in the world. You deserve the absolute best and I know that James is that for you. And James, I'll say this again because sometimes you don't take me seriously. I will literally kill you if you hurt her. So stop doing it. I'm serious this time." She pointed at him.

He held up his hands, showing his innocence.

Melissa laughed. "But seriously, the second one is for keeps. I believe that counts for marriages too. Except for in Penny's case. One is definitely enough. Because you two couldn't be more perfect for each other. Here's to the happy couple." She raised her glass in the air.

"I'm so sorry," I said as I clinked my glass to his.

James laughed. "I loved her speech. I wouldn't have expected anything less from her."

"She called me a cat lady and threatened to kill you."

"It's the future lawyer in her."

I shook my head.

"How's everyone doing tonight?!" Rob said into the mic.

"I'm sure I'll have to apologize to you after this, though," James whispered to me.

"Man," Rob said. "I'm so much happier doing this the second time around. For a girl that James is actually in love with and excited to be married to."

I couldn't help it. I found James' mother in the crowd. She was absentmindedly picking at her salad with her fork. She couldn't have looked any more bored. I turned back to Rob. I wasn't going to focus on any of that negativity.

"My brother is a hard person to get to know," Rob continued. "All of you probably think you know him, but you don't. Just a handful of people really do. Me, Jen, Mason, and Matt, and that's just because we grew up with him. The lovely Penny is the only person to get to know him recently. She was the first person to ever break down his walls. It's probably the really kinky weird sex they have."

Holy shit.

A few people laughed.

"Or maybe the fact that she's sexy as hell."

Fucking stop.

"Or maybe it was the whole student/professor relationship they had going on. I mean...that's fucking hot. The sneaking around. The forbidden aspect of it all. I mean damn, that will get anyone turned on. I bet James went into the class he taught her in with a hard-on every day."

James cleared his throat.

"Oh, sorry, I got distracted. Right, right. Obviously it's deeper than just a physical connection. I've never seen a couple that cares so unconditionally about each other. I thought my brother was crazy when he left New York.

Especially for Delaware. I mean, what the hell is in Delaware? Well, drum roll ladies and gentleman. Penny was in Delaware. He was meant to go there to meet her. And I truly believe that. Because without Penny, I'm not sure I would have ever gotten my brother back."

I didn't think most people knew what Rob was referring to. And it didn't matter, because I did. James said I had saved him. I knew Rob thought I did too. Maybe it was true. I liked to think that I helped.

"I love you Penny. Not in a weird way. As a sister and most importantly as a friend. I'll always have your back. So don't you ever doubt that again." He turned to James. "And now James. My favorite sibling."

"Hey!" Jen said.

"What? He's getting married, Jen. Let him have his moment."

Everyone laughed.

"Seriously, James. I love you, man. I look up to you. You've always been there for me. I'm so grateful for everything you've given up for me. And I'm so happy that you finally found someone that makes you happy. Because that's what you deserve. A smoking hot girl that makes you happy all day long, if you know what I mean."

James laughed.

This was so inappropriate in front of our families.

"From a professor and his student to one of the most adored couples in the city, you two are quite sensational. And I wish you both a lifetime of happiness. And I cannot wait to be an uncle to all the kids you're certainly going to have since James never wears a condom." Rob winked at me.

My face had to be scarlet. *Why? Why did he think this stuff was okay to say in public?*

James' arm seemed to stiffen around me. Just the thought of kids entirely freaked him out. Rob was going to be waiting a long time to be an uncle.

"I bet fifty dollars that they're going to sneak off at some point during the reception to get it on. Talk to me if you want in on the pool. And here's to the happy couple," Rob said and lifted his glass.

James laughed and clinked his glass against mine. "Wow, I'm sorry about all that."

"How do you not get mortally embarrassed whenever he talks like that? Our parents are listening."

"We've been living together for over two years, Penny. Everyone knows we're having sex."

I shook my head. "Still."

"And that's why I apologized on behalf of him."

"That was way more embarrassing than Melissa's speech."

"Maybe I can make it up to you and let Rob win a bunch of money all at once?"

I laughed. "There's people everywhere."

"Leave the details to me. We can probably sneak away for a bit when the dancing starts."

"You don't want to just wait until we get back to the hotel?"

"I'm pretty sure this will be more memorable." He was staring at me so intently.

I still couldn't say no to him. I'd bend over backwards to make sure he was happy. And he was right, too. Sneaking away somewhere here would be more memorable. "As long as it's still romantic."

"When have you and I ever not been romantic?" He lightly bit my earlobe.

I was completely, hopelessly in love. Just his words made me want him right here on this table. I took a bite of my salad to distract myself from the desire to rip off his tuxedo. I looked out at all the people that had come to celebrate with us. Everyone was laughing and smiling. Today couldn't be more perfect.

CHAPTER 15

Saturday

As the day slowly turned to night, the reception grew even more magical. I could even just make out the stars in the sky, which was a New York City miracle.

"Let's welcome the happy couple to the floor for their first dance," the D.J. said.

James stood up and put his hand out for me. Hands Down by Dashboard Confessional started when we stepped onto the dance floor. I knew it was an unconventional wedding song, but this was our song. We shared our first dance to this song the first time I visited New York with James. Someone had been playing it on their guitar in Central Park. And we had danced under the stars just like this.

James spun me around and then pulled me in close. We swayed slowly despite the fast beat of the song. I stared up into his dark brown eyes. I had never seen him look more handsome, or more perfect than in this moment.

"My heart is yours to fill," James said with a smile, quoting the lyrics. He grabbed my hand and twirled me around again.

I laughed as he pulled me back into his strong arms. I loved the feeling of his hands on my hips. We went to functions that had dancing all the time. James was an exceptional dancer. And somehow he made me seem okay at it too. I was elevated just from being near him.

"The words are hushed, let's not get busted," he whispered.

That was one of my favorite lyrics. It made it seem like the song was made for us. Sneaking around with him when he was my professor had been fun. But I loved now even more. I clasped my hands behind his neck, savoring the feeling of his skin beneath my palms.

"Hands down, this is the best day I can ever remember," I said, quoting the lyrics back to him.

"Baby, you have no idea." His hands tightened on my hips and he lifted me up in the air.

I laughed again as he slowly turned in a circle. I heard a few cheers from our guests and a splattering of applause.

James slowly slid me back down his torso. Before my feet had even touched the ground, he kissed me. Full and deep as he held me tightly in his arms.

I felt a little dizzy when he pulled away.

"Find me after your dance with your father."

"Where are you going?"

"I'll be setting up something romantic." He kissed my cheek and slowly released my hand. I watched him wander through the crowd of people and disappear into the restaurant.

***

"Jen?" I said when I walked down one of the hallways of the restaurant I hadn't tried yet.

"Oh, hey, Penny," Jen said and looked over my shoulder. She ran her fingers through her bangs and adjusted the strap on her dress.

"Oh my God."

"What?" She awkwardly cleared her throat.

"You just had sex."

"I did not," she said and then immediately laughed.

"I dared you to ask Ian on a date. Not to have sex with him!"

She laughed. "Fine you caught me. You were right about Ian."

I smiled. "You two didn't waste any time."

"We're both adults and we've both liked each other for years. What's the point in waiting when you know it's right?"

"There is no point."

"Exactly. Besides, we're at a wedding. Of course we were going to sleep together. I mean, have you seen him? He's mouthwatering."

I laughed.

"Hello, ladies," Ian said.

"Hi, Ian." I smiled at the fact that Jen had probably asked him to give her a head start so it wouldn't look like they had just slept together. "I'm going to leave you two alone." I stepped around them and walked down the hall. Love was certainly in the air tonight. And I couldn't judge them at all. I was about to do the same thing with James.

"James?" I whispered as I opened the door to the room that he and his groomsmen had been in earlier to-day. I had already tried the small room that I had finished getting ready in, but it had been dark and empty. That wasn't the case here. Dozens of candles were lit in the small room. It reminded me of when James had proposed. The only thing missing was him.

"James?" I whispered again and slowly turned around. He definitely wasn't here. There weren't even any places he could be hiding. I couldn't explain it, but it felt like something was wrong. James had to have been the one that had set this up. So, where was he?

My pulse quickened. What if something had happened to him? What if Isabella had shown up and...what? Hurt him? I just had this awful feeling that something terrible had happened. I tried to take a deep breath, but it just made my heart race even more. I had passed Porter on the way into the building. He would help me find James. I quickly opened up the door and ran straight into Porter.

He grabbed my arms to steady me. "Are you alright, Mrs. Hunter?"

It was the first time someone had actually addressed me that way. But I was too upset to savor how great it sounded. I shook my head. "Where is James?"

"Isn't he in there with you?"

Shit. "No. Porter, something is wrong. Is it possible that Isabella is here? I just have this awful feeling..."

"No," he said with a frown. "Briggs is doing a border patrol and we have extra security posted everywhere. No one is getting onto the premises that wasn't on the guest list. Mr. Hunter must have just slipped past me. Give me a second." Porter touched something on his watch. "Who has eyes on Albatross?" He placed his finger on his earpiece.

I swallowed hard. Normally I'd find something like that codename hilarious, but my stomach was twisting into knots.

Porter nodded and let go of his earpiece. "He's at the bar getting champagne, ma'am."

"Getting champagne?" *Oh, thank God.*

"I'm sorry," Porter said. "He told me to keep my eyes on you. I shouldn't have..."

"No, it's fine. I was just overreacting." I wasn't sure why I was so on edge. Everything was fine. I took a deep breath.

"I promise we have everything under control," Porter said. "He just slipped away from me."

"Thank you, Porter. I know you do. I'm sorry that I bothered you."

Porter smiled. "It wasn't a bother. And here he is now."

I turned my head to see James coming down the hall. He was holding two glasses and a bottle of champagne.

I didn't want him to know how worried I had been. This moment wasn't going to be tainted by a stupid fear. I took a deep breath to calm my nerves and opened up the door for him.

James walked into the room and placed the glasses and champagne bottle down on the table. I heard the pop of the cork. But I didn't want champagne. I wanted him.

I grabbed his arm so that he'd face me. Nothing mattered right now except for us. We had both been waiting for this moment for so long. "You're my husband."

The smile that spread across his face was contagious. "And you're my wife."

I grabbed his tie and pulled him toward me. "There's still one more thing we need to do before it's official."

"And what is that? I just thought we'd have a private toast and take a few moments to talk."

"Seriously?"

He laughed. "Fuck no." He grabbed my waist and pulled me against him. "If it was up to me, I'd be making love to my new wife for the rest of the night." He leaned down and kissed me softly.

I wanted to make love to him too. But I was amped up from worrying. I grabbed a fistful of his hair and deepened the kiss. I was on edge and I knew that the only thing that would calm me down was him deep inside of me. I reached down and unhinged his belt.

He groaned into my mouth as he pushed my back against the wall.

I made short work of his zipper and ran my fingers to the waistline of his pants.

He grabbed my hands and lifted them above my head. "Not so fast, baby." He pressed the backs of my hands against the wall.

"You have your whole life to torture me." I squirmed under his grip. I wanted to touch him.

I felt him smile as he kissed the side of my neck. "I promised you that I'd make love to you tonight."

"At the hotel, later. Right now we're just consummating our marriage real quick." I hooked my leg around his waist.

"No, not quickly." He kissed the side of my neck again and slowly left a trail of kisses down the front of my chest and between my breasts.

"I need you, James. You have no idea how much I need you."

"Then you know how I feel all the time." He grabbed my ass and lifted my legs around him.

I could feel how hard he was. His erection was pressed against my stomach as he lowered me onto the table.

"I've been waiting my whole life for this moment. I'm going to savor every second of it." He bent down in front of me and kissed the inside of my ankle as he slowly pushed my dress up.

I wasn't going to be able to take his torturous ascent. "James, please."

"Insatiable as ever," he said once he reached the inside of my knee.

I knew my whole body was trembling with want. All I could feel were his lips on my skin.

"I like this," he said and snapped my garter against my thigh.

I squirmed and he tightened his grip on me.

"It's hard to know how I should make my lovely wife come first." His breath was hot between my thighs.

He grabbed the sides of my thong and slowly lowered it down my hips.

"Your cock."

I felt him smile again as he kissed me just beside where I needed him most. "That'll be the last of the three. So you'll have to choose what's first. My fingers," he lightly stroked his fingers against my wetness, "or my tongue."

I felt his hot breath again. I didn't want to go slowly, but I did want that. There was never a moment where I didn't want that. "Your tongue."

"I was hoping you'd say that." He placed a long, slow stroke against my wetness.

Fuck.

He expertly swirled his tongue, hitting all my walls. He knew exactly what to do to make me putty in his hands.

I tilted my head back and moaned.

He responded by thrusting his tongue deep inside of me. He gripped my thighs firmly in his hands and spread them as far as they would go, allowing him to go deeper still.

God yes.

He was completely devouring me. I was moments away from release. He wrapped his hands around my thighs and pulled me to the edge of the table, changing the angle again. I could barely control myself. And then he gently rubbed his nose against my clit.

I came. Hard. I gripped his hair as I screamed his name. It was almost embarrassing how fast he could make me come. But I was never embarrassed about my reaction to James. And I knew he loved it just as much as I did.

"There is nothing better than the taste of you," he whispered and placed one last slow stroke against my aching pussy. "And now for my fingers."

"James, please, I need you."

"Baby, trust me, I know exactly what you need." He slowly encircled my wetness with one finger.

I whimpered as he sunk his finger deep inside of me.

"And it makes me even harder each time you tremble in my arms. The look on your face when you come makes me want to do it over and over again to you." He thrust a second finger inside of me.

"James," I moaned.

He began to massage my clit with his thumb. "Penny Hunter. God, I love the sound of that." He kissed the inside of my knee and then stood up so he could peer down at me. The new angle just made his fingers go deeper. He moved his hand slowly at first and then faster and faster, driving me toward the edge.

"I love how flushed your cheeks get when you're about to come. And the way your lips part ever so slightly."

He knew me even better than I knew myself.

"Look at me when you come, baby." He curved his fingers, hitting the spot that always made me come.

Yes! I could feel myself start to pulse around his fingers. A small smile curled onto his lips when he felt it too. I let myself collapse back onto the table, but didn't drop his gaze. I could feel the heat of his stare. Each time my pussy throbbed against him, it made him want me more and more. And it was an intoxicating feeling. I loved that he got aroused at my pleasure. It made me feel so sexy.

He slowly slid his fingers out of me and put them in his mouth, sucking off my juices. "I've never seen you more beautiful than in this moment."

The room was only illuminated by candlelight. His face danced in the shadows, somehow making him look even more perfect.

He slowly lowered his pants, revealing his massive erection. "And I've also never wanted you so badly."

I reached behind my back, searching for the zipper on my dress.

"Keep it on," he growled and stepped forward. He spread my thighs apart again. "I want you just like this."

"Then take me." I grabbed his tie and pulled his lips down to mine.

He groaned into my mouth as he slowly sunk into me.

Fuck, yes. Even though he had just had me with his mouth and his fingers, his thick cock always seemed to stretch me even wider. And I loved the feeling. I loved being completely possessed by him.

"I was made for loving you, Penny," he said against my lips. "I'll never stop. I'll love you until the day I die." He grabbed my hips as he slowly started sliding his length in and out of me.

All I could think about was the friction that I had craved ever since I had stepped into this room. All I could feel was the heat between us.

"You're so beautiful." His fingertips dug into my hips slightly as he quickened his paced. "Fuck," he groaned.

"Don't stop. Please don't stop." I wasn't even sure if I was talking about right this second or our entire future. I just wanted him forever.

"Baby, I'll never stop. I'm yours. Forever and always." He kissed me hard as he slammed into me more forcefully.

There were no doubts anymore. There were no more what-ifs. He was mine and I was his.

His fingertips dug into my hips even harder as my toes started to curl. He exploded inside of me with a force I had never felt before. And I came just as hard.

"My beautiful wife," he said and kissed the tip of my nose. "I promise to love and cherish you every day."

I felt so full. Full of his love and everyone else's that had come to our wedding. I couldn't stop the tears that fell down my cheeks.

"I was made for loving you too, James. You're my everything. My perfect husband." I put my hand on the side of his face.

He rubbed his thumbs under my eyes to remove my tears. "Thank you for saying no to Las Vegas. This was so much better."

I smiled, remembering him asking me to run away with him in my dorm. "This was perfect. Do you think we can sneak away now, though?"

He laughed. "Let's cut the cake and throw your bouquet and get the hell out of here." He grabbed my waist and pulled me to my feet.

I quickly pulled my thong back on as he put his belt back through the loops of his pants. I reached up and straightened his tie and ran my fingers through his hair.

"What, you don't want me walking around with sex hair for the rest of the night?"

"Rob's speech was enough inappropriateness for one night, don't you think?"

James laughed.

CHAPTER 16

Saturday

"Don't you dare do it, James." He was holding the piece of cake close to my face and it was way too big of a piece for me to eat.

"Do what?" He smashed the piece of cake against my mouth.

I leaned forward so it wouldn't get all over my dress and laughed. I immediately grabbed his piece and shoved it against his lips, smearing the icing across his cheek.

He laughed. "Delicious. You have a little something there," he said and touched the tip of my nose with his hand that was covered in icing.

I laughed and grabbed a napkin. "Chocolate cake was a terrible idea," I said. I licked the corner of my mouth. But he was right, it was delicious.

"But it looks so good on you." He handed me a cloth that a waiter had just given him.

I quickly wiped away the mess along with most of my makeup. Luckily most of the pictures had already been taken. "You missed a spot," I said and wiped my finger across his cheek. I put my finger in my mouth and licked off the icing.

"Are you just trying to make me forgo the hotel again?" He raised his left eyebrow and snatched the cloth back from me.

***

The song had slowed down and I was swaying in James' arms. I had been staring into his eyes the whole time. I couldn't seem to stop. He was my husband. James Hunter was my husband. It was hard to wrap my head around it. I was married to the man of my dreams.

James smiled. "What are you thinking?"

"That I can't believe I married my professor."

"Any regrets?"

I shook my head. "None."

The song stopped. I thought another would start up, but instead, I heard the thump of the mic.

"It's time to see whose wedding we'll be celebrating next!" the D.J. said. "Someone get a chair in the middle of the dance floor."

Rob dropped Daphne's hand and pulled a chair up to me and James.

"This should be properly embarrassing," he said with a wink.

Embarrassing? There was nothing embarrassing about this. Unless I threw the bouquet too hard or something. I had seen someone throw it into the rafters before. But we were outside. I'd be fine.

"Mrs. Hunter, take a seat and let your new husband find your garter."

I laughed and sat down in the chair. James kneeled down in front of me and lifted up my skirt slightly. He bent down and his head disappeared beneath it. I hadn't even thought about how horribly awkward this would be. God, Rob was right. This was definitely embarrassing.

James kissed the inside of my knee and then my thigh. He was purposely taking a long time just to mortify me. He knew exactly where it was from earlier.

I felt his fingers slowly wrap around the garter and he pulled it gingerly down my thigh. He reappeared a second later and made a face like it had been hard work.

He laughed and smoothed my dress back into place.

Everyone seemed to think it was hilarious. "Ow, ow!" all the groomsmen yelled.

James winked at me and stood back up.

"All the single men please make your way to the dance floor," the D.J. said.

"All those sexy bachelors!" Justin said and clapped his hands.

I couldn't help but laugh.

"And all the single ladies, stand on the other side of the dance floor," the D.J. said.

I saw all my friends make their way to the dance floor.

"You or me first?" James asked.

"I'll go." I turned away from the group of girls. I threw my bouquet behind my back and immediately turned around to see who would catch it. It landed straight in Melissa's arms without her even trying to grab it. She laughed awkwardly and tried to hand it to Bee, but Bee shook her head.

Melissa shrugged and smiled at me.

As soon as I was back from my honeymoon, we would have that conversation I promised her. Just thinking about it made my stomach twist with guilt. And not just because of the fact that Tyler had left her because of me. It was also because this was the first time all day that I had even thought about Tyler. But it was better that he wasn't here. It wouldn't have been right. Maybe one day we could be friends again. The way I thought we had been this whole time.

James shot my garter belt into the group of bachelors.

Matt jumped up and caught it. He smiled as he walked over to Melissa. He grabbed her waist, pulled her in close, and kissed her.

A few people gasped. They were supposed to share a dance, not a kiss.

But in a few seconds, Melissa grabbed the back of his neck, ensuring that he wouldn't stop.

"Wow, I did not see that coming," James said and put his arm around my shoulders.

I smiled. "I think they'd actually be really good together."

"Yeah? They're both such strong personalities though."

"I'm just saying I could see it."

Melissa laughed as Matt kneeled down in front of her. He lifted up her skirt and slid the garter up to her thigh. She put her hands on his shoulders to steady herself and squealed when he kissed her thigh.

"Now it's time for the bride and groom to go get busy!" the D.J. said.

"Oh God." I put my hand over my face and James kissed my cheek.

When I opened my eyes again, everyone had formed two lines for us to walk between. And everyone was holding sparklers.

I thought the night already looked magical. But with those, it was just perfect. James grabbed my hand and we laughed and ran through all the smiling faces. When we reached the end of the line, James grabbed me and kissed me. Everyone cheered. It felt like I would never stop smiling. Like life could always be this perfect. James let go of my waist and we turned to wave to everyone.

I heard a loud boom. *Fireworks!* I turned to look up in the sky. But nothing was there. Just the stars that had magically appeared for our wedding. I felt James's hand on my shoulder. A second boom rang out before I had even turned back toward him.

When my eyes met his, I could see it in his face. Terror. Pain. His hand on my shoulder grew even heavier as he stumbled forward. He coughed and blood splattered onto my dress. I looked down at the red that was spreading across his dress shirt. *No. No!*

It wasn't like you see in the movies. He didn't whisper my name and say he'd always love me. It was just fear in his eyes. A terror that had to match my own. And time didn't slow down. If anything, it sped up.

Everyone started screaming. Sirens wailed in the distance.

"Get down!" someone shouted.

"James." A third shot rang out and he fell to his knees, pulling me down with him. "James!" I screamed. I pressed the skirt of my dress against the wound I could see. "Somebody help him! James, stay with me." I pressed down more firmly on his wound, but it just seemed to make it worse. His stomach was covered in blood. His arm was covered in blood. His chest was covered in blood. "Baby, please. Please." It wasn't desperation in my voice. It was despair. Because he was no longer looking at me. He was staring blindly at the stars.

DEVOTION

The sparklers fizzled out as I watched the life drain out of my husband's face. The darkness of the night seeped in around us.

PART 2

CHAPTER 17

Saturday

Someone pulled me off of him.

Porter bent down over James and ripped his shirt open. I could see the hole in his stomach. I could see the hole right below his chest. There was so much blood. Porter pulled off his jacket and pressed it against both of the wounds as he put his ear to James' chest. "Briggs!" he yelled.

Briggs released me from his grip. His hands replaced Porter's as Porter began performing CPR.

James wasn't breathing. *This can't be happening.* I felt frozen. I kept blinking, thinking what was happening in front of me would change.

An ambulance screeched to a stop and paramedics burst out of it.

Briggs stepped out of the way of the paramedics and scanned the top of the buildings that surrounded this side of Central Park as Porter shouted instructions.

"West side," Porter shouted. "Check the rooftops."

Briggs cursed and took off running.

I closed my eyes. *Please let me be imagining this.*

"Penny," Porter said and grabbed my arm. "Get in the ambulance. We'll meet you at the hospital."

"Is he going to be okay?"

"You need to get in the ambulance."

That was a no. James wasn't going to be okay. He was dying. James was dying. Tears streamed down my face. I quickly climbed into the back of the ambulance as soon as they had lifted James into it. I watched them press down on James' body with electrical paddles. James' body jolted.

"James," I whispered and squeezed his shin. "James, you can't leave me." I cringed when his body jolted again beneath my hand. "James, please, wake up."

"Turn it up," one of the paramedics said as the ambulance came to a stop outside of the hospital. His body jolted again as the doors flew open. His gurney was lifted out of the ambulance and he was rolled into the hospital.

I ran after the paramedics. A doctor leapt onto the gurney and started performing CPR as they disappeared behind swinging doors that stated hospital personnel only. I was left alone in the empty hallway, watching the doors swing until suddenly they stopped.

I fell to my knees and let myself cry. I had sensed that something was wrong earlier. If I had told James that, maybe he would have let us leave. Maybe we would have stayed inside for the rest of the evening. My thoughts flooded with maybes. I could sense that she was there somewhere. Isabella. And she was still out there. She'd rather James be dead than with me.

Someone needed to come back through the doors. Someone needed to tell me what was happening. Tears cascaded down my cheeks and I didn't bother to wipe them away. Someone needed to tell me he was okay.

"Penny."

I shook my head.

"Penny." Rob lifted my face so that I would look at him.

"Rob," I sobbed and I started crying even harder.

He put his arms around me and held me. He didn't bother telling me everything was going to be okay. We both knew that it wasn't. He ran his hand up and down my back. It didn't calm me down at all.

I wasn't sure how long he held me, but eventually he pulled back. "Come with me," he said and stood up. "Maybe someone will have an update for us." His eyes were red too. I had never seen Rob cry before. And it made me even more unsettled. He was crying because he thought James was gone too. He was crying because he thought he had lost his brother.

I grabbed his hand and he pulled me to my feet. I turned back toward the doors James had disappeared through. *Please, James. Please don't leave me.*

Rob put his arm around my shoulders and walked me toward the front desk. I stood there listening to the commotion of the emergency room as Rob was handed forms to fill out.

"No," Rob said. "I asked how he was doing. Not this," he said and slammed the clipboard down on the counter.

"Sir," the woman said. "We will have someone come talk to you as soon as we know."

"Can't you just check?"

"That's not my job."

"How about you get off your ass and..."

"Rob," Mason said and put his hand on his shoulder. "How about you sit down and let me talk to them?"

Rob ran his hand through his hair. "They won't tell us anything."

"Penny." I turned around to see Bee. She was crying almost as hard as I had been. "He's going to be okay. He has to be."

I shook my head. She was trying. But her tears gave her away.

She immediately put her arms around me. "He's strong. He'll pull through." She was one of the few people that knew just how strong James was. But her words didn't calm me down. Nothing could make it feel like I wasn't sinking.

I glanced at Rob in the waiting room. His elbows were on his knees and both his hands were in his hair. When he was distraught he looked even more like James.

I just felt numb. What if I never got to see James upset again? What if I never got to see him happy again? I pulled away from Bee's hug. Nothing would console me right now. I needed to see him. I just needed to see him.

Mason was now arguing with the same woman that Rob had been.

"You encouraged her!" Rob yelled.

I looked back over at the waiting room. Rob had just shoved his father in the chest. "This is on you. James is dying because of you!" He shoved his dad again.

A security guard started toward them.

"Rob!" I ran over to him and put my hand on his shoulder. "Please calm down. You can't get sent to prison tonight. I need you here. Please, I need you. Please."

He shook his head and wiped under his eyes with the back of his hand. He grabbed my arm and pulled me to the other side of the waiting room, away from his parents. "It's their fault," he said and collapsed in a chair. "They fed her delusional mind. Why aren't you angry?"

"Because I don't have room for that right now. Because I'm upset and scared and..." my voice cracked. "Because I'm trying so hard to be hopeful."

He was the only one that understood. He was the only one that loved James as much as I did. "I'm sorry." He pulled my head onto his shoulder and let me cry again. He kept his arm wrapped protectively around me.

I tried to block out the sounds of Jen yelling at the reception desk. Apparently they were taking turns. I closed my eyes tightly. I pictured James saying his vows. I pictured James proposing. I pictured him running into me at the coffee shop. And it all just made my chest hurt even more. It all just made the possibility of losing him that much more painful.

"Pen." I opened my eyes and saw my dad kneeling in front of me. He was handing me his handkerchief. "Melissa brought you a change of clothes. How about you go change into something more comfortable." He put his hand on my knee.

I shook my head. I didn't want to change. I wanted to make love to James in our hotel room because it was our wedding night. I reluctantly grabbed his handkerchief.

"He's in surgery," Jen said and sat down next to me.

That wasn't much of an update. I had assumed that when time started to pass. "Does that mean he's breathing?"

Jen grabbed my hand. "They wouldn't have put him into surgery if he didn't have a pulse. It's a good sign."

I nodded. James was breathing again. That was definitely a good sign. His heart was beating. He was alive.

"Sweetie," my dad said and patted my knee again. "Your mom and I are here. Just let us know what you need."

James. I need James. "Thanks, Dad." In that moment I wanted to be a kid again. I wanted to go back in time. I wanted someone to fix everything for me. Because the thought had started to settle on me that all of this was my fault. Isabella hated me. If James was single, this wouldn't have happened. If I hadn't flirted with him in class, he wouldn't have fallen for me. He wouldn't be in a hospital bed dying.

Stop. I closed my eyes again. *He can't die. He can't leave me.*

***

Hours passed. Saturday turned into Sunday. A doctor came out and I again lifted my head in expectation, but he went to another family. I swallowed hard. I was losing my mind. I needed to know if he was okay.

All I could hear was the ticking of a clock on the wall. Seconds passing. James could be taking his last breath, and I wasn't there with him. I needed to be with him. We couldn't end like this.

I ducked out of Rob's arm. Like most of the people in the waiting room, he had fallen asleep. But sleep wasn't going to come for me. Not until I knew. I walked up to the front desk. "Do you have any updates?"

She typed something into her computer. "He's still in surgery."

"Is that a good thing?

She shook her head like she didn't know.

"You must know. You work here."

"I'm just a nurse. I've never even worked in the E.R. portion of the hospital until tonight."

It was her first night. I thought about everyone screaming at her. But at that moment, I didn't care. She was the only person standing in my way of knowing where James was and how he was doing. But I didn't have any fight in me. All I felt was this sense of doom. Of loss. I couldn't shake the feeling. I couldn't stop hearing the clock ticking.

"Please." I could feel the tears forming in my eyes again.

"As soon as I know, I'll tell you. I'm sorry."

"Can't you get someone to go check? Can't you take me to go see him?"

"Once he's out of surgery."

"But what if that's too late?" My voice cracked. *What if that's too late?*

"I'm sorry."

"Penny," Melissa said and touched my shoulder.

I hadn't known that anyone else was still awake.

"Let's go get you cleaned up, okay? You'll feel better when you change into something more comfortable."

Feel better? Nothing would make me feel better except rewinding time. What if our first kiss as husband and wife was one of our last kisses? What if our first dance was one of our last?

"Come with me." She grabbed my arm and pulled me toward the restroom.

I didn't want to change. James was supposed to take off my wedding dress. We were supposed to be sharing one of the best nights of our lives. *Keep breathing, James. Please keep breathing.*

I stared at my reflection in the restroom mirror. No wonder everyone kept asking me to change. I looked like I was a bride from a horror movie. Blood was splattered on my dress and chest. It had seeped into the bottom of my dress when I had tried to apply pressure to James' wounds. It was on my hands and arms. I was a reflection of everything bad that had happened tonight. A walking memory. I couldn't bear to look at myself.

I pulled down the straps of my dress and reached behind me to unzip it. My fingers were trembling and I couldn't undo it. "Get it off me."

Melissa's hands replaced mine.

Tears streamed down my cheeks and I turned away from the mirror. "Get it off!" I croaked. As soon as it was unzipped I pushed the straps down my arms and let it pool around my ankles. I bent over the sink and began scrubbing the blood from my skin. *Get it off.*

"Penny, stop." Melissa said from behind me.

I continued to wash my hands.

"Penny, stop, you're hurting yourself." She turned off the water.

I looked down at my arms. My skin was red from where I had been scrubbing it.

"Put these on." She handed me a pair of leggings and a tank top.

It was what I almost always wore to my college classes. I'd do anything to go back to those days. I thought about James in my dorm, asking me to marry him in Vegas. Why did I say no? If I had said yes, he'd still be beside me. This was the wedding I had wanted. He was dying because of me.

"It's my fault."

"It's not your fault."

"He's dying because of me."

"He's not going to die." There was no doubt in her tone. Melissa was strong. She always believed what she believed. And she was usually right.

I needed to be strong right now. I needed to borrow some of her strength. I looked up at her.

"He's not going to die," she said again.

I nodded my head. *He's not going to die. He can't die.* I slowly changed into the clothes she had given me. She placed a pair of flip flops on the ground as she folded my dress and put it into the bag she was carrying. I wanted to tell her to throw it out or burn it or cut it into a million pieces. I never wanted to see that dress again. I wanted to pretend that today had never happened. I unstrapped my heels and slipped my feet into the flip flops.

"Good," Melissa said. "Now you're dressed so that we can run around and try to find him."

"What?"

"If no one's telling us, we'll go find out ourselves."

"Melissa?"

She turned toward me.

"Thank you." I put my arms around her.

"It's going to be okay." She rubbed her hand up and down my back.

Her confidence was exactly what I needed. I almost believed that what she was saying was true. I wanted to believe it was true.

"Come with me," she said and looped her arm through mine. She turned right toward the swinging doors. Someone crying made me turn my head back toward the waiting room. It was my mom. My family and friends were standing in front of a doctor.

My mom was crying. Why was my mom crying? I let go of Melissa's arm and ran toward them. It felt like my heart was beating out of my chest. "Is he okay?" My voice sounded strange and high pitched.

The doctor turned to me. "He's stable," she said. "But we had to put him into a medically induced coma."

"What does that mean?"

"One of the bullets punctured a lung. We were able to repair it. We probably avoided the need for a transplant, but the next few days will tell us for sure. Another of the bullets ruptured his spleen and there was internal bleeding. He's had a blood transfusion. We've removed his spleen without further complications. The third bullet was just a flesh wound on his bicep. It only needed stitches."

"Is he going to be okay?" None of what she was saying made sense. I didn't know the severity of any of it. I just needed to know if James was okay.

"We've done everything we can. We induced the coma because he was unresponsive."

"What does that mean?"

"It means he needs to fight."

I swallowed hard. James was a fighter. He'd always fight to be with me. He'd wake up. He had to. "Can I see him?"

"Immediate family only, two at a time."

"Okay." I grabbed Rob's hand. I needed him with me. I needed him to keep me calm. Because I couldn't afford to break anymore. If I wanted James to be strong, I needed to be too.

CHAPTER 18
Sunday

It didn't seem like it was him. Maybe that's how I was able to keep so calm. James looked pale and lifeless. A tube was down his throat and he had IVs in his arm. More wires disappeared underneath his hospital gown. He didn't look like James. He didn't look like my husband anymore.

"What is the tube for?" Rob said quietly.

"To help him breathe," the doctor said. "We want to put less pressure on his lung while it's healing."

"Is he breathing on his own?"

"Yes," the doctor said. "He's stable, he's just unresponsive."

I didn't know what any of that meant. But I didn't have any questions right now. I just needed James to know I was here for him. That's what he needed from me. To know I was here. To know I was being strong. "Can I hold his hand?"

The doctor nodded. I let go of Rob and slid my hand into James'. It was warm, but lifeless. I was used to him squeezing my hand back. I was used to him rubbing his thumb against my palm. "James," I whispered. "I'm here. Wake up, baby. Come back to me. Please." I knelt down and kissed the back of his hand. "Please, James."

"If you'd like the next two people to come in, I can go get them," the doctor said.

They couldn't make me leave him. I'd never leave him. "I'm staying," I said.

Rob put his hand on my shoulder. "Do you want me to send Jen in?"

I shook my head. "Please stay. He'd want you to stay." *Don't leave me too.*

"Okay." Rob grabbed a chair and pulled it toward me. I kept hold of James' hand as I got off my knees. I was vaguely aware of Rob pulling a chair up to the other side of James and grabbing his other hand.

And we both sat there, holding James' hands. We didn't say anything else. There was nothing to say. James knew we were here. That was enough.

***

I woke up with my stomach in knots. I was going to be sick. I put my hand over my mouth and ran toward the bathroom. I had just opened the lid of the toilet when I threw up everything I had eaten last night. *Fuck.* I grabbed my stomach as I hurled some more.

"Penny?" Rob said and tapped on the bathroom door. "Penny, are you okay?"

Of course I'm okay. I'm not the one sitting in a hospital bed with three gunshot wounds. Tears stung my eyes again. "I'm fine." *Be strong.*

I choked as more vomit came up.

"Penny?" Rob banged on the door a little louder. "I'm coming in."

I heard the door open. I looked away as I grabbed some toilet paper to wipe my face off.

Rob kneeled down beside me and lightly touched my shoulder. "I'm going to go get the doctor."

"No, I'm fine."

"You're not fine."

I swallowed down anything else that wanted to come up. "I am." My stomached seemed to churn. *Shit*. I turned to the toilet and threw up some more.

Rob rubbed my back and helped me stand up when I had finally finished emptying my body of every horrid thing possible. He left me alone as I washed my face. I knew he was going to get a doctor despite what I had said.

When I walked out of the bathroom, James' doctor was already standing there. She was looking at a chart and jotting down something on James' monitor.

"How is he?"

She looked up. "The same." She set her clipboard down on the counter by his bed. "How about you come with me for a second?"

"I'd like to stay with him."

"He's more likely to get sick now without his spleen. Spleens help fight bacteria. Right now he can't be exposed to any viruses. We'll be giving him some vaccines if his condition improves."

If. I looked at Rob. He was sitting beside James again. I wasn't going to risk making James any worse. It killed me, but I followed the doctor out of the room.

"My stomach has been upset the last few days. But otherwise, I'm fine. And I feel better now that I threw up. I think it was the wedding and then...this."

The doctor didn't say anything as she opened a door for me.

I followed her inside.

"Please sit down," she said.

I sat down in the chair she gestured to.

She ran a thermometer across my forehead. "Normal," she said. "Stick out your tongue for me." She poked my tongue with a wooden thing. "Normal," she said. She pulled out a small light from her coat pocket and checked the back of my throat and my ears. "All normal." She frowned for a second. "You said you feel fine now?"

"Yes." I did. After throwing up I felt so much better. I just wanted to be with James.

"Have you been feeling any differently than usual besides for the upset stomach?"

"A little emotional, maybe. But I was just nervous about getting married. This whole week has been a little overwhelming."

She nodded. "Okay, here's what I'm going to do. Let's run a blood test and a urine test really quick. If you come back clean, you'll be allowed to go see him again."

"And if I don't?"

"We'll give you whatever medicine you need to improve your condition and once you're well, you can see him again. It's just a precaution." She was already preparing a needle.

I turned away as she sunk it into my arm. The last thing I needed was to be sick right now. James needed me.

She placed a band aid over the spot she had just taken blood from and handed me a small cup. "Pee in that." She gestured to the bathroom.

This was ridiculous. What sickness could they see from my urine? I closed the bathroom door and quickly peed into the cup. The sooner this nonsense was over with, the sooner I could be back by James' side. I walked out of the bathroom and handed her the cup.

"I'll be right back," she said and left the room.

I went back into the bathroom and washed my hands again. It still felt like I was covered in blood. I closed my eyes and took a deep breath. *Be strong.* I scrubbed my hands and arms until my skin was red again. I wiped away the tears that had formed in my eyes. *Be strong.* James needed me. I wasn't going to be sick. I wasn't going to do anything but be by his side until he woke up. Not if. *When.* I took a deep breath and walked out of the bathroom.

"Well, you don't have an infection."

"Thank God. Can I go see him again?"

"I think maybe you should take a seat."

I shook my head. I wasn't sick. She couldn't make me stay in here. No, she didn't say I wasn't sick. She said I didn't have an infection. Normally my mind would be racing from possibilities. But I was tired. And upset. And completely focused on James. Nothing she said was going to sway that. Whatever horrible thing she was about to tell me, it wouldn't change that. And I knew it was horrible. She was looking at me like she pitied me. I didn't need her pity. I needed to see my husband. "Please let me go see him. Whatever this is, it can wait." I started to walk past her.

"It can't wait. I'm sorry, but it can't."

I folded my arms across my chest. "What's wrong with me?"

She gave me a small smile. "Nothing's wrong with you. Penny, you're pregnant."

Suddenly my throat felt dry. I tried to clear it. "What?"

The doctor smiled again, but it didn't quite reach her eyes. "You were experiencing morning sickness. And your fluctuating hormones were probably the cause of you feeling more emotional than usual."

No. This can't be happening.

"If you'd like, I can send a nurse in to do an ultrasound to tell you how far along you are. But based on the morning sickness, you're at least a few weeks."

"I'm not pregnant. Can you do the test again?"

"Your blood test and urine test both confirm it."

I can't be pregnant. Not now. How did this happen?

"I can send in a counselor if you'd like. I know this isn't exactly the ideal time for this news when your husband is in recovery."

"No." I shook my head. "I just need to go see him."

"Okay." She nodded. "Just tell me if you need someone to talk to. You can go see him now."

My feet didn't move. Now I understood the pity in her eyes. She pitied me because I was pregnant and my husband was dying. *She knows he's dying.* "Is James going to be okay?" I didn't have the courage to ask anyone that yet. But I needed to know.

"It's up to him to wake up now. We've done everything we can."

"What's the likelihood of that happening?"

The doctor pressed her lips together. "In his state, 50/50."

A fifty percent chance? I swallowed hard. "Thank you." That was finally something I understood. There was a 50 percent chance my husband would wake up. There was a 50 percent chance that my baby would meet his or her father. *Fifty/Fifty.* "Thank you," I said again.

She may have said something else, but I didn't hear her. I walked as quickly as I could back to James' room. I needed him. And now this baby needed him. *His baby.* I couldn't live without him. I couldn't raise a child without him. The thought made me feel nauseous again. James didn't want this baby. He didn't want to be a father yet. *How did this happen?*

"Are you okay?" Rob said as I walked back into the room.

"I'm okay," I said, and didn't look him in the eye. I sat back down next to James and grabbed his hand. *Wake up. You have to wake up!*

"I know you're lying."

I looked up at Rob.

He wasn't supposed to be the first person I told that I was pregnant. It was supposed to be James. It had to be James. "Wake up," I whispered. I started to silently cry again as I clutched his lifeless hand.

"What did the doctor say?" Rob said.

"I'm not sick."

"Penny, what did she say?"

If I had learned anything the past few days, it was that I had family and friends that I could count on no matter what. I didn't want to cut anyone out anymore. And I needed to tell someone before the agony swallowed me whole. Because now it wasn't just me that needed James. It was this baby inside of me that needed a father. I wanted to be strong, but I didn't know if I was strong enough for all three of us. But I couldn't do it. I needed to tell James alone.

Rob sighed. "You can talk to me. You can tell me anything, Penny, you know that."

I nodded. I'd tell him soon, but I had to tell James first. "Can I be alone with him for a second?"

"I'll go give everyone an update." Rob stood up and stretched.

"The doctor said he has a 50 percent chance of waking up." I didn't look up at Rob. I just stared at James' face.

"He's going to wake up," Rob said. "I know he will. I'll be right back." I heard the door close behind him.

My lip started to tremble and I pressed my forehead against the back of James' hand. "James, please wake up. I need you to wake up." The beeping of the machine was driving me crazy. I knew it meant he was alive. But it was teasing me. He was alive, but he wasn't here with me. "I know you can hear me," I said. I lifted my head. "Baby, I know you can hear me." I stood up and leaned forward, kissing his forehead.

I took a deep breath. James didn't want children yet. But I knew if he was awake, he'd be excited. He'd want this one. He or she would be good and kind and loving just like him. I kissed his forehead again. "I'm pregnant." I ran my fingers through his hair. "We're going to have a baby." My voice cracked on the last word.

It killed me to see him like this. It made my chest hurt. I wanted to see him smile again. I wanted to hear his laugh.

"Come back to me. Please come back to me."

***

I didn't hear what anyone said as they filtered in and out of the room. I just kept my hand in James' and continued to whisper to him.

"Mrs. Hunter, we need to have a word with you."

I didn't look up.

"Mrs. Hunter?"

I slowly lifted my head. It was a police officer. Not the same one as we had met from the precinct. But similar enough. I immediately hated him. I had a tendency to blame myself, but this was their fault too. They wouldn't listen to us about Isabella. They wouldn't let us get a restraining order.

"I have nothing to say to you."

"Well, I have some questions for you."

"Get out."

"Excuse me?"

"Get out." I had never heard myself sound so authoritative before. But the officer almost seemed to shrink at my words.

"Another time then," the officer said and retreated out of the room.

I saw Porter standing outside the room. He turned his head and we made eye contact for a second. I could see it in his eyes. He felt guilty for what happened. But I couldn't talk to him right now. I couldn't talk to anyone. My own guilt was eating me up.

I ran my hand across my stomach. How had I let this happen? The pain was too much. I was sinking. Only James could save me. I put my forehead on his hand. *Please wake up.*

CHAPTER 19

Monday

No change. I stared at James' handsome features as the doctor walked out of the room. They weren't strained with stress or worry. But he didn't look peaceful. He looked lifeless. The thought chilled me to the core.

CHAPTER 20

Tuesday

His hand felt colder. Or maybe mine did. It felt like we were both slipping into the unknown. I was weak. I was so weak without him. The fear of losing him was swallowing me whole.

CHAPTER 21

Wednesday

"Penny, it's the tenth time he's called." Rob was standing by the door holding my cell phone. I couldn't stand hearing it ring so I had given it to him. I couldn't talk to the press. I couldn't talk to James' lawyer. I couldn't talk to anyone.

"Tell him I'll call him back."

Rob hesitated by the door. "He's one of your best friends. Don't shut people out right now. The cops have been hounding him. He just needs to know you're okay."

"Well, I'm not okay." I bit my lip to prevent myself from crying again.

"Then tell him that." He held the phone out to me.

I stood up and walked over to Rob. He handed me the phone and left the room. I wanted to press the end call button. But Rob was right. Tyler deserved to know what was going on. Especially if the police were badgering him about this.

"Hi, Tyler," I said softly into the phone. I turned to look at James.

"I saw what happened on T.V. I..." his voice trailed off. "Penny, I'm so sorry."

I didn't say anything. I had heard so many people say they were sorry. Sorry for what? This wasn't their fault. Sorry for my pain? No. I wasn't who they should be feeling sorry for. Sorry wasn't the right word. I looked away from James and stared out the small window.

"Penny?"

"I'm here."

"How are you holding up?"

"I'm okay."

"You don't sound okay."

"What do you want me to say, Tyler? That I'm dying inside? That I can barely look at him because it hurts too much?" I put my hand down onto the windowsill. I couldn't hold it together anymore. I couldn't do this.

"I'm coming back to New York."

"Don't do that."

"I want to be there for you."

"Come back when you're ready to come back. Not like this. Not right now."

"I'm sorry," he said.

I cringed at the words.

"The police want me to come in for questioning anyway. I have to come back."

"No. You don't." I couldn't imagine Tyler coming to the hospital. I knew James wouldn't want him to be here. My grip tightened on the windowsill.

"Of course I do. I have to do what the cops want."

"Just ignore their calls. Stop picking up the phone."

"I can't do that. It makes me look guilty." His words hung in the air. "I'm not, Penny. I would never do something to hurt you."

"I know. And James has people looking into it. Just...don't come back. Don't answer their phone calls. I'm taking care of it." *I'm going to take care of it. After I sit with James for a few more minutes.* I just felt so tired. All I wanted to do was wait for him to open his eyes. And I needed to be here when that happened.

"He's going to wake up, Penny."

I nodded but didn't actually say anything into the phone.

"Call me if you need anything, okay?"

"I will." I swallowed hard. "How...how are you doing?"

"I'm okay."

He wasn't okay. I could hear it in his voice. But I wasn't going to question him like he had me. Because I couldn't handle anything else right now. I felt guilty enough as it was. "Call me when you find the sunnier place you've been searching for."

"Yeah. As soon as I find it."

"Bye, Tyler."

"Tell James he'd better wake up. Tell him to fight."

Before I could say anything, Tyler hung up the phone. I turned away from the window. James was my sunny place. And I knew I couldn't exist in the dark.

CHAPTER 22

Thursday

"She has an alibi."

I looked up. I hadn't even noticed Mason come in. No one but immediate family had been allowed to visit him yet. I wasn't sure if he had sneaked in or if they had let him back. I was supposed to be taking care of everything like I had told Tyler, but I hadn't left James' side. It felt like I was frozen in time. I couldn't do anything. It was like time was standing still until he came back to me.

"What do you mean?" I asked.

"I mean, someone vouched for Isabella being in another state on the night of your wedding."

"That's impossible. I know it was her."

"I have some guys looking into it."

I didn't need to ask any questions about that. I knew Mason would hire the best of the best. "Who vouched for her?"

"Her boyfriend I think."

I took a deep breath. Austin? Was Austin her boyfriend? I shook away the thought. I couldn't put any more blame on myself. I was already drowning. "Why would they believe someone close to her?" Austin and I hadn't ended on good terms but that was on him. Why was he trying to ruin my life? Why would he do this?

"We'll get her. In the meantime, you need to go talk to the police."

"I'm not talking to them."

"You have to."

I squeezed James' hand. "They already had a chance to listen to us. They chose not to."

"Penny, they just arrested Melissa."

"What?" I immediately stood up. "For what?" I imagined her yelling and screaming in the halls of the hospital demanding answers. I had been held up in here for days. I should have been out there keeping everyone updated.

"Conspiracy to commit murder."

"What are you talking about?"

"They're saying it was her. Because of the speech she gave. Because of her relationship with Tyler."

Fuck. "Stay with him." I walked past Mason.

"Hey," Mason said and caught my arm. "We both know it was Isabella. I'm going to prove it." He handed me an envelope that was already opened. It was a manila envelope. The same kind Isabella had been sending me. It was addressed to me.

My hand shook as I pulled out the note inside. It was written in the same font as all the rest.

"I was aiming for you."

I couldn't seem to stop shaking. "Where did this come from?"

"Melissa went to pick up your mail. This was in with everything else. That was the last evidence the police needed. They think she put it in with the rest of your mail. I opened it because James had told me about everything that was going on. I thought you needed to see it."

"She's trying to kill me."

"And I'm not going to let that happen. Go talk to the police. And then I'll work on getting Melissa out of jail. Penny, you have my word. I'm going to take care of this." He put his hand reassuringly on my shoulder.

"Don't leave him."

"I'm not going to leave his side until you're back."

I glanced once more at James and then ran out the door. Isabella had been trying to kill me. The guilt I had already felt weighed even heavier. My best friend was not going to go down for this. Tyler wasn't going to go down for this. Isabella was going to pay. Even if I had to kill her myself.

I recognized the detective that had tried to talk to me a few days ago in the hospital waiting room. And standing right next to him was Officer Daugherty, the detective that wouldn't take us seriously at the precinct. They were both talking to James' father.

"Penny." James' dad put his hand on my shoulder when I reached them. "Penny, we're taking care of this. Go back to him."

No. Everyone was "taking care of this." Yet, Isabella was still out there. And my best friend was in jail.

"You said you had a few questions for me," I said to the detective that had tried to question me before.

He glanced nervously at James' father and then nodded his head. "Yes. We wanted to talk to you about your friend, Melissa Monroe."

I dug my nails into the palm of my hand to distract me from my anger. I was going to lose it. I tried to take a deep breath, but it just made me even more upset. "You mean the fact that you're here to apologize for arresting the wrong person?"

"Besides for Tyler Stevens, she's our lead suspect in the threats and shooting..."

"Suspect? Isabella is the lead suspect. Why isn't anyone listening to me?"

"Is it true that Miss Monroe threatened to kill James during her speech at your reception?"

"What? No."

"And I quote, 'I will literally kill you if you hurt her. So stop doing it. I'm serious this time.' " The detective stared at me.

"She was joking." I thought about what Melissa had said during the rehearsal dinner. How I should be enjoying it while I could because it could disappear in an instant. I knew she didn't do it. But she had been saying weird stuff. What if Tyler had been in on it? What if he had told Melissa? What if she had known this was about to happen? *No.* They were just twisting my thoughts.

"Given the circumstances, we have to take her threat seriously."

"And what about Isabella? Why don't you take my concerns seriously given the circumstances?"

"We talked to Isabella this morning," Officer Daugherty said. "She's on vacation in Maine. She wasn't even in the state this weekend."

"And the only person who verified that was the person she's currently having sex with? Check your sources."

"Mrs. Hunter..."

"Don't you dare. Don't you dare show me the respect you should have when we came to you with this problem in the first place. My husband is dying in the next room because of you. And your incompetence."

"You gave us a dead end. We're trying to determine who was actually behind the threats and the shooting, but you keep putting up road blocks."

"Just because Isabella wasn't here doesn't mean she didn't hire someone else to do it. Of course I don't think she was actually behind the gun."

"We're still trying to get a hold of Tyler Stevens. And we already have Melissa Monroe in custody. The investigation is going well. Go be with your husband. We'll continue our discussion with the victim's father."

Fuck you. "Officer Daugherty, Tyler didn't do this. And neither did Melissa. If you don't investigate Isabella further and it turns out to be her, which it definitely is, I will...sue you."

Officer Daugherty laughed. He was staring at me like I was insane.

No, I didn't know if I could sue the police. I didn't know if that was even possible. But how dare he laugh at me. At my grief. At my pain. I would end him and the stupid detective next to him that was trying to hold back a laugh too. My hand was already in a fist. I tightened it even more and was about to pull my hand back when James' father grabbed my arm.

"Penny, go be with James. Let me take care of this while you go take care of my boy. He needs you."

But I'm not strong enough. I tried to take a deep breath. "She'll never stop." I handed Officer Daugherty the manila envelope. I had never felt so defeated. *She's never going to stop.*

CHAPTER 23

Friday

"Wake up, James." Tears rolled down my cheeks. "Please. Please, I need you." I gripped his hand a little tighter. It killed me that his fingers didn't intertwine with mine. I dropped his hand and put my face in mine. My hope was fading. I was drowning. Darkness was encroaching and I had nothing left to fight it off. Nothing.

CHAPTER 24

Saturday

A knock on the door made me look up. Everyone had just been coming and going. No one ever knocked.

Porter slowly put his head in. "Can I come in?"

I nodded.

He closed the door behind him and walked over to the opposite side of the bed that I was on. His eyes locked on the monitor that was showing James' pulse.

There had been no change. The doctor said that each day that passed, the likelihood of him waking up again went down. It had been a week. I didn't know what that meant for the likelihood now. A fifty percent chance was bad enough. And I didn't have the courage to ask. I tightened my grip on James' hand. *Wake up. You have to wake up.*

"Cole."

I looked up at Porter. "What?"

"My first name is Cole." He gave me a weak smile.

"Cole Porter? Like the composer?"

"Yeah." He laughed and sat down across from me. "And Briggs' first name is Paul. Like the Australian boxer."

I laughed. It sounded weird. I realized I hadn't laughed since my wedding night. I closed my eyes.

"We really just go by our last names because we both have embarrassing full names."

I shook my head. I was pretty sure that wasn't true. But I could tell he was trying to cheer me up. The only problem was that it wasn't working. Nothing could cheer me up except James opening his eyes. "Thanks for telling me."

"James and I met in A.A. He knows those things about me. You should know them too." He gave me another small smile.

"This isn't your fault, you know." Maybe he had just come in to tell me his first name and to help me preoccupy my mind with anything but worry. But it seemed like he needed to hear that the blame wasn't on him. Because it wasn't. It was on me. It was all my fault. I bit my lip so I wouldn't start crying in front of him.

"It is, ma'am."

And just like that, he was back to being formal. "It's not. And please call me Penny."

He nodded. "All right, Penny. I just needed you to know that I was sorry. I thought...well, I didn't think. That was the problem. We had the perimeter checks and guest list..."

"You couldn't have known."

"It's my job to know."

I didn't know what to say to that. We all felt guilty about what had happened. It helped me to know that I wasn't the only one.

"He'll want me to hand in my letter of resignation once he gets out of this. And he will get out of this. But I'm not leaving until then. I won't let anyone into this room that doesn't have permission. I won't let anything happen to you. That was always Mr. Hunter's first priority. You should know that."

I did know that. But hearing it made my chest hurt. Because it felt like he was lying in that bed because of me. "You don't have to resign. I want you to stay."

He looked at me curiously for a second. Maybe he didn't believe I had the authority to make that decision. I probably didn't.

He nodded. "Thank you, Penny. But we'll see what he has to say when he wakes up." His optimism sounded forced.

I couldn't be the only one that believed he'd wake up. I needed someone that believed in him as much as I did. "Can you find Rob and tell him I need to see him?"

Porter nodded and stood up. "Of course. I'll go get him for you." He gave me one last smile and left me alone with James. Maybe it was just me, but his hand felt a little cooler. The beeping of his heart rate monitor sounded just a little slower.

"James, you need to be strong. Please wake up." I kissed the back of his hand. "Please, James. I need you to be strong for us." I ran my palm against my stomach. I was about to be strong. I was going to tell Rob about the baby. Maybe if I was strong enough to do that, James would be strong enough to wake up.

"Hey," Rob said as he came into the room. He looked exhausted. "Penny, I have some bad news."

Nothing could possibly be worse than what had already happened. "What is it?"

Rob pulled up a chair beside mine. "You got a call from James' lawyer this morning."

I had given Rob my phone. I couldn't handle the endless ringing. And I couldn't bear to talk to anyone. "What did he say?"

"Apparently James has a DNR."

"What's that?"

"Do not resuscitate. If his heart stops, he doesn't want them to restart it."

"No, he wouldn't have that. Maybe before he met me, but not now."

"I'm sorry, but he does have one. It was written before he met you, but he didn't change it. And he has updated his will since he's been with you."

I shook my head. "He was depressed. He had to have been depressed when he agreed to that. He wouldn't do that now. He must have just forgotten when he updated his will. Besides, they already restarted his heart when he got here. They already broke the DNR."

"They didn't know. It's not in his medical record. But the lawyer is forwarding them a copy of his DNR now."

I shook my head. "Rob, you can't let them send that to the hospital. If something happens, they'll just let him die. You have to do something."

"There isn't anything I can do. It's what James wanted."

"No. He wouldn't want that. He wouldn't leave me without fighting. He promised he wouldn't leave me."

"Penny," Rob said and put his hand on my knee.

I immediately stood up. "Don't I have some say in this? I'm his wife."

"I'm sorry."

"You can't let them send it."

"I've tried everything."

"I need him. I can't. Rob, there have been so many times I thought I lost him. And I know I can't. I can't live without him. We can't live without him."

"If this is what he wanted, we can be strong for him."

"Stop giving up on him!"

"I'm not giving up on him!" He stood up too. "You think I want this? You think I want to watch my brother die without anyone doing anything? Penny, this is killing me too. Like you just said...we can't live without him."

"No. You don't understand." It felt like I couldn't breathe. I swallowed hard. No one understood.

"What don't I understand?" He put his hands on my shoulders. "What aren't you telling me? What have you been hiding from me ever since we got to this fucking hospital? Why won't you let me in? Why won't you let me help you?!"

"I'm pregnant." My voice was an exasperated sob.

"Shit." He immediately put his arms around me.

I wasn't sure if he had meant to say it out loud, but his words seemed to echo around the small room. *Shit.*

"I'm going to be an uncle?"

I nodded into his chest.

"I'm going to be an uncle," he whispered wistfully. He sighed and rubbed my back before releasing me from his hug. "Okay. Fuck James' wishes. I'm going to go burn down his lawyer's building."

"What?"

"Unless you have a better idea."

"Find out when he submitted the DNR to his lawyer. And hire your own lawyer to figure out if I can veto it as his new wife."

"I'll do that first. You're right, arson should never be the first option."

I smiled and sat back down. It seemed like years had passed since I had heard Rob make a joke.

"I'm going to be an uncle." His smile was contagious. "Do you know if it's a boy or a girl yet?"

"No, I haven't had an ultrasound. I'm going to do it when James wakes up."

"Okay." He nodded vigorously. "Good thinking. I'm gonna go make a few calls. I'm gonna fix this."

"I haven't told anyone else yet. Can you maybe just keep it between us right now?"

"Of course." He was already at the door. But he quickly rushed back over and kissed my forehead. "No matter what happens, you're not alone, Penny. You'll never have to raise it alone."

I nodded. His words were comforting, but they made me cringe at the same time. I couldn't raise this baby without James. I couldn't. "Thank you." I nodded again.

I watched him run out the door and then I grabbed James' hand again. Telling Rob made it seem more real. I was pregnant. James and I were going to have a baby. "It's time to wake up now. James, you need to wake up. We need you."

CHAPTER 25

Tuesday

Mason and James' father had done what they promised. They had gotten Melissa out of jail on bail. But she wasn't allowed anywhere near the hospital. I didn't ask Mason how much bail was, but I knew it had to be a lot. She was still their prime suspect. At least she was out, though. Shaken up, but out.

Unfortunately, I wasn't allowed to be relieved. They couldn't find any evidence that Isabella was behind the shooting. And each day that passed, I had this eerie feeling that someone was watching me.

But the worst part was that nothing seemed to be able to wake James up. Nothing.

Rob couldn't bury the DNR. The hospital had gotten it this morning. I had told James' doctor that I wanted her to disregard it. She had explained to me that she always has to do what's in her patient's best interest. But I didn't understand. How could it be in his best interest to leave this world? When he was finally happy? When we were finally allowed to be happy? And what the doctor didn't realize was that if James died, I'd die too.

It hurt so much, I couldn't even think straight. And the longer James lay there, the worse I felt. I couldn't eat. I couldn't keep going without him. I just couldn't.

I let the tears run down my cheeks.

I felt so ashamed. I should have been stronger for the baby. But I couldn't be. Not without James. He was the only reason I was still breathing. And when he stopped, I knew my heart would too. I was nothing without him. I was weak. Because there was no me without him. There couldn't be.

CHAPTER 26

Wednesday

I woke up in the middle of the night freezing cold. I was hunched over in the chair beside James' bed, curled up in a ball. My eyes blinked in the darkness. The only light in the room was the medical equipment and the moon shining in through the windows.

I felt like I needed to throw up again. But I didn't have anything left to throw up. I was going to be a bad mother. Because I was selfish. Because I didn't know how to live without James. And every day that passed it seemed more likely that I'd need to.

The beeping was all I could hear in the room. The constant beeping. The beeping that was slowly driving me insane.

I wrapped my arms around myself and stood up. Despite how cold I felt, that wasn't why I had woken up. I was dreaming of our wedding night and what could have been. I let a small smile unfold on my lips. I pictured his hands on me, whispering that I was his wife. And he had let me slowly take off his tie and tuxedo jacket. I had unbuttoned his shirt and found his tattoo. His wedding present. The present I had completely forgotten about.

I glanced at the door. No one was going to come in right now. I needed to find it. I needed to see his gift to me. I slowly climbed onto his bed and lay down beside him.

He didn't smell like James. He smelled like the cheap shaving cream they had let me shave his face with and the soap I sponged him with. I ran my fingers down the scruff that was already forming on his face again. I wanted to kiss him, but there was a tube down his throat. Instead I gently ran my index finger across his bottom lip.

"Wake up, James. Please. You promised you wouldn't leave me. You told me this love was forever and always."

Nothing.

Every time he didn't respond, it killed me a little more inside. I slowly pulled down the front of his hospital gown, revealing tons of wires attached to his chest, monitoring his heartbeat. The tattoo wasn't on his chest. I kept pulling.

First I saw the bandage on his ribcage. Where they had fixed his punctured lung. I gently kissed the bandage. Then I saw the larger bandage on his stomach, the evidence of his ruptured spleen. I gently kissed the second bandage. But there was no tattoo.

I had the strangest feeling that maybe this wasn't James. Maybe this was some imposter, and James was somewhere happy and healthy. Somewhere away from me. Somewhere where no one would try to hurt him. But I knew that wasn't true. I knew every contour of his six pack. I knew the line of his happy trail.

I tried to swallow down the lump in my throat as I pulled the gown down his arms. There was the bandage on his arm. Stitches. I should have been counting my blessings, not my husband's fatal wounds. All three, so close to his heart that it broke mine even more.

Again, there was no tattoo. Where was it? I moved his arm slightly and looked along the inside of his bicep. And that's when I saw it. On the side of his chest, hidden by his arm. Because it was personal. It was only for me to see. Because he was mine and I was his.

"James." I ran my finger up and down the pulse of the tattoo. "You promised me forever. Getting married was supposed to be our new beginning. Not the end." I was choking on my words. "It's too soon! You have to wake up. I need you. I need you!"

I splayed my hand on his chest. "Wake up! You have to wake up! I need you. Baby, please, I need you." I pressed the side of my head against his chest. I needed to hear his heartbeat. I needed to know he was going to be okay. "Please, James. You promised. Please don't leave me like this. Please don't leave us."

And that's when I saw it. His index finger moved.

CHAPTER 27

Wednesday

"It's not like you see in the movies," the doctor said. "It takes a long time to come out of a coma. Give him time. Keep talking to him. And you need to eat something."

It took me a second to realize she was reprimanding me. "Yes, absolutely," I said.

"Penny, I meant now. You're not doing James any favors by starving yourself and your baby."

I stared down at James' face. He was going to wake up. He was fighting to come back to me.

"His mother and father have requested to come see him. Maybe head down to the food court and get some breakfast?"

I didn't want to be anywhere near James' mother. I couldn't handle her negativity and her harsh glances. She never said it, but I knew she blamed me. I had somehow broken her perfect daughter-in-law. What she didn't seem to realize was that this was who Isabella was all along. Manipulative, conniving, toxic. I didn't do that. And if anything, James' mother fueled her behavior.

I looked back up at the doctor. "But he's going to be okay? He's going to wake up?"

"It's looking good." She gave me a reassuring smile.

I nodded. "Okay. I'll be back in a few minutes." I glanced once more at James before leaving the room.

Porter and Briggs were both outside James' hospital room, with their arms folded across their chests, looking very much the part of security guards.

"Is it true?" Briggs asked. "He's moving?"

"He's been tapping his index finger and thumb. The doctor said it was a good sign. He's going to wake up." It was the first time I had said those words, and a smile spread across my face. *He's going to wake up!*

Briggs closed his eyes and leaned his head back against the wall. For some reason I wouldn't have guessed he was a religious man. But he seemed to be thanking God right now.

"I'm going to go get some breakfast. Do either of you want anything?"

"I'll come with you," Porter said.

"No, that's okay. I'm just grabbing something to eat."

"I'm coming with you." He nodded at Briggs and started walking toward the elevator.

Briggs smiled at me and I quickly followed Porter. I was happy to have them both around. I still felt on edge. Every now and then, I'd get this eerie feeling that someone was watching me. I glanced over my shoulder before stepping onto the elevator.

Porter was silent as the elevator descended.

"Thank you," I said. "For staying outside the room. And making sure no one came in."

He nodded and looked down at the ground.

"He's going to be okay, Cole."

He looked up at me and smiled. "I still prefer Porter."

"James is going to be so surprised that I was able to trick you into telling me your first name."

"I was trying to cheer you up."

I shrugged my shoulders. "It still counts."

He shook his head as the doors dinged open.

"What would you like to eat?" I asked as I stepped off the elevator.

"I've already had breakfast, Penny." He leaned against a wall and folded his arms.

For some reason I had thought he'd be eating with me, not just watching me. But he had called me Penny instead of ma'am or Mrs. Hunter. That was a good start. "Are you sure?"

"Rob is over there," Porter said and nodded toward a table in the center of the cafeteria.

I turned my head. I knew the doctor had told everyone the good news already, but I hadn't seen Rob yet. I had requested to be alone with James while she told everyone. I just needed to be close to him. I always needed that.

Rob was sitting with Daphne. She had her hand on the side of his face and they were smiling at one another. Seeing Rob like this made me so happy. I liked Daphne. She seemed so grounded and that was exactly what Rob needed. I had never seen him look at anyone the way he was looking at her right now. He was in love. I would never ask him if he was, because I wouldn't want him to freak out about it. But that's what I was witnessing right now. *Love.*

I didn't want to intrude on their moment. I had already monopolized his time in the past week and a half, begging him to stay with me and James. I hadn't even thought about the fact that he was probably missing her. Actually, I hadn't thought about anyone else at all. I touched my stomach. I needed to eat. When James woke up, I wanted to tell him that we were having a healthy baby. After breakfast I'd ask to have the ultrasound.

I turned toward the line of food.

"Penny!"

I turned around to see Rob running toward me. When he reached me, he immediately wrapped his arms around me and lifted me into the air. "He's going to be okay!" He laughed as he spun me around in a circle. "Oh, shit." He immediately set me back down on my feet. "You don't think that hurt the baby?"

Not more than me not eating for the past week. "No. Of course not." But I really had no idea what I could and couldn't do while I was pregnant. I knew literally nothing about being a mother. And I suddenly felt completely unprepared.

"Hey," Daphne said and gave me a hug. "Let me get you something to eat. You must be starving."

I could have imagined it, but it seemed like she had glanced down at my stomach. I stared at Rob as Daphne walked away.

He looked guilty.

"Did you tell her?"

He shrugged. "I'm sorry. You can't tell me something like that and expect me to keep it to myself. It's exciting news. Everyone should know."

"And everyone can know as soon as James does."

Rob nodded and gave me a big smile. "I'm going to be an uncle."

I laughed. "Yes. So who else did you tell?"

"Just Daphne, I swear. I have this thing where I don't want to keep anything from her. Everything just kind of spills out."

I smiled. "That's good." In a lot of ways Rob was like James. I was glad to know that they didn't share the keeping secrets from their loved ones trait. Nothing good ever came from that.

"Yeah. But I'm sorry. I shouldn't have said anything."

"No, it's okay. It's sweet that you wanted to share the good news with her."

"And she won't tell anyone. She's always just hanging out with me anyway."

"Rob, that's incredibly sweet."

He shrugged. "Why does everyone seemed surprised when I do something sweet? I'm a sweet guy." He winked at me.

"Because usually you're acting inappropriate."

"Me?" He pretended to look shocked. "What are you talking about, my new favorite MILF?"

"And there it is." I rolled my eyes at him.

He laughed and pulled me in for another hug. "He's really going to be okay?"

"The doctor said it was looking good. He's waking up. It's going to take a few days, but, he's waking up." I could feel myself getting teary eyed. *He's coming back to me.*

Rob kissed my forehead and then released me from his hug.

"I have a favor to ask. At first I thought I should wait for James. But I haven't been eating and I'm worried maybe...I don't know if...I just want to make sure the baby is okay."

"I'm sure it's fine."

"Right. Yeah, never mind. I was just being silly."

"No, what were you going to ask me?"

"Would you maybe come with me for the ultrasound? I know it's a strange thing to ask, I'm just kind of scared to do it by myself. And if something's wrong I'm going to need..."

"Me?"

I smiled. "Yes."

"Just tell me when and I'll be there."

"Okay. I was going to talk to the doctor after breakfast. If it's too weird, you don't have to come. I don't want to make you..."

"I told you I'll always be there for you." He lightly tapped the bottom of my chin. "I want to come see my nephew."

"Why do you think it's a boy?"

"I just want it to be a boy."

"What would be so wrong with a little me running around?"

"One of you is quite enough, thank you."

I scowled at him.

"See. You're so dramatic."

I lightly punched his arm.

"Here you go," Daphne said and handed me a bagel. "I heard you're a big fan of bagels."

"I am. Seriously, this is perfect." I took a huge bite.

"What were you two talking about?" Daphne seemed a little nervous.

"It's okay," I said. "Rob told me that you know about the baby."

"Oh, thank God. I'm so sorry, Penny. He was acting all frantic a couple nights ago and he wouldn't get off the phone and I made him tell me what was wrong. It wasn't his fault."

I smiled. "It's okay. Really. I'm glad you know too. Now I just need James to wake up before he's the last one to know."

Daphne smiled. "I promise I won't tell anyone. And I'm so excited for you. I can't wait to have kids." Her eyes suddenly grew wide. "You know, like way in the future."

Out of the corner of my eye I noticed Rob was smiling at her. I had been trying hard not to talk about labels and love or anything like that around Rob. But maybe I was wrong about him being scared to settle down. Maybe he just hadn't found the right person yet. He was excited to be an uncle. Maybe he'd be just as excited if he was finding out he was going to be a dad. The thought made me smile. It would be nice if my friends had kids soon so that our children would grow up together.

Rob slipped his arm behind Daphne's back. "Way in the future? Who will my new nephew grow up playing with then?"

Daphne immediately blushed.

"You don't know if it's a boy, Rob," I said.

"It's definitely a boy."

I shook my head and took another bite of the bagel. "This is so good." I hadn't realized how hungry I was.

Daphne laughed.

"Rob? Penny!"

I turned around to see Bee running toward us. Her eyes were red and I could see the fresh tears on her cheeks.

No. I knew what she was going to say. I had this horrible feeling in my gut. I had left James for a few minutes and now...and now...

"Something happened," Bee said. She looked distraught. She could barely get the words out.

"What?" My voice came out as a croak.

"I don't know. God, I don't know. He stopped breathing. Something about his lung. You have to come." She grabbed my hand and pulled me toward the elevator.

James couldn't die without me by his side. He'd think I had abandoned him. Why had I left him? It felt like everything was in slow motion as the elevator rose.

When the doors opened, I saw them wheeling James away. I started to run after him. But someone grabbed my waist, preventing me from pushing through the doors.

"Penny. Penny, you have to stop!" Mason said.

"No." I was sobbing now. "She said he was going to be okay. No!" I struggled in Mason's arms until I fell to my knees.

Mason knelt down beside me. "His lung collapsed. They're going to fix it. Just like they did before."

I shook my head. "She said he was going to be okay."

"He's going to be okay."

"I left him. I thought...I thought..."

He put his arms around me. "You didn't leave him. Penny, he knows you didn't leave him."

"They're going to let him die. They're not going to save him."

"His heart didn't stop. He was just having some trouble breathing."

"What if it does? You can't let him die. Don't let them do this." My tears streamed down my cheeks. "I thought he was going to be okay."

"He is." He pulled my face to his chest and didn't flinch as I soaked his shirt with tears. "He is," he said soothingly.

"I need him."

He continued to rub my back. "Penny, the waiting room is full of people who are here for you and him. Come talk to everyone."

"I can't." I had been doing my best to avoid the waiting room. Everyone's sad stares. Everyone giving up on him. This morning I thought we could all be happy in the good news. But now... I squeezed my eyes shut. *No.*

"These are the times when you're allowed to lean on others. Penny, you're not alone. We're all here for you." Mason wasn't philosophical. It sounded more like something James might say.

I slowly looked up at him. "You sound like James."

Mason smiled. "That's because James said that to me once."

I wiped away the tears under my eyes. "Why?"

"He was sitting in a room like the one all your friends are in when my dad had a heart attack. We all thought we were going to lose him. I'm used to being strong. And I felt so weak."

"I feel weak."

He nodded. "So lean on us." He gave me a small smile.

I looked down at my lap and realized that Mason was wearing sweatpants. I had never seen him in anything less fancy except when he went for runs with James. I looked back up at his face. For the first time ever I saw the worry lines around his eyes and the scruff on his face for forgetting to shave. He looked exhausted, like he hadn't been sleeping either. I saw the pain that reflected in my own eyes.

I wasn't the only one hurting. I wasn't alone in my grief. Why was I acting like I was alone?

"I'm sorry, Mason." I put my hand on his forearm. "Thank you."

"Come with me." He slowly stood up and put his hand out for me. He pulled me to my feet.

As soon as we walked into the waiting room, I was embraced in hugs. But nothing seemed to warm me. An icy feeling had covered my entire body. I squeezed my eyes shut. *He'll be okay. He's fighting to come back to me.* I tried to slowly breathe in and out as everyone said encouraging things to me. But it felt like I couldn't breathe. *He won't leave you.*

"Penny?" Daphne saying my name seemed to pull me out of my trance. She put her hand on my shoulder. "Take a deep breath, okay?"

I nodded. I tried to focus on my breathing.

"Do you want me to go get you something else to eat? Or maybe some water or something?"

I shook my head. She wasn't saying it was going to be okay. She wasn't throwing out meaningless words to try and make me feel better. And for the first time I realized why. She knew what loss was. James had said she had lost her brother. She knew this suffocating feeling. The first thing I wanted to say was, "I'm okay," but I knew that was almost as bad as hearing it from someone else. Instead, I said, "I feel like I can't... breathe."

"Sit down," Daphne said and gestured to a nearby seat. "Try to take another slow breath."

I nodded my head.

"Here, this might help distract you. Something just came for you." She handed me a manila envelope.

"Where did you get that?" Mason said. I hadn't realized he was standing next to us.

"The UPS guy dropped it off a few minutes ago."

"Where did he go?"

"He left through the doors he came in through." Daphne gestured to the door that led to the exit of the hospital.

Mason sprinted toward the doors.

"What was that about?" Daphne asked.

But I barely heard her. I opened up the letter and pulled out the note. It read:

"If I can't have him, no one can."

I put my hand over my mouth. Did she know his lung collapsed, or was it just impeccable timing? It felt like she knew. It felt like she was watching me. I looked over my shoulder. *How does she know everything?*

"Penny?" Daphne put her hand on my shoulder. "Penny, what's wrong?"

"Who's telling her?" I whispered.

"Who's telling who what?" Daphne said. "Penny, breathe in for five seconds and then release."

"Who's telling her?!" I screamed.

"Hey," Daphne said and put her hand back on my shoulder. "Please take a deep breath."

Mason came back into the waiting room and shook his head.

"No." I pushed Daphne's hand away and stood up. "One of you is telling her. One of you is telling her!" It felt like I was breaking.

"Hey, Pen, calm down, okay?" my dad said and lightly touched my arm.

I flinched and stepped back. The cops suspected Tyler. They suspected Melissa. Mason knew about the envelopes. Had James told him? Or was he a part of it? Daphne had given me this one. Austin had given me one. Who else had? I tried to remember. There had been one at the office. A switch seemed to go off in my head. Zach. Zach had been the only one at the office when I had gotten one of the manila envelopes there. And he had continuously badgered me about James being abusive. He had been at our wedding too. And James had a fucking list of people who were potential threats. What if the cops were right? What if this wasn't Isabella? What if it was someone else? And what if it was someone in this room? "No."

"Pen."

I didn't trust anyone. I took another step away from my father. "It's one of you."

"Sweetie," my mom said. "What are you talking about?"

"Someone call Officer Daugherty right now. I need to speak with him."

"Okay," my mom said and pulled out her phone. She put her cell to her ear and started talking on it. But I didn't hear what she was saying.

"Hey." Rob gently touched my back. He was the only one I knew for sure wasn't doing this. He loved James. He loved me.

"It's one of them. She knows. How else would she know?" I handed him the note.

He quickly read it. "That doesn't mean she knows what just happened. This could have just been because

James is here. There's no way she could know about his lung collapsing. It just happened."

"Unless someone told her."

Rob frowned. He grabbed my arm and pulled me out of the waiting room and into an empty hallway. "So you're accusing one of our closest friends and family of conspiring with Isabella?"

"I don't know. How can we know? She just keeps sending me stuff. And James is in surgery again. And...I don't know." I shook my head. It felt like I was losing my mind. But what if I was right. What if someone was feeding her information?

"No one out there would do that."

"How are you so sure? The cops aren't sure. I'm not even sure anymore."

"Penny, you're just upset about what happened. This," he raised the note in the air, "is still Isabella. She's the one behind all of this."

"But what if it's not even her?"

"Penny, what are you talking about?"

"What if it's someone else? One of them knows something. Rob, I can't explain. I just know. One of them is lying. One of them is talking to her. They're telling her everything. She's not doing this alone."

Rob ran his hand through his hair. "No one else would write this note though."

"I know." I tried to take a deep breath like Daphne had instructed. I nodded my head. "I'm sorry, I'm just freaking out. I just..." I let my voice trail off.

"But I don't think you're wrong either."

Goosebumps ran up my arms at his words.

"I've been feeling like someone's watching me. What if...fuck, what if you're right?" He turned his head toward the waiting room.

"I've felt it too. I just have this eerie feeling. She watched me before with this undetectable camera. Maybe that's it again. Maybe it's not another person." I noticed Officer Daugherty walk into the waiting room.

Rob sighed. "Let's go tell the cops to question everyone. And to search for a camera. If you're right, maybe that's what will finally lead us to her."

"But you've felt it too?"

He lowered his eyebrows as he nodded. He didn't realize that all his small gestures killed me inside. The similarities between him and James hit me the hardest.

"I need to tell you something," he said slowly. "It's been bothering me. And now that you're questioning things, I feel like I need to tell you."

I looked up at him. "Tell me what?"

"James asked me to take care of you if something ever happened to him."

I didn't doubt that James would do that. But I did have one question. "When did he ask you that?"

"He asked me twice actually. Once right before you two moved to New York. I didn't know you that well, but I was already grateful for what you had done for him. I don't think you realize how happy you made him."

I tried to blink back my tears.

"And he asked me again the night before you two got married."

That was sweet. But it made my stomach unsettled. Why would James ask him again?

"I just need you to know that he didn't need to ask me. I'd never let anything happen to you."

"Rob."

"But..." he let his voice trail off.

"What?"

"I'm wondering why he reminded me. I'm wondering if he knew something was going to happen."

I shook my head. "I mean, he was worried about what Isabella might do. But he didn't know. If he knew, he wouldn't have let us get married. He wouldn't have put himself in danger."

"Penny, the night before your wedding, he also told me that he'd die for you."

"That's a figure of speech."

"But what if it wasn't? What if he just wanted to marry you? As the last thing he could do? As the last choice he could make?"

I shook my head. *No.*

"What if he was getting notes too? What if she had threatened him? What if he knew?"

"He would have told me. Especially after I told him." But would he have? He was always trying to protect me. He was always keeping me in the dark. *Oh my God.* I thought about the words James whispered against my lips on our wedding night. *I'll love you until the day I die.* Did he know it would be soon? Had he known all along?

"But what if he didn't? What if there's evidence somewhere else? Somewhere in your house? Or in his office?"

"What does it matter? That won't save him."

"But it'll get him justice. We have to get her put away. She can't get away with this. If he dies..."

I tried to swallow back my tears.

"Think, Penny. Is there anything else that he said to you? Did it seem like he was holding something back?"

No. It felt like he had given me every piece of him. And then I remembered. "She did send him pictures. Like she sent me. Compromising photos. He made it seem like she gave them to him in person. But maybe she sent other things like she did with me. Which means maybe she threatened him too."

"Okay. You go talk to the cops. I'm going to go to your apartment and search for the pictures and anything else that might help. Call me if you get an update on James."

"Wait." I grabbed his arm. "Can you stay for a second? I'm having trouble catching my breath."

"I'll go get the doctor."

"No." I closed my eyes and leaned my back against the wall. "Just tell me something good. Tell me something that will calm me down."

"You're having a baby."

Possibly without a father. I opened my eyes. "Something else. Tell me about you and Daphne. Distract me."

He smiled. "What do you want to know?"

"How serious are you guys? Do you really like her?"

"I more than like her. She gets me in a way that no one ever has before. She laughs at my jokes. She...grounds me. I feel more centered ever since I met her. And more useful, more needed, like I finally have a purpose in life. Making her smile makes me happier than I've ever been. And I get this weird feeling in my chest when we're apart. I haven't even told her this yet, but I know that I love her. Penny, I'm going to marry that girl. Shit, why are you crying?"

"I don't know." I tried to wipe away my tears. "I'm just really happy for you."

He laughed and pulled me in for a hug. "James is going to be okay, you know. We're going to be going on double dates in no time."

"Yeah." But my heart wasn't in my words. James was in surgery. And if he didn't make it, I wasn't going to make it either.

"I have to go, Penny."

"Can't it wait? He needs you here. I need you here."

"If Isabella did threaten to kill him and she didn't succeed, she's not going to give up. She's always been determined to get her way. It can't wait. She'll come here. And they'll let her, because the cops aren't even fucking looking at her. They haven't even asked her to come back to the city for questioning. And if someone out there is talking to Isabella..." he let his voice trail off. "Don't tell anyone about this, okay?"

I nodded.

"No one."

"I won't."

He gave me one more swift hug. "Call me the second you know anything." He handed me my phone that he had been holding on to for me. "Don't look at me like that. You don't have to answer any of the calls except the ones from me. Ignore the press. Ignore it all, okay?"

I nodded. "Call me when you find the proof that we need."

"I will." He patted my back and left me alone in the hallway with my thoughts. I didn't want to believe that James knew Isabella was going to try to hurt him. But it made sense. Normally I would have been mad at him for something like this. But not today. Today, all I could think about was how sweet it was if it was true. How he wanted to marry me so badly he put himself in danger. And how much guiltier it made me feel. Rob was right. We needed to get to the bottom of this. We needed to make sure that when James woke up, everything was taken care of. And he could just focus on healing.

I looked back at the swinging doors. *When. Not if.* My husband was going to come back to me. He had to.

CHAPTER 28

Wednesday

"No one else would have sent me this message," I said.

Officer Daugherty shook his head. "This could be any bachelorette in this city. They're all jealous of you. There's a lot of crazy people out there."

"You're kidding right?"

"No. This doesn't mean anything." He handed the note back to me.

"What other evidence could you possibly need?"

"Solid evidence."

I tried to stay calm. Rob was working on getting that. Hopefully he'd find something. I had pulled Officer Daugherty into the hallway that I had been talking to Rob in so that no one would overhear us. But this wasn't going the way I would have hoped. Maybe he'd listen to what I had to say next. "Rob and I have both felt like someone's been watching us."

"We have a team outside the hospital. Melissa isn't allowed within 50 feet of the building."

Still not working. "What I mean is that someone in the waiting room is feeding Isabella information. Or there's a camera or something."

"Mrs. Hunter, I don't know how many times I have to tell you that Isabella isn't..."

"Okay. Fine. Then not Isabella. But someone is telling whoever has been sending me these notes what's been going on here." *And it's Isabella!*

He nodded. "Could be. I'll ask everyone a few questions. See what I can turn up."

"Thank you."

Officer Daugherty glanced at his phone. "Looks like there was no record of that shipment with UPS. It must have just been someone that was dressed like a UPS guy."

"Aren't there cameras in this hospital? You could probably get an angle of his face. Run it against your system?"

"You've been watching too many crime shows. How about you leave the detective work to us? And I recommend you get some sleep."

Condescending asshole. "Thanks, Officer Daugherty."

***

"I heard what you said to Mason. You're not weak," James' father said as he sat down next to me.

I kept my eyes on Officer Daugherty. He was having a conversation with Jen. It definitely wasn't Jen. Or anyone else here. What had I been thinking? None of these people would betray me. I sighed. "You don't know me very well." It was a cold response. But I was trying to focus. I was trying to see if anyone was texting or slipping away too often for the restroom.

"James came to our house once a month for the past two years trying to convince us to meet you. I know more than you think."

I turned toward him. "Really?"

"He didn't tell you?"

I was starting to think that James still didn't tell me a lot of things. "Not exactly. He told me he was trying, though."

"He was pretty relentless, in fact."

I smiled. "That sounds like James."

Jon shifted in his seat. "I owe you an apology."

"You don't. It's between you and James." I wasn't going to interfere anymore. I just wanted James to wake up. I just wanted him to be happy.

"No." He shook his head. "Well, yes, but I'm not talking about that right now." He awkwardly cleared his throat. "When Susan and I were in the room with James, something came up. I know it wasn't the time or place to confront her, but at the moment it seemed necessary."

"You were arguing in his room?" I had left James alone to hear his parents screaming at each other. To hear the chaos that he grew up with and so badly wanted to escape.

"Yes, but..."

"Why would you do that? The doctor specifically said to talk to him quietly. Not yell."

"I'm sorry."

"Why? Why couldn't you put your son first for five seconds?"

"It's not what you think. I was trying..."

"No, that's exactly the point, Jon. You weren't trying."

He lowered both his eyebrows. I hated how much it reminded me of James. I hated how that small action made me want to forgive him, to comfort him. But Jon wasn't James. Rob wasn't James. James was back in surgery. With a DNR and no more chances. My husband was dying. And his own father's yelling caused it. His parents screaming at each other. I refused to sit here and listen to Jon's lame apology. Because I didn't have it in my heart to forgive anyone.

"I don't think he stopped breathing because we were arguing. What I was trying to apologize for was that we moved our argument out of the room."

"He was alone when it happened?"

"I'm so sorry."

He was alone? Tears pricked at my eyes. Mason was wrong. I couldn't lean on any of these people. Because none of them seemed to have James' best interests in mind. Any one of them could have been conspiring alongside Isabella. Any one of them could be the enemy.

"Penny, if you would just let me explain," Jon said.

But I was already walking away. I needed to be alone in my grief. I needed to be alone in my weakness.

CHAPTER 29

Wednesday

"Penny?" my mom said and knocked on the stall door. "Can you please open the door?"

There was no escaping in this hospital. And I couldn't leave. I needed to be here. I needed to be close to him. I clenched my eyes shut. I couldn't do this right now.

"You know," my mom said, "when you were little and you got upset, you used to lock yourself in your room. No matter what we said to try and console you, you refused to come out. Until you got hungry."

I shook my head. I wasn't a kid anymore. And I wasn't refusing to come out because I was upset. I was refusing to come out because it felt like my life had stopped. It felt like my legs wouldn't work. It felt like my world was black. I was drowning in my grief. I was drowning in my weakness.

"Sweetie, I know you're in pain. Please come out and talk to me."

"I can't talk about my fears because it makes the possibility that much more real."

"Sweetie." My mom touched the stall door.

For some reason the door between us made it easier. It reminded me of going to confession when I was little. I was always so terrified of talking to the priest. Not because I was upset about anything I had done. I was just terrified of him judging me.

I looked down at the notebook on my lap. I had been reading my vows to him again. And trying to make sense of the scribbled, tear stained notes of how he made me feel. The day before our wedding I thought I needed to capture those moments on paper because he had broken up with me. I had actually written quite a bit. But the notes didn't do him justice. And this was so much worse than just us being broken up. Maybe I could have kept going knowing he was out there, alive and happy. But not like this. I couldn't keep going if he died. I couldn't do it. I stifled my sob. "What if he dies, Mom?" It came out as a whisper. It really did feel like I was in confession.

There was no response. My mom just sighed.

"What if I lose him?"

"Then you have to choose to keep living."

Everyone had been telling me that he wouldn't die. That everything would be okay. No one was able to confront the possibility of James dying. "I can't keep living without him."

"You can. And you will."

No. "You don't understand."

"Of course I understand. I love you with all my heart. And I love your father the same. The possibility of losing one of you is terrifying."

"He's my whole world. He's everything."

"Penny, you have family and friends that love you dearly. I understand how it feels like he's everything. But that's the whole reason you keep living. You keep going in order to keep the memory of him alive. And your family and friends help to make that happen."

I touched my stomach. *To keep the memory of him alive.* If James didn't come out of this, I had to keep living. So the memory of him wouldn't die. I couldn't let the memory of him die. So why did I feel like curling up in a ball and dying beside him? Why was I so weak when I was begging him to be strong and fight his way back to me? I took another deep breath. I needed to shake this feeling. I needed to be stronger than this. I wasn't sure I could keep going without him beside me. But I needed to try. I needed to stop giving up. I needed to stop being so pathetic. "I think I'm hungry now."

My mom laughed. "Then come out and let's go down and get some dinner."

I stuffed my notebook back into my purse. Maybe I wasn't strong enough to keep living without him. But maybe I could write more down. More memories, more feelings, more words to eternalize how wonderful he is. So that no one could ever forget. So that the memory of him would stay alive, even if I couldn't. I took a deep breath and walked out of the bathroom stall.

My mom had tears in her eyes. And somehow I felt closer to her than I had in years. We had grown apart when I went to college and when I moved away to the city. But I was still her child. I was still allowed to need my mom. And I really needed her right now.

"Mom, I'm pregnant."

"What?" She put her hand over her chest. "Does James know?"

I shook my head. "I found out here. I had been feeling nauseous and emotional and...well, I guess that was why."

She embraced me in a huge hug. "Sweetie, this is the kind of news that allows you to keep fighting."

But it had made me feel weak. *Be strong.*

"Now we definitely need to get you something to eat."

***

I sat in the waiting room with my eyes closed. All I could hear was the clock.

Tick tock.

Tick tock.

Tick tock.

"Penny." Bee nudged my arm.

I opened my eyes and saw the doctor walking toward us. She looked exhausted. Her face was completely unreadable. Time seemed to slow down as I stood up.

"As you know, James' lung collapsed," she said. "We thought that we had fixed the puncture before, but it wasn't strong enough. We've repaired it again and removed the air from his chest cavity. There was no tension in his chest, which was a good sign. But his heart stopped during surgery."

It felt like my heart stopped while I was listening. I felt Bee grab my hand. I felt someone else touch my shoulder. Without their support I would have been falling. But it didn't stop the despair inside of me. *No. This can't be happening.*

"You are all aware that James has a DNR. In all cases we have to respect the patient's desires."

No. God, please no.

"But, it's also a judgment call on our part. The DNR was written a few years ago. And..." she glanced at me, "there were other factors to consider. With that said, we did not follow James' desires. We restarted his heart. And he woke up." The doctor smiled.

I put my hand on my chest. It felt like I could breathe again. *He's awake.* Even before she said it, I could feel him. Despite everyone around me, I fell. I fell to my knees and cried away my fears. I cried away the feeling of despair.

Everyone around me started cheering and laughing. And I just continued to cry. "Can I see him?" I croaked. "I need to see him."

The doctor crouched down beside me. "He's asleep right now. He needs his rest. But you can go be with him."

"Thank you." I tried to wipe my tears away, but I couldn't seem to stop crying. All my worries from the past few days seemed to seep out of me. And I was filled with this underlying hope.

She nodded. "It's in his best interest to meet his baby."

"Thank you," I said again. I threw my arms around her. "Thank you so much."

"You can thank me by not letting him sue the hospital."

"He wouldn't. I know this is what he wanted."

"I'll need you to get him to sign a few papers when he wakes up saying that's true. But how about right now you go see him?"

I nodded and slowly stood up. I didn't feel weak anymore. I felt strong again. Like I could face anything. And the realization hit me hard. I was strong because of him. James gave me strength. He really was my everything.

I followed the doctor to the door.

"Don't wake him up, Penny. It's very important that he gets rest."

"I won't." I went into the room.

There was no longer a tube down his throat and the color was back in face. He looked like James again. He looked like my husband.

I didn't say a word. Right now he needed rest and silence. *Thank you. Thank you for coming back to me.* I let my tears fall again. I thought marrying him was the happiest moment of my life. But it wasn't. This was.

PART 3

CHAPTER 30

Thursday

"Penny," James whispered.

I was dreaming again. James and I were sleeping in our bed. I didn't want to wake up. I didn't want the memory to fade. The sun was streaming through the windows. He tucked a loose strand of hair behind my ear and kissed my forehead. I was surrounded by warmth. The sun on my face and his body intertwined with mine. But nothing came close to the warmth in my heart. The simplest of moments were my favorites. The lazy mornings. Making pancakes for him on the weekends while he pretended to help. I closed my eyes even tighter. I didn't want the memories to fade. I couldn't let the memories fade.

"My beautiful wife," James said and touched the side of my face.

And the realization hit me hard. It wasn't a dream. He had never gotten to wake up in the morning and say those words to me. Until now. My eyes flew open. He was staring at me. James was awake. "James." I didn't try to hide the worry in my voice or the tears in my eyes. And especially not the joy in my heart.

"You haven't been eating," he said slowly. His voice was hoarse. He barely sounded like himself.

"Neither have you."

He laughed and then immediately groaned. "Stubborn as always, I see."

"You're awake." I had almost forgotten the curves of his lips. And the dimples in his cheeks. And that intoxicating way that he looked at me.

"What, you thought I'd leave you?" He smiled again, but it didn't hide the grimace. He was in pain.

"Let me go get the nurse, okay?"

"No." He grabbed my hand.

It felt like a lifetime since he had grabbed my hand. I relished the warmth of his skin and the strength behind his fingers.

"Don't cry. It hurts me to see you cry."

I quickly wiped my tears away. *Be strong.* "I thought I lost you." *I thought you had left me.*

He shook his head. "Come here." He patted the bed beside me.

I didn't hesitate. I was tired of dreaming of his arms around me. I thought I'd never get another one of these moments.

He cringed as I climbed onto the bed.

"James, let me get the nurse."

"No. I just need you." He moved his arm so that I could rest my head on his shoulder.

I slowly lay down, trying not to hit any of the wires that were attached to him.

He groaned softly. I wasn't sure why he wouldn't let me go get the nurse. But I wanted this moment too. I just hoped I wasn't hurting him too badly.

"Does it hurt?" I asked.

"I'm okay."

It didn't really answer my question, but I knew what he meant. Everything was going to be okay now. We were both alive. That's all that mattered.

"Am I thirty yet?"

Is he? I tried to count the days in my head. I had lost track of time. I had lost track of everything.

"Did you forget my birthday?" He ran his fingers through my hair.

"No. No, it's on Sunday. Today's only Thursday." I closed my eyes and listened to his heart beating. I had a million questions for him. I wanted to know why he still had a DNR. I wanted to know if he had known Isabella was planning on hurting him. But right now, I just wanted to hear his heart beating.

"I guess I woke up just in time to get those meggings?" He laughed and then coughed. "Ow."

"James, I'm going to go get the nurse. They'll give you something for the pain."

"I don't want anything for the pain." His words hung in the air.

"I don't want you to hurt. James, I don't want..."

"I made you a promise in my vows. That you could always rely on me. I won't ever jeopardize that. You're all I need right now. I mean that."

I lifted my head up and ran my palm against the scruff on his chin. "I don't like seeing you in pain."

"Now you know why I hate to see you cry." He gave me a small smile.

I nodded. No more tears. If he was being strong, I could be strong too.

"That wasn't how I pictured our wedding night ending," he said.

"No. I pictured it very differently."

He smiled. "I'm sorry. I'm sorry that I ruined..."

"You didn't ruin anything. I'm just so glad you're awake." *I'm so glad you came back to me.*

We stared at each other in silence for a moment. I hadn't felt this content since our wedding. And I knew that James couldn't just walk out of the hospital right now. He'd have to recover. He needed to heal. A part of me wanted to tell him about the baby. But I wasn't sure how he'd react. Right now he needed to stay calm. So I let the perfect silence settle around us. I stared into his dark brown eyes and let everything slowly shift back to us. Back to the night when he was almost taken from me. Back to what I should have been feeling at that moment. I had this sense of peace. And I knew he had woken up because of me. And he knew I would have died without him. We didn't have to say anything at all. This moment was all that we needed.

"You should eat something," James finally said, breaking the silence.

I smiled. "I don't know how you're worried about me when you're the one with three bullet holes."

"I can barely feel it." He pressed his lips together. "But I could use some water."

"I'll go get you some."

"No, don't...please don't leave."

We locked eyes for another moment. I had no idea what it was like to be in a coma. Had he felt alone? Had he known I was by his side the whole time?

"I think there's a button somewhere." He nodded with his head toward the nightstand.

I reached over and pressed it. "I was with you the whole time, James. Except when they forced me to go shower and eat." I gave him a small smile.

"I know. I must be in major need of a shower."

"No, actually. They let me sponge bathe you."

"That's slightly demeaning." He raised his left eyebrow at me.

"The nurse offered to do it. But you're my husband. I don't want anyone else to see you naked."

"Your husband." He smiled. "Well, you did marry an older man. You better get used to it."

I laughed. "Not that much older than me."

He kissed my forehead. I took a moment to breathe in his scent. It was still diluted by hospital soap, but now that he was awake, it was almost like I could smell him again.

"I could feel it," he whispered. "I don't really know how to explain it. I just...I knew you were there. And I could feel that you needed me."

"You know that I always need you, James."

He kissed my forehead again. "I'm sorry, baby. I'm so, so sorry."

Why did he keep trying to apologize? I thought about what Rob had said. That maybe James knew Isabella was going to try to hurt him. But before I could ask him, the nurse walked into the room.

She immediately frowned at me.

I sat up and stepped down off the bed.

"How are you feeling, hon?" the nurse asked.

"Thirsty. And tired."

"You need to let him get his rest," she said and looked at me.

James laughed and then coughed again.

She handed him a glass of water.

James took a long sip. "When can I get out of here?" He tried to sit up and clenched his teeth together.

"Not anytime soon." The nurse grabbed the glass from his hand. "Not if you don't get your rest."

"I'm fine, really." He grimaced again as he readjusted himself on the bed.

"On a scale of one to ten, how is the pain?"

James shrugged. "Ten as the worst?"

"Mhm."

"Maybe a three then."

She looked at him like she didn't believe him at all. "Go back to sleep, hon. Maybe you'll start making sense once you get some proper rest. The doctor will come in shortly, she's just finishing up a surgery."

James nodded. It looked like he was already about to fall back to sleep.

"And you stay off his bed, missy," she said to me before she left the room.

"Really, how much does it hurt?" I asked and slipped my hand back into his.

"It's not so bad." He yawned and grimaced again.

"James."

"It hurts like hell."

I pressed my lips together. "Go back to sleep, James," I said and kissed his cheek.

"Come back up. I want to hold you."

I wanted to follow the nurses instructions, so I sat back down in my seat. I wanted him to get better. "I'm not going anywhere. I'll be right here when you wake up."

"Promise you'll stay?" he asked as his eyelids grew heavy.

"Of course." I squeezed his hand.

"I love you, Penny." It was almost a mumble.

"I love you." I watched him slowly fall asleep. For the first time in a long time, I realized how tired I was too. I laid my head down next to his hand. I felt at peace. I felt safe. I felt whole again.

***

Something buzzing woke me up. When I realized it was my phone, I quickly grabbed it and slid my finger across the screen so that it wouldn't wake James. But it wasn't a phone call, it was just a text. I clicked on the message that Rob had just sent.

"Penny, I've got it. You have to come see this."

I looked down at James. He had asked me to stay. But settling this mess would give him such a sense of peace. I didn't want him to have to worry about anything while he was recovering.

Another text came through. "It's enough to put her away for a long time even if they can't link anything else to her. It's over."

I let a breath escape that I hadn't realized I had been holding. *It's over.* I leaned down and kissed James' forehead. "I'll be right back," I whispered.

He moaned in his sleep.

No one would ever hurt him again. Ever. I left the room as quietly as possible.

"How is he doing?" Porter asked once I was in the hall.

"Good. He's sleeping. I'm going to run by our apartment real quick. I'll be back in half an hour."

"I'll come with you," he said.

"You don't have to. I'm meeting Rob there. He thinks he found evidence to convince the cops that Isabella was behind all of this."

Porter was already talking into his watch. He touched his earpiece. "Briggs will be here in a minute and we can head over."

"I think it's better if you both stay here." I felt guilty for leaving James alone when I had told him I'd stay. I wanted to make sure he was okay while I was gone.

"You're always our first priority, Mrs. Hunter. Mr. Hunter has made that very clear."

Briggs ran up to us. "How is he?"

"He's sleeping. But he's good." Porter clapped him on the back.

Briggs nodded. He looked relieved. "Have you asked him about us?" he asked.

"He's not going to fire either of you." Not after he knew how protective they had been since our wedding night. Not after he found out how much they cared.

"I'm taking her to the apartment," Porter said. "No bathroom breaks."

"I'm feeling much better today," Briggs said.

Porter nodded. "You ready?" He started walking before I had even answered.

"What was that about bathroom breaks?" I asked as I caught up to him.

"Briggs' stomach got really upset yesterday and he kept leaving his post. I have it under control."

"You guys are allowed to take breaks."

"Not at the same time, though. Would you like me to call Ian or would you like to drive with me?"

"I'll drive with you." Every time I went home to shower he'd ask me the same thing. And I always said I'd drive with him. He had even started letting me sit in the front seat with him. Besides, I knew Ian and Jen were spending time together before she had to fly back to California. I didn't want to interrupt that.

Porter opened up the passenger door for me and I climbed into his SUV. It was strange driving through the city today. The last few days had been hell. Everything looked bleak around me. But today I noticed how green the grass was in Central Park. And how happy the joggers looked. Soon that would be James again. He'd be better in no time, I knew it.

"Are you married, Cole?"

Porter barely winced when I called him by his first name. And he didn't reprimand me anymore either. There was no way I was going to let James fire either one of these guys. They had only just started to warm up to me.

"No, I'm not married."

"Are you dating anyone?"

He glanced at me for a second as he hit his turn signal. "You're asking a lot of questions today."

"I just feel like when James is all better you're going to get all serious again. It's my last chance to get to know you." I saw a small smile on his lips.

"I have a girlfriend. We've been together for almost five years now."

"What's her name?"

"Last name or first name?" He smiled again.

"First name, of course."

"Julie."

"I'm sorry we've been keeping you away from her. Everything's going to go back to normal soon."

"Briggs and I both wanted to be there. You never even asked us to stay. As far as I was concerned, we were volunteering."

"We're going to pay you for your time."

"That's not necessary. It's my fault that he was in there in the first place."

"That's not true." I looked out the window. "It was mine."

"I don't think so, Penny."

I liked that he was continuing to call me by my first name. "We agree to disagree then."

He gave me a small smile. "I guess so." He pulled up in front of our apartment building. "Do you want to just call him and tell him to come down? When James wakes up he'll be wondering where you went."

"Good idea." I wanted to get back to James as soon as possible. I clicked on Rob's name in my phone. It went straight to voicemail. "His phone must have died. I'll just go up real quick. I'll be back in a minute."

"Let me come up with you." He unbuckled his seatbelt.

"No, it's fine. His phone dies all the time. He never charges it. Sometimes I'm surprised he even has a cell phone at all. Besides, I wanted to go up anyway to grab a few things for James in case he's allowed to change out of his hospital gown."

"Okay." He nodded at me as I climbed out of the car.

For the first time in ages I was actually happy to enter our apartment building. Cliff, the man at the front desk, didn't stare at me like I was a charity case this time. Someone must have reported that James had woken up. It was probably all over the news.

"Good afternoon, Penny," Cliff said with a smile. "I have some mail for you."

"Good afternoon, Cliff." I grabbed the mail from his hand. No manila envelopes. No more Isabella. Soon this would all be behind us.

"And just to let you know, Rob and your cleaning lady are both in your apartment. They were both on the list that Mr. Hunter wrote up so I let them in."

"Yes, that's fine. And her name is Ellen." I hated when people addressed her in any way as our help. She wasn't that to me. Ellen was family. She had stopped by the hospital every day. I had told her she didn't need to work at all, but she insisted that it kept her mind off worrying. And that she wanted the apartment to be perfect for when James came home. She was one of the sweetest people I had ever met.

"Right, yes I have her name listed here. Ellen. I'll make a note to call her that. Actually," he said and cleared his throat. "I was wondering...do you know if she's single?"

My first reaction was to laugh. Cliff was even younger than me. And Ellen had to be at least 60. But of course, there was no way he was asking for himself. He was probably asking for his father or some older relative. "She's single."

"Oh wow. Okay great." He looked slightly embarrassed. "I'm happy to hear that James woke up."

I smiled. I couldn't even express to him how ecstatic I was. "Thanks, Cliff." I walked toward the elevator with the mail. I thought about Bee and Mason, Rob and Daphne, and Jen and Ian. And possibly even Melissa and Matt.

Love was in the air. Ellen loved James like a son, but she didn't have any children of her own. Her husband had passed away a few years ago. Maybe there could be some love in the air for her too.

The last week and a half I had felt so depressed walking into our apartment. It felt empty and lifeless without James. It wasn't a home without him. Really, the hospital felt more like home than this did. Wherever James was, that was where home was.

I stepped off the elevator and grabbed my keys. I walked into the apartment and tossed the mail and my purse on the kitchen counter. "Rob?"

There was no answer.

"Ellen?" I couldn't wait to tell her that Cliff had asked if she was single. Her first reaction would probably be to giggle too.

But again, there was no answer.

They must have both been upstairs. "Rob?" I called again as I walked out of the kitchen. I turned the corner toward the staircase and saw him. He was lying at the bottom of the stairs. There was a pool of blood under his head and his leg was twisted at an awkward angle. "Rob!" I ran toward him and crouched down. "Oh my God, Rob." I was afraid to touch his body. I didn't want to injure him any more than he already was. There was so much blood underneath his head. And it was smeared around beneath his hands like he had tried to get up and failed. *No.*

"Wake up. Rob, you have to wake up. Ellen!" I screamed up the steps. "Ellen, help!" I gently put my fingers to Rob's neck, trying to find a pulse. My eyes were blinded by tears. "No, Rob, wake up."

"Don't move."

Her voice made my whole body turn cold. *Isabella.*

"Stand up, Penny."

I let my fingers fall from Rob's neck. I hadn't had time to find a pulse. Or maybe I just didn't want to believe what I had really felt. Nothing. There was no pulse. And I suddenly felt so weak. I didn't want to stand. I wanted to throw myself on Rob to protect him. A million thoughts flashed through my mind, but what stuck with me were some of the last words Rob said to me. "I'm going to marry that girl." He had finally found himself. He was finally happy. He couldn't die now. He just couldn't.

"Put your hands in the air and turn around."

"Where's Ellen?" I thought about Ellen lying somewhere else in the house. Unconscious. Or worse. All I could do was stare at the pool of blood expanding around Rob's head. *This can't be happening. Rob can't be dead.* Tears streamed down my cheeks. *He can't be.*

"I said put your hands in the air and turn around."

For a second I thought about running. It wasn't just my safety I had to think about anymore. But I couldn't escape this. There was only one door out of the apartment. And she was in my way. And I couldn't leave Rob. I stared down at his body. *Please be okay.* I slowly stood up, lifted my hands in the air, and turned to face her.

A cruel smile crossed her lips. She looked as perfect as ever, even though she was wearing something I never thought I'd see her in, a pair of faded jeans, a tattered t-shirt, and yellow latex gloves. She was dressed like a cleaning lady. Yet not a single strand of her hair was out of place and her makeup looked like a professional had done it for her. I always felt insignificant around her. I thought that feeling might fade after James and I got married. But it hadn't. Or maybe it was just the fact that she was pointing a gun toward me.

"I never much liked him," she said and nodded toward Rob's body. "It's a pity though, I didn't expect anyone else to be here."

"Is he dead?" I needed to know if Rob was okay. I needed to know if he was breathing.

"How should I know? He certainly doesn't look good. Luckily I always come prepared. Although, I certainly didn't expect to see you. Shouldn't you be with your new husband? Especially after you left him alone the last time?"

How does she know about that?

"One thing I do love about you is how utterly transparent you are," she said. "You think I don't have connections? You think I had no idea what was happening to my own husband in the hospital? Think again."

Her own husband? She had lost her mind. She was completely insane. "Who's feeding you information?"

"The question is, who isn't, dear. God, this was all too easy."

I swallowed hard.

"So, let's see. Hmmm. How should I have this play out? I originally just came here to plant evidence to frame you. But this is so much better. I'm thinking a lover's quarrel. Maybe the two of you were sleeping together behind James' back? Maybe the baby is actually Rob's?"

"How do you know that I'm pregnant?"

"Weren't you listening? I know every move you make."

"Who were you working with?"

"The press will report anything I tell them," she said, ignoring my question. "But I do love a scandal. Poor

James. His new bride and his letch of a brother screwing around behind his back. And the worst part is James will believe it. Because I'll be by his side helping him recover. And I'll be reminding him every day how awful you were. How you only wanted to be with him for his money. And how his brother lived off his wealth. How Rob always resented his big brother's success."

"That's not true. You were the only one that was ever after his money."

She made the same noise with her throat that James' mother always did. "I have my own inheritance. I don't need the Hunters' fortune. And you won't be there to trick him anymore, putting false ideas in his head about me. Besides, James certainly doesn't believe that you could possibly love him if he doesn't even love you."

"He does love me."

"No. That was the problem the whole time. He's addicted to you."

"He's not addicted to me."

"Yes he is! And now that I know the only way he's capable of a connection, I can easily win him back. I'll make him crave me in a way he couldn't possibly crave you."

"He's not addicted to me," I said more forcefully. I was sick of hearing that. James was not addicted to me.

"You're so naive. I almost feel sorry for you, if it wasn't for the fact that you fucked my husband while I was still married to him." She lifted her gun a little higher.

"And you're delusional."

"Is that what you think? That my trying to win my husband back is delusional? I'm fighting for him. I'm fighting for us."

"There's nothing left to fight for!"

She shook her head. "It was always me and James. Always. Ever since we were children our futures were set in stone. We have the greatest kind of love story. Yes, we've had our issues. And that was on him, not me. He projected his problems on me. He wouldn't touch me. He made me feel awful about myself. So yes, I found solace in other men. But he pushed me there. Because he couldn't face the fact that he was sick. And now he's gotten help. Now he's better. And now he can truly love me in a way I never thought possible. The way that you did. So it's only fair that he comes back to me. It's only fair."

"Life isn't fair, Isabella." I wanted to lunge for the gun. My mind was racing. What was the best way to reach for it?

"You think I don't know that? If life was fair I wouldn't be standing right here with you. I wouldn't be arguing with an immature girl about my husband!" Her hand was shaking.

For the first time I thought she might actually not shoot me. Maybe she was realizing how crazy this whole thing was.

"Isabella, we don't have to be arguing about this." I took a step forward.

"Don't move." She grabbed the gun with her other hand to steady it.

My phone started vibrating in my purse. Isabella glanced over toward the kitchen counter.

"Who's calling you?" she asked.

"I don't know."

She pulled my phone out of my purse and looked at the screen. "Is Porter still at the hospital?"

"No. He was waiting in the car downstairs."

"Shit." She tossed my phone down on the counter. "Enough chatting. Stand next to Rob." She raised her gun again.

"Isabella, you don't have to do this."

"Of course I do. I've already tried to kill James. And I failed both times. Now I'm going to kill you instead."

"Both times?" *She tried twice?*

"Kneel down next to Rob," she said, ignoring me.

"Isabella."

"Now!"

I heard the click of her gun being cocked. *Fuck.* "Okay." For some reason my fear hadn't switched on until that moment. I was worried about Rob. But now, now I realized what was going to happen. She was going to kill me. She was going to get her way. I was going to die. My baby was going to die. I tried to blink back my tears. I tried to think of anything I could do to prevent this from happening. But there was no hope. I glanced down at Rob's lifeless body. This was it. James and I were never supposed to happen. I was his student and he was my professor. Everything had always been against us. We weren't allowed to be happy. Life was a cruel joke.

I looked back up. I noticed the front door slowly opening. *Porter! Oh, thank God.* "You don't have to do this," I said. I needed to distract her. I couldn't let her hear him coming in. "We can just tell the cops it was an accident. You won't have to go to jail."

"Nothing I do will send me to prison. People like me don't end up in jail."

Criminals? I thought about James' rap sheet. He never ended up serving time. Maybe she was right. People like her didn't end up in prison. I needed to think of something to stall her. "Who's been telling you everything?"

"It's not just one person, Penny."

"Who then?"

"This is really what you want to know on your death-bed? As your whole meaningless life flashes before your eyes? I pity you."

"At least tell me how you got up here." *Please let this be working.* Isabella seemed happy about the way she had tricked everyone. She seemed to like to brag about her connections and tricks.

"You really are quite dense. Why do you think I'm dressed like this?" She gestured to the yellow gloves. "It's crazy what a little flirting at the front desk will get you. Men have always been easy for me to manipulate."

"Of course they have."

She laughed. "Flattery isn't going to save you, Penny."

I glanced at Porter who was slowly turning the corner into the kitchen. I didn't even realize my mistake until it was too late.

Isabella smiled and shook her head. She quickly turned around.

"Porter!" I yelled.

Three shots rang out and Porter fell to his knees. Three holes appeared on the front of his shirt.

"Porter!" I choked. I didn't want to be weak in front of Isabella. But I had just gotten to know Cole. He was sweet and kind. He had a girlfriend that he was missing. He stood by James' hospital door every day to make sure he was safe. I owed everything to him. He put himself at risk every day for me and James. And now... I watched Porter's lifeless body fall forwards and hit the ground with a sickening thud. Now, he was dead because of me. I let my tears fall down my cheeks. I let the guilt swallow me whole. Because nothing mattered now. Porter was my only chance at surviving this. Isabella was going to kill me next.

"Kneel on the fucking ground, Penny." She grabbed Porter's gun and slid it into her pants pocket.

I knelt down in the ever expanding pool of blood by Rob's head.

"Porter's body complicates things slightly." Isabella sighed. "We'll need a new scenario now." She tapped her gloved finger to her lips. "Okay, here's what happened. You and Rob were fighting upstairs. You didn't want him to tell James the truth. So you shot him at the top of the steps." A shot rang out as she shot Rob in the shoulder.

"No!" *God, Rob.*

Isabella laughed. "Don't worry. Odds are he's already dead." She cleared her throat. "And after you shot him, the force of it made him fall down the stairs. Dead. Porter rushed in because he heard the gunshot. So you decided to shoot him too. Because you're the fucking worst! God, you really are a bitch. And then you realized you made a terrible mistake. You realized that you just murdered two people in your crazy rampage. There's no coming back from that. Such an awful feeling. It just ate you up inside. Your only redemption was to kill yourself after it's all said and done."

She smiled her cruel smile. "And the best part? Everyone will think you were the one that tried to kill James on your wedding night. Maybe Rob persuaded you to run away with him. And then after your plans went south, you changed your mind. This bloodbath was the only way out in your delusional mind."

"I'm not the delusional one."

"In the eyes of the whole world, you're about to be."
She lifted her gun.

"Okay. Okay, Isabella, you win."

"Of course I win. I wouldn't have played this game if
it was possible to lose. Everything is always stacked in my
favor. I'm Isabella fucking Hunter."

"I'll divorce him. You don't have to kill me."

"Maybe that would work if you didn't get knocked up
like the slut that you are. But James has a soft spot for
children."

She really didn't know him at all. "He doesn't. He
doesn't even want kids. And he doesn't know I'm pregnant. He doesn't need to know. I'll disappear. You'll never
see me again." I was lying through my teeth. If she let me
go, the first thing I would do would be to find a police
officer at another precinct. One that she wasn't in bed
with.

Isabella eyed me coolly. "He really told you that he
doesn't want kids? That's rather ironic since it was the only
reason he married me."

My heart seemed to skip a beat. "What?"

She laughed. "He never tells you anything, does he?"

Don't listen to her. My last thoughts would not be about
James lying to me.

"I told him I was pregnant. He always believed everything I told him. That's probably why he has such a hard
time trusting you."

"Were you actually pregnant?"

"Of course not. I would never risk my figure for children. That's what surrogates are for." She waved her hand
dismissively. "And when I told him I lost the baby, it

brought us closer together. That was the happiest time in our marriage."

"When he was depressed about losing a child?"

"No. When he leaned on me. When he needed me." She took a step forward. "And it all made sense when I found out you were pregnant. He was marrying you out of obligation instead of love. It gave me the hope I needed."

"He doesn't know that I'm pregnant."

"You're a terrible liar."

Out of the corner of my eye I saw Porter stir. *He's alive. Oh my God, he's alive!* "I'm not lying. James doesn't know. And he never has to."

"Exactly." She took a step forward.

"You don't have to do this."

"It's already done." She smiled. "Your fate was set as soon as you slept with my husband. As soon as you decided that you were more important than the rules. As soon as you gave into temptation."

As she inched closer, I knew it was now or never. This was my one shot at escape. I had to grab her gun. But I didn't have to do anything.

Porter had stood up. He quietly stepped forward and grabbed Isabella's gun from behind.

"Get off me!" She yelled and pulled the trigger.

I closed my eyes as a shot rang out. But I didn't feel anything. My eyes flew open.

Isabella was squirming in Porter's arms. And I did the first thing I could think of. I grabbed a pan off the kitchen counter and whacked it hard against the back of her head. Isabella went limp in his arms.

"Jesus Christ." Porter shoved her off of him and she fell to the floor. "Are you okay?"

"I'm fine." The pan fell to the floor with a clang. "But Rob..."

"Call 911." Porter was already crouching down next to Rob's body.

I fumbled with my phone, spilling out all the information to the operator on the other side.

Porter lifted one of Rob's eyelids.

"Is he okay?"

Porter didn't respond.

Rob couldn't die. Not like this. I didn't know anyone as full of life as him. I didn't know anyone as kind and selfless as him.

Sirens wailed in the distance.

CHAPTER 31

Thursday

I stared down at the blood. But it wasn't the puddle of it that wrenched my heart. It was Rob's bloody handprints on the wooden floor. Where he had struggled to get up. Where he had been knocked back down. That's what the detective said. Rob had gotten hit on the head at the top of the stairs and fallen. He had tried to get up at the bottom but Isabella had hit him in the head again. I couldn't seem to stop staring at Rob's bloody handprints.

A flash made me blink my eyes. The crime scene investigators were taking photos of the blood.

"Penny." Porter lightly touched my shoulder. "Let me take you back to the hospital."

"This was my fault." I put my hand over my mouth.

"This was not your fault."

"It was my fault!" I shrugged away from his hand. "There were a million signs. There was no reason for Rob to ask me to come here. He would have just brought the evidence to the hospital. And the texts didn't sound like him. He didn't even use any funny jokes. And even the guy at the front desk asked if Ellen was single. I thought he was asking for his dad or something. I never thought..." I was choking on my tears. "It is my fault. What happened to Rob..."

"You're acting like he's dead. He's not. He's just unconscious. He may already be awake."

"I just...he's one of my best friends." I hadn't realized it before that second. But it was the truth. There was no one else I could ever confess my worries to as much as I could Rob. Sometimes it was even easier to talk to him than it was to talk to James, because he understood my fears about James being an addict. He understood me. And he always had my back. He was always there for me.

"And he's going to be okay." Porter touched my shoulder again. "He's going to wake up. Just like James did."

He didn't know that. "If you hadn't been wearing a bulletproof vest, you'd be dead. I never could have forgiven myself."

"You can't live your life in what-ifs. I'm not dead. I'm fine. And Rob's going to be fine too. None of this was your fault."

"I should have seen it."

"You can't blame yourself for not thinking like a criminal."

I shook my head.

"Look, it's not your fault because it's mine. And Briggs. Aren't you wondering why I came up?"

"No. I just assumed you were worried when I didn't answer my phone."

"Yeah. Partially. But I was calling to tell you something. When you didn't answer, I did assume the worst. Because while I was waiting in the car for you, I got a call from Briggs. Apparently after some digging from the investigators that James and Mason hired, the hospital announced that there was a malfunction with the ventilator that was helping James breathe. It randomly stopped working. That's why his lung collapsed. Briggs made them pull the video footage of when it happened. I was on break at the time. And Briggs had gone to the bathroom because his stomach was upset. He thought James' parents were going to stay with him. He never would have left his post if he knew James was going to be alone."

I already knew where this was going. Isabella had said she'd tried to kill James twice.

"There's footage of Isabella slipping into James' room right before the malfunction," Porter said. "And she left the room right after the ventilator apparently stopped. There are no cameras in the actual hospital rooms, just in the hallways. Her timing was so impeccable that we're almost positive that Isabella somehow slipped something into Briggs' coffee so that he'd need to use the restroom. Especially since he feels so much better today. He'd still be sick if it was the bug that's been going around.

"This," he said and gestured to the blood on the floor, "is enough to put her away for a long time. There still isn't proof that she was behind the shooting. Her being in James' room when the ventilator malfunctioned is suspicious, but not damning. But she's still going to prison for what she did today. She's still going to pay."

"She told me she had tried to kill him twice. She said she had failed both times she tried. That must have been the second time. Isn't that proof enough?"

"It's her word against yours. I believe your word will hold better in court due to what happened today, but it's still not guaranteed."

"She tried to kill my husband."

"And there is no hard evidence to support that."

I thought about what she said. That people like her didn't end up in jail. "They'll send her to a hoity-toity pris-on. She'll get off soon for good behavior. She'll come after us again. Rob thought that there might be evidence here. What if he found it? Or what if it's still here?"

"Then we'll talk to Rob when he wakes up. Right now, I'm taking you back to the hospital."

"Just give me five minutes. I think I might..."

"I'm sorry. I have strict instructions to bring you back immediately. James has been calling me nonstop for the past half an hour. We're leaving now."

"Excuse me," the detective working with Officer Daugherty said. "I found this at the top of the stairs. Does this mean anything to you? Possibly about why the assailant may have attacked the victim?"

I took the crumpled slip of paper from his hand and quickly read the brief note:

"If you marry her, I will end you. There is no coming back from this."

"He knew," I said in a whisper. James fucking knew. Rob was right. James knew and he let it happen.

"Penny, as far as we knew it could have been about ending his reputation," Porter said.

"You knew about this?" I held up the note.

"We were briefed on it, yes." Porter quickly explained its significance to the detective.

The detective agreed to run it for prints. But I wasn't listening to their exchange.

Of course Porter knew. Of course Briggs knew. Because why would James tell me? He never told me anything.

I had been avoiding going back to the hospital. But it wasn't because I was shocked by what had just happened.

Or that I was horrified that my new apartment was now a crime scene. I was still standing here because I was furious. The whole time James was unconscious, I blamed myself. I thought that it was somehow my fault.

But Porter was right, this wasn't my fault. It was James'. He had hidden something from me again and I was so angry I could almost feel the anger pumping through my veins. Rob came here because he could feel it too. The secrets. Rob was hurt and unconscious because James hid something important from both of us. And I knew there was no solid evidence of that, or whatever people kept telling me. But I had a piece of paper from Isabella saying she'd try to kill him if he married me. That was the interpretation. And I knew James. I knew that he thought that's what it meant too, but he decided to keep it from me. And at this moment, I hated him for that. I hated him for what had happened. I hated that he always tried to protect me when I didn't need protecting. All I needed was the truth.

And I wasn't just mad about that either. I was mad at him for having a DNR. I was mad at him for thinking he could control everything in both our lives and that he'd just be willing to leave it without asking me. He had changed his will after he met me. He had left me all his money. But that was the whole problem. He had decided to leave it to me because he decided that if he got hurt he'd leave me without trying to fight. He willingly decided to give up on the life we created together without even asking me what I thought.

And the worst part was that he'd lied again. Because that's all he seemed capable of. It hurt me to the core that he was still keeping things from me. Yes, maybe he didn't want children because he thought he'd be a bad dad. His father had been awful to him growing up. His role model was crap. I understood that. I understood that he was worried his addiction problem might put his children in jeopardy. I understood it all because that was the crap that he fed me. But it seemed to me that he didn't want a child because he thought he lost one. That he was still silently grieving a baby that never existed. And I hated him for not sharing that with me. I hated him for not sharing his pain with me. I loved James more than I thought I could ever love another human being. But I fucking hated him too.

"You're right. Let's go back to the hospital." I needed to have a word with my husband.

CHAPTER 32

Thursday

When I arrived back at the hospital, James was arguing with the nurse. He was trying to stand up and the nurse kept telling him to stay in bed. He looked pale from the effort. I wanted to be able to comfort him. I wanted to be able to tell him that everything was going to be okay, but I didn't know that it was. I didn't know that it could be.

He glanced at the door and spotted me. "Penny! Are you okay? I've been trying to reach you."

I swallowed hard and walked into the room.

"You need to sit down, Mr. Hunter," the nurse said. "This is your last warning or I'm going to have to sedate you."

James stopped trying to get past her and sat down on the edge of the bed. He was breathing heavily when I reached him.

"Are you hurt?" He winced as he reached up to touch the side of my face.

"I'm fine."

"Is Rob okay?" he asked. "Is he going to be okay?"

I could hear the pain in his voice. But all I could think about was the fact that he shouldn't just be upset. He should feel guilty.

"I don't know. He's unconscious. His leg is broken and he has a bullet in his right shoulder. There was so much blood." I pressed my lips together. I wasn't going to cry right now.

The pain wasn't just in James' voice. It was all over his face. He did feel guilty. He knew this was his fault. But he wasn't saying anything. He wasn't telling me the truth. And he certainly wasn't letting me in. I wanted to hug him and slap him at the same time.

"Do you know why Rob was there in the first place?" I didn't give him a chance to answer. "Because he thought his big brother was dying. And he wanted justice for you. He was searching for evidence that Isabella was behind the shooting. Because of something that you said to him. About how you wanted him to watch out for me if something happened to you. And that you were willing to die for me."

"Penny..."

"Because you knew what Isabella was planning to do! You knew." My voice cracked on the last word. "You knew, James."

He didn't say anything.

"Rob got hurt trying to find evidence to put Isabella behind bars. He got hurt trying to protect you. Because you thought lying to us protected us. It didn't, James. It only ever hurts me. It hurts me."

"Penny..."

"No, James. I spent every day by your bed torturing myself. Blaming myself. Agonizing over my mistakes. It almost killed me. Every time you tell me something new, I feel like it's the last secret you have. That you finally trust me completely. But that's not the case. It's never the case. Now's the time for you to throw out insults and push me away. Go ahead. Tell me to leave. Kick me out of your life. Tear me down like you love to do. Because pain is easier for you than love."

"Penny." He coughed. "Damn it." His knuckles were turning white, holding himself up on the bed.

I should have gone to him. I should have comforted him. But I couldn't. "We're broken, James. You broke us."

He didn't look sad anymore. He looked angry. "What was I supposed to do, Penny? I wasn't going to let Isabella dictate how I lived my life. I wasn't going to let anyone do that ever again. I'm so sick of people telling us we can't be together. Choosing to be with you is the only good decision I've ever made in my whole fucking life. No one is ever going to tell me that we can't be together. Fuck that."

"Then why would you risk your life knowing you had a DNR? You basically signed your death certificate. You never really wanted this. That hurts even more than the secrets and lies. The fact that you'd leave me without fighting. The fact that you'd throw this all away. How could you?"

"I don't have a DNR."

"Stop lying to me. I thought we were finally on the same page. I thought we were finally okay. I'm going to go see how Rob is."

"Don't walk out like this. You told me you'd stay with me. You shouldn't have been in our apartment anyway. Why did you go when you said you wouldn't?"

"Because I was trying to take care of you!"

"And that's no different than anything I did."

"I didn't purposely put myself in danger, James."

"Well you were in danger anyway. Penny." He reached one of his hands out to me. "Please."

"And you should have told me about why you really married Isabella."

"I did tell you."

DEVOTION

I shook my head. "I know about the baby."

He sighed. "You don't understand. Give me a chance to explain."

"I've given you a million chances." I couldn't look at him anymore. I couldn't see him in pain and feel so much anger toward him. It was too hard. I couldn't do this.

He called after me as I closed the door. Nothing he could say could make me understand.

***

"Are you going to come in or just stare at me?"

I hadn't realized that Rob had seen me. I was lost in thought. I smiled and walked into his room. The doctor told me that he had woken up as soon as he got to the hospital. They had put a cast on his leg and taken the bullet out of his arm. He had a concussion and a lot of blood loss. But he was going to be okay. And he already looked more animated than James. "How are you feeling?"

"Like shit." He laughed. "I can't believe I got beat up by a girl."

"I heard she took you by surprise and whacked you in the back of the head."

"Still. It's embarrassing."

"Does it help to know that I knocked her out with a frying pan?"

He smiled. "A little, yeah." He stared down at the cast on his leg. "The doctor said I would have bled out if someone didn't find me."

I wasn't a hero in this scenario. I had been so blind to not see what had been unfolding. "Rob." I sat down next to his bed and grabbed his hand. "I thought...I thought you were dead. I've never..."

"Being beat up by a girl is embarrassing enough. Being murdered by one? Now that's an awful way to go."

I laughed. "I'm being serious."

"I hate serious."

I shook my head. "Still. I was so upset that I'd never get to tell you that you're one of my best friends."

"One of your best friends? I'm honored. Does that mean I get to sleep with you like Tyler did?"

"Ugh." I removed my hand from his and gently slapped his forearm. "Seriously, I didn't have siblings growing up and I just feel like you're the brother I never had."

"Stop getting sentimental on me, sugar tits."

"You're the worst," I said with a laugh.

"Is that the kind of thing you say about one of your best friends?"

I sighed and leaned back in the chair. "Where's Daphne?"

"Getting me pizza."

"Are you allowed to be eating pizza?"

Rob shrugged. "Ow, fuck." He looked down at his shoulder. "When have I ever not done something I wasn't supposed to?"

"Fair point."

"So..." he let his voice trail off as he looked at me.

"So, what?"

"Did you tell James that he's going to be a dad?"

"We didn't get around to that yet."

"What? How could you not have told him that immediately when he woke up?"

"He was supposed to be resting. And I didn't want to upset him. And now...now I'm too mad at him. He knew, Rob. He knew Isabella was going to try to hurt him."

"I knew that he knew. That was the whole reason why I was looking for the evidence."

"You could have been killed."

"But I wasn't." He flashed me a smile. "So what's the problem?"

"I'm so mad at him."

"Then why are you in here talking to me instead of fighting with him?"

"I don't want to fight with him. He's supposed to be resting."

"And when has James ever not done something he's not supposed to?"

I put my chin in my hand. God, they were so similar. "I want to tell him on his birthday. All the presents I got him suck."

"You've never been good at getting him gifts. I'm telling you, for the hundredth time, all he wants is head."

I rolled my eyes.

Rob smiled. "But telling him you're pregnant might beat it."

"Yeah?"

"I'd do both just to be safe."

"You're the worst."

Rob laughed. "I love you too."

CHAPTER 33

Thursday

"I'm sorry," James said as soon as I walked back into his room. He was lying in his bed again. He looked completely out of energy.

"Me too." He didn't invite me, but I climbed up onto his bed anyway and rested my head on his shoulder.

He immediately put his arm around me, placing his hand firmly on my hip. I hadn't realized how much I had missed this. I needed his touch. Somehow it was the only thing that sustained me.

"I'm so sorry," I said. "With everything that's happened...I was just so overwhelmed. But all that really matters is that everyone's okay."

"What about us? Are we okay?"

"Just because I'm mad at you doesn't mean I don't love you. I'll always love you."

He stayed silent. I listened to the sound of his heart beating. It seemed to be the only thing that could calm me down recently. My emotions were everywhere. The doctor had said that was normal. Apparently my hormones were crazy right now. She had even said the word crazy, which made me feel even crazier.

"I should have told you about the baby," James said. "I don't like to think about that time in my life. It's hard for me. And when Isabella lost the baby, that was hard too. Especially because I never really believed her. I thought she had been lying about being pregnant. And when she lost the baby I felt so guilty for never accepting it in the first place. For being mad at it. That baby was just another reason why I had to marry her. I still feel awful about what happened. I still feel guilty for never wanting it in the first place."

"James, she was never pregnant."

"She was. And I'm sorry I didn't tell you..."

"No, she lied. She told me that she faked it. All of it."

He exhaled slowly. "God, I'm such an idiot."

I lifted my head so I could face him. "She's very convincing. I understand why you believed her."

"I should have known. I had already suspected it. But then I was so blinded by my guilt. Fuck, she must have seen that too." He looked up at the ceiling.

"You would have been a good father."

He laughed, exasperated. "No. That's the whole thing, Penny. I didn't even want it. I think I proved that I'd be a terrible father. Everything else I told you is true too, though. How I'm worried about being like my dad. How I'm worried I won't be present because of my own issues. I'd make a shitty father."

"That's not true."

"I like it just being the two of us. Father's have to be selfless. And I'm too selfish. I want you all to myself." He kissed the top of my head.

I blinked away my tears. "James, you are selfless. Everything you do is to protect me. That's kind of the whole reason we were fighting in the first place."

"I'm not selfless. Being an addict has put my family through so much pain. A selfless person wouldn't have done that. I wouldn't have been so consumed with my own pain that I stopped caring about everyone else."

"Everyone makes mistakes."

"You don't. You're perfect."

I laughed. "I'm not perfect."

"No." He tucked a loose strand of hair behind my ear. "If you were perfect, you'd be kissing me right now. Because we haven't kissed since our wedding day."

I put my hand on the side of his face. "James, I'm sorry about earlier. I'm just so happy that you're awake. I'm so happy that..."

He grabbed the back of my head and lowered my face toward his until our lips met. It was everything I had been missing. He had looked completely spent, but his kiss made it seem like he wasn't. I let myself melt into him. I tried to completely forget the horrific events of the day. But there was still one thing bothering me.

I pressed my forehead against his and breathed him in. "James, why did you have a DNR? It hurt me so much to find that out. I just don't understand why you'd have that."

"I don't know why you keep saying that." He ran his finger across my lower lip. "I don't have one."

I lifted my face away from his. "You do. Your lawyer had the forms."

He lowered his eyebrows. "I had one. Years ago. Before I met you. Because I wasn't happy in my life. Because I didn't have anything I cared about. But I got rid of it when I moved to Newark and filed for divorce. I was trying to start over. I'd never have one now. You know that."

"I don't know what to tell you. You do have one. The hospital is worried that you're going to sue them for restarting your heart. I had to beg the doctor. And if she didn't know..." I cleared my throat. I'd tell him on his birthday. Not right now. "If she hadn't made that decision, you would have died."

"Well, the lawyer was wrong."

"Rob basically harassed him trying to get him to change it. He was rather insistent that he couldn't." Isabella's words came back to me. When I had asked her who was working with her. "Does Isabella have the same lawyer as you?"

"No. I got a new lawyer during our divorce."

"I bet she somehow convinced your lawyer to change it."

"He'd get disbarred. There's no reason why he'd agree to that."

"Yes there is. Money."

James nodded.

"We need to talk to the police."

"Isabella is in jail. Right now we're safe. And I'm exhausted. We can talk to them in the morning. Please."

"Of course." I rested my head back down on his shoulder.

"Don't leave this time." He yawned.

"I won't. I promise."

CHAPTER 34

Friday

"Hey, lovebirds," Mason said.

Bee laughed.

I slowly opened my eyes. James was smiling. He looked so handsome. He looked just like himself again. Everything was going back to normal. Everything was good again.

"Hey, guys," I said and sat up. "It must be a good sign if they're letting non-family visit."

"I think so," Mason said. "Although we would have snuck in either way. Doctors are the worst."

He looked so much better than he had the other day. I knew it was his investigators that had helped find out that Isabella had snuck into James' hospital room. It was because of him that Porter had come up to my apartment. It was because of him Rob and I weren't dead. But before I could say anything, James cut in.

"Congratulations, you two," James said and tried to sit up. He grimaced a little less than he had yesterday. "I'm so sorry I missed it. Tell me everything."

"What?" Bee said.

Mason was rapidly shaking his head.

"Still a little out of it?" Bee asked and sat down on the edge of the bed.

"Yeah, I guess."

"We were so worried about you. You really didn't miss much. We've just been waiting for you to wake up." She smiled at him.

"Yeah, man," Mason said. "We only left the hospital to eat and sleep. He put his hand on Bee's shoulder. When Bee turned back toward us, Mason shook his head again and repeatedly mouthed what I thought was, "Shut the fuck up."

James yawned. "It's so good to see you guys. Thanks for sticking around. Sorry I made you wait so long."

"Nowhere we'd rather be," Mason said with a smile. Whatever he had been secretly trying to tell James, he seemed content that James had gotten the hint. "You gave us all a scare."

"Getting shot will do that, I guess."

"It's seriously too soon to joke about it," Bee said. "Can we get you anything?"

"No. You guys should go home. Spend some time just the two of you."

"What the fuck?" Mason mouthed silently at him.

"Are you sure?" Bee said. "We thought maybe we could all have breakfast together."

"We have to talk to the police anyway," James said. "There's still a few more things we need to sort out."

"I think we're being dismissed," Bee said with a laugh.

"Yeah," Mason said and gave James a death stare. "Let's go home. I really am exhausted." He wrapped his arm around Bee's waist. "And I could use some alone time." His hand slipped to her ass.

"Oh my God." She shoved his hand away. "We'll be back later. Stay out of trouble, you two."

"Maybe we should be saying that to you," I said with a laugh.

Bee laughed and Mason pulled her to the door.

"I'll be back in one second." I slipped off the bed and ran after Mason.

"Mason!" I said. He turned around and gave me a small smile. Almost as if he had put on a show for James. So that James wouldn't really know how much Mason cared. I'd never understand men.

"Thank you, Mason. For everything." I gave him a big hug.

He patted my back. "What exactly are you thanking me for?"

"Porter came up to the apartment because of what your investigators found out. If it wasn't for you..."

"You mean, if I hadn't interfered James would be single right now? I finally could have had him all to myself!"

"Mason!" Bee said and lightly shoved his shoulder.

"I'm just kidding, Penny."

"And thank you for being here. For both of us."

"I meant what I said. There was nowhere else I'd rather be." He squeezed me and then released me from his hug.

"And thanks, Bee." I gave her a hug too.

"These past few weeks have been such a rollercoaster ride," she said and hugged me back. "I hope that you know you can count on me now."

"I know. And I already knew it." I stepped back. "I love you guys."

Bee smiled. "We love you too."

Mason nodded. "Go back to your husband. I'm feeling weirdly emotional and if you ever saw me cry I'd never live it down."

"Maybe if Rob saw you cry. I wouldn't judge you."

"Not a risk I'm willing to take." He winked at me.

I laughed. "I'll see you guys later." I watched them walk away toward the waiting room. James and I were so lucky to have them in our lives. I slowly walked back into James' room and sat down on the bed beside him. "So, what was that about?"

"What was what about?"

"You congratulated them. And then Mason kept shaking his head."

"Yeah, I don't know. I guess I must have had a weird dream or something."

"I know that you're lying. And now that we're married you said you could break bro-code." I lay down next to him.

"I probably should have never agreed to that."

I laughed. "Come on, tell me. I'm not going to stop nagging you until you do."

He smiled. "I thought they'd be engaged."

"What?"

"They were supposed to meet us in Venice last Saturday. Bee's always wanted to go to Italy too. I'm guessing they didn't go?"

"They've been here this whole time, waiting for you to wake up."

"Shit. He's been planning it for over a year. Or at least, he's been worrying about it for over a year."

"You know, he said there was nowhere he'd rather be than here."

James laughed. "Yeah that was nice, but he didn't mean it. I fucked everything up."

"James, he did mean it. You should have seen how upset he was when you were in your coma. I've never seen him like that."

James' lips parted like he was about to say something, but then he closed them again.

"Besides, I'm sure he has a backup proposal plan," I said.

"I don't think he thought he'd need one. And he's been so nervous about it."

"Why would he be nervous? Bee is definitely going to say yes."

"That doesn't make it any less scary. I was terrified when I proposed to you. I thought you'd say yes, but it had only been two months. And even if we had been dating for a few years, I still would have been nervous."

"I would have said yes no matter when you'd asked." I looked up into his dark brown eyes. "And I don't think you need to worry about ruining anything for Mason and Bee. This city is where they met. It means so much to both of them. He really should be proposing here. I mean, isn't it nice that we can go visit Main Street whenever we want to reminisce? You even bought the coffee shop so that it would never change."

He smiled. "That's true."

"Actually, I have a bet for you."

"And what is that?"

"I bet you that he ends up proposing at the top of the Empire State Building. Whenever Bee and I pass it, she still gets stars in her eyes. She told me that everything changed for them when he took her there on the Valentine's Day after they met. Actually, she said she had been worried he was going to propose and that it was too early. But I bet she wouldn't be worried this time."

James laughed.

"I feel like I should text Mason and tell him that."

"That would be cheating on our bet. Besides, I've been interfering in their relationship since the very start. Let him do this his way."

"He probably will propose there without me saying anything at all. It just makes sense. Besides, if I've learned anything the past couple weeks, it's how sweet and caring Mason is. Behind that rough exterior. I still remember when I first met him. When we ran into him in that hotel. His gaze chilled me to the bone. I'm pretty sure Bee saved his soul."

"Saved his soul?" James looked like he wanted to laugh.

"Yes. Like I saved yours."

"Is that so?" He raised his left eyebrow.

"Don't look at me like that, James."

"Like what?"

"You know like what. You're in a hospital bed."

"I'm pretty sure last time we were in a hospital bed together and the roles were reversed, I told you that I loved you for this first time. And then I made love to you." He lightly touched my cheek. "I like that I can still make you blush."

"I'm not blushing." I tried to hide my smile.

"You are." His fingers slid to my neck.

"James, you're supposed to be resting."

"I'm tired of resting." His hand slid down my neck.

"The doctor hasn't cleared you for that yet."

"Have you asked?"

"Of course I haven't asked."

"You're blushing again." He gave me one of those smiles that instantly made me wet.

Damn it. "Don't be ridiculous."

"You're allowed to ask when you're allowed to make love to your husband."

"Yeah, when we leave the hospital. You only just woke up. And you can't even stand up without grimacing in pain."

"I'm pretty sure that will make me feel better."

I laughed and stood up as someone knocked on the door of James' room. My smile faded when someone I didn't know walked in.

"Excuse me Mr. and Mrs. Hunter. I'm Detective Lee. I've been assigned to your case after the arrest of Isabella Hunter. I have a few questions for you."

"Of course," James said. He didn't look like he was in nearly as much pain as he pushed himself up into a sitting position.

"After yesterday's incident and a statement from Cliff Stern, we know that Isabella impersonated your maid, Ellen Price, in order to gain access to your apartment. Rob Hunter arrived at the scene after Isabella was already inside. He was hit in the back of the head with her gun and proceeded to fall down the staircase where he struggled to get up and was then shot in the shoulder and hit again in the back of the head until he lost consciousness."

"He was shot after he was already unconscious."

"You were present for the shooting?"

"Yes. I already told Officer Daugherty all of this. Isabella was trying to stage a scenario that made it look like I was the one that was behind James' shooting."

Detective Lee scanned his notes. "Officer Daugherty must have left that out of the notes. Or maybe I'm missing a page. I'll give him a call this afternoon. Isabella is currently being questioned by him at the precinct. For now, could you just run through said scenario again for me real quick?"

Shit. I had already told Officer Daugherty all of this. He had talked about how the scenario didn't make any sense because they would have found out that I wasn't pregnant during my autopsy. So I had to tell him that I was pregnant. I didn't want James to find out like this. "Could we maybe talk in private?"

"Of course," Detective Lee said.

"Baby, it's okay," James said and lightly touched my back. "I want to know what happened."

I exhaled slowly. This didn't really matter. Officer Daugherty already had my official statement. I wasn't even sure why Detective Lee needed to know this. "Yeah, of course. She just wanted to make it seem like Rob and I were having an affair or something. The whole thing was ridiculous."

"Got it," the detective said and jotted something in his notebook. "After you left the crime scene yesterday, we located a duffle bag underneath your bed with a sniper rifle in it. There weren't any prints on the bag or gun and the rifle wasn't registered. Does it belong to one of you?"

"No," James said. "I would never own a gun."

I shook my head. "Isabella was wearing cleaning gloves. That's probably why there weren't any prints. She had broken into the apartment to frame me."

"So there was no premeditation of violence?"

"No, but she didn't hesitate at all to escalate it to that. She tried to kill both Rob Hunter and Cole Porter. And if it wasn't for Cole, she would have killed me."

"Okay," he said and jotted something else into his notebook.

"She mentioned that she had a lot of connections. It made it seem like there were a lot of people working with her. And James and I both found it odd that his lawyer insisted that he had a DNR, since James is insisting that he does not. Could you look into that? Maybe he's one of them?"

"What's your lawyers name?"

"John Litt," said James. "He's a name partner at the law firm Ellis Litt. I really can't imagine him being behind any of this."

"But we'd appreciate you looking into it," I said.

Detective Lee looked back and forth between us and jotted something in his notebook. "I'm going to try again to get a hold of Officer Daugherty to get the rest of the paperwork and an update on the questioning. Hopefully Isabella will be willing to cut a deal to name some of her accomplices."

"A deal? What kind of deal?" Isabella had been right. She'd never end up in prison. We'd never be able to get away from her.

"We'll have to see. I see the situation with Mr. Porter and Mr. Hunter as attempted murder, but there are defenses against that. Your brother, Mr. Hunter, not you Mr.

Hunter." He suddenly looked a little flustered. "We're still trying to link her to the other crimes. Was there anything else that you forgot to mention to Officer Daugherty yesterday? Anything at all?"

I frowned. "What about the note where Isabella threatened to end James if he married me? That was a blatant threat. Isn't that enough to prove that she tried to kill James? She even told me she tried to kill him twice."

"We're still looking into it. Unfortunately, like all the other notes in evidence, there were no prints. Is there anything else?"

Neither James nor I said anything.

"Very well. Your doctor wanted to have a word with you. I'll let her know I'm done questioning you. Thanks for your patience with this. We're doing everything we can to sort all of this out."

I found his statement ironic. Because I wasn't being patient at all. And I was furious with the way they were handling this. When he left the room I turned to James. "What if they let her go? What if..."

"Penny. It's going to be okay. We have to let them do their job."

"Since when do you trust them?"

"I don't have the energy to not trust them right now."

It broke my heart to see him in his hospital bed. It broke my heart that I couldn't fix this. "But you have enough energy to have sex?" I wanted him to laugh. I wanted him to not worry about anything. I needed to step up and handle this.

He gave me a small smile. "That's different."

I shook my head. "How about we focus on getting you out of here, okay?"

"That sounds like a great idea," the doctor said as she walked into the room. "How are you feeling today, James?"

"Great." He sat up and kept a level face, not showing his pain at all. But I could see it in his eyes. "Much better. When can I get out of here?"

She picked up his chart and looked at it.

"His birthday is on Sunday," I said. "Is there any way he could be home for that?"

"I think we can arrange that. Even though you were unconscious, your body has been healing for two weeks."

"What about Rob? Will he be able to get out of here soon too?" James asked.

She smiled. "I've already agreed to discharge your brother tomorrow morning. He won't stop pestering me to come see you, but I told him I'd change my mind if he refused to rest. But the injuries you sustained were much more serious than your brother's."

"How is he doing?"

"He's acting like he's perfectly fine. The bullet in his shoulder had a clean exit and the break in his leg was also fairly clean, but it's pretty miraculous how quickly he's recovering. I'm sure he'll be stopping by first thing tomorrow morning."

James nodded.

"I'm going to have the nurse come in and give you a few vaccines. And according to your chart you're also behind on some of your regular immunizations. We'll have her administer those too. It's important that you stay on top of those from now on. After a splenectomy, it's much more likely to contract infections. You're at a much greater risk now."

James nodded again.

"And we need to discuss your blood pressure."

"What about it?"

"I have your most recent checkup information from your primary care physician. Which was from six years ago. Your blood pressure was already borderline then. And he had recommended you come in the next year for a follow up. Which you did not."

"It's hard for me to get time off work."

The doctor gave him a stern stare. "Well, James, it's not borderline anymore. You have stage 1 hypertension. Although it is not proven that stress causes long-term high blood pressure, before you woke up, your blood pressure was fine. As soon as you came out of your coma it sky-rocketed again. So in this case, I feel like it is related. If you don't make active changes, this is going to become an issue."

"This situation has been stressful. That's all."

"And six years ago? Most people in your physical condition in their early twenties don't have this problem."

James pressed his lips together.

"There are medications we can prescribe to lower..."

"No," he said. "I don't want any medication."

"Then you need to actively pursue a less stressful lifestyle. I'm recommending that you take at least the next two weeks off to fully recover from your splenectomy anyway. And we'll continue to monitor the healing of your lung. Take things slowly. You'll be able to tell when your body can resume normal physical activity. You'll be running again in no time, I'm sure."

"And what about intercourse?" James said without a hint of embarrassment in his voice.

I was mortified.

"As newlyweds, I don't think anything I could say would dissuade you from that," she said and smiled. "But maybe keep it to positions where you exert less effort, though."

Oh my God.

"I'll send the nurse in."

As soon as she walked out I lightly slapped James' shin.

He smiled and slowly put his hands behind his head. "I think reverse cowgirl counts, don't you?"

"What is wrong with you?"

"I'm pretty sure she just said we could do that."

"She also said the nurse was about to come in."

"I stopped listening after that. But maybe that would be good. You always have been excited by the thought of people watching..."

I ignored his last comment. "Well, she also said your blood pressure is too high. That you're too stressed out. I think we need to talk about that."

"I was thinking we should do something besides talk."

I laughed as he pulled me down into his arms.

"I was stressed out when you left me. And I was worried when I woke up. That's it." He put his hand on my cheek. "I'm not stressed out now. I'm sure if she took my blood pressure right now it would be excellent."

"Excellent, huh?"

He pulled my face toward his. "Excellent." His lips gently brushed against mine.

I immediately scooted off the bed when the nurse walked in. I held his hand and looked into his eyes. He didn't even flinch when the nurse started to give him his first shot. For a second I wondered if he had ever taken drugs that way. But I didn't really want to know the answer. That was who he used to be. *The man in front of me right now is who he truly is.* I was optimistic that nothing would get in the way of our future again. I was still worried about how he'd react to hearing about the baby. But I knew he'd eventually be excited. He had to want it.

***

James had fallen asleep early. When he was in his coma, it had been agonizing to watch him. But it wasn't like this. Now he looked peaceful and happy. Whenever I woke up before him, I always asked him what he had been dreaming about. He always said he had been dreaming of me. I knew that couldn't really always be true, but I loved when he said it.

My phone buzzed and I looked down at the screen. I quickly answered it before it buzzed again. "Hey, Tyler."

"Hey. I heard he woke up."

"Yeah." I smiled at James and then walked over to the window so I wouldn't disrupt his sleeping.

"How is he doing?"

"Good. He's a lot better today than he was yesterday. And I think they're going to discharge him for his birthday."

"And how are you holding up?"

"Better now that he's awake."

He was silent for a second. "The cops stopped calling me. I saw what happened on the news. How Isabella broke into your house. Are you okay?"

"I'm good. And yeah, they arrested her. They shouldn't be bothering you anymore."

"Thanks, Penny."

"How are you?" I held my breath as I waited for his response. *Please be good. Please don't be hurting because of me.*

He was silent again. "Better. Actually, I met someone."

"Really?"

He laughed. "Don't sound so surprised."

"I'm not. Any girl would be lucky to be with you."

"Oh, no, we're not dating or anything. She actually just needed a ride to the west coast. We're just friends."

"What's her name?"

"Hailey."

"So you're on a road trip with a relative stranger. Are you trying to get yourself killed?"

He laughed again. "No, just learning how to live again."

"You're having fun then?"

"Yeah. I'm having lots of fun."

"Good."

"This was exactly what I needed."

"Hailey or the trip?"

He was silent again for a second. "Both, maybe. I should go, Penny."

"When do you think you're coming back?"

"I don't know. I'll stay in touch, though. Tell James I said I hope he makes a speedy recovery."

"I will. And don't pick up any scary hitchhikers."

"I think I'm good with just the one. Bye, Penny."

"Bye."

It wasn't our normal flow of conversation, but he did sound better. I wondered what Hailey was like. Hopefully she was sweet and caring and loyal.

"Who was that?"

I almost jumped at James' voice. I thought he had been sleeping. "Tyler. He wanted me to tell you that he hopes you have a speedy recovery." I sat down on the edge of James' bed.

"I shouldn't have punched him."

"Next time he calls I'll tell him you're sorry."

"I never said I apologized. I just said I shouldn't have done it."

"What's the difference?"

"I should have had enough control not to do it. It doesn't mean he didn't deserve it."

"I don't think you're going to be getting into any fights for awhile."

James smiled. The way the moonlight shining through the blinds hit his face made him look even more handsome.

"And it sounds like he's met someone."

"Yeah?"

"Mhm. Her name is Hailey. He didn't actually say it, but I could tell that he really likes her."

"That's good."

I lay down next to him. "James, you're all that I think about. There's never been enough room in my heart for anyone but you. You never had anything to worry about. And now that we're married? It's a done deal." I smiled up at him.

"A done deal?" He yawned and kissed my forehead.

"I'm sorry that I woke you."

"It's okay. Actually, I almost forgot to ask you. How did you find out Porter's first name?"

I smiled. I had been wondering when he'd ask me that. "I'm just very persistent."

"He's a rock. I know that's not it."

I shrugged. "He could tell how upset I was. He was trying to cheer me up."

"Hmm."

"He told me how you two met too."

"He wasn't supposed to divulge any personal details about his life."

"Have you ever thought that you may have too many rules? It's probably stressing you out."

He laughed.

"I'm more comfortable with first names. And he saved my life. Calling him Porter is way too formal."

"I haven't gotten a chance to thank him yet."

"It's the middle of the night. Go back to sleep."

"He's out there, isn't he?"

"Paul and him have been taking turns watching your door, yes."

"And you're calling Briggs Paul now?"

"That's his name."

"Well, if Porter is out there, he's already awake. Go tell him to come in."

"He was worried you were going to fire him, you know." I slid off the bed.

"Really?"

"He probably thinks you don't like him because you call him by his last name."

"He asked me to call him by his last name. And I'd never fire him. He saved your life."

The way James said it made it seem like there was nothing in the world that could outdo that. Because he felt the same way I did. He was my whole world. And I was his.

"I'll go get him." I opened up the door. The hallway was completely empty except for Briggs. And he was sitting on the floor. Crying. I let the door close behind me.

"Paul, what's wrong?" I put my hand on his shoulder.

He cleared his throat and stood up. But he didn't look any less exasperated.

"Are you okay?"

He shook his head. "Penny, I'm so, so sorry."

"I already told you that there's nothing to be sorry for. You couldn't have known what was going to happen. Please don't be upset about that."

"No." He pulled out a handkerchief as he shook his head. "I'm sorry for this." He placed his hand with the handkerchief in it over my mouth and pushed me back against the wall.

I tried to scream, but his hand muffled my voice. A strange smell filled my nose.

"They threatened to kill my wife and daughter," Briggs said.

I clawed at his hand.

"I know you understand that. I know you'd do anything to protect him. You have to understand."

I kicked him as hard as I could and reached for his throat. He was so much bigger than me.

"Please forgive me."

I thought my mind would grow fuzzy. Or I'd start to fall asleep. But nothing really happened. My body just felt strange. And the smell was everywhere.

He glanced over his shoulder and pulled out his phone. "It's done." He hung up the phone and looked back at me.

"I didn't have a choice, Penny." His eyes had never stopped looking teary. His face looked distorted as everything started spinning. He let go of my mouth. I tried to tell him not to leave, but nothing came out of my mouth. I tried to scream, but again there was only silence. My body slumped to the ground. The ground twisted in front of me and my eyelids grew heavy. The last thing I saw was Isabella walking toward me.

CHAPTER 35

Friday

"He's so handsome, isn't he?"

I slowly opened my eyes as James' hospital room came into focus. I had a terrible headache. I tried to lift my arms but I couldn't. I looked down at my hands. My wrists were bound to the chair handles with duct tape. My eyes flashed toward the voice.

Isabella was smiling at me. Her hand was on the side of James' face. "Wouldn't you agree that he's handsome?"

"James!"

"No use yelling."

"What did you do to him?" Why was James sleeping? He looked like he had when he was in his coma again. What had she done to him?

"The nurse didn't just give James vaccines earlier. She injected him with a slow release sedative. He's knocked out cold." She ran her fingers through the scruff on his chin.

"Get your hands off him." I tried to move, only to find that my ankles were taped to the chair too.

"You don't like when I touch him?" Her hand slid to the side of his neck. "It must haunt you that I've touched every inch of his skin. And that he's touched every inch of mine."

I swallowed hard.

She ran her index finger across his lips. "And not just with his hands. He's kissed every inch of my skin too. I always liked how fierce he was in bed. How passionate he was. Is he like that with you too?"

"Go to hell, Isabella!"

"I'm only going to ask you once to keep your voice down. And I won't be dying today, Penny. It's actually going to be you that will be entering the gates of hell in about," she looked at the clock next to James' bed, "ten minutes. First I get to have some fun." She pulled down the front of James' hospital gown. "And his muscles. They're enough to drive a girl crazy." She ran her fingers down his six pack.

I wiggled my wrists, trying to weaken the duct tape. I was going to kill her. I was going to fucking kill her.

"What's it like to see another woman with your husband? Stings, doesn't it?"

"He had filed for divorce before I even met him."

"And if he divorced you, wouldn't you still be jealous?" Her fingers wandered down his happy trail. "Possessive even?"

"Stop touching him."

She smiled. "I'll take that as a yes." She sat down on the edge of his bed. "It must drive you crazy knowing that he used to scream my name. That he used to crave my lips. That I used to satisfy him in every way imaginable."

I shook my head. "I can't change the past."

"No. You can't. But you can change the future. Or rather, I can." She smiled her cruel smile. "This is really for the best. You weren't good for him. You just fed his sickness. All this ever was between you was addiction."

"He's not addicted to me!"

"No, I guess not. He's just addicted to sex. You're just something he's going to use and cast aside. Just like he did with me. Now, I did tell you that I'd only ask you once to keep your voice down. There will be consequences for that. Slow, painful consequences. Which I'll enjoy, so thank you."

I tried to ignore her threats. "He's not addicted to sex either. He's been clean for years."

"No? Maybe we should ask him." She picked a needle up off the nightstand that I hadn't seen before.

"What are you doing?"

"Giving him adrenaline to counteract the effect of his sedative slowly. Very slowly. So that he'll be able to watch me kill you and won't be able to do anything about it. He'll almost be paralyzed, if you will. He might even just think he's dreaming." She put the needle into his arm. "It'll just be a few minutes now. Let's play a game while we wait, shall we?"

I continued to struggle against the duct tape. It was ripping at my skin. I bit my lip, trying not to focus on the pain.

"Here's the game. If you could have one phone call right this second, who would you call?"

"The cops."

"Hmm. Wrong answer. How do you think I got here in the first place?"

"By forgetting to take your meds?"

She laughed. "I didn't realize you were funny. But no. Take a guess at why the cops would be the wrong phone call. I'll give you a hint. I'm supposed to be in custody, yet here I am."

"Because you're working with them?"

"Bingo. Officer Daugherty is a very dirty cop." She winked at me.

Fucking asshole. I knew he hadn't been helping us. This whole thing had just been a joke to him. I cringed as the tape bit at my skin.

"You'd be surprised at what someone would do for a few million dollars. And the best part is, all the money I've had to spend wasn't even mine. You gave it to me. So in a way, you really are responsible for everything that has happened to James in the past few weeks. It's been so much fun watching you fall apart. And suspecting your friends. It was priceless. And I'm a huge believer in everything having a price. I guess in this case it was actually 20 million dollars."

I needed to buy time. Someone would come in here to check on us soon. But I had a sinking feeling in my stomach. If the nurse was in on it, she wouldn't be coming. And Briggs certainly wouldn't be coming. He had betrayed us. He had drugged me. But I needed to believe that someone would come. Because I was stuck in this fucking chair. "Why did you try to frame Tyler and Melissa?"

She smiled. "Because I wanted you to feel completely and utterly alone. I wanted you to be paranoid. I wanted you to push everyone away. Because I know girls like you. You're weak. You need people around you, telling you how wonderful you are. Because you're a conceited narcissist. And you only care about yourself."

Me? That sounded more like her. "You don't know me. I didn't have many friends growing up. I found solace in reading books and escaping into their stories. My best friend used to tell me I was going to grow up to be a cat lady. I've never needed anyone until I met James. He changed me. He made me better." *He saved me.*

"How sad. I almost pity you. If you weren't such a whore."

James groaned.

"Good. He's waking up." She leaned toward him. "Good morning, baby," she said and placed a kiss against his lips.

Fucking bitch! I pulled as hard as I could, tearing at my skin. But I was still stuck to the chair. *Fuck!*

James groaned again.

He's drugged. He doesn't know it's not me. He doesn't know what's happening.

"I knew he missed me," she said and smiled at me. "He used to groan like that all the time when we were together."

"Stop."

"You should have seen the way I kissed him when I snuck into his room when you left him all alone. It was probably a foolish move when I could have had someone else mess up his ventilator, but it was so easy that I couldn't resist. Besides, I just needed to see my husband." She smiled at me. "I needed to taste him."

"Stop," I said more forcefully.

"You know what my favorite thing used to be?"

"Please stop." I continued to struggle with the restraints.

"The way his fingertips dug into my skin when he'd fuck me. He knew just how to make my toes curl. I think that was his favorite thing too. Punishing me. Being in complete control of me. God I loved that."

My whole body felt cold. I loved that too. I was letting her get in my head. I was letting her win. *Focus.* I pulled on the restraints again. I almost cried out at the pain.

She laughed. It was cold and cruel. "Everything he's done with you, he's done with me first. You know, I think I actually want him to be a little more alert for this. I want him to experience the same amount of pain he's caused me." She plunged another needle into his arm and his eyes flew open.

He immediately closed his eyes and shook his head. He opened his eyes again and stared at me in horror.

"Honey, take it slow. You've been heavily sedated." She ran her finger across his collarbone.

He closed his eyes again.

"We were just having a discussion, James. Penny doesn't think that you're addicted to her. I think it's time that you told her the truth."

"No." His voice was croaky.

"James, it's only fair that she knows the truth. Tell her."

I could tell he was trying to move. But his body wasn't responding. He opened his eyes again and gave me a pleading look.

Isabella walked toward him and put her hand on his shoulder.

He grimaced at her touch.

"Tell her," Isabella said.

He shook his head. "I'm not addicted to her."

"James." My eyes were filled with tears. This wasn't the time for him to finally realize that. I shook my head. *Lie to her. Tell her what she needs to hear.*

Isabella frowned. "Baby, you know that's not true. Tell me the truth." She ran her hand down his bare chest.

"I'm addicted to her." He wasn't staring at me. He was staring at her.

I knew it was a lie. But it still stung. And it hurt to see them together like this. With her hands on him. With his eyes on her.

"Don't tell me, James. Tell her."

His eyes darted toward the button to call the nurse.

"Tell her, James." She grabbed his chin and turned his face toward me.

James' eyes slowly met mine. "I'm addicted to you, Penny." He lowered both his eyebrows. Almost like he realized how truly wrong it was. Like he understood that it was more than that. This couldn't be the last thing he ever said to me. I couldn't let this be how we ended.

"And the only way to get rid of your addiction is to get rid of the temptation, to kill the root of the problem. In this case, Penny."

"No. Isabella, no. Let Penny go. Do whatever you want with me. But don't hurt her."

"We'll get her out of our way. We can be happy again."

"We were never happy."

"Of course we were. Before life got in the way. Before your problems became bigger than both of us."

"My problems? You ruined our marriage."

"You ruined me, James! As soon as you said you were in love with her, you ruined my whole reputation."

"You ruined your own damn reputation when you screwed around behind my back."

"But baby, you never complained about how much better the sex got. All the new techniques." She put her hand back on his chest.

"Don't fucking touch me!"

Isabella didn't remove her hand. "Look at me, James. Don't look at her. For once in your life, focus on me!"

James' eyes left mine. Originally Isabella had said I'd be dead in ten minutes. But it seemed like more time than that had passed. Maybe James' sedative would wear off soon. Maybe someone would show up and help us. My world was filled with maybes. But maybes weren't going to save me. I pulled my arms as hard as I could and accidentally let a whimper escape from my lips.

"Penny." The agony in James' voice brought tears to my eyes.

"This isn't about her!" Isabella yelled. "This is about us!" She pulled out a gun from her purse and pointed it toward me.

"Isabella, please just let her go. And we can talk."

"Is this about the baby? If you want a baby, I'll give you a baby. We were always good at practicing."

"What are you talking about?"

Isabella turned toward me with a smile on her face. "He really doesn't know?" She laughed. "This just got so much better."

"Know what?"

Isabella slid off his bed and walked toward me. "She didn't tell you? She's pregnant."

The moment I had planned in my head for telling him about the baby had been ripped from me. This would be his last memory of me. Me not telling him something. It would tear him apart. If Isabella didn't kill him, that would.

James just stared at me. He didn't say a word. The color had drained from his face. And I realized he wasn't really staring at me. He was looking past me. This wasn't how this was supposed to go. I had it all planned out.

Look at me. Please look at me. "James, I was going to tell you on your birthday. I..."

"That's quite enough." Isabella pressed the gun against the side of my forehead.

Oh God. My heart was pounding. It was all I could hear. And all I could think about was how mad I'd been the past few days. And how it was such a waste of time. Such a horrible waste of time to have anger in my heart. I should have been counting my blessings. I should have been with him the whole time. I should have been savoring it.

"Isabella, stop!" James yelled. "Please stop. You win. You win, okay? I'll do whatever you want."

"I want you to be with me. I want us to be what we used to be. I want everyone to be jealous of me again. I want my fucking life back!"

"Okay. Me too. I want it all back. I want you back."

"But what about the baby?"

"I never wanted kids. And I don't want that one. She knew that. She knew that and she got pregnant anyway. I don't want anything to do with her or that child. You know me, Isabella. You're the only one that really knows me. You're all that I want. It's always been you."

James! Look at me! I struggled against the duct tape.

Isabella pressed the gun harder against my temple. "You'll go back to her."

"No. I'll never want her as much as I want you. You know that, baby. I'll file for divorce. We can go wherever you want. Just...please come here."

The gun slowly dropped from my forehead. "I just don't understand. Why were you ever with her then? Why would you hurt me like this?"

"I pitied her. She was weak. I liked that she was young and naive and didn't know better. Because she was everything that you weren't. And it killed me that you didn't want me anymore. That someone so strong willed and sexy had cut me down. I was just trying to forget by dating someone that was so opposite of you. But I could never forget you."

Young. Naive. Weak. It was everything I didn't want to be. It was everything that I was. *Look at me James. Show me that you don't mean it.*

"I know how unforgettable I am." She ran her fingers through his hair.

And he smiled. That smile was like a knife in my heart. They looked so natural together. I looked away. Maybe he was just telling her what she needed to hear. But maybe...

"Then kiss me," he said. "Let's start over. Let's put all of it behind us. We'll be better than we ever were."

I watched as Isabella leaned down a little closer to him. And I died inside. Isabella was right. The thought of him with her had always haunted me. And now that I was about to see it? It was seared into my brain.

This couldn't be what he really wanted. This couldn't be. So why did he ask her to kiss him? To give me a chance to escape? There was no escape. I pulled my wrists as hard as I could. It just made me cry more. *Young. Naive. Weak.* I was so weak. I gritted my teeth as I pulled again on my restraints. Nothing. All I could do was watch the man I love tilt his head toward the woman he was professing his love for.

It happened in a flash. James pulled out his IV and wrapped the cord around Isabella's neck right before her lips met his.

She dropped the gun on the floor and it skittered over to the window.

"You tried to kill me, you fucking bitch!"

"James!" I screamed as Isabella struggled in his arms.

"You tried to kill my brother!" He tightened the cord around her neck. Blood trickled down his hand where his IV had been.

"James, stop!" A part of me wanted him to kill her. She had put us through hell. But this wasn't James. He would never do something like this.

"You tried to kill my wife. You threatened my family," he was choking on his words. "I was forced to give up my life to be with you once. I'll never make that mistake again. No one will ever tell me how to live my life again." He replaced the cord with his hands.

Her face was turning purple.

"James, you're not a murderer! Stop!"

"She'll never leave me alone! She'll never leave us alone." His voice cracked on the word us.

She was starting to sag in his arms.

"This isn't who you are, James!"

He let go of her throat and pushed her off the bed. Her body slumped to the ground. But I could see her chest rise with each breath. She was alive. Just unconscious.

"Did she hurt you?" James said as he ripped off the rest of the wires that were attached to him. "Are you okay?" He stumbled out of the bed and caught himself on the edge of it. "Penny?" He fell to his knees in front of me.

I couldn't respond because I was choking on my sobs. This wasn't the end. I wasn't going to die. We were going to be okay.

He ran his fingers along my skin as if searching for some sign of injury. My arms. My legs. My face. He grabbed something to cut away the duct tape and he pulled me down into his arms.

"I'm okay," I whispered. "I'm okay."

The tears in his eyes just made mine fall even faster.

"Penny." His voice sounded so hoarse. "I'm so sorry. I'm so sorry, baby."

"You're bleeding."

He smiled through his tears. "I'm fine. We're fine." He pulled my face to his chest. "You're shaking." He wrapped his arms tighter around me. "It's okay now. We're okay."

"For a second I let myself believe that the things you were saying were true," I said into his chest. "I thought, I thought..."

"No. No, Penny. I didn't mean any of it." He leaned back and put his palm on my stomach. "None of it." He was staring at my stomach. "Are you really pregnant?"

"I didn't want you to find out like this. I wanted to surprise you. I was going to give you this little onesie I picked up in the gift shop for your birthday and tell you. And I know you don't want kids. At least, not for a long time. I was stressed out before the wedding and I must have forgotten to take my birth control and..."

"Penny." He grabbed the sides of my face. "I want everything with you. All of it. And if you're pregnant, I want kids now. I want it."

"You're not mad?"

"Mad? Why would I be mad?" He laughed. "No. This baby is going to be every part of you. Sweet and kind and good. No, I'm not mad."

"I thought you'd be upset."

"No, baby." He kissed the side of my neck and pulled me against him again. "Never. I'm going to be a dad." He buried his face in my hair.

"You're going to be a great dad."

He just held me in response. I let myself cry against his shoulder. This was all I needed. For him to hold on to me. This was all I ever needed.

"Are you sure you're okay?" he whispered.

"I'm okay." I was holding on to him like he was the only thing keeping me afloat.

"And the baby? Everything's okay?"

I pulled back. "I don't know. I found out I was pregnant right after you came to the hospital. I was a mess. I couldn't eat. I... I don't know."

"I'll go tell Porter or Briggs to get the nurse."

"No." I grabbed his arm before he could get up. "Briggs was working for her. She threatened his wife and daughter. And the nurse drugged you. I don't know if she knew what she was doing or if it was an accident..."

"Is Briggs out there right now?"

"I don't know. The last thing I remember was him putting this cloth over my mouth and..."

"That son of a bitch." James grabbed the edge of the bed and slowly stood up.

"James, you need to sit down. Your stomach is bleeding." There was a blood stain on the front of his hospital gown.

He looked down at the blood.

"Something must be wrong with your stitches. You have to sit down."

James tried to walk past me but I grabbed his arm.

"James, please just sit down. I'll go get someone."

The door burst open and Briggs rushed in holding a gun. He was completely out of breath.

My heart was filled with fear. Because the gun was pointed directly at me.

"Jesus Christ," he said and kept his gun pointed at me.

James stepped in front of me.

"Get down!" Briggs yelled.

"Briggs, you don't have to do this," James said.

"I said get down!"

The room echoed with the burst of his gun.

I screamed and pulled James down behind the side of the bed. I heard glass shatter behind us. I turned my head. I'm pretty sure James saw it the same time that I did because he tried to push me behind him again. Isabella was standing in front of the broken window with the gun in her hand.

"Drop it!" Briggs shouted. "Now!"

She smiled and lifted the gun toward me and James.

Another shot echoed in the room and hit Isabella right in the chest. A third shot hit her in almost the same spot. The gun fell from her hand. She stumbled backwards and crashed through the broken window.

We heard people screaming outside and a sickening crunching noise.

"Are you both okay?" Briggs said. He knelt down next to us. He put his hand on my shoulder.

"Thank you," James said and clasped his hand.

"I'm so sorry, I..."

"It's okay. I understand. I'd do anything for my wife and baby too."

"Baby?" Briggs turned his head to me and smiled. "You're pregnant?"

I nodded. None of this news was happening the way that I had planned.

"Congratulations," he said with a big smile.

I couldn't think about this right now. I tried to run through everything Isabella had said to me in my mind. "Officer Daugherty was working with her," I said. "And possibly the nurse. I'm not sure she knew what she was doing. Find Detective Lee."

"I already called it in when I was hightailing it back here after checking to make sure my family was okay. Detective Lee is on his way. And..."

"You piece of shit!" Porter yelled as he came running into the room. He grabbed Briggs by the collar of his shirt and pushed him onto his side. He landed a hard punch across Briggs' jaw. "I trusted you!" Porter yelled as he landed another punch.

"Cole! Stop!" I tried to stand up, but James put his hand on my shoulder.

"Porter, he just saved our lives," James said.

"And you wouldn't have needed saving if he had done his job. He was behind the whole thing!" he spat and grabbed Briggs' collar again.

"Both of you stop!" James said affirmatively.

"I wasn't behind the whole thing, man," Briggs said. "Just today. She threatened my family."

"And what about when Isabella snuck in here the first time and tried to kill him?" Porter said. "Because of your stomach issues. Bullshit." He pushed him back down on the ground.

"That was true. I didn't...she didn't threaten me until today." He ran his hand down his face.

"You can tell it to the cops," Porter said and pulled him to his feet. "I'll be right back," he said and he walked Briggs out the door.

"I'm sorry," Briggs said as he was pulled out of the room. "I'm sorry!"

"We can't let him get sent to prison for this," I said.

"He drugged you." James ran his palm along the side of my face.

"And he saved you." I swallowed hard. "Is she dead?"

"I think she was dead before she even fell."

"It's over." I pressed my head against his chest.

"It's over."

CHAPTER 36

Saturday

Isabella was dead. I shouldn't have felt at peace with that. But she had been my hell. She had been James' hell. And we were both breathing easier now. I wasn't happy that she was dead. But I was happy that James and I didn't have to live in fear. I was happy that there wasn't a shadow over us. I was happy that maybe, just maybe, there was a little less weight on James' shoulders.

We had just given our statements to the police and now a silence had settled over the new hospital room they had put James in. My head was resting on James' shoulder and I was staring out the window at the sun rising.

"It's beautiful," James murmured against my temple.

I hadn't realized he was watching it too. I tilted my head up to look at his face. He smiled down at me and kissed the side of my forehead.

"Is it horrible that I feel so peaceful?"

He lowered his eyebrows slightly. "No." He pulled me in closer to his side.

"She needed help. She needed..."

"You can't get someone help unless they accept that they need it."

I nodded my head against his shoulder.

"For the first time in a long time, all I see is light." He grabbed my chin and tilted my face toward the sunrise.

I blinked away my tears. "Me too."

We both sat in silence, watching the colors stretch out over the horizon. No one was going to try to hurt us again. Everything was going to be okay. It was truly, finally over.

Rob came bursting into the room and we both turned toward him. He had kicked the door open with his cast and was now cursing under his breath.

"Rob, just wait one second!" Daphne said from behind him as she tried to grab the door to hold it open.

James laughed and Rob's face immediately looked more at ease.

"Is the troll really dead?" Rob said. He was balancing a crutch under one arm. His other arm was in a sling.

Daphne made an apologetic face.

James gripped my shoulder a little tighter. "She's dead."

"Good riddance." Rob collapsed in a chair. "Sorry it took me so long to come see you. The doctors kept delaying my discharge for no reason!" he yelled over his shoulder.

Daphne quickly closed the door.

I laughed and she started to laugh too.

"And when I finally did get discharged, the po-po wouldn't let me come in and see you until right this second. Something about collaborating witnesses or something. Trust me, I was giving them hell."

"Well, the investigation must be coming to a close if they're letting us talk now," said James.

Rob nodded. "Right, right." He glanced at me and then back at James and raised both his eyebrows.

I was just about to let James know that Rob knew about the baby when James cleared his throat.

"I'm really happy you're both here," James said. "We actually have some news."

Oops. But I didn't bother telling James they already knew. I was excited that he was so excited about it.

"Penny's pregnant. We're having a baby!" The joy in his voice was almost palpable.

"What?!" Rob said in a weirdly high pitched voice. "That is totally a huge surprise to both me and Daphne! We didn't know about that at all! How exciting!"

James laughed. "You already knew?"

"Your baby mama has a big mouth. Right, Daphne?"

Daphne's eyes got wide. "I'm not sure that's exactly what happened." She laughed awkwardly.

Rob laughed.

James turned toward me and I was surprised to see his smile vanish. "Don't cry, I'm not upset with you for telling them." He slowly wiped his thumb under my eye. "Why are you crying?"

I hadn't realized I had gotten tears in my eyes. "No, it's just...I'm so excited that you're excited."

The smile returned to his face.

Rob slowly stood up out of his chair and hobbled over to James. "You're going to make a great dad. You know you are." He clapped him hard on the back despite the fact that they were both hurt. "And my main MILF." He gave me a hug too.

James groaned.

"You don't approve of her new nickname? You better get used to it." He grabbed both sides of James' face. "You beautiful, beautiful man."

"Stop touching me."

"I'm just so happy you're alive."

"You're freaking me out," said James. "Are you still on pain killers?"

Rob laughed and released James' face. "Actually yes, yes I am." He patted James' cheek again.

"Okay, maybe I should be getting you home," Daphne said.

"If that means your house, then fine," Rob said. "Home."

Daphne wouldn't have been able to hide her smile if she had tried. I felt like I had just witnessed a big moment. He had called her place his home.

"Call us if you need anything at all," Daphne said.

"Thanks." But everyone needed to spend some time away from the hospital. I glanced at James. It looked like he was having trouble keeping his eyes open.

When Rob and Daphne left I helped him adjust his pillows so that he'd be lying down and snuggled up next to him.

"Did you catch that? He called Daphne's place his home."

"My baby brother is growing up." James yawned.

I smiled as I watched him fall asleep. We were all growing up.

CHAPTER 37
Saturday

We waited as patiently as possible in James' room. His doctor said he could probably be discharged from the hospital tonight. While we were still at the hospital, we decided we should go ahead and get an ultrasound. James was excited, but I was super nervous. I just hoped the baby was healthy. I hoped I hadn't jeopardized anything. I was absentmindedly tapping my heel against the leg of the chair waiting impatiently for the doctor to show up. I almost jumped up when the door opened.

But it was James' father. He gave us a small smile and walked over to us. "How are you feeling today?" he asked James.

"Good. Better." James smiled. Their relationship was still strained. But at least they were talking, "Actually," James said, "the doctor is about to stop by. If you could give us a minute, we'll be right out."

"Well, there's one last thing we need to discuss with Detective Lee. I asked him to meet us in here and he mentioned that he was stopping by in just a minute anyway. He said he was ready to brief us on what they had found."

"What's this about?" James asked.

"Something I had told Officer Daugherty. I'd prefer if we waited for Detective Lee." He looked down at his hands. He seemed upset.

I was too jittery to focus right now. I was excited for the ultrasound. It was all I wanted to talk about. I nudged James with my elbow. "Let's tell him," I mouthed silently.

James smiled and shrugged his shoulders.

"Jon," I said.

He immediately looked up at me.

"We have some exciting news." I smiled up at James.

"Penny's pregnant," James said and squeezed my shoulder.

A smile spread across Jon's previously distressed features. "You're having a baby? Congratulations, James." He stood up and gave James a hug.

I was almost surprised by how long it lasted. James even awkwardly patted his back.

"And Penny," he said. "I knew you'd be giving me grandchildren in no time." He gave me a hug. "Wow." He exhaled slowly as he sat back down. "I..." he laughed. "I don't even know what else to say. Congratulations. I think we all needed some good news. Penny, I know you're going to be an amazing mother. I know it." His smile seemed to disappear again.

"Really, Dad, what's this about?" James said.

Jon shook his head. "Maybe I should just discuss this with Detective Lee in private. I shouldn't have..." but his voice trailed off as Detective Lee walked in.

"I heard you get to go home today?" he said with a smile and sat down next to Jon.

I think we're all ready to get out of here," James said with a smile.

"Right, right. Well I won't keep you longer than necessary. But I have some great news. As soon as we arrested Officer Daugherty, everything started to fall into place. I wasn't doing the questioning, but apparently he sung like a canary, trying to get himself a deal to walk away scot-free. Don't worry, we won't let that happen. But it did let us round up everyone that was part of what happened to you the past few weeks. Isabella had paid Officer Daugherty five million dollars to help her. He had a gambling problem that he had kept hidden from the force and was in terrible debt. He didn't need any more convincing than that.

"You already knew about Briggs. And he hadn't been lying about not being involved the whole time. There was video footage of the nurse slipping something into his coffee to upset his stomach. Her name is Linda Vega. She's the mother of Brian Vega, one of the guys on James' threat list. We were aware that James had gotten numerous death threats from him after Hunter Tech's advancements had tanked Vega's stock price. But no one had put it together because Linda got the nursing job under a fake name. She told Isabella what to do in order to make James' lung collapse again. And she fed her information on his health status and injected James with that slow release sedative."

I squeezed James' hand. His face looked a little pale. It was a lot to take in.

"Brian Vega was involved too," Detective Lee continued. "He hacked into the bank transfer to make it seem like the money had been sent to an account owned by Tyler Stevens. But it really went into an offshore account that your lawyer, John Litt owns. Litt had a copy of the restraining order against Vega, which was how Isabella was able to find someone else who wanted James dead. Apparently John Litt and Isabella had been sleeping together ever since James and her divorce hearing. Litt will almost certainly be disbarred for accepting bribes, releasing personal information, and forging the DNR. Or just for the scandal. He's already hired the best defense lawyer in the city, but don't worry, I'll make sure he sees jail time for this.

"We took your information about the threats against Briggs' family and have decided we agree that he acted upon duress. He was an unwilling accomplice. We are all set to drop the charges against him if that's what you're sure you want to do."

Without hesitation, James nodded.

"We have already dropped the charges against Melissa Monroe and Tyler Stevens. Is there anything you would like to add about Linda or Brian Vega?"

"No," James said.

Detective Lee nodded as if expecting that. "They've both plead guilty already. They'll be behind bars for a long time."

James exhaled slowly. I hadn't realized how much stress he was still holding on to. "Thank you," James said and stuck out his hand to Detective Lee.

"Just doing my job, sir." He cleared his throat awkwardly. "Jon," he said, turning to my father in law, "you said there was one more thing you'd like to discuss?"

"Yes, actually, I was hoping it would come up in the briefing. But since Officer Daugherty was the only one I ever told, I feared it might not. I had talked to him the other day, and I wasn't sure why nothing was being done about what we discussed," he said. "I thought it was the proof that we needed. And if I had known he was dirty...if I had talked to someone else...maybe none of this would have happened." He shook his head. "Penny, that's why Susan and I were fighting the other day in James' room. I was confronting her about something. And she stormed off. I had to go after her. I had to confirm my suspicions. And I'm sorry I left. I'm sorry I left him alone." He shook his head again and looked back down at his hands.

"And what exactly did you tell Officer Daugherty?" Detective Lee asked.

I grabbed James' hand. I knew this was going to be bad. I knew this was going to hurt him.

"About all the texts between Susan and Isabella."

Shit. James' mother helped her?

"He didn't divulge that information during his questioning," Detective Lee said. "What texts?"

Jon looked at James for a second and then looked back at the detective. "There are texts on Susan's phone encouraging Isabella to do whatever it took to stop the wedding from happening. They never mentioned violence, and I'd like to think she didn't know what was going to happen. But even after James was shot...she kept Isabella informed on what was happening in the hospital. She fed her delusions. She encouraged her. She was a part of all of this."

Detective Lee looked up from his notes. "Do you want to press charges against your wife?"

I noticed Jon glance at my stomach.

"Yes," Jon said. "I want to press charges."

"Dad?" James said. "You don't have..."

"She encouraged Isabella even after she stole from you. Even after she hurt you. I know that Susan didn't believe Isabella was behind that. In part because Officer Daugherty insisted that Isabella wasn't. But, James, she knew. Or she at least should have been concerned. She put us all in danger." He glanced at my stomach again.

"We'll go talk to her now. If you're sure," Detective Lee said.

"I'm positive," Jon said.

The detective nodded. "I'll go tell her she needs to come in for questioning."

"And I'll get out of your way," Jon said and started to follow Detective Lee out.

"Dad." James got up and walked over to him. "Thank you." This time James hugged him.

Watching their exchange brought tears to my eyes. I could feel that this was the start of something better. Maybe Jon would start being a good father right before James became one. I put my hand on my stomach. *Be okay. Please be okay.*

It looked like they said something else to each other, but I couldn't make it out. James sat back down next to me with a smile on his face.

"Are you okay?"

"Yeah." He put his hand on my thigh. "I'd like to say I was surprised by what my mom did. But I'm not. I'm okay, though. My dad was trying to protect me. I'm just going to focus on that instead."

"What did he whisper to you?"

"He told me to try to be better than him. For you. For the baby."

"I don't think you have to try."

"Maybe." He put his hand on my stomach. "When do you think you'll start showing?"

"I have no idea. I don't even know how far along I am."

"Who else knows already?"

"I told my mom, so my dad probably knows too. And you already know I told Rob who told Daphne. That's it."

James smiled. "I'm excited to tell people." He spread his fingers out, covering my whole stomach with his hand.

I put my hand on top of his. "You're really excited about this?"

"I think maybe this baby is everything I didn't know I wanted. I can't stop smiling. I promise that I'm excited." He kissed my cheek as the doctor walked in.

"You ready to get out of here now that all the excitement has calmed down?" she said.

"Yes." He said it more to me than to her. "I'm ready."

I hadn't expected James to be so accepting of this situation. But after everything that happened the past few weeks, maybe he was just counting his blessings too. He was embracing our future because we were lucky enough to have one together.

"You already know you have to come back in a few weeks to get your stitches removed and get a few more vaccines," she said as she looked up from her chart. "And more important than that, you need to get your stress under control. I can't emphasize that enough."

"I will." James rubbed his thumb against my stomach. It reminded me of when he'd do that to my palm. It was equally soothing. I had the feeling that he was doing it for the baby. To show him that he was there for him. *Him.* I wanted a little James running around. Apparently Rob's thoughts were rubbing off on me.

"So, now for the baby?"

"Yes." James stood up and grabbed my hand. He helped me onto the bed and squeezed my hand when I lay down.

His excitement was contagious. But I was still a little apprehensive. What if it wasn't okay?

"Normally we don't do ultrasounds until a few months in," the doctor said. "But this will give us an idea of how far along you are. If you could just lift your shirt for me?"

I pulled my tank top up so that my stomach was bare.

She put some weird jelly looking stuff on my stomach and ran the wand over my stomach. "And don't be alarmed if I can't find anything. It just means you're not that far along."

I nodded. But as the seconds passed, I started getting concerned.

"Wait," she said as her hand stopped. "There it is." She pointed to the monitor. "That tiny little oval."

It was the smallest little dot on the screen.

James squeezed my hand again. "It's so small." His voice was full of awe. I turned away from the monitor to look at him. His eyes were glistening. He smiled down at me and kissed my forehead. "Can you tell how far along she is?"

"Based on the size, she's probably just about four weeks. Which would put her due date in mid February. Probably right around Valentine's Day."

I found that completely fitting. I squeezed James' hand.

"Can you tell what sex it is?" James asked.

"I don't want to know," I quickly said.

"What? Why?" He was smiling down at me.

"I want it to be a surprise."

He nodded. "Okay."

"It's too soon to tell either way," the doctor said. "We can verify that closer to halfway through the pregnancy. If you change your minds and want to know, that is. But everything looks good. You should make an appointment with your gynecologist in a month or so. They'll be able to give you a more precise due date and make sure everything is progressing normally. Did you want a print out of this?"

"Yes," James said immediately.

She smiled and pressed a button on the keyboard.

"We're going to be parents," James whispered to me. He pressed his forehead against mine.

I put my fingers in his hair. "You're going to be a great dad."

He laughed and placed a soft kiss against my lips. "God I hope so."

CHAPTER 38

Saturday

It was late when we finally left the hospital. There was something so wonderfully normal about being in the back seat of our car with Ian behind the wheel. It made the past few weeks seem like a terrible nightmare. Except for one thing.

I leaned my head against James' shoulder. "Thank you."

"For what?"

"For being so excited about this."

"You really thought I wouldn't be?" He ran his fingers through my hair.

"I was nervous that you might not be. And I really didn't mean for it to happen, I..."

"Penny." He tilted my face toward his. "We're lucky to both be alive. This is a blessing."

"I love you. I love you so much, James."

He responded with a kiss. Soft and slow. The kind of kiss that builds in the pit of your stomach and spreads in every direction until your whole body tingles with desire. I grabbed the back of his neck to deepen the kiss. I had been so worried the past few weeks. I hadn't felt this fire since our wedding day.

"You have no idea how badly I want you right now," he whispered against my lips. "All I did was dream of you. All I ever do is dream of you."

"Let's pretend it's our wedding night. Let's pretend nothing bad happened." I felt like we had been robbed of one of the best moments of our lives.

"Baby, I'm already one step ahead of you." He opened up the door. I hadn't even realized that the car had stopped. James leaned over and unbuckled my seatbelt. "Come with me." He stepped out of the car and put his hand out for me.

I grabbed his hand and let him help me out of the car. We were standing outside the hotel we visited the first time he had brought me to the city. It was also where Mason and Bee lived. But I had a feeling we weren't here to see them.

"What are we doing here?"

"Come with me."

We walked hand in hand up the front steps and into the ornate entrance.

The concierge immediately stepped out from behind his desk. "Right this way, Mr. and Mrs. Hunter."

I glanced up at James, but he wasn't giving anything away. He just smiled down at me as we followed the concierge. I heard the music before we reached the door.

"Our song?"

"We don't need to pretend it's our wedding night. Tonight is our wedding night." He pushed open the doors.

A single guitarist was in the ballroom, playing Hands Down the way that we had first heard it together in Central Park. The lights dimmed as I stepped into the room. It was like I was transported back in time to when we visited New York back when I was James' student.

James lightly touched my wrist, sending shivers up my arm. "Penny, may I have this dance?"

I turned around and smiled up at him. "Of course." I clasped my hands behind his neck. "How did you plan all this?"

But he silenced me with a kiss as he pulled me closer toward him. His hands slid down my back stopping right above my ass.

The song ended and the lights cut off, but he didn't stop kissing me. I couldn't see him, I could only feel his hands on me, his lips on me, him pressed against me.

He groaned as I leaned into him and his hands slipped to my ass.

I needed him. He was right, we didn't have to pretend. We had never had our wedding night together. This was it. "Do we have a room here?" I said breathlessly.

"We do. Or we can go home. Or we can go to the airport and go on our honeymoon. Anywhere you want to go. I just want to be with you."

"Let's go upstairs."

"I was hoping you'd say that."

I could feel his smile against my lips. He grabbed my hand and we walked as quickly as we could toward the elevators.

The concierge looked up as we passed. "Mr. Hunter, do you need..."

"We're good," James said as we stepped onto the elevator. As soon as the doors closed he pressed my back against the side of the elevator. "We're so good." He lifted my hands above my head and kissed me hard. He kissed me like he had that very first time in the pouring rain, pressed against his car.

I'd never get enough of this passion. Or this overwhelming feeling of finally being his. When we first met, I had this feeling that this was something big and scary and perfect. I knew it all along. But I never thought I'd be this lucky. I never thought I'd really be his. And I certainly never thought that he'd be mine.

The doors dinged open and he pulled me into the hall, stopping in front of the same room we had gotten almost three years ago. I grabbed the keycard from him and slipped it into the door.

"Wait," he said before I could open the door. He lifted me up into his arms.

"James!" I laughed. "You're not supposed to be lifting anything."

"I'm carrying my new bride through the threshold."

I saw the strain on his face. And the effort he was putting in was admirable, but completely unnecessary. "Put me down. You're going to pull your stitches out again."

"It's tradition, Penny," he said through a clenched jaw as he kicked the door open with his foot. He was breathing heavily as he placed me down on the bed.

"James, sit down."

He didn't protest as he sat down next to me on the bed. "I'm sorry. I wanted tonight to be perfect." He coughed into his hand.

"It is perfect." I straddled him on the bed. "Just take a minute to catch your breath." I put my hands on his shoulders and watched him as his breathing became more steady again. "Why did you bring me here?" I glanced over to the window. I remembered him fucking me against it. I remembered him saying he wanted the whole city to know I was his. The memory sent goosebumps up my legs. I needed him to catch his breath, but all I wanted was for him to do that to me again.

"I was thinking about what you said about Mason and Bee. About how he should propose to her on top of the Empire State Building because it means something to them. And, well, this place means something to me."

"Yeah?" It meant something to me too. That day we had come here was the first time I got to really see him as more than my professor. It somehow made this love seem bigger than us. "What does it mean to you?"

He ran his hand down my back. "Remember the last time we were in this room? You chose a ten dollar comedy show and a walk in Central Park."

"I remember." I somehow knew what he was going to say next and my eyes were already teary.

"It was in that moment that I realized just how good you truly were for me. How much you really cared about me for me. For the first time in forever, I wasn't depressed in New York. Because I had you by my side. And I knew that we could go anywhere in the world and be happy as long as we were together. And I knew I could never let you go. I knew that I needed you in my life forever. You're my light, Penny. You've always been the light to my darkness."

"James, your soul is brighter than you realize."

"I'm sorry I said I was addicted to you. I'm sorry. This is so much bigger than that." He put his hand on the center of my chest. "I'm sorry I ever doubted that. This is love." His hand slid between my breasts and stopped on my stomach. "This is love. Because it's not that I can't live without you. It's that I don't want to. I don't want to live without either of you." He spread his fingers across my stomach. "Because I love you. Baby, I love you so much."

I grabbed both sides of his face and kissed him, knocking him backwards onto the bed. This moment meant more than any other. This was the moment I had waited for my whole life. When our love wasn't clouded by social expectations or issues from our pasts or secrets that we had unwillingly held on to in order to protect ourselves. This moment was pure just like our love was, just like it always would be.

I slowly pushed up James' t-shirt and leaned down to kiss the stitches on his stomach and on his ribs. He pulled his shirt the rest of the way off and grabbed the hem of my tank top.

I lifted my arms in the air as his fingers slowly traced up the sides of my torso. He pulled it the rest of the way off and unclasped my bra. He watched it slowly fall down my arms. The way he looked at me made me feel like the sexiest girl he had ever seen. Like the only girl he ever saw.

He grabbed my hips and rolled over on top of me.

"James, you're supposed to let me be on top. The doctor said..."

"Fuck that. I'm making love to my beautiful wife."

"James..."

"Don't worry. I'm going to do it slowly." He put his lips around one of my nipples and lightly tugged.

God yes.

"Very slowly." His breath was hot against my skin as his fingers slipped below the waistline of my shorts. "You're so fucking wet, baby." He sunk a finger deep inside of me.

"James," I moaned. It felt like forever since I had gotten to be with him, since I had gotten to feel this way.

He sucked hard on my nipple as his finger thrust deep inside of me.

I didn't want to wait another second. I couldn't possibly. I pushed my shorts and thong down my hips.

"Eager as always."

"Make love to me, James. I thought I'd never get another one of these moments. I thought I lost you. I need you, James. You have no idea how much I need you."

"I waited my whole life for you. I'll never leave you, Penny." He gently kissed my stomach.

He'll never leave us. Somehow his gesture made this moment even more intimate.

He leaned down and kissed the inside of my thigh.

"James please."

"I love when you beg me." He moved between my legs. "But you never need to beg. I'll always give you what you want." He leaned forward, pressing his erection against me. "Always, Penny." He slowly slid his length inside of me.

I let my fingers dig into the muscles of his back.

He groaned as he thrust deep inside of me. "God, I've missed you."

"I've missed you too." I grabbed both sides of his face and brought his lips to mine.

For the first time in a long time, there was no urgency in his kisses. Just passion. Just a need that matched my own.

He grabbed my thigh and began to slide in and out of me a little faster.

I should have told him to slow down, but I couldn't make him stop. I was too caught up in the moment. All I knew was that I wanted him closer to me. I wanted to feel him all around me. I wrapped my legs around his waist.

He buried his face in my neck. "You drive me crazy, baby."

I grabbed a fistful of his hair as he slammed into me harder.

"I'll never get enough of you." He shifted so that he was staring down at me. "You're so beautiful."

"Don't stop. Please don't stop." I ran my fingers down his muscular arms. I loved every inch of this man. All of him.

He smiled down at me. "I love you, Penny. I love you with everything that I am."

I looked up at the man above me. The man I loved. The man I'd do anything for. "James." I put my hand on his chest. His heart was beating so fast. "I've waited my whole life for you too. I love the man that you are. I love everything about you. And I love the way you love me." I put my feet on the edge of the bed and tilted my hips up.

"Fuck." His fingers dug into my hips as his lips met mine again.

I poured my heart into this man's hands. And I didn't regret a single second of our time together. Everything that we had been through just made me appreciate him even more. My life was dull and gray before he came along. And now? My life was an explosion of colors.

He thrust into me hard.

So fucking explosive.

He kissed my neck, my collarbone, my breasts as he drove me to the edge of oblivion. "Come for me, my beautiful wife."

I wrapped my legs around him again as his hand slid to my ass. I could feel myself tightening around him. I was so close.

And then he came. I felt the familiar warmth spread up into my stomach and let myself let go.

"James!"

"God, Penny."

Explosive was definitely the only word to describe it. He was the one doing all the work yet I was completely out of breath.

He collapsed beside me. "I'm out of shape."

I rolled onto my side and perched my head up in my hand so I could look down at him. "No. You're healing."

"Was that the wedding night you dreamed of?"

"Better. James, tonight was perfect." I intertwined my fingers in his and smiled as he pulled my hand up to his lips and kissed it.

"I can't believe that we're married." He kissed the back of my hand again.

"Married and expecting. Time flies."

James looked down at my stomach and then back up to me. "You can't tell at all. No one would ever guess that you're pregnant."

"Will you still love me when my stomach is huge?"

"I love you more each and every day. So...yes." He leaned over top of me and kissed my stomach.

The position made his tattoo visible. I reached up and ran my finger along the pulse lines of it. "When did you get this?" I had been wondering when he had gotten it the whole time he was in his coma.

"The morning after our fight."

"You got it when you thought we were done? Why?"

"Because even if you left me, it didn't make it less true. My world changed when you walked into it. For the better."

"James. That just makes it that much sweeter."

He smiled. "I forgot that you hadn't seen it yet."

"I have already seen it."

He raised his left eyebrow. "Did you rape me in the hospital?"

I laughed and pushed his chest so that he was lying down again. "No. I wanted to find it. I just stripped you a little, that's all. And just for the record, you started to wake up right after that. Apparently you just missed having my hands all over you."

He smiled. "Oh, I definitely missed that."

"But seriously, James. That is the sweetest gift you've ever given me. How am I supposed to compete with that? And your birthday is tomorrow."

"This is pretty good." He kissed my stomach. "Actually, this is really, really good. I love it. I couldn't have asked for a better present."

"It is a little terrifying though."

"It's okay. We're going to be fine."

"How do you know?"

He pulled me into his arms. "Because everything's alright as long as you're with me."

I sighed as I listened to his steady heartbeat. There was no better sound in the world. No better feeling than his arms around me. Nothing at all was better than this.

"Thank you for tonight, James. It was perfect."

He kissed my forehead. "Thank you for taking a chance on me." He yawned and pulled me even closer.

"Thank you for choosing me," I whispered against his chest.

"I'll always choose you."

***

I slipped out from underneath his arm and grabbed my phone. I needed to make his birthday special. Despite what James said, I needed to give him something great. I wanted to surprise him. I clicked on Rob's number in my phone and held it to my ear.

"It's a little late," Rob said and cleared his throat. "Daphne's going to think I'm getting a booty call. Wait, is this a booty call? Am I dreaming?"

"I'm sorry to wake you, but I need a favor," I whispered, ignoring everything he had just said.

"Whatever you need, baby mama."

I laughed and sat down on the couch. "I'm going to have to get used to that nickname. I was wondering if we could somehow manage to put together a last minute surprise party for James? Maybe at Mason and Bee's? James and I stayed at their hotel last night..."

"Done."

"You didn't even ask them."

"I'll make it happen."

I smiled. "Thanks, Rob. And can we maybe make it a small thing? Just our closest friends?"

"You want me to uninvite people?"

"What do you mean uninvite people? I only just told you about it."

"I already sent out 150 invites while we were talking."

"What?"

"I'm just kidding. I'll take care of it."

I couldn't tell if he was kidding or not. But when he said he'd take care of it, I knew he would. "How are you feeling?"

"Tired. But I'm super excited to be an uncle. And James seems really excited about it too."

I glanced at the bed. "Yeah, he does." I smiled at the thought. He wanted the baby. He hadn't been upset at all. He was just happy. We were happy.

"You're going to make great parents."

"Thanks, Rob."

"But it's not even going to compare to how awesome of an uncle I'm going to be. Speaking of which, are you going to do that thing where all your friends also call themselves aunt and uncle to the baby? Because I kind of like the idea of being the only uncle. Since I'm technically the only actual uncle."

"I'll talk to James about it."

"I'll take that as a yes. Mason and Matt can suck it."

I laughed.

"Okay, I have to go. I have a lot to do. Plus, I need to buy James a bunch of presents that I originally wasn't sure I was allowed to buy because I didn't know if he knew yet. You know?"

"Shouldn't you be taking it easy? Maybe..."

"My older brother only turns 30 once. And I didn't...I mean, I didn't know if he was going to get to. I want to make it special."

I closed my eyes. He was right. It had to be special. "Thanks, Rob. I'm sure whatever you get him he's going to love."

"Lots of tequila and strippers?"

"Please don't do that."

"Ugh. Fine. Go back to bed, Penny. I got this covered."

"No strippers."

"What was that? I'm going under a tunnel. I think I'm losing the connection."

"Didn't I just wake you up? Hello? Rob?" I pulled the phone away from my ear. The line was already dead.

CHAPTER 39
Sunday

I slowly opened my eyes to see James staring at me.

"I'm the luckiest man alive," he said with a smile.

I blinked, letting his face come into focus. "Happy birthday, baby." I reached up and ran my hand against the scruff on his chin. "You're also the handsomest man alive."

He turned his head to kiss my palm. "I was thinking for my birthday that I just want to relax and hang out here today."

"Are you sure? I thought maybe we could go out to dinner somewhere and tell everyone the good news."

"I don't think you've ever turned down a lazy day in." He lowered both his eyebrows.

"I wasn't the only one that almost lost you. Your friends and family experienced that pain too. They want to see you."

"Mhm." He yawned and slowly sat up. "I think you're planning something."

"I'm not planning anything." I smiled at him. "I'll even let you choose the restaurant."

"Okay. But we're going home right after dinner."

"You turn 30 and suddenly your new bedtime is 8 o'clock?"

He laughed. "I just want to be alone with you. Maybe we can go for a walk in Central Park tonight?"

"That sounds perfect. The simplest things are my favorite things to do with you." I gave him a swift kiss on the lips. "Now get dressed, old man, we have places to be."

I squealed as he pulled me on top of him.

"What's the rush?"

There was no rush. Right now all I wanted was for us to get lost in each other again.

***

"Oh, I almost forgot. Bee accidentally left her sunglasses at the hospital. I told her we could drop them off for her." I pressed the button for their floor after we stepped onto the elevator.

"We can just give them to her at dinner tonight."

"But we're right here. It'll only take a second."

James shrugged his shoulders and I tried to hide my smile. The doors dinged open on Mason and Bee's floor.

I knocked on their door, but there was no answer.

"I guess she's at yoga or something. Which means Mason is on a run. One sec." I pulled out the key I had to their place. Bee had given it to me for when they went on business trips together. They had one plant in their apartment, and Bee was terrified of killing it. She said it was her practice baby. I smiled as I put the key into the lock. Maybe I needed to get myself a plant too.

"Are you sure it's okay for us to just go in? What if they're...you know." He winked at me.

I laughed. "Then they should have answered the door. Besides, that's what spare keys are for. Returning your friend's sunglasses if you happen to be in the neighborhood."

"I guess," James said and put his hands in his pockets.

I opened the door to an empty apartment.

"At least they're not naked," James said with a laugh as he walked in.

Awkward. It reminded me of when I had almost given James head in front of a houseful of surprise guests for my graduation party.

"Surprise!" everyone yelled as they jumped out of their hiding places.

James laughed and wrapped his arms around me. "Do you think they heard my naked comment?" he whispered in my ear.

"I have no idea."

He laughed again and kissed my cheek. "Thanks for the surprise. I knew you were acting weird."

I smiled up at him.

"Happy birthday!" Jen screamed and threw her arms around his neck. "Oh, God, I'm sorry," she said and pulled back. "Does it still hurt?"

"I'm okay," James said.

"I hope it's alright that I invited Ian," she said.

James glanced at Ian who was standing off to the side of everyone else. "When did that happen?"

"You were unconscious for a long time. Come with me." She grabbed his hand and pulled him toward Ian.

James smiled at me from over his shoulder.

"Whoa let me help you," I said and grabbed a huge gift wrapped box from Rob. He was holding it with one arm while balancing a crutch. "Geez, what's in here? This is ridiculously heavy."

"It's a surprise, but you probably shouldn't be lifting it either. You can just put it on the ground." He adjusted the sling on his arm as I placed the box down in front of me.

"And you should probably sit down." I looked down at the cast on his leg.

"I keep telling him to sit down. Hi, Penny," Daphne said and gave me a hug.

"How do I suddenly have so many women meddling in my life? Last time I checked, I still had my spleen so..."

"Very funny. Thanks for putting this all together," I said and gave him a hug.

"Anything for you guys. You know that." He kissed my cheek. "But yeah, maybe I should sit down."

Daphne looped her arm behind his back.

"Being an invalid does have its perks," he said to her and she smiled up at him.

"You guys are adorable," I said.

"Adorable?" Rob scrunched up his nose. "I hate that word. To the couch!" He pointed to where everyone else was gathered.

James was already sitting there. He had saved a space beside him. I sat down and rested my head on his shoulder.

"To James," Rob said and lifted up his glass. "The best brother and friend a guy could ask for."

Everyone clinked glasses and I took a sip of my water.

Mason cleared his throat. "James, you had us all worried sick. And the past few weeks have been...well, frankly, fucking terrible."

James laughed.

"It's not funny yet, man. But, either way, I thought we could all use some positivity. James, two years ago you gave me some advice. The best advice I've ever gotten, really. And even though I never ask for your help, you're always there for me. Bee and I wouldn't be together right now if it wasn't for you. And I don't want to steal the show in any way. But Bee and I have some news."

"We're engaged!" she shrieked and turned her hand so we could see the huge ring on her finger.

"Oh my God!" I got up and gave her a hug. "I'm so happy for you. And you, Mason." I gave him a hug too.

"Thanks, Penny," Mason said. "And it's because of you too. If James hadn't met you, he never would have given me the advice that he did. And seeing you and him together, it made me realize what I was missing, you know? So, thank you."

For some reason I started crying. "That's so sweet of you to say."

"Don't cry." He smiled at me.

"Sorry." I quickly wiped away my tears. "I've just been really emotional recently."

"I think we all have."

I wiped away the rest of my tears and looked back at Bee. "Your ring is beautiful. Tell us everything. How did he propose?"

"It was so romantic." She smiled up at him. "He proposed at the top of the Empire State building."

I glanced back at James. I rarely ever won one of our bets.

He shrugged his shoulders.

I took a second to soak in this moment as I looked around the room. Mason and Bee were finally engaged. Rob was in love. Melissa was snuggled up next to Matt. They seemed to be hitting it off really well. And Jen and

Ian looked so happy together. I sat down next to James. "Let's tell them our news a different day," I whispered. "Let's just enjoy this moment right now."

"I was thinking the same thing." He touched the bottom of my chin so that my lips met his.

"Okay, okay," Rob said. "Congrats you two. But you said you didn't want to steal the show, so stop stealing the show. I want James to open the present I got him."

Mason laughed. "Yeah. Sorry. We just couldn't not tell you guys."

"I'm so happy for both of you," James said. "And thanks for what you said. That means a lot to me."

Mason walked over to him. He leaned down and gave him a hug. "I meant every word."

They did that thing where they slapped each other on the back.

Bee and I smiled at each other.

"Where's the present you got him?" Mason asked.

"By the door. Could someone go grab it for me?" Rob asked. "I've been told I'm not allowed to get up anymore."

Mason laughed. "The Hunter men have suddenly rendered themselves useless." He walked over to the door and grabbed the box. "Shit, this actually is pretty heavy. What the hell is in here? Bricks?" He put the present down on the floor in front of James.

"It's a surprise," Rob said. "Actually, it's kind of a surprise for all of you. Open it."

James tore the paper and slowly opened the box.

"So, I was doing some research, and these are all the best books," Rob said. "About what to expect and everything. Things you should and shouldn't do. And there's some vitamins in there that Penny needs to start taking immediately."

James laughed as he lifted up the bottle of prenatal vitamins.

"Vitamins?" Matt asked. "Why did you buy Penny a present?"

James smiled at me. "Well, we weren't going to say anything yet. But Penny and I have some news too. She's pregnant."

"What?!" Melissa screamed. "Ah!" She attacked me in a huge hug. "You're going to be a mom? This is crazy." She hugged me again. "You're going to be such a great mom, Penny. Are you so excited?"

"We're very excited," James said and rubbed my back.

"I'm so happy for both of you." She gave James a hug. "You two didn't wait very long at all. I didn't realize that you wanted kids right away. But I'm so, so happy for you."

"We didn't really plan it. But I couldn't be more excited. It was the best possible surprise. I'm sorry Mason and Bee, we didn't want to steal your thunder. We weren't going to say anything..."

"Are you kidding?" Mason said. "I'm going to be an uncle?"

"No," Rob said. "Technically I'm going to be the only uncle."

"Congratulations," Mason said, ignoring Rob. "You really can't tell at all. Are you sure?"

"We're sure," James said. "It's this tiny little dot, but it's there. Here, let me show you." He pulled out his wallet and handed the picture of the sonogram to Mason.

I hadn't realized that he had put the picture in his wallet. Everything he did just warmed my heart so completely.

"Do you know if it's a boy or a girl?" Jen said. "This is so crazy exciting!"

"It's definitely a boy," Rob said.

I laughed. "No, we don't know."

"When do you get to find out?"

"Actually, we want that to be a surprise too."

"You seriously don't want to know ahead of time?"

"It's more fun this way." James rubbed my back again.

He was saying everything I felt. I didn't need to say anything at all. Instead I looked through the box that Rob had given James. There was everything from naming books to actual books for the baby. So that we could read him bedtime stories.

"How does it feel to be knocked up?" Matt asked.

Melissa punched his arm.

"I'm just so happy. And hungry. We haven't eaten breakfast yet."

"Oh, we'll go get the cake," Bee said and quickly stood up. "You know this means we have to hop on the kid train soon too, Mason. We want our kids to grow up and be friends."

"We have a little time," said Mason. "Matt and Rob are three years younger than James and me. And we all get along great. But yeah. I'd like our kids to grow up together. Which means all of you have to speed things up too," Mason said to Matt and Rob.

"Well, Daphne and I are moving in together," Rob said. "Babies are next after that, right?" he said with a laugh.

"You're moving out of your place in Newark?" I asked.

"Well, yeah. James asked me to run Hunter Tech. I kind of need to be here. And I want to be here." He put his arm around Daphne.

"You asked him to run Hunter Tech?"

Rob laughed. "I think you two have a few things you need to talk about. Let's all go help with the cake."

Daphne helped Rob to his feet and everyone went into the kitchen.

"You asked him to take over?" I asked. I couldn't hide my excitement. This had to mean that he was going to teach again. That he finally realized what truly made him happy.

"Yeah. He wants to settle down. I think he was looking for an excuse to move here so that it wouldn't seem so crazy fast with Daphne. And he needs a little structure in his life. Besides, he was handling all my emails and stuff while I was in the hospital and he really took care of things for me. Thanks for having him handle that, by the way."

"I never asked him to handle it."

"You didn't?"

"No. I guess he just...did it."

James smiled. "Even more reason why he'll be a great fit. And he has a lot of great ideas for the company."

"And what about you?"

"The doctor said less stress. And I want to be there for you and the baby. I don't want to be working all the time."

I smiled. "Won't you be bored?"

"I may have applied for a few local teaching jobs," he said with a smile.

"Yeah?"

"You sound surprised. I told you I'd think about it before the wedding. I thought about it...and that's what I want."

"You're going to be a professor again?"

"Well, we'll see. I haven't heard back yet or anything. And I don't want to start anytime soon. I think I need some time off."

"James, you don't even understand how happy that makes me."

"I think you just want to be able to call me Professor Hunter all the time again."

I laughed. "I'll never tire of calling you that. But no, that's not why. It's because you finally realized what you love."

"I love you."

"I mean besides me. You love teaching. It's what you were meant to do."

"I kind of feel like I was meant to be a father too. I know I said I didn't want kids for a long time, but I'm not lying when I say I'm excited. I'm really, really happy."

I smiled. "I know. And, I have something for you. I'm sorry I didn't wrap it. I was going to if we had gone home last night, but," I grabbed the onesie from my purse, "this was what I was going to give you to tell you I was pregnant."

"God, it's so small." He unfolded the onesie I had picked up from the hospital gift shop. It had the Giants logo on it. "I'm pretty sure this is for a baby boy."

"I don't know if it's just been Rob's incessant talk about it being a boy or what, but I feel like it's going to be a boy."

He lowered both his eyebrows. "Yeah?"

"You look disappointed."

"No. No, I just...I want it to be like you. Everything good in this world." He put his hand on my stomach.

"And that's why I want it to be a boy. So that it'll be like you. Everything I love in this world."

"Right now it's just a tiny dot. I can't believe that dot is going to be a baby. Our baby."

I put my hand on top of his.

"I don't want to mess it up. I don't want to disappoint it."

"You couldn't possibly, James. And it makes me so happy that you want to spend time with him before he's born."

"It's going to be a girl." He smiled at me.

I shrugged. "Maybe."

"But you're going to let me raise it as a Giants fan either way?" he said.

"Just don't tell my dad."

He laughed. "Thank you, Penny. This really is the best gift. But I wanted to ask you one more thing."

"Yeah?"

"I want you to stay home with me for the next few weeks. I know that you're supposed to finish your internship. And if you want to do that, of course you can. But I thought we could both use a vacation. You could always finish the internship in the fall if you'd like."

"Actually, I wanted to talk to you about that too. The day before our wedding, I was terrified I'd never see you again. I started writing down all this stuff about you and the way you made me feel. I just...I didn't want to ever forget. And when you were in the hospital, my mom told me that it was my job to keep living. In order to keep the memory of you alive. That really stuck with me. But at the same time, I knew I wasn't strong enough. I don't know how to live without you."

"Hey." He wiped the tears from under my eyes with his thumbs. "You don't have to live without me."

"I know. And I'll never forget how lucky I am that you woke up. How blessed I am that our story didn't end there." I pulled a notebook out of my purse. "I know it's silly, but I thought that if you didn't wake up that I'd just suddenly die too. And I felt guilty for not being able to keep your memory alive. And I started writing about, well, our story. Of how we met and...well, all of it. And how we have this huge scary everlasting love. The kind of love that people dream about."

"I didn't know you enjoyed writing."

"Honestly, I didn't either. But I've always loved reading. And when I started to write about you, I just couldn't stop." I looked up into his dark brown eyes. "And I think people might like hearing all about you."

"Me?" He laughed.

"Yes. About how we started. The truth that no one else seems to believe."

"The truth?"

"About our love. How we overcame all the obstacles that everyone put in front of us. How true love has it's struggles too. And how it's so worth it."

"Hmm." He kissed the tip of my nose. "Do you really think anyone would be interested in reading about us?"

"Of course they would. Maybe it could even be a whole series."

"Is there really that much to say?"

"About you? Absolutely." I placed the notebook in his lap. "It's barely anything yet. But I think it could be something great. I've been trying to find my thing after graduating. And really, James, all I've ever been passionate about is you. I want to write this book. And raise this baby. And be the best wife I can possibly be to you."

"If that's what's going to make you happy."

"Nothing would make me happier. I don't ever want to go a day apart from you. And I don't want the memory of you to ever completely fade. This will make that possible." I tapped the top of the notebook.

"Can I read what you have?"

"Yeah, well, it's super rough. It's mostly just notes. All I know is that it's going to start at the coffee shop. Where our lives both changed forever. When I finally learned what living truly was." I smiled. "When I decided to break all the rules and fall head over heels for my professor."

He put his hand on the side of my face. "The best day of my life. God, I love you, Penny."

"I love you with everything that I am, Professor Hunter."

He smiled as he wiped away my tears with his thumbs. There was suddenly a hunger in his eyes that hadn't been there before. It reminded me of when I was his student and he was my professor. I had sometimes thought he was the hunter and I was the prey. That the whole thing was a game. But despite what he thought, I never saved his life. He saved mine.

We never were able to agree on who tempted who. But there was truth in both our stories, and together, it came down to two things. Two unmistakable truths that led us to this moment. This perfect moment. I looked up into his eyes. I was the hunted. But I had willingly let him hunt me.

PROFESSOR HUNTER

Want to know what Professor Hunter was thinking when he first met Penny?

Find out in *Professor Hunter - Temptation* from James' point-of-view!

To get your free copy of *Professor Hunter*, go to:

www.ivysmoak.com/devotion-pb

WHAT'S NEXT?

James and Penny face their biggest hurdle yet when her pregnancy has life-threatening complications. And for the first time ever, see their story unfold through James' point of view.

James and Penny's story continues in *The Light to My Darkness*...available now!

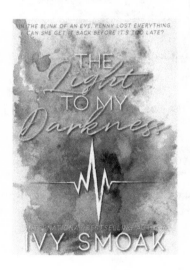

A NOTE FROM IVY

My relationship with my husband was a little rocky when we were first dating. People from his past haunted me. We definitely had our ups and downs. But I never stopped loving him. Wanting him.

And at the end of 2017, we danced to Hands Down by Dashboard Confessional at our wedding. He's the light to my darkness. He gave me the confidence to follow my dreams and write these novels. I feel like we can all relate to the struggles that come along with love. But it is so freaking worth it.

Devotion is for you guys. You've been devoted to these characters from the very beginning and I am so grateful to all of you.

Ivy Smoak
Wilmington, DE
www.ivysmoak.com

ABOUT THE AUTHOR

Ivy Smoak is the international bestselling author of *The Hunted Series*. Her books have sold over 1 million copies worldwide, and her latest release, *Empire High Betrayal*, hit #4 in the entire Kindle store.

When she's not writing, you can find Ivy binge watching too many TV shows, taking long walks, playing outside, and generally refusing to act like an adult. She lives with her husband in Delaware.

Facebook: IvySmoakAuthor
Instagram: @IvySmoakAuthor
Goodreads: IvySmoak

Recommend *Devotion* for your next book club!

Book club questions available at:
www.ivysmoak.com/bookclub